HARTFORD PUBLIC LIBRARY
500 MAIN STREE
HARTFORD, CT 06103

D1110039

STONE COWBOY

STONE COWBOY

a novel

MARK JACOBS

This novel was inspired by a short story of the author's which first appeared in *The Atlantic Monthly* in 1989: "Stone Cowboy on the High Plains."

Copyright © 1997 by Mark Jacobs.

All rights reserved.

Published by
Soho Press, Inc.
853 Broadway
New York, NY 10003

Library of Congress Cataloging-in-Publication Data
Jacobs, Mark, 1951–
Stone cowboy : a novel / Mark Jacobs.
p. cm.
ISBN 1-56947-098-7 (alk. paper)
I. Title.
PS3560.A2549S7 1997
813'.54—dc 21 97-20257
CIP

10 9 8 7 6 5 4 3 2 1

For Anne Bulen Jacobs
and Robert Ready

6904

STONE COWBOY

ONE

Two days before he was released forever from el Panóptico Prison, in La Paz, Bolivia, Roger the stone cowboy became aware that he had been talking to God. A Swedish mercy nurse who spoke terrible Spanish was binding up his forearm where one of the troll crazies had sliced him, in an argument in which Roger himself had played no part. As the earnest, homely blond woman worked, he could feel his pulse thunder the length of the hurt arm. They were in a room the trolls called the infirmary, which meant it had a bed nobody slept in. (All Bolivians were trolls, Roger had decided a long time ago. They were short and dark and strange, not like people, really, but humanlike to a certain extent.) Light the color of clear, thin honey came through the single window high in the prison wall and dripped down on them. Roger felt sticky.

The honey light dripped, his pulse thundered, the mercy nurse babbled bad Spanish. An odd lull had occurred in the afternoon bitch and hum in el Panóptico. Before the woman released his arm, Roger became aware that he was saying something into that lull: Give me back my heart. It was not really what he would have thought of as a prayer. Definitely it was no prayer. He didn't care what it was. More interesting was where he was sending it. In a slow roll, like revelation, he realized that he had indeed been mumbling to God. No answer came back, of course. That would have been too much to expect. He returned to his pallet in a kind of daze.

He was giving up dope. All kinds, not just the coke cigarettes the trolls smoked, called *pitillos*. All shit, shit in all its manifestations. That was a lot for a stone cowboy who had made himself high, by his own best estimate, in twenty-three countries and twenty-five American states over a period of more than ten years. So he was giving up a lot, and that was hard. He had some insurance, but he wasn't touching it. He wished he had remembered to keep track of how many days he had stayed down now, but he hadn't. His mind had become his body, and it was acting funny. Then that mumbling.

"When they let you out, in two days, what are you going to do?" the Swedish woman asked him.

He shook his head, not because he didn't want to be sociable but because he was preoccupied. His mind had become his body.

"Did you hear me?"

"I heard you." You you you you you . . . et cetera.

"Do you have any idea of where you are going to go?" she persisted.

Give me back my heart is what he thought, but he said nothing to her, because he did not want her to misunderstand him.

"Will the people from your consulate help you?" No way, Josefeen. He would not go back to Gringolandia. Not until he had calmed down a little more. He knew the trolls wanted him out of Bolivia, but when the vice-consul showed up to escort him to his doom, he slipped, skipped, did not trip. It was easy.

He had only a few bucks in troll money, so he had to get a job. First to eat and sleep, then money to move on with. He had his insurance but wasn't touching any of it. So he took a yellow unpsychedelic bus with black stripes up out of the canyon of La Paz, up the highway toward the Altiplano. He wanted to get a good view of the Andes, something he had craved his whole time in jail. The Altiplano was a desert that had gotten lost, squeezed in between two ranges of the Andes at fourteen thousand feet. The ultimate natural high was what Claude, a French doper in el Panóptico who understood Bolivia better than most Bolivians, had called it. Real people couldn't survive long at that altitude, just llamas and alpacas. And trolls. Real people needed air with something in it their lungs could chew on.

Three-quarters of the way up the *autopista* the bus broke down. The engine shuddered like Claude had done one night at the tail end of a bad chemical experience, and that was it. The trolls filed off the bus like religious fatalists, and Roger followed last, because he had to. Most of the trolls went up the hillside on a footpath alongside a concrete culvert down which no water coursed. A few walked the highway in hopes of a ride. The driver, who apparently had no plan, sat by the roadside and chain-smoked cigarettes. Roger watched his face for a sign of distress, but none was there. That was a troll for you. He wished the man would offer him a cigarette, but forget that. When his half pack of smokes was gone, the driver stood up and left, walking on the highway berm without looking back or hoping for a ride. No good-bye, because no hello. Give me back my heart. Roger crossed the highway and sat down cross-legged on an outcropping of shaly rock. Below him, in the brown bowl of the canyon, the lights were going on in La Paz. The skyscrapers downtown looked ridiculously little in the vastness of brown earth around them. Toothpicks of light. On the far horizon the outlines of the mountain Illimani were filed smooth in the twilight. For all the smoothness, the mountain dominated the city. The Indians worshipped the mountains as gods, someone had told Roger once, but that might have been pure bullshit, some tourist's stone fantasy. He sat and watched the night fill up the canyon as if he had no place else on earth to be, nothing better to do. The air had begun to get cold.

Eventually he recognized a certain pressure inside his head, as if he were not alone, or as if he had been trying to communicate something to someone without knowing it. It was not a prayer. He remembered the way his body had looked when he saw it in a mirror by chance at the prison: dead-white skin, pudgy like pastry. A real shock. He looked like weakness in the flesh. He was twenty-nine years old, but ten years' extra wear seemed to have been compressed into every one of those years. That was the dope, no doubt. He was a veteran cowpoke, a long-time outrider of the world's high plains.

The pressure and the indefiniteness of the sensations he felt bothered him as he sat. The entrancing scene of La Paz at night, even after his long confinement, could not hold him. Though he wasn't hopeful, he went back to the highway and stuck out his thumb. Anyway, he felt better moving.

After ten minutes a pickup truck stopped, and the troll driver motioned for him to get into the back, which he did, happily. The truck engine laboring, they climbed the last quarter of the highway out of the canyon and passed through the toll booth, after which Roger expected the driver to stop and let him out. The man, a fat-bellied troll Indian with a flat hatchet nose, did not stop. Because he could think of no convincing reason to get out at any particular place along the road, Roger acquiesced.

They went slowly through the muddy urban sprawl of the city of El Alto. The pickup, whose shock absorbers had died in 1970, bounced like an amusement-park ride. WELCOME TO EL ALTO, THE CITY OF THE FUTURE, read one enthusiastic mural, which displayed troll workers in an attitude of defiance, holding their tools like weapons. If this is the future . . . Roger said to himself archly, but could think of nothing compelling to complete the thought. What it was was an Altiplano mud village multiplied several hundred times: the same crumbly adobe huts and walls, the same mud streets, the same Indians in their Andean stupor going about the business of surviving. The city lacked only llamas in the streets; he saw plenty of pigs and dogs, and a few oxygen-starved chickens.

The sign said RIO SECO—Dry River—but they were all dry in this part of the country. A real river hadn't coursed through the Altiplano since the dinosaurs used to wander down to the banks and lap up the polluted water after a hard day defending their territory. With no warning, the troll driver stopped at an intersection of two crater-pocked streets. Roger jumped out and down.

"Gracias," he said to the man, who waved an enormous hand as if irritated and drove off trying to avoid the craters, which were full of dust that rose up in clouds like smoke signals.

Although he felt weak, Roger was not hungry at all, not even thirsty. He liked walking, so he walked, keeping careful track of the things he saw. A blind man with no legs sat on a street corner, holding his upturned hat for change. He must have been a miner. Dynamite victims were strewn all over La Paz, like debris from an unnatural disaster. Next to the man was a crippled yellow cat. Roger put some change into the hat, at the same time resisting a strange urge to kick the helpless, ugly cat, whose fur was stiff with dirt.

As he walked he kept up his inventory: A blond-haired doll like Barbie, with no limbs, lying on her back in the mud like a rape victim. Three men teetering as they shared a bottle of beer, with the one glass building a communal buzz. An underemployed hustler with bad teeth and a tight skirt that could flatter no one. Boys playing soccer in the street with a scuffed ball that needed air. A woman in a heavy shawl, baggy skirts, and a black bowler hat, sitting in a huddle alone in her corner store, next to tall bottles of soda pop in rainbow colors. Alongside those bottles the woman had no face in his imagination, and probably didn't feel the lack.

Attracted either by her or by the almost cheerful yellow light inside her store, Roger went inside. He bought a small bottle of warm Coca-Cola and poured it into the greasy glass the woman handed him. She had a face after all, but it was the typical face of a troll, illegible and hostile in a disconcerting blank way, just like the Altiplano and the Andes. For a moment Roger wanted not to go, but to be, home. In prison he had learned a little Aymara, so he spoke to the shopkeeper woman politely in that language.

"Can I find a hotel nearby?"

Surprised to hear the Aymara, but unwilling to show the surprise, she shook her lowered head.

"Anyplace to rent a room?"

"What for?" she asked him in Spanish.

"To sleep, that's all," he said in Aymara. He had a good ear; he knew that his accent was pretty good, and that she must be impressed. The pressure in his head was unsettling, as though he had lost his equilibrium. He had felt like this his first few days in La Paz, before his body adjusted to the dehumanizing altitude.

"Why to sleep?" she asked him. Stupid damn question, but that was her way of holding up the conversation. She had spoken in Aymara, which minor triumph of diplomacy pleased Roger unnecessarily. "Because my body is tired." His mind was still his body, and it had been invaded.

"You're a foreigner," she said, also unnecessarily.

"Guess from where."

She shook her head. She was about forty, maybe, and she had a striking, angular, womanly face, if you could get used to the idea of the shape of her body, which was a bunch of connected lumps below all those mysterious cloaking skirts.

"I'm a Russian," he said.

"Liar."

"Then what?"

"A gringo."

Something in the way the trolls said that word was offensive, as if they were the human ones and Americans were some low breed of dog.

"Why to sleep?" she asked again, so that he knew she liked him.

"Because I'm tired."

"I have a room in back."

"I don't have a lot of money. "

"All the gringos have money."

"That's a lie. I was in jail."

"In el Panóptico?"

"That's right."

"Then you're a drug addict."

"I'm not. It was a mistake, a case of mistaken identity."

"Liar."

"I'm not a liar, and I'm not a drug addict, but I am a gringo. Is that wrong in some way?"

The last he had to say in Spanish, because he was reaching the end of his dexterity in Aymara, which was a backwards, upside-down kind of language.

"All the gringos have lots of money. How did you come to Bolivia?"

"On an airplane."

"See?"

"How much for the room, for one night?"

She told him a price that was half what he had expected to hear from her, and he accepted by pulling change from his pocket and placing the coins flat on the wooden countertop.

"I'm really a Russian," he said. "I'm a Communist. We're going to invade your country. I'm the first of the first wave. Shock troops, you know? Follow that?"

His body was two hundred and ninety years old. He had his insurance but wasn't touching it, so he bought from the woman a bottle of troll wine, terrible stuff but strong enough, strong as Robitussin. Because he liked her, he wanted to tell her that he had once been raped by identical redheaded twins in a county jail in Alabama, after he had been picked up for possession of a little dope, but he could not bring himself to that confidence. The twins had had ugly freckles all over their similar fish-white bodies. Fuck that noise, he warned himself. He let himself be led through the back room of the store to a dirt patio, where a couple of detached rooms were suspiciously hidden. She showed him into the first, which had an iron-spring cot and a comfortable cotton mattress, better than anything he had slept on in el Panóptico except for the week when some troll disease had made him sick enough to get into the infirmary, where the consul had visited him with old *Time* magazines he never read. All news was bad news.

When the woman left, he lay on the cot on his side and opened the bottle of wine, which he drank very slowly, sucking on it almost, like a nursing baby. Soon the alcohol began to reduce the obnoxious pressure inside his head. He could feel the mellow redness seep into the cracks between his nerves, where all the irritation was, like a rash. He would not go home to Gringolandia until he had sorted through some things and could think in a straight line.

He must have drifted off, even though a little wine was left in the bottle. When they shook him awake roughly, he wanted to hit.

"This is my husband," the store woman said to him in Aymara. "His name is Don Eloy."

Don Eloy looked down with tremendous disdain at the stone cowboy on the cot. He was big for a troll, as wide as he was tall. He looked the image of a decadent Indian on a reservation in the United States, dour and sour and dreaming of eagles. His black eyes were fierce, his ruddy face fiercer.

"What are you going to do tomorrow?" he asked Roger, as though he had a right to know.

"What do you care?" After the initial urge to strike out, he felt halfway okay. Enough wine had filtered between the nerve cracks to prevent chafing. No use resenting a troll.

"You want a job?"

"Doing what?"

"At my lumberyard."

"But doing what?"

"Working."

"How much will you pay me?"

"Ten pesos a day."

"I'll try it."

"I'll pick you up in the morning. Listen, little gringo, you shouldn't get drunk. My wife tells me you're a drug addict."

"I'm not."

"When we are working, you are going to tell me about life up north."

That sounded fine. Even on ten pesos he could save money to leave Bolivia. It was a question of discipline. He didn't have it, but he would find it. Before he fell back to sleep, he imagined the way he'd feel crossing the border, knowing that he would never see an ugly troll face, never have to talk to a troll again in his life.

The work at Eloy's small-time lumberyard was not too bad. He had done the same sort of thing in dozens of places, dozens of times: lift fetch carry, drop hold hammer, bend push pull. The dust was awful and the hours longer than you would work anywhere in the States; those were the only bad parts.

"How much a day are you going to charge me for the room and my food?" he asked Eloy his first day on the job.

"Don't worry about it, *gringuito*," the big man said, pulling on his long front teeth with one dirty hand.

Roger, the stone cowboy, tried to pin him down but did not succeed. And he was too tired to persist. He was weak. Not for years had he worked for so long with his hands and all his body. El Panóptico and the world's garden house of dope had run down his two-hundred-and-ninety-year-old body considerably. The little strength he had left over he used to defend himself from Eloy and his men—

scurvy trolls, all of them, who derived a deep, stupid satisfaction from riding him. He was not just the Gringo, he was the Worthless Gringo, who could not keep up by half with the trolls when they were lifting and stacking boards, let alone do anything requiring more skill of body.

Decadence was Eloy's explanation for Roger's miserable condition. During a break he explained his theory both to Roger and to his other hired men. Roger was not sure whether he was trying to be sarcastic, but he thought not.

"Alienation," Don Eloy said. "It's obvious. Capitalist society produces alienated individuals, because the workers are alienated from their work."

"Bullshit," Roger said, defensive though he did not have to be.

"Shut up," Eloy said. "Alienated people take drugs to escape their alienation. That's a false escape, of course, but they can't know that, can they?"

They were sitting in the lumberyard on wooden chairs. Don Eloy's chair had a fabric cushion. The hired men's chairs did not. Roger had no chair. He sat on the ground and tried to breathe slowly. The exertion had made him weak. It was July, what the trolls called winter: cold and windy and dry. The dust swirled in the yard, coated Roger's body, got down into his throat so that he coughed.

"Where did you pick up ideas like that?" he asked his new boss. Couldn't let them get away with more than the minimum of trash. "University of Moscow?"

Baiting him worked. The break was stretched appreciably, and Roger sensed the satisfaction of the other men when Eloy wound up and delivered. The basic idea, from what Roger could discern, was that Bolivia and the trolls were dirt poor because the imperialists up north—the Yankees—were filthy rich. It was that simple. The standard of living and conspicuous consumption that characterized the United States were the consequences of an economic arrangement that made the trolls dependent for crumbs. Nothing new there: Roger had heard the same song sung in el Panóptico when they wanted to get down on him there. Look at the tin, Eloy ranted. Bolivian miners coughing their black lungs out produced cheap tin so that the United States could win the Second World War, and here in the Andes only a few families, oligarchs in cahoots, made any money.

The break lasted for half an hour.

He wanted to get straight with Eloy about the pay arrangement, but that night he was too tired. Looking for discipline, he bought no wine. Eloy's wife's food was about the same as prison food, to which he had become accustomed, so he ate and went to sleep.

The second day and the rest of his first week were more of the same. Eloy got puffed and holy talking about the crummy way the gringos had treated the trolls. The other men laughed like first-graders about how weak the drug addict from el Panóptico was, but they didn't push as hard as they might have, because they appreciated the long breaks they got when Eloy started spouting. At night he drank at most a little wine, no more than half a bottle, and some nights he had none at all. Roger's body felt like Bolivia after it had been tromped on and raped by a hundred thousand imperialist mineral pirates. But even that exhaustion became the cause for a little self-satisfaction: He would ride it all out.

He had his insurance but wasn't touching it. Whenever the day was quiet, he felt the pressure in his head, but he had almost become used to that; the pressure was company.

After a week he asked for his pay, and got it. Six days times ten pesos should have been sixty pesos, but Don Eloy gave him thirty.

"Thirty pesos for room and board?" Roger protested. "That's outrageous."

"Do you have a better offer?"

They were standing in the little store that fronted the dusty street. Roger was part, now, of the yellow light that had attracted him the first night. Little tremors of weakness ran up and down his legs. Don Eloy's wife hung her head, so Roger could not tell whether she was ashamed of the way her husband was taking advantage of him.

⸙

"This is your idea of a political lesson," Roger said to Eloy. "That's what it is, isn't it? You're trying to prove something."

"You have a better offer?"

"I have black lungs."

"From smoking drugs."

"I don't do drugs."

"Liar," piped up the wife.

"I'll get my own place to stay," he told them both, feeling almost as stubborn as he was tired.

"Go ahead."

"You'll pay me ten pesos a day without taking anything out? No more screwing me?"

"Ten pesos."

"Guaranteed?"

"Where are you going to sleep? It's cold."

"That's my problem, not yours."

The next day was Sunday, a day more or less of rest. Eloy closed his lumberyard and sat in a contraband chaise longue in his wife's corner store, drinking beer slowly and growing predictably sullen. The problem, evidently, was the lack of an adequate object for his anger, for which frustration Roger almost pitied him. But he was glad to get away from the big man's domestic sulk. He went walking.

On earlier walks he had seen the blue tents, and that was what gave him his idea. Out-of-work miners had come to El Alto looking for relief or a job, and those who found neither would sometimes shelter their families in tents of blue opaque plastic that they set up in the empty fields that could still be found in El Alto. No rent, no room deduction, no one taking unfair advantage. They carried their water in jugs from a tap somewhere and hunkered down into a refugee's life.

The Altiplano wind was blowing hard, stirring dust devils all across the shabby brown city. The day was still young. The sun was flat in the east and the shadows were cold, making Roger think of mornings in el Panóptico, a memory like death itself. He walked with his hands in his pockets, head down, until he saw one of the blue tents, in front of which a troll picked something from his wife's long black hair. She leaned back peaceably in the man's lap as he poked, while around them a handful of midget trolls lolled like unimaginative slaves. A quality of domestic intimacy about them impressed Roger powerfully. So he asked them for help.

When they understood that he was not making fun of them and that he had no intention of taking over the land on which they had squatted, they helped him locate some plastic and build his tent, smaller than theirs but big enough for a single man to live in. At the nearby Sunday market they helped him buy two blankets, a tin pot, and a plastic jug for water, all at reasonable prices. He spent the day with them, feeling as if he had stumbled upon the family of some uncle whom he had not expected to like.

When the sun went down, early, he crawled into the new tent, almost at peace but feeling maudlin and alone. For a long time he lay on his back and listened to the wind bang through El Alto, the City of the Future. It was not much colder than the room at Eloy's, but it was damn cold. Though he was tired, he could not sleep. The desolation of this place wanted to overwhelm him.

For the first time since he could remember, he began to plan, gingerly—the way a person might exercise after a broken leg had healed. He would not walk away from Don Eloy's exploitation yard, because his body, inside which his mind still stalked nervously, had begun to crave work. Just as important, next week he would have the entire sixty pesos, and he thought he could save more than he would spend. He would work a few more weeks, buy some dollars, and get out of

Bolivia. In Peru he would do the same, getting stronger and more disciplined. He would go north, working his way and getting younger. The trip would take maybe three months, with luck, but once over the border into Gringolandia, he would buy a hamburger and a milkshake, and then hitchhike home to Flint, where his high-school friend Danny was probably still working as a foreman in one of the car plants. Danny would wangle Roger a job, and Roger would grow up to be president of the United States of America of the North. His first official act would be to bomb Bolivia off the fucking continent, starting with El fucking Alto.

That night, when he eventually got tired, he had reached a weird equilibrium that balanced the wind outside with the windy pressure inside his head. Danny, he realized, would never believe this, nor could the story be told. The desolation wanted to get at him, get him good, but he was learning stubbornness. In a way he was glad it was too cold to get out of the tent and go find a bottle of wine somewhere. Thus one dollar saved.

Eloy and his men sucked the marrow from the big bone of pleasure when they learned that Roger was living in a blue-plastic tent in an empty field. His fortune was their revenge for all the miners who had died from black lung, for the hundreds of years of eating small potatoes, for their condition of perpetual trollhood. At the end of the second week, however, Roger felt as if he had beaten them all. Don Eloy handed over sixty Bolivian pesos—no discount, no comment. Roger sewed an extra sock to the inside of his jeans, at the waist, into which pocket he tucked the money. He was a miser, and no bottle of bad wine tempted him. He went to sleep early, stronger and younger than he had been for years.

At the end of the third week he asked for a raise. In response he received a boring, gritty lecture from his employer about economic dependence, about the inhuman face of imperialism, about the revealing analogy between workers against capitalists and poor countries against rich countries. When Don Eloy offered him one peso a week extra, he accepted the offer and felt that he had won a tactical victory.

By September the weather had warmed, at least during the day, and the nights were bearable, even on the Altiplano. The change of season made Roger restless, and he decided he would work another week and then take the bus to Peru.

"I'm leaving next Sunday," he said to Eloy.

"Where to?"

"The United States."

"They'll never take you back. They were glad to see you go."

"I just thought I ought to tell you."

"You're going to start taking drugs again, I bet."

"You bet wrong."

"You're an insolent bastard."

Roger cursed him in nicely accented Aymara, and the troll lumberman bellowed with pleasure.

That night in his tent Roger thought seriously for the first time about destroying his insurance: two hits of windowpane acid that Claude had passed to him in el Panóptico as a way of vicariously celebrating Roger's release. Too soon. He felt more superstitious than vulnerable, but he could not yet let them go.

Thinking made him restless, almost nervous. He crawled out of his tent to take a walk, and he found the city in the grip of a power failure. Rio Seco and all of El Alto were as dark and desolate as his worst mood. Overhead the southern stars were splendid, Orion lying on his side like a drunken veteran. For some reason the sight of the stars robbed Roger of his confidence. For a long minute he considered doing the acid, after which he felt unreasonably tired. Rather than walk, he crawled back inside the blue plastic cocoon and slept. The pressure and the presence in his head had diminished as he grew back into health, and that almost disappointed him. He felt more abandoned than ever, as if some important quiet self inside were sitting with his legs crossed and his hands folded, waiting for an answer, and all he got back was the silence, on the far side of which was nothing. Give me back my heart, he heard rather petulantly.

Although they were careful not to speak a word, Roger knew that Eloy's men were the ones who broke into his tent and took the money. He remembered nothing unmistakably identifiable about any of them. Not a human smell, or an individual cough. They fell on top of him and clamped a hand over his mouth, and for a moment he thought that they were going to rape him. Impatient hands tore down his jeans, but what they grabbed was the small wad of his money, which he had changed into dollars the week before. Before they left, Roger wondered how they could know so surely where to find his money. In another life he would have cried.

Instead, he went after Eloy, whom he found stumbling drunk in a broken-shouldered restaurant that smelled of garlic. A single woman from one of the Altiplano towns worked there in the evenings. For no reason that anyone who knew Eloy found convincing, she liked to flirt with the married lumberman, even though she had no expectation of any kind of gain from the transaction.

"I want my money, " Roger told him, wondering whether the man could hear or understand him through the alcoholic vapor.

"Fuck you, little gringo."

"I want my money."

But Eloy was not capable of holding up even that much conversation. Maybe to impress the woman on duty, whose one gold tooth shone strangely in the lamplight, he dove at Roger and hugged him like a lover. The force of the embrace knocked Roger down, and Don Eloy fell on top of him. Sitting on his chest as if sober, he began to slap Roger in the face, while cheerful Altiplano pipe music bubbled in the background. Left side, right. Left side, right. No punches, just hard slaps. Roger felt the blood begin to run somewhere. Concentrating intensely, as if doing some Oriental meditation exercise, he drew his strength to a single point in his arms and pushed the heavy troll off. Don Eloy rolled along the floor like a barrel with arms while the waitress screamed theatrically. Roger kicked him hard once, then left running.

His mind had become his body again, after a long period of improvement and strength and great discipline at saving money. Walking after he became winded, Roger began to age again, and the speed at which he regressed terrified him. At the same time, the pressure came back into his head, stronger than it had been before. Why are you doing this to me? he asked, conscious of aiming the question precisely, an arrow into a void.

No answer, none expected.

The lights had come back on in the city, what few there were. The yellow domesticity seeping through cracks and over transoms both attracted and repelled him. He got lost. Better not to go back to his tent. If Eloy sobered up he might remember who had kicked him and send his hired trolls back to mess him up. Anyway his brain worked better with his legs moving. Before he found a place out of the wind to lie down in he had aged a good two hundred years.

The sun woke him early, his body stiff, his eyelids crusted with blown dust. A bulky waddling *cholita* lent him a tin basin of cold water to wash in, and he wandered the streets of El Alto again. Don Eloy would be in bed with a hangover, and his men, knowing that, would show up late for work. For the moment Roger was safe from hostile trolls. All he needed was something to eat. With something in his stomach his brain would be able to come up with a plan. The main thing was not to focus on the money he had lost, because that would lead him to think about how close he had come to getting back to Flint and safety, and desolation would freeze his feet to the stony ground.

He couldn't help walking past places offering breakfast: hot *llaucha* pastries and that gooey purple liquid the Bolivians called *api*. It was Roger's favorite, better than Froot Loops with bananas. Eventually someone would turn his back for a moment, and Roger would swipe just enough to stay human, just enough to keep his brain engaged. One more marauder from the north would take advantage of a southern victim. No.

Despite his setback, he was not the same stone cowboy who had walked in a daze out of el Panóptico. He owed Don Eloy and his lumberyard that much, which was the little discipline he had worked his way into. If he stole some breakfast, odds were some sharp-eyed troll would catch him. He imagined a herd of angry, skirted *cholitas* tearing down a mud street in hot pursuit, holding on to their bowler hats in the wind of their own outrage, while the stone cowboy ran tossing warm, incriminating pastries the way he had once tossed dime bags of dope under similar duress. And if the Bolivian police picked him up again and checked their record books, the closest he would ever get to Flint and normalcy would be in a sad stone fantasy lying on his back in the dark in el Panóptico. He had already lived through several centuries in that particular prison. He let his stomach growl.

Resolution made, intuition lit him up. Why was he in El Alto in the first place? Because that's where the airport out of Bolivia was. Without his thinking much about it, the City of the Future had seemed to be the first step up and away from exile in La Paz. But there was no chance in the Andean world that he could get out of the country the way he had come in. The way out, therefore, was the way down. Back down into La Paz. The truth chastened him.

Not enough to hold him back, though. It took a long hour to get his bearings, and then to find a street that led to a road that ran into the *autopista* going down the lozenge-shaped canyon back into the city. Back. He had easy luck hitching. A solo bearded gringo with the eyes of a zealot, watery blue and fixing, picked him up in an old green Jeep and told him Jesus was a revolutionary. The man had the face of a fish with a one-track mind, a pike maybe, at home in cold deep water.

"Don't go looking for him in your suburban Yankee malls," he lectured Roger, as if that were a likely temptation from which he had to be warned off. "His skin is brown, brother, and he's with the people that get hurt for a living. Our brother Jesus hangs with the world's oppressed."

"Amen," Roger whispered straight ahead into the bug-smattered windshield. Past the windshield was the city he thought he had escaped: dirty cobbled streets on which malnourished dogs picked through heaps of garbage, *barrios* of stone buildings climbing the steep walls of the canyon as if to get away from something deadly in the center. Odds were what they were afraid of was real, where they thought it was.

"You're hungry, aren't you?" the fish-faced man told Roger when he dropped him downtown in front of the big San Francisco Church.

Roger's stomach turned over in anticipation. He nodded, not trusting himself to say a word that might deflect charity.

"I figured so," the man told him, stroking his thin beard. "Well, guess what?"

"What?"

"You're going to stay hungry until you stop looking for Jesus in the malls and start seeking him where he is truly to be found. That's the pure unvarnished truth, *amigo*. Chew on it for a while and see if you're not comforted."

Inside the stone cowboy was a candle burning low; he could feel its little heat keeping him alive. Any unnecessary excitement just might blow it out, so he closed the door of the Jeep softly and walked away. By the time he reached the middle of the plaza in front of the church he had come up with all kinds of lancing comebacks, but he opened his clenched fist and let them go, watched them flutter up and dissolve in the thin, bright air, butterflies that weighed nothing, which was what they were worth.

He had gone without food before. One time years before in Ames, Iowa, he had gone thirty-six hours on a pack of Twinkies when leaving the room he had rented might have caused some painful complications in his life. He knew that for a long time it was the idea of eating more than the food itself that got to a person. So he didn't take too seriously the complaints his body was making. He swallowed, bringing back the sickly sweet taste of the Twinkies in Iowa. The problem was what the hunger was doing to his ability to think in a straight line.

If sunlight could be sharp it was falling sharp on the plaza that morning, little jabbing needles on Roger's face, his bare arms. He found a place in the flat diagonal of shade cast by the church and pushed his attention outward, away from his body and its discomfort. Anyway the plaza was almost always good for a gape, full of trolls with grim expressions going about their troll business, plus tourists with cameras, suckers and hunters of something they could snap and call ex-fucking-zotic. Roger watched a crowd gather around a tall, gaunt man in a bright red poncho with black fringe. An Argentine, from the exaggerated way he talked. The Bolivians watched him unpack a suitcase, set up a collapsible wooden stand on which he stacked jars full of a viscous blue liquid that shimmered in the sun. Then out came the snake.

From the grainy diamonds on the snake's back Roger would have said rattler, but there were no rattles on the end of the tail, and the Argentine in the poncho handled the beast without much care. Maybe it was the Great Andean Squeeze, a famous imaginary snake that haunted the dreams of traveling gringos, and other dark places. For a long time Roger watched the salesman hustle his crowd, letting the snake out of its cage to wander over the stone pavement, winding its way among the crowd making everybody nervous. When a woman screamed or a man cursed, he would pick up the snake and return it to its cage without locking it, letting the snake discover again that it was free to escape, sort of. The bottles of blue liquid, whatever they were, were selling at a respectable clip. Hunkered in the shade, absorbed by the spectacle, the stone cowboy forgot himself, which was all to the good.

"Excuse me, please. Do you speak English? Are you an American? Do you know this man? Have you seen him?"

Something in that voice set him off from the start. It was the voice of a schoolmarm, the voice of her red fingernails scraping down a blackboard to get your attention when you spaced out something basic, like the year George Washington chopped down the cherry tree. It was the voice of Florence Nightingale, another mercy nurse with an overblown idea of what she was doing for the suffering world. And she looked the part, from the ground up: Sensible sandals by Dr. Somebody or Other, a denim skirt ideal for rough-and-ready traveling in third world shitholes, just rinse and hang it up to dry and you're ready for your next danger-packed outing among the natives. A white blouse that neutered.

Not that she was homely. She had her little mystery, her unknown secret quality that made her attractive. Her brown hair, long, was almost blond. He liked the way brown twisted into blond and back again, like camouflage. Her brown eyes, too smart to be the eyes of an animal, took him in the way they must be taking in everything that crossed her field of vision. She was the kind of self-contained woman he liked to ride next to on a bus, inventing an identity for her, and a story that ended in her naked need for somebody like him. Not this one though, not in a million years.

Roger took the photograph preserved in plastic wrap that she handed him and studied it for a moment. On the periphery of his vision the Great Andean Squeeze snake made its winding way among a crowd of hayseed Bolivians who wanted their bottle of blue goo. A woman screamed, but it was a phony scream, a scream that said I really want this snake to keep wrapping himself around my feet, just pay me lots of attention. Instinct, he told himself. When in doubt it's the crutch you walk with.

"He's your brother, isn't he," he told the woman, who stared down at him in neutral, waiting to see whether this one would do her any good, find her what she needed to find.

"He's my brother," she nodded.

"And you came to Bolivia to find him . . . "

"Please. Have you seen him?"

The stone cowboy studied the face intently. "Why do you want to find him? Is that a fair question?"

"It's personal." She took the photo from him impatiently, tucked it into her sensible leather purse, which was probably also the place she kept her cash stash. Unless she was wearing it next to her skin in one of those nifty pouches people like her bought before going abroad. If she was, then that was where she kept her passport, too. Roger knew a place in La Paz where he could get enough cash for a gringo passport to buy a plane ticket to Miami, or close. It would be a victimless crime. All she had to do was go to the window at the consulate and tell them some dangerous druggie attacked her in the street and they would issue her a new one on the spot. He would have sold his own passport but that was trickier. The vice-consul would laugh in his face when he heard that a band of antiimperialist trolls had mugged the stone cowboy in a dark alley in Villa Miseria, beating the shit out of him in retribution for what the United States of Imperial America had done to Bolivia over the long, sad centuries.

"Wait," he told her when she turned away. "I know him, I've seen him."

"You're lying."

"Why would I lie?"

"What's his name?"

"He never told me his name. He said it was bad luck, and there were people after him. He's superstitious, isn't he?"

She nodded, couldn't help it even though her people-judging instinct told her to walk away. She wanted very badly to find this brother, who must be a bum to go away from a stand-up sister like this without leaving a forwarding address.

Chances were where you found them, what you made them. Before she could get away Roger stood up and took her arm lightly, led her away from the plaza. The idea was to trick her body into thinking they were heading for the brother, who had to be within walking distance. Trucking uphill from the plaza he guided her up Sagarnaga Street, ascending into another level of strangeness. The things for sale by *cholitas* in bowler hats and skirts were things a woman like this would not have imagined, not even in her dreams: red-eyed fish with jointed bodies made of silver, weavings that told the story of the creation of the universe, devil's head masks with outlandish bulbous features covered with spangles and beads, dried and preserved llama fetuses in baskets lined up together like some gruesome animal gallery, exotic powders and potions and unguents with weird names in Aymara.

"Please," she said once, "if you don't know where my brother is, just let me go. I'm not good at this."

"At what?"

"At traipsing around a place like . . . like this place is, looking for somebody who doesn't want to be found. I don't speak Spanish, and people try to take advantage of me. I like things to be in their places, and nothing is in the right place here, is it? That's the kind of person I am, am I not?"

"How am I supposed to know what kind of person you are?"

"Because I'm transparent. That's what everybody says. I'm good and I'm responsible and you can see right through me. If you can't, it's because you don't want to, and because you're mean spirited. Ask anybody who knows me what I'm like and they'll tell you. I'm Agnes the self-effacing miracle worker, and I'm transparent as the light of heaven."

He heard the panic rising in her, a song she would have to sing eventually and be a better woman for it. Having panicked himself a few times—his first day in el Panóptico they wound up calling the American consulate; they thought he was going to explode in messy little chunks of fried gringo flesh all over their filthy fucking prison—he recognized the feeling, and the feeling's need to come out.

"You have to take it easy," he warned her, "until your body gets used to the altitude up here. There's no oxygen in the air, you know. No joke. The trolls' bodies are different, it doesn't bother them."

"Trolls?"

"The Bolivians. The CIA has this top-secret report that says Bolivians aren't humans, they were dropped here by a spaceship from Mars. The U.S. government has all kinds of shit like that they never tell their citizens about."

He had pushed too far. Angrily she pulled away from the false security of his arm in hers. She looked at him too upset to spit out the nasty things she wanted to be saying, walked away down a side street picking her way past cardboard boxes jammed with llama fetuses. How many dried llama fetuses did one country really need, for Chrissake?

Roger watched her go, but not out of sight. She was his only option. He trailed her long enough to realize that she was only wandering, trying to walk off the bad mood he had put her in. When she stopped at a little troll restaurant he came in and quietly took a seat next to her.

"I'm sorry," he told her. His repentance was real. "It's just that I haven't talked to an American for a long time. I'm out of practice."

The place she had picked was a typical low-grade La Paz eatery, four little tables on spindly legs, a woman knitting behind a counter pretending they weren't there. The customer is always invisible, Roger reminded himself; the first rule of Bolivian business. His stomach was hallucinating. The trolls made great soups, and those white-flour rolls were good enough to write home about. *Dear Danny: How's tricks on the assembly line? Have you Motor City hardheads finally figured out how to make cars the way the Japs do? Anyway you wouldn't believe where I'm writing you from.* Right, Danny would not because he could not.

Roger tried to start over. "What's your name?"

She shook her head, not at his question but at something private Roger didn't hear. He wished he could; that would help him understand her, and to get what he needed it would help to understand her.

"The thing is," he told her, "I was in jail here for a while."

That was the last thing he wanted to tell her. Now she would never trust him. To a woman like her he was just an ex-con, some shady character she sort of remembered from the day she stayed home sick in sixth grade and watched a movie on the tube way back in black-and-white days when people like Roger were called hardcases. But he couldn't keep his mouth shut. "Just before I got out," he told her, "this very weird thing happened. It was like all of a sudden I was talking to God."

Her purse lay on the table between them. Not Roger but his fingers picked it up, played with it a little. Touching it felt like violation.

"Are you going to hurt me?" she asked him, calm as a judge.

It was a relief not to have to lie. "I don't want to hurt you," he told her. "I want to help you find your brother. My name is Roger. I'm the stone cowboy. Now you tell me your name."

"I told you, my name is Agnes," she told him, "and people admire me because I do social service work and I'm dutiful and respectful to my elders, and so far I haven't believed a single thing you said." She pointed at his restless fingers. "Except that you were in jail. If you steal my purse you won't find anything in it that will help you out of the fix you're in, whatever it is."

"I'm hungry," he said, and without comment she bought both of them big bowls of thick, hot soup in which lumpy orange tubers floated, each the shape of a differently deformed man. It was the best soup he had ever eaten, and he was grateful.

"Go away now," she told him when they left the little restaurant, but he understood that he didn't have to. He stayed half a step behind her on the way to the *pension* where she had rented a room.

They got to the Empire of the Andes just in time to hear Doña Inocencia remember her vision. Doña Inocencia ran the *pension*, three stories of cold stone sandwiched between identical locked warehouses. Roger had spent enough time in Bolivia to understand the place, which was a rookery of relatives and friends coming in from the country looking for jobs, finding them, losing them, going back to their insufficient patches of Altiplano land. There were times when he actually felt sorry for the trolls, who were always drawing the shortest stick.

"Do you speak Spanish?" Doña Inocencia demanded of Roger in the downstairs common room. She sat in her chair like the queen of a very small kingdom. The woman didn't dress like a *cholita*. She wore a regular human house dress, and there was light in her eyes, not the sullen hostility he was used to finding there. But Agnes was embarrassed. She was sure the Bolivians would think she was bringing a man to her room to satisfy her basic human needs. She tried to disappear but the landlady wouldn't let them go. This was Doña Inocencia's world; if you passed through you paid your tribute. The furniture was pre-Colombian, the indoor air cool and slightly stale, the light from a single ceiling lamp pale.

Roger answered her in polite Aymara, and all the relatives tittered. He was a hit. "Then tell the *señorita gringa* to sit here, next to me," the old woman patted a chair, "but she has to be careful she doesn't smoosh the bird."

Doña Inocencia, it turned out, had two crippled legs. Her relatives took turns trundling her every morning in a wheelbarrow down treacherous streets through the market to the Prado, where she begged. The bird, a clay-colored pigeon with clipped wings, kept her company. Not sure what she was being roped into, Agnes took a seat stiffly next to her landlady.

"Relax," Roger told her, "this is just trolls being sociable." He sat in a chair that sagged, next to a man who had to be a miner. Both his hands lacked fingers from an accident with dynamite, which had also left his face in a permanent scarred grimace.

"How did it go today, Doña Inocencia?" the stone cowboy inquired politely.

"Not as well as it should have. At noon here comes this foreigner, one of yours he must have been, with a piece of good fresh bread in his hand. But he meant it for the bird. Can you believe it? I showed him the pocketful of grain she was sleeping on and said could I eat the bread myself? He lifts the bird out of my pocket and pets it. He shakes his head and gives me some change and says something in Spanish, very bad Spanish, about how hard life in the colonies is, thinking he was talking way over my head. But we're not that stupid, are we?"

"Tell the North Americans about your vision, Aunt Inocencia," a woman in a lacy black shawl urged her, eyes studying the ceiling.

"These foreign people don't care about all that."

"Yes we do," Roger encouraged her. He translated for Agnes. "She had a vision, and she wants us to hear it. You want to listen, don't you?"

Agnes nodded slowly, and Doña Inocencia shook her head to toss off her pretense of doubt. "You have to understand what it meant when the gringos went in their rocket ship to the moon. What year was that? It doesn't matter, a long time ago already. You see, the good Jesus has always had a camp up there. He likes to spend the night there when he gets restless in Heaven, worrying about all the world's wickedness, *que hay de sobra pues*. So when the gringos landed on the moon it spoiled his peace."

"What does Jesus look like?" Roger asked her. Serious question. He wouldn't want to go through the experience again, but life in el Panóptico had given him an open mind.

"He is a tall man with no hair on his head, and no beard. He wears a long gray saint's robe that covers his knees. The fabric is very smooth. In the pockets of the robe he carries corn. His skin is red, and he makes a person feel scared and happy and sad and holy all at once just by seeing him. Last night I saw him in a vision when he came down to the earth to speak with the Pachamama. They went up into the mountains together. I saw the two of them sitting together on a peak. The Pachamama was crying. I couldn't make out the words, but I had the sense that she was lamenting the bad things being done to her. Helicopters, she told him, and soldiers from the North were tearing up the coca plants. She told Jesus it felt to her like they were tearing the hairs from her head.'

"Jesus said nothing, of course. It's not very often he will actually speak. What he did was point to the sky—I saw all this quite clearly—and the clouds that had been up there parted, and in the open space out came a full moon, blacker than the night itself and shining."

Roger wanted to hear more, but Doña Inocencia had said all she was going to say. She retreated into herself, and the relatives scuttled. Hanging back sociably, the mangled miner whispered to Roger that he was from Potosí, and he knew more about Trotsky than any *yanqui* intellectual ever thought of knowing, and what did Roger think about dialectical materialism?

"I think the world is a whale," Roger whispered back. "And the whale is swimming in space, and if you don't hold on tight you'll fall off and get drowned."

When it was safe to escape he followed Agnes to her room, which was on the minimal side. An iron spring cot with no mattress, a piece of twine hung from wall to wall from which dangled a single hanger. A crockery bowl and pitcher. The walls were a chalky rose, with water stains in suggestive shapes running in every direction. It looked like home. It had to be home, which was the place he needed.

He watched Agnes set up a small gas stove and boil water for tea. She was the kind of person who didn't need to fill up the empty air with nervous words. She was self-contained, an admirable trait that ticked him off, for some reason. From a plastic bag folded several times she took a Red Rose tea bag. "We'll have to share," she said when she handed him a pale blue enamel mug with a chipped rim. "So was it prison that taught you to speak such good Spanish?"

"You're not going to get very far here if you can't speak, Agnes. No troll is going to go out of his way to give you a hand. They'd just as soon see you bleed to death in the street as offer to help."

"What is it you have against the Bolivians?"

"Not a goddam thing. It's what they've got against me."

"Then why don't you leave?"

"I'm working in that direction."

"What was that woman, Doña Inocencia, saying downstairs?"

"She's a mumbo-jumbo queen. She sees visions and tells people about what she sees and they believe her."

"Well, what was the vision?"

"The Aymara have a god here. They call her the Pachamama. She's the Earth Mother."

"Why do you like to run everything down?"

Roger's policy was never to answer a question head on. Too dangerous.

"According to Doña Inocencia the Pachamama is angry. She's royally pissed off at the gringos, which includes you and me, by the way. If they thought they could get away with it they'd lynch every foreigner in the country and make soup out of the carcasses."

"Why is she angry at the gringos?" This was like taking a test in school, an essay test where you had to give something away you'd rather hang on to. Way back before the world began, Roger had always liked the multiple choice kind better, because he was fairly good at guessing.

"It's the coca thing," he explained reluctantly. When she took the mug back from him to take a sip he noticed a little mole on the underside of her wrist. Seeing it made him uncomfortable, as though he had caught her undressing. Somewhere the wings of an unusual bird beat in darkness, and Roger shivered.

"You don't express yourself precisely. Is that because you don't want to? Or because you think I won't understand what you have to say? What do you mean when you say 'the coca thing'?"

Never head on, not ever. "You think the Bolivians like having nine thousand gringo grunts in camouflage uniforms and their helicopters and trucks and riverboats with guns and millions of dollars worth of high-tech equipment invade their country to wipe out a plant that's been sacred to them for thousands of years?"

No answer.

"There was this guy in el Panóptico that told me every time a coca plant is torn from the ground by the roots it's like raping the Pachamama's body. He wasn't a troll, he was French, but he understood how the trolls think. He was a friend. He gave me a present once. I still have it."

"Don't you think the government of the United States has a moral obligation to fight the drug traffickers on their own territory? Do you think we should let them just go on poisoning us with their cocaine so that they can get richer?"

This was like trying to talk back to somebody on TV. The opinions expressed by the high-strung lady looking for her brother in Trollandia do not necessarily reflect those of the frigging management. Roger wanted to change the channel. He didn't, couldn't. He was home.

"This French guy, he was a serious doper but fairly intellectual. He said down in their subconscious, wherever that is, the trolls believe that the Pachamama wants them to get organized and throw out the invaders. They're always talking about reclaiming their lost cultural heritage and all that revolutionary shit. Watch: When they say 'lost cultural heritage,' what they really mean is gringo blood should be running in the streets of La Paz. It's code, so CIA types and your average dumb gringo don't understand what they're really getting at."

Agnes nodded. "This helps."

"Helps what?"

"It helps me understand why my brother came here, what it was that attracted him to the place."

"You mean he's into the Bolivian subconscious?"

She looked at him hurt. He hadn't been trying to make fun, not enough to hurt, anyway. She breathed in the way the heroine in a movie did before being led out to the wall to face the firing squad. No blindfold, please, I can take what's coming at me, because my cause is just. "My brother," she said slowly, "is a magician."

A slow glow of satisfaction warmed Roger on the inside, but he gave nothing away. Home was the place he wanted to stay.

"Our father is a minister in the Unitarian Church, and he teaches philosophy at the university. He is an unusual man, gentle and intelligent and perceptive and understanding. Jonathan has worked very hard for a long time to be sure he wouldn't turn out to be a son his father could be proud of."

"I get it. The old man isn't into magic as a career. He thinks the kid should have gone into insurance."

Roger couldn't remember the last time he had had a conversation like this one, with a gringa like Agnes. Maybe never. He liked not liking her, which was not the same as trying to hurt her, which he was not doing. He liked it that she called him on everything.

"What is the poison in you that makes you mean? Is it drugs? Have you taken a lot of drugs?"

What he couldn't explain was that he was still the stone cowboy but he was coming down off the high plains, looking for a valley, hopefully green and sheltering. All he really needed was to get out of Trollandia to get soothed and straight.

"The Bolivians believe in magic," he told her instead. "Up on the Altiplano in the villages there's all kinds of magic men. They have all these ceremonies where they burn llama shit and coca leaves and do all kinds of weird things. The French guy said it's not bullshit, they really believe it. He kind of believes some of it himself."

"But you don't . . ."

I believe the world's a whale, he didn't tell her, didn't tell her he wasn't going to fall off because he was an expert at hanging on. "When did your brother come to Bolivia?"

That was the way with her, keep turning her back to her brother and the reason she was there. "Jonathan was never one for staying in regular touch, not with anyone. We got postcards sometimes, from different places across the country. He never said anything like I'm doing fine, don't worry about me. His handwriting is very small. He filled up all the space on the back of the post card with his mystical gobbledygook."

"Your brother sees visions like Doña Inocencia?"

"In his case I don't think he really sees them. He imagines them and then tries to convince himself they were real. His postcards always included profanity, and they always had something calculated to upset our father. But three months ago we received one, the last one, written in plain English. There's no more magic in Gringolandia, he said. The car manufacturers and the war manufacturers have exterminated it from the North American continent, and he for one couldn't live without magic in his life."

He let her catch her breath without trying to work his knife into the hole she left open. What he heard in her voice wasn't bitterness, exactly, it was the thin hard thing left over after the bitterness was reamed out. She poured more hot water on the tea bag in the mug, and he stared at the mole on her wrist. It was cold in the room but not as cold as it was sleeping on the street in El Alto, and he felt himself slipping into neutral.

"He said there was still magic in South America, if you got far enough away from the pollution zone to feel it. That's what he called our country, the pollution zone. Can you imagine how that made our father feel when he read it? Our father fought in the Navy in the Pacific Theater in the Second World War, and he calls the United States mankind's noblest experiment-in-progress, and his son calls it the pollution zone. You're falling asleep, aren't you."

"Not everybody can be a Republican," Roger told her.

"Our father is a registered Democrat, and he marched in Selma in the sixties. He doesn't have a Republican bone in his body. You don't understand a thing I'm saying, do you?"

"I understand you paid big money for an airplane ticket and came all the way down here because your loser brother wrote Bolivia on the back of a postcard once. That doesn't make a whole lot of sense to me. Don't you think you might have jumped the gun? For all you know he changed his mind at the last minute and went to Katmandu. He'll show up. They always do. I might even show up myself some day, if I can get the cash together to get out of this shithole of a country."

"Go away now, please. I gave you something to eat, and I've let you rest and get warm. But you have no idea who my brother is or where he is, and that's all I can care about right now."

She was scared of him, a little; he saw it in the way she held herself away from him as she sat, heard it in a quiet backbeat behind the rhythm of her words. He didn't take that personally. He was the kind of guy, for her, who used to show up at the house looking for her brother so the two of them could go get into some serious trouble. But he needed badly the resting space she could give him.

"I want to help you find him," he said. It wasn't a lie. If he wasn't as hard up as he was, he would have been the shiniest knight. "Anyway how do you expect to find him if you can't speak Spanish? Let me sleep for a couple hours here, and then we'll start looking. Cross my broken heart."

He had her. She was smart enough to see he was the cheapest translator she could hope to find in Trollandia, where nothing ever came cheap. "I speak some Aymara, too," he said. "Not a lot, but enough to ask some questions. If your brother's really here and hanging out with the magic men, they won't speak much Spanish."

She pointed to the bed, so he took his shoes off, crawled under her covers, and lay on his back watching her sit rigid in the chair, which she moved across the room as far from his body as she could. She wrapped her hands around the enamel mug and squeezed until her knuckles puffed pink and white. He was the hardcase prisoner in his cell, and she was the warden with no sense of humor. Slipping into sleep was the sweetest release.

⸙

It was still light when he woke, but just barely. The light in Agnes's room was gray and feathery, like Doña Inocencia's pigeon, and cold. Somewhere to the west, the sun made a tiny clinking noise dropping over the far side of the canyon wall. She wasn't there, which was more of a break than he had expected or deserved. He got out of bed, pulled on his shoes, and searched her suitcase. Incredible. There it was, tucked in between her extra skirt and a pair of rolled up jeans. She had gone out leaving her passport to be safeguarded by a stone cowboy, and inside the passport were five one-hundred dollar bills, so new they were stiff. In-fucking-credible.

He shoved the passport into one jeans pocket, wadded the money into the other, grabbed his jacket. Out of there. But he stopped to look at something she had written, left lying on the seat of the chair.

Dear Father: I don't quite know how long this will take to reach you through the international mail. Maybe I'll be back with you before it arrives, I'm sure I will, but it does me good to talk with you this way. As I write I imagine you reading in your room. I pray that Doctor Avery will have told you already that you can get up and start walking around a little, but if he hasn't, please please don't. What can be accomplished by strong will to speed your recovery you will accomplish. But you have had a serious heart attack, Father, and I worry that you will pooh pooh what Dr. Avery tells you and tell him you know best. I can just see you screwing your mouth down tight and looking righteous thunderbolts at him all the while saying, Mind over body, Avery, mind over body. But this is your heart, and I am not ready to give you up yet, even to God.

I thought I would keep you abreast of what happens as I go along. I know how your restless mind needs something to chew on as you lie there in bed, and besides, it will help me think clearly. I will admit that I have been mightily discouraged here from the outset. No one is friendly, and almost no one speaks any English, and all I've managed to do is bump about blindly asking whether anyone has seen Jonathan. But today I've had my first stroke of luck, and I intend to put it to good use.

This morning I met, entirely by chance, an American who speaks wonderful Spanish and even, he claims, some Aymara, which is the Indian language spoken hereabouts. He has spent a great deal of time in Bolivia and appears to understand the country better than most. He has offered to help me track down my brother, and I see no reason not to take him up on his generous offer. For the first time since the plane touched down I feel as though the optimism I told you I had is justified. At any rate the hardest part of this, which is doing all the asking, is now going to be enormously simplified for me. I know you are reluctant to use the word prayer, *but in the course of communicating with your Maker in the way that you do I hope you will pass on my grateful thanks for what has happened.*

Please don't take my worrying like this, long distance, as some kind of emotional fussbudgetry. My head is clear even though my heart hurts. I came to Bolivia to find Jonathan so that I could tell him his father has had a serious heart attack and wants very badly to see him again to put to rights all the bad things, all the hard feelings, that have happened between the two of them over the years. For his father there is nothing more important in his life, and nothing will ease him the way making peace with his son will. It is the same for Jonathan himself: There can be nothing more important to him, not even his magic, and I am confident that he will understand that when we finally get a chance to talk.

. . . I just reread what I've written and I sound to myself like some sort of little miss prim, chastising to beat the band and pointing out the obvious to her tolerant father. It's not like that, I'm not like that. I know you worry about my being alone in a place like this but don't. Anyway I'm no longer alone. I have my translator and trusty guide. . . .

Shit. He folded the letter, lay it flat on the chair seat, smoothed an end that had curled up when he read it. For a moment he panicked, felt trapped the way he had felt the first weeks in el Panóptico when he woke up in the lonesome middle of the long night and remembered he was still in hell and no way out. But this was something different, and it was happening in a different place, quiet in a spooky way, as though someone was listening to the scraping sound his thoughts made as they turned in the track of his two-hundred-and-ninety-year-old brain. He realized he was going to have all the time in the world to make up his mind, and that made him angry. Stupid woman, he said aloud but immediately regretted the assault on the silence that filled up the room. Everybody in Doña Inocencia's pension had died and gone wherever trolls went when they died.

He let his hands think for him, make their own decisions. He watched them pull the passport and the still stiff hundreds from his pockets, replace them in Agnes's suitcase, close the lid gently. Then take just the passport out again. It was his hands that found an honorable compromise. On their own they put the passport back into the suitcase and took instead a nifty flashlight with a compass and a clock and some camping gadgets in the handle; he could sell it for ten or fifteen bucks on the street. Ten bucks was four hundred and ninety less than five hundred, but it would get him away from her and give him another day to come up with an escape plan.

Out of there. Taking his jacket. He was. In the lobby the only troll in sight was the scarred miner, who asked him what he meant about the whale and wasn't it an insult somehow? If it was, why didn't he say flat out what he meant? Your existence on the frigging planet is an insult, Roger whispered to him in unintelligible English, relieved to have someone to be mad back at. Peace, he told the miner, put your faith in plastic surgery. Gone.

Except in the street here came Agnes swinging her ignorant innocence in a sack of many colors. "You really needed the sleep," she told him. "I was too restless to stay in the room. I went down to the Prado asking people if they had seen my brother."

"Any luck?"

She shook her head, as if she had only just then realized it. Maybe she walked all the way from the Prado to Villa Miseria in a state of suspended animation, lying to her body to keep it plugging away uphill. Roger understood how that worked, had done it himself many times. Her father had it all wrong. Body over mind was how things were. Your mind was a feather, and your body was all the air in the world, and the wind blowing it.

She bit her lip, making him think of a disappointed kid, some girl in a birthday dress, only her sadness was scarier. "Where are you going, Roger?"

"Going?" He did not feel bad for taking the flashlight gizmo, not when he could have cleaned her out. Going.

"You'll be back, won't you?" Having panicked himself so recently, he understood how that strange pipelike sound came up like a controlled scream out of her warm and vulnerable insides. That was the worst thing about thinking, imagining how things could be for somebody else.

"Back," he told her, working to keep it from sounding like a question flung back at her own ignorant, innocent question. He found a whole sentence to say, almost. "Be back," he told her. "Good luck."

Gone. He was two blocks, three maximum, from a place he knew where they would be happy to give him green gringo dollars for her high-tech flashlight. In the place where his heart had been he wished her all kinds of luck finding her flaky magician brother, who had to be the earth's scummiest scum. Luck. She watched him walk away.

TWO

Sitting on a bench next to a hundred-year-old *cholita* with a hunched back who smelled like bread, watching a herd of Bolivians line up to visit the criminals in their families, Roger swore himself a promise. When he got back to Flint—and he would—he would do whatever it took to make Danny understand what twelve bucks worth of troll money could buy. Which was not much: a full belly and just enough space to catch your breath in.

In prison once—across the street from where he sat, in a cell called Hell—he had read in *Time* magazine that all the *yanqui* factories were being taken over by the Japanese. Pretty soon all they'd be producing was some kind of robot, a metal-munching monster that made life easier for the owners of everything and put real people out of work. On break, Roger would slip up to the roof with Danny to smoke a joint and steal some sunshine and get away from the Nip foreman, a mean little bald guy who carried raw fish in his lunch bucket. The fish stank. Down below, their friends would be griping about the Japanese lessons piped into the plant at lunch hour. They knew their brains were being washed, but no one could quit because they had mortgages and car payments and half a life to keep going. Meanwhile up on the roof, floating above all that flapping noise, Roger would explain to Danny what it was like to be twelve dollars away from disaster.

The food was stoning him, but he had to stay out of Fantasylandia. Get real, stay real, get out of Bolivia. It was a stupid idea to come back to el Panóptico, the place he hated most in the country he hated most of any, most of all. Criminals were supposed to return to the scene of the crime, not the place they paid for it. Coming back was like fooling around with a gun held up to your own head; it produced a tingle in a tender place that felt pretty good, but you still might get blown away.

The idea was to walk in straight lines. If you could see them. With the twelve bucks they gave him for Agnes's fancy flashlight he had filled his stomach with soup and bread and salty meat. There was enough left to buy a joint, but he did not. What he had was breathing space, just enough time, if he was lucky, to figure out how he was going to get out of Bolivia. You could breathe on a bench in front of your ex-prison as well as you could anywhere else in La Paz, which was not too much. Some hustling businessman could make a killing filling up empty bottles with air and shipping them to the Andes.

He watched a woman in the visitors' line take off her bowler hat and hit her kid on the head, hard, with the brim. No reaction from the kid; that was the troll way, hunker down and take it. He realized that there was something about the Bolivians he didn't hate. He didn't want to think about what they had in common. Nothing was something.

He thought about getting paper and a pencil, writing a message to Claude in Spanish and sending it into the prison with one of the visitors. He could pay somebody to smuggle it in. But there was no way to know whether it got there. There was no reason, based on experience, to trust anyone to do anything.

Fuck the drugs, 'cuz they are fucking you. That was the main message. Claude was a semimystical person. They had never talked about it, but Roger thought it was likely that he believed in mental telepathy, which was basically a way to get messages across without stamps. He concentrated. If Roger thought hard enough, focused the right way, Claude would know he was there outside the walls, and he'd listen for the message.

The line moved slowly, a snake being sucked in by a big, patient stone beast. Then from a side door Roger watched a man step out into the free air. He held one hand palm up as if to check for rain, then buttoned up his jacket and slunk away like the sleazy criminal he was. El Verdugo, the trolls in el Panóptico called him. The Executioner. He was bald, lumpy, mean. His skin was tough, creased deep as an alligator hide. One afternoon during a minor misunderstanding he had knocked Roger down and kicked his body with steel-toed boots until Roger realized he had to play dead to save himself. He died convincingly, and eventually el Verdugo walked away to pick on somebody else.

Roger told the *cholita* on the bench good-bye first in English, then in Aymara, followed the prison guard down the street, staying in spitting distance. Luckily he was going downhill. Roger was weak again, which meant vulnerable, and incapable of doing much distance. He worried that the Executioner would suddenly flag down a bus, or a taxi, and he would lose him. But he kept slogging on foot, square shoulders out like a general on horseback, and the stone cowboy followed.

Revenge, if it worked, would be sweeter than clean sex. When the prison guard got to his house, which had to be the domestic equivalent of el Panóptico, his wife weeping and wailing in dirty rags while his kids, chained to filthy stone walls, did their homework in ink made from their own blood, Roger would stop him on the doorstep. He would identify himself as the messenger of death and retribution in the name of all the people the Executioner had hurt, hit, or shat on in el Panóptico. He would break his arms, break his legs, burn a peace sign on the bastard's tongue. He would rip a page from the school notebook of his oldest son and write a message in el Verdugo's blood, something like DEATH TO TROLL OPPRESSORS!

No. On a corner he stopped. In a slow-moving herd of trolls who all looked depressed in the same spooky way, he thought he saw Ceferino, one of Don Eloy's men. It wasn't, but even if it was Ceferino there was nothing left to take from the stone cowboy. He thought for a moment of the money he had lost that would have taken him out of Bolivia, and the thought made him weaker still. Then he thought, for no reason he could figure, of Agnes's father in his sickbed back in Gringolandia. It was like being there to see it: the sick man's long bony fingers looking yellow against the white sheets, sunlight coming through a half-open window, and the songs of birds like angels perking up his dreams. He let el Verdugo escape to ruin other prisoners' lives. Not that there was any connection between one thing and the other.

In a little park with steep steps leading down to the Prado, Roger lay on a bench and slept. The good thing was nobody would bother to rob him. About certain kinds of things people were smart. They knew, for example, when you had nothing worth taking. The park was loaded with birds, black ones with beaks like syringes, but they refused to come into his dreams, which moved like slow water toward a place too far downstream to imagine. Pulled by the undertow, he dreamed panic: He was stuck in a place that had no air, and the people around him had no faces, just the same hostile mask, behind which they were laughing at the gringo who had nothing in his pockets.

Cold air woke him. The sun had gone down, and there he was: still in Bolivia with a few bucks, two hits of windowpane acid, and an idea. He walked uphill again in the direction of San Francisco Church, killing time until the *peña* opened.

All the bands in La Paz started late. Even after the place opened he had to wait while couples and little crowds of party people drifted into the club. The smell of the food they ordered made Roger dizzy. He was used to living lean. The Paceña beer he ordered took more money than he had to waste, but it was an investment in his idea.

"I know you," she admitted when she finally came in with the musicians. She was dressed like a gypsy in a long, shifty dress decorated with amoeba-shaped purple paisley. Her limp blond hair was hidden under a kerchief, and from one ear a silver hoop dangled. A little green-and-yellow parrot with glass eyes sat in the hoop, swinging when she moved her head.

"You read my fortune once, in the plaza."

"Was I right?"

"You said I was going to get out of Bolivia."

"You will," she said, "if that's what you really want."

The members of the folklore band she played in hauled their instruments onto the little stage and began warming up. Roger felt the eyes of the *zampoña* player on him, hard and suspicious. "He doesn't like you talking to me."

"Ernesto? There's lots of things Ernesto doesn't like." She tapped the inside of her tambourine with nervous fingers. "You can't tune a tambourine."

"Your name is Cherokee. I remember."

That impressed her, impressed him, too, given the more or less decrepit condition of his brain. "I have to ask you something."

"I can't talk now. We're going to start in a minute. I'm part of the band."

"It's important."

"Then hang around till we break."

"I can't afford to sit here and drink, and if I don't drink they'll throw me out."

Ernesto was talking to the guitarist, an arrogant-looking guy in a black poncho with red stripes. Before her keeper could notice, Cherokee took some money from the pocket of her dress and left it on the table. She picked up her tambourine and climbed the stage looking like a person who didn't owe anybody anything.

Roger had heard enough Bolivian folk music to last a lifetime, but it was pleasant to sit there drinking on Cherokee's money, watching her charm the Bolivians in the audience and the musicians next to her on the stage and even Ernesto, who was doing a pretty good job of hiding, for the moment, his possessive instinct.

On the band's first break she came back to his table. "I can't stay long. Do you like what we're doing?"

"How come you stay with the guy if he won't let you breathe?"

"I need a place to rest," she told him. That much he understood. "You didn't like the music, did you."

"I'm trying to find somebody. A magician. He used to hang around Sagarnaga Street. You do magic, don't you?"

"I do magic. That's my job. The band is just to keep Ernesto happy, plus I like standing in a place where I can look down on people."

"Do you know the guy I'm talking about? A small blond sort of guy that takes himself real seriously? A pain in the ass kind of guy. He didn't like anybody talking during his act. One time I saw him light into a troll for whispering in the middle of a trick. He was a real intense kind of person."

"What's a troll?"

"A Bolivian. That's their secret identity no one will ever admit."

"I can't talk right now. Besides, you make me feel jumpy, like all of a sudden you're going to explode."

"There's not enough of me left to explode. You should have known me a couple hundred years ago."

"Go outside and wait."

"What about Ernesto?"

"Ernesto is my problem."

By the time Cherokee stepped out of the *peña* into the cold night air of La Paz Roger was shivering. Not from the cold but because he was wearing down. But the way up, he still believed, was the way down. She was carrying a blanket.

"What's that for?"

She didn't like head-on questions any more than he did. "Follow me," she told him, and took off toward the Prado. She flagged down a taxi, an old green 1970-something Dodge, and opened the back door for him. Roger could not conceive, any more, what it would be like to have enough money to take a taxi.

"They don't give me any money for playing in the band," she told him as the driver made a big deal out of getting into first gear. "But I do magic during the day, and I keep whatever I get from that."

"You're rich," Roger told her. He meant it. He admired her for being able to do a little more than survive in a place as hostile as La Paz. Maybe you were born being able, or not; the idea that that might be true depressed him.

They got out of the taxi at the base of a city landmark called El Monticulo, climbed steep stone steps in the dark to the park at the flat top of the hill. El Monticulo was a lookout kind of place, with paths past marble statues, under enormous eucalyptus trees. In the daytime the peaks of the Andes stood up like prison guards over the city, keeping people in. At night the lights of the city lay like bright flowers on a deep lake of darkness. The wind blew high and hard.

Roger followed Cherokee until she found the bench she wanted, out of the way of the wind, almost, but with a view of the sloped city below. She unfolded the blanket. Inside, the tootsie in the roll, a bottle of red wine. She uncorked the bottle, told him to sit. She sat beside him and wrapped the blanket around both their bodies.

"This is going to cause you all kinds of grief with Ernesto, isn't it?"

The wine warmed him fast. He knew its strength was temporary, but under the circumstances it was stupid to turn down any consolation that came his way.

"Ernesto is temporary in my life. He did me a major favor one time."

Under the blanket their jeans touched, and he felt her hand travel until it found his. He was holding hands with a gringa fortuneteller at the windy top of the world. He wished he had someone to tell that to. He sent up a thought balloon toward Danny in Flint, but the wind took it, whipped it south until it popped in the dark.

"When I saw you at the *peña* I thought you wanted to hustle me, but you don't, do you?"

He did not.

"Who are you?"

"I was in jail here, in el Panóptico. They let me out, but I don't have any money to get out of this shithole of a country."

"Bolivia's okay, you just have to make an effort to understand it. The magician you're looking for, his name is Flame. Flame believes Bolivia is where the magic went after the Industrial Revolution happened up north. If he's right, then that explains all kinds of things."

She put the wine bottle in his mouth and tilted it gently until he could drink. That made him feel like a baby, sucking and being taken care of. There were worse feelings. Cherokee inspired confidence.

"Just before I got out of el Panóptico," he decided to tell her, "this weird thing happened. I was in the infirmary, and it was like I was talking to God or something. I wasn't trying to, it just happened."

"That's the magic working, is what Flame would tell you."

"Do you believe in the magic?"

She shook her head, drank from the bottle. "Not the way Flame does. It's like, everybody has to have a story to make life tolerable, you know what I mean?"

He knew. "Like the trolls all believe they are the oppressed good guys with all kinds of soul, and the gringos are the bad guys, the ones that do all the oppressing because they don't have any soul so all they can think about is making money off the backs of Bolivians. I had to listen to all kinds of that shit in el Panóptico. They wanted to make me feel guilty for being a gringo. I had one friend, a French guy, a real committed doper. Don't take it seriously, he was always telling me. It's just dust in their eyes, it's the illusion that keeps them sedated."

"Dross," said Cherokee.

"What's dross?"

"That's what Flame called the dust in their eyes. But he thought if you got past all the dross you could get close to the magic, the real thing. I'm not saying you can't."

A little wave of wind got in under their blanket, and Roger realized how frigging cold it was. The cold made him turn toward Cherokee at the same time she was turning toward him, and they kissed.

"I like the taste of your spit," she told him. "It makes me think of drinking Campbell's soup when I was sick when I was a kid."

He ran the palm of his hand down her back, felt that she was wearing no bra.

"We could make some love up here and nobody would ever come by and notice," she said, thinking it through aloud. "But that's not what's happening, is it?"

It wasn't. What was happening was different: It was giving and taking comfort in a condition of exhaustion. "It's like my system is shut down inside," he told her.

"Mine too. But that's okay. That's why I knew I wanted to come up here with you and be under this blanket. We're the same, aren't we?"

"You mean shut down?"

"It's probably not forever. I wish I believed in the magic the way Flame does. It would make things better."

"Better?"

"More interesting, or more exciting. I don't know."

"Will you tell me where Flame is?"

"Tell me why you want to know, first."

"I'm a spy for the Industrial Revolution. They sent me to bump him off before he gets his hands on the magic and turns it against us." He wasn't sure why he didn't want to tell her the simpler truth.

"Flame is the one who brought me to Bolivia," she told him. "We met in this convenience store I was working in. He gave me my aura name. That's how come I know I'm Cherokee. I went with him when he did a tour in the U.S. We did two swings across the country, one north, one south. He's real good at his magic, plus he believes in what he's doing. He was always restless, though. Even in his dreams he used to talk about the magic men in Bolivia. It gave me the creeps. I didn't want to come with him when he told me to get a passport."

"But you did."

She laced her hand into his again, and the intimacy came close to sex, came close to waking up something inside that he was not ready to wake up. He put his tongue into her mouth, let it explore, wondered what the chemical reaction might be when two different spits sloshed around together in the same small place. They drank some more wine.

"I came to Bolivia with Flame because I didn't want to go back to stacking dogfood cans in a convenience store."

"And?" It pleased him to know there was an and.

"And because I liked the idea of the magic even though I didn't believe in it the same way Flame did. Does. I don't want to tell you any more about Flame unless you tell me why you want to find him. Is he in trouble?"

"He's in trouble if he doesn't find the magic, I guess."

She pulled away from him on the bench, taking the blanket with her. The abandonment was more than Roger could handle, just then. But years of experience with people he had no right to trust had made him reluctant to tell simple truth. He got as close as he could to that. "His mother is here in La Paz. She's looking for him because his father had some kind of heart attack or something. He might be dying. He wants to see his son before he goes, to make peace with him, I guess. His real name is Jonathan."

"Johnny," she corrected him. "That was his name before he found his magic name."

"The way I understand it, Flame and Father Flame never got along real well. It had something to do with Flame not wanting to follow in the old man's footsteps selling insurance."

"What does all that have to do with you, though?"

He wanted to tell her that he had his own code name, that he was the stone cowboy, but he was hurt when she pulled her body and her blanket away from him. The wind was eternal, it was the actual idea of wind blowing itself real. "Let's finish the wine," he said.

"I have a joint," she told him. "One of the guys in the band gave it to me last night."

He came close. In the low place he was crossing on foot, a million feet down below the high plains of Bolivia or anywhere else, a single toke would power him up, get him going. He would recover his imagination, which was pretty much gone. But he knew that would be a mistake. One hit and one day, sooner or later, he would die in Bolivia.

"How come you didn't smoke it last night?" he asked Cherokee.

She shrugged, moved back in his direction. He lifted the blanket to take cover with her once more, touched her breast lightly in a way that meant respect, meant *in another time*. She understood the gesture, and its tact. It was like talking a language he had forgotten he knew. It occurred to him that maybe he hadn't.

"It's like the sex," she told him. Taking on such confidence came close to killing him. He had been too alone for too long.

"I understand," he warned her.

He didn't want to hear more, but she wanted to say it. "It's too dangerous, right now. I have to stay shut down. You know what I mean? It's like there's something good inside you that has to grow first, before you let yourself go, but it won't grow unless you're shut down for the right amount of time, which you don't really know what it is. Does that make any sense to you?"

More than he wanted it to make.

"Why won't you tell me what finding Flame has to do with you? You don't like being straight with people, do you."

"Flame's mother is paying me to help her look for him. She doesn't speak Spanish. She's helpless in Bolivia. The trolls will take all kinds of advantage of her, and she knows it." It was the kind of truth he was capable of.

"And the money she pays you is what will get you out of Bolivia."

He nodded. It seemed true, and tempting.

"I left Flame because he was hitting me," Cherokee told him.

"That's a pretty good reason."

"It took me a while to figure out how to survive here, and until I did I stayed away from him. I thought maybe he had left La Paz. Then one day I was out walking on the witches' street and I saw him. He didn't see me. I followed him. He went into this building up near Little Miami. It looked like some kind of warehouse. It was dark and grungy and it gave me the creeps, but I went in after him."

"How come, if he was beating you?"

"Flame has this power, not just over me, over lots of people. He draws you in. Partly it has to do with what he knows and what he tells you, all that magic stuff that he can make you believe. But there's something else inside the guy. The spooky thing was, there was nobody else in the warehouse. He didn't seem surprised to see me, either. He was way up there. When he gets up like that he can't help looking down on you. He made me feel like a stranger to him, somebody he maybe ran across once but he can't remember where, not the woman who came to Bolivia with him.'

"He told me not to talk, this was his waiting room. Waiting for what? I asked him. He looked at me like I was insulting him, and I saw how wasted he was. He must have been doing lots of dope and not eating. He used to go through this phase when all he'd take into his body was dope and fruit juice. But this was the worst I ever saw him look. It was like he was old, and I had this fantasy that maybe he really did find the magic but they made him trade away his youth for it, you had to be old and wasted to see what was there."

Roger had a vision of the guy in a dark warehouse in La Paz waiting for some illumination that wasn't coming, and he saw again Agnes's father in his sickbed waiting for his worthless son to come home, and he saw Agnes herself waiting in the hotel room for someone to help her put the pieces of her family back together. He found in himself no wish to help. He liked it better when his imagination didn't work.

"Flame went into this long rap about how close he was getting, and he had finally come across some Bolivians who were willing to help, but he had to be ready for what was out there. He was worried about some big catastrophe, though. It had to do with the coca plant."

"I've heard all that shit before. Some of the trolls believe it, too. That's probably where Flame picked it up. You know, you can go crazy if you don't talk to your own kind once in a while."

She looked at him wondering whether he meant her. "Next door to the warehouse is a magic shop," she told him. "The woman that runs it knows Flame. If he's still around." She told him how to find the warehouse.

"Thanks. What's going to happen to you when you go home to Ernesto?"

"I can't go home tonight. He drinks when he plays. It'll be okay tomorrow morning. He's weaker in the morning. He won't admit it, but he likes my blond hair."

"So what are you going to do all night?"

"I'm going to sit here under the blanket and think about a house in Lockport, New York. That's where I'm from."

"What's in the house?"

"Tall windows with sunlight coming through, and spider plants, and all kinds of musical instruments, and a Siberian Husky, and a man who doesn't hit women."

Roger knew the odds of such a place existing were about the same as the odds of Flame the magician's finding his ultimate super-buzz illumination in a La Paz warehouse, or Roger himself working on the line again in Flint with black boots and a lunch bucket and health insurance, but he respected Cherokee's need to dream, which seemed to him to be a fairly pure impulse. They held each other for a while and finished the tail end of the wine. Nothing to say, which relieved Roger. He had said more, listened to more, than he was used to doing.

For a moment he held her breasts in his hands, and she closed her eyes, and they rocked a little on the bench under the blanket. Her breasts felt good, like stones with just the right amount of give to them. But it couldn't go any farther—shut down meant shut down, and for a reason, even though neither one of them might understand it—and it was stupid to think of spending the night next to her there when she was going to get up in the morning and go home to Ernesto the *zampoña* player, who was taking some kind of care of her.

"See you in Lockport," he told her, but he wasn't sure whether she understood the compliment.

It cost Roger all the strength he had picked up from the wine and proximity to Cherokee's body and her house in Lockport to get himself down from El Monticulo, then up the Prado again back to the Empire of the Andes. Locked. In the one low light left on in the lobby he made out the mangled miner from Potosí asleep on a couch. From his face-up position Roger knew the man was snoring, dreaming about dialectical materialism, which was only another way of saying sour grapes, if you thought about it.

He knocked politely but loud. The miner shifted on the sofa. He knocked harder. The miner sat up, rubbed his face with one wounded hand, looked at Roger in the street. He shook his head and lay down again, pulled a pillow over his head.

Roger pounded on the glass hard enough to rattle it. "We will bury you," he screamed in English. He knew the miner could hear him, and he felt a wave of the anger that used to run through him at el Panóptico when one of the trolls hassled him and there was nothing he could do to defend himself, let alone get even. The door of the Empire of the Andes was half glass, loose in its frame, and so thin that enough pounding might break it. He pounded.

His fists on the rattling glass made plenty of noise, but he thought there should be more. No way was he spending the night in the street. Agnes wouldn't want him to. He cursed in Aymara, he cursed the little that he knew in Spanish. The miner pulled the pillow tighter over his head and rolled over so that Roger had to look at his miserable back, the scarred neck, the vulnerable tailbone that made him look like some kind of burrowing animal. He wanted to curse in English, but what came out was a song. He had forgotten all the songs he used to know. The one that came back surprised him, but he was too wound up to take much notice except for the peripheral pleasure of remembering "I'm A Little Teapot" all the way through. On the last verse, before he started "I've Been Working on the Railroad," he won.

"The sky is falling," he told the miner in Spanish when he came to the door.

"You're not registered here."

"My sister is. Agnes. You know her."

"Your sister?"

"All I want is to tell her something. Then you can throw me out."

The miner shook his head. "You're a liar. What you want is a free bed."

"Then put it on my sister's bill."

Doña Inocencia would not want him to turn down anybody's money. Pretending to be more reluctant than he really was, the miner finally let him in. "Hang on tight," Roger told him, meaning to be friendly. "The world's a whale. All you have to do to stay alive is keep hanging on."

Outside Agnes's room Roger hesitated. He had to let the anger drain out, or what he wanted to accomplish with her would be spoiled. When he knocked, the speed with which she responded made him think she must've been lying there awake in the dark.

"It's me, the stone cowboy." Your guide and interpreter, he held himself from adding.

"Go away."

"Let me come in, please. I have good news."

"You stole my flashlight, and then you lied to me. You told me you were coming back. But you went out and sold the flashlight, didn't you."

She should have been grateful he didn't take the five hundred dollars and her passport, but he didn't think she would see it that way.

"I'm back," he said. "I'm back now."

"Please go away. If I let you in you'll only steal something else, and for some reason I have a hard time stopping you."

"I found somebody who knows your brother."

"Liar."

Everyone thought he was a liar, especially when he was telling the truth. "He goes by the name of Flame, and he's still in Bolivia. There's a magic shop up near Little Miami, next to this warehouse. The woman who owns the shop knows your brother. She knows Jonathan."

She opened the door. In the hall light he saw she was wearing a blue terrycloth robe, tied tight, and thick glasses that blanked the beauty that was in her face if you paid attention and were watching when it came out in her expression. He figured she must wear contacts during the day, and it pleased him to see her the way she was, without them. It was a kind of nakedness he could handle.

"The name of the magic shop is La Cueva. That means the Cave. I know how to get there."

"Who told you?"

"Please let me come in, Agnes. My legs are giving out on me, and I'm freezing."

"Who told you?"

"The gringa girl who came down to Bolivia with him. Her name is Cherokee. That's the name your brother gave her. She left him."

"Why?"

He didn't like the mean sense of satisfaction it gave him to tell her, but he told her. "Because he beat her."

It was as though he had hit her himself, and the satisfaction evaporated. From under her thick, ugly glasses tears dripped. From the face of another woman, in another life, he would have wiped those tears away. Now, in this life, the main thing he had to do was get inside. He moved toward her while she was distracted, and she let him enter.

The bulb in the room would not turn on, so Agnes felt in the dark for a candle and matches. Roger felt bad about the flashlight. If he had known, he would have taken something else, something she would not have immediately missed.

"Why did you lie to me?" she wanted to know.

It wasn't a lie, it was a truth that took longer to happen than maybe it should have. But he knew she would not have the patience for that sort of explanation so he didn't try. "I'm a different kind of person," he told her.

"No, you're not. That's just it, you're the same as most people."

"And you were hoping I wasn't."

"Why didn't you steal my money?"

"I thought about your passport," he admitted.

"If I let you sleep on the floor, will you take me to La Cueva in the morning?"

He promised, and she blew out the candle. It wasn't too bad on the floor, because she gave him her sleeping bag. Rooms at the Empire of the Andes came with plenty of blankets. He lay trying to calm his body, letting a little cocoon of warm air build up against his skin. With the warmth, and the homey quiet of Agnes's room, the shaking almost stopped. He drifted, not to sleep but to a place like peaceful waiting. The first time she spoke, he didn't catch what Agnes said. He thought it was thank you but it was something else.

"Voiceprints," she repeated. "Did you ever hear of voiceprints?"

He had not.

"They're like fingerprints, only more precise because they tell you more about a person."

"Now who's lying?"

"Did you ever know two people to have the identical voice?"

He was learning; he would not have guessed that she liked to play, not like this or at all. Stuffed into her bag, he identified the separate smells of wool, and dust, and sweat, and something faintly sweet he couldn't place.

"To capture the print accurately, I need to hear the *r* sound distinctly," she told him. "Repeat after me."

He repeated: *"Round the rampant rugged rocks, rude and ragged rascals run*."

"Good," she told him. "Say it again."

"I don't like talking in code."

"It's not code, it's poetry."

"Same difference."

"Say it again, please."

He said, "So tell me what my voiceprint says about me."

In the absorbent dark he could hear her sigh. "Thank you for coming back, Roger."

But he wanted to know his voiceprint identity.

"Your voiceprint tells me that you're not as tough as you want to be, that you can be nicer than you pretend to be, and that you honestly believe the reasons you give yourself for telling lies."

But he didn't like the way she was heading. "Don't," he told her.

"Don't what?"

"Don't make me into something I'm not. Don't pretend I'm what you need me to be."

"It's not me," she insisted. "It's in the voice."

"I can do yours."

"Go ahead."

"It works different for me. I have to hear the *f* sound."

"Okay."

"Say Fuck the frigging faggots when they fart in your face."

She surprised him by saying it without hesitation. Maybe the darkness helped, loosened something that needed loosening to work right. He asked her to say it again and she did, more slowly. Coming out of her schoolmarm's mouth it sounded sweet, and good, and inventive.

"So what do my voiceprints tell you?"

"That this is your three-hundredth reincarnation."

"What was I before?"

"You want all three hundred of them?"

"Yes."

At least she had an ego, which he assumed was all to the good.

"The thing about reincarnation is you don't necessarily go up or down on the scale depending on how good you were in your previous life."

"I know that."

She knew that . . . "One time you were a fox, I'm pretty sure of that."

"Is that up or down on the scale?"

"No idea. But it left you with something this time around. You're smart, and you know how to hide it, which keeps you out of trouble. If I'd been a fox things would have been a lot easier on me this time around."

"What else was I?"

"You were a Bolivian."

"Is that good or bad?"

"How come you think everything has to be good or bad?"

"Because your answer will tell me something I want to know about you."

"You were a *campesino*."

"What's that?"

"A *campesino* is a small-time farmer who's born poor and dies poorer after living a fairly miserable life. In your case you lived on the Altiplano growing potatoes and herding a couple llamas. One cow. You had thirteen kids but seven of them died on you, and your wife didn't like you very much. She wanted to marry your older brother but he didn't want anything to do with her, so she took you instead and never forgave you for it."

"Second best."

"But since you were already a fox you knew how to hide all the things that could cause you any grief."

"Such as?"

"Such as the bad feeling you got laying on top of your wife in your shack up there on the high plains when you were absolutely one-hundred-percent sure she was thinking about your brother, who was good looking—in a troll way—and knew how to make everybody in the village laugh."

"Who else was I?"

"Aren't you getting tired of this?"

"No."

"Your father rode you pretty hard, didn't he."

"Don't say anything about my father. You wouldn't understand him, not the first thing. He's a Unitarian."

"What's a Unitarian?"

"A person who would like to believe God is a person but can't."

"Are you married? At home, I mean."

"I'm not married."

"Living with anybody?"

"I'm not living with anybody."

"You shut down?"

"What do you mean by that?"

"Nothing."

"Do you want me to tell you who you were in one of your earlier reincarnations?"

"No."

She told him anyway, but he blotted out the story of who he might have been by concentrating on the memory of what it had felt like to be under Cherokee's blanket on the top of El Monticulo, the giving hardness of the fortuneteller's small breasts, and the wind that seemed to blow specifically at him, and the unsayable satisfaction of recognizing he had something in common with her, which was the fact of being shut down inside.

In the morning Agnes's cheerfulness hurt, nails on a blackboard. She watched him eat the breakfast she bought him in Doña Inocencia's dining room, the walls of which were covered with folk art that Roger despised: dancing devils with leering faces and twisty horns, flat-faced wood carvings of noble Indians, paintings in which the Andes looked tame and inspiring instead of what they really were, which was the most hostile landscape on the face of the earth.

"You eat like an animal that hasn't been fed for a week," Agnes told him, bubbling. "You know, Roger, this is the first progress I've made since I've been here. All of a sudden I feel sure that Jonathan is still in Bolivia, and that I am going to find him, and that he will go home in time to see our father. And that Father will be at peace about . . . things in general."

Eating food she had paid for, he saw no reason to contradict her with anything that would puncture the big pink balloon of her fantasy. Without consciously thinking it through, he had come to a decision that he thought was fair, and straightforward, and involved no lying.

"I'll take you up to La Cueva and translate for you," he told her.

"Thank you."

"After that, I have to be going. I need to get out of this country. I'm going back to Flint. That's where I'm from, sort of. Where I used to be from."

"Of course," she said slowly. "I have been writing down some simple sentences in Spanish that will help me ask people about my brother. You can help me by looking over the sentences and fixing the grammar."

"I don't know shit about grammar."

"All I need is for you to tell me whether people are going to understand what I'm writing."

He resented what he heard in her voice: hysteria with a cap on it, and she would never lift the cap. He wondered how he could ask her for enough money to get across the border into Peru. Lima was a big city, and they didn't know him there. He could lose his passport there and the consulate people would have to put him on a plane back to Gringolandia. That might work, unless he was in their computers, in which case he would have the same credibility problem he had in La Paz. But he would worry about that one in Lima.

"I'll be glad to look over your sentences," he told her gently. He knew he couldn't ask her for money, even for a loan. If she didn't offer, he would get into her pack and make the loan himself. If things worked out that way, he would take down her father's address and send the money to her there once he got set up in Flint. Before he got set up. Danny was the kind of guy who would front him the money no questions asked.

It took longer than he had expected to find the warehouse and La Cueva, and when he did come across the place, Roger almost blew it for Agnes because the woman who ran the magic shop reminded him of Don Eloy's wife. She was shaped the same, but all the *cholitas* had that same pyramid shape. It was the way she inhabited her place of business, as though nothing outside her walls mattered at all. Everybody on the planet was born with a certain amount of imagination, though the amount varied. What they did with what they had was what mattered. The owner of La Cueva had shrunk hers to fit inside her shop. It was ironic, if you remembered that her business was magic supplies.

The place was loaded with paraphernalia that Flame would know the use and meaning of: boxes full of dried llama fetuses of various sizes. The empty eye sockets followed him around the room making him feel like a shoplifter. Not that there was anything worth ripping off: Sacks of leaves and heaps of bright-colored powders and dusty books in Spanish and a barrel filled with wooden flutes and Pan pipes and something else that looked like a blowgun for poison darts.

"What do you want to buy?" the woman asked them.

Roger wanted to rag on her the way he had liked to rag on Eloy's wife, but the point was not to make him feel good, it was to find out something useful about Agnes's no-good brother.

"What is she saying?" Agnes asked him.

Roger could scarcely tolerate her eager enthusiasm. "She says she's sorry she's so ugly and her store is such a rat hole, but that's life in Bolivia, that's troll life in general and there's no use fighting it, is there?"

Agnes unwound layers of plastic from the photograph of Jonathan, of Johnny, of Flame, the Mystical Gringo. "Ask her if she knows him."

Not that easy, not with a troll. The woman shook her head and asked them again what they wanted to buy.

"I'll buy something," Agnes said impatiently. "Anything. Pick something out."

But that would be a mistake. If they gave in too easily to the *cholita*, she would never tell them anything. He took charge. "See this woman with me? She speaks no Spanish, and her Aymara is even worse."

If trolls could giggle, this one did. Roger was encouraged. If she had any sense of fairness, Agnes would pay him for what he knew, which was exactly what she needed, at the moment.

"The guy in the picture she's showing you," he told the owner of La Cueva, "is her husband. They're from New York City. You know that big statue of the woman with a torch?"

"The Statue of Liberty."

"It's huge, you know, it's enormous. The guy in the picture is an artist, a sculptor. He and his wife were living inside the Statute of Liberty. Right up inside the torch, in an apartment, for inspiration and to save money. But he couldn't take it. He flipped, ran out on her. He left her with five little kids to raise by herself. He told her he needed to find some magic."

She nodded fiercely. He had her. Zing zang zung. "He's crazy," she told him. "He has no idea of magic, not the real magic."

"Do you think it's fair of him to run off and leave his wife with five kids?"

She shrugged, and Agnes wanted to know what she was saying.

"Go wait in the street," he told her. She went.

"No luck," the *cholita* said to her vanishing back. "She'll never get that one back."

"How come?"

"Because he wants to be gone."

"Is he still in La Paz?"

She shook her head, and Roger felt more disappointment, for Agnes's sake, than he would have expected to feel. He could see her chasing the Mystical Gringo down to Tierra del Fuego and maybe farther, all the way down to the South Pole, the home of negative Santa Claus. The *cholita* was right. The farther Agnes chased him the harder he'd run, without even trying. Meantime their father drifted closer to the genuine edge. It was sad, if you thought about it; reason enough not to think about it.

"Cochabamba," she offered. It was a gift, unasked for, and he appreciated her generosity.

"He's in Cochabamba?"

"They like him."

"Who likes him?"

She shrugged her shoulders expressively, meaning she wanted to tell. "The ones who use the warehouse."

"What do they use the warehouse for?"

"To keep things."

"Do they ever talk to you when they come by?"

"Not to me."

"But you know who they are."

She knew one. "He only came once. In a Mercedes, blue, with those black windows you can't see into. Did you ever see a car like that? That's a car for someplace else, someplace with good streets. Not for La Paz. The rest of the time it's just his men that come."

While Agnes fretted and paced in the street, Roger exercised the patience that was required to get what he needed to know. It was a question of listening sideways. The *cholita*, he finally figured out, was not really like Don Eloy's wife. She was an open-minded kind of person. He took what she had to give, and if he had had some money of his own he would have bought a blowgun from her as a way of saying thanks.

"He's in Bolivia, isn't he," Agnes said. "I can tell by your face. What's wrong? Is he hurt?"

He changed his plan again. What he needed to do was get away from her before he got stuck. If she offered him some money he would take it. But he would not rip her off. Several cruel ways of telling her about her brother came to him. He used none of them. A troll carrying a devil's head mask with three-foot horns and confetti streamers came up behind them and ducked into La Cueva, and Roger wished it was as simple as being in Flint.

"Your brother's mixed up with some drug dealers," he told Agnes. Straight was best. "Cocaine. He's with them in a place called Cochabamba, near the Chapare."

"What's the Chapare?"

"That's where they grow the coca leaves and make the paste that they make cocaine from. It's an ugly place: It's a jungle, only it's full of coca paste labs and buyers and sellers and gringo DEA agents and UMOPAR police—that's the Bolivian version of DEA."

She shook her head. "My brother is stupid and selfish and misguided, and I'm sure he likes drugs, but I can't believe he would become a drug dealer."

"Let's walk," he told her. She looked like she was going to wilt and drop. They walked across Little Miami paying no attention to the piles of contraband crap people wanted to sell them.

"It's not that your brother's a dealer," he explained when he thought the blood was pumping in her again. "He's like, kind of like the entertainment."

"I don't understand."

This was hard, had to be. Roger had a sense of doing the right thing and nobody around to notice or care. Give me back . . . he heard someone whisper. Not him. Not now. "One of the big-time paste buyers is a rancher from the Beni. They call him el Grán Moxo. He's an albino. He has to keep moving, so he has houses all over Bolivia. One of his houses is in Cochabamba." He felt like a teacher in history class, which was a reasonably good feeling because not something he had experienced with any frequency.

"El Dorado," she said.

"I don't follow you."

"El Grán Moxo is the name of the legendary king of Paititi, the place the Spaniards thought they were going to find when they went hunting for El Dorado. The Golden City. They never found it, because it probably never existed."

"That's something you just happened to know. . . ."

"I read it in a guidebook on the way here. On the airplane. There was nothing else to do."

"Whatever." She was definitely the kind of person who read guidebooks about places before she got to them. "From what I understand, the Grán Moxo is one of those insane guys, unpredictable, the kind of person tough guys look up to. People in el Panóptico were always talking about him. He's the kind of guy that'll either kill you or give you ten thousand bucks depending on which way you rub him. They say he's got enough cash to pay off the Bolivian national debt."

"What about Jonathan?"

"Apparently he likes your brother's magic, or his rap, or something. That part's not real clear to me. Anyway the woman at La Cueva heard that el Grán Moxo took your brother with him to Cochabamba. Kind of like the team mascot, you know? What else would you expect from a bunch of Bolivian druggies? Their mascot is a gringo magician. Hey, are you okay ?"

"I'm okay," she told him, and the amazing thing was that she was. Almost.

He took her arm to stop her. "So now what, Agnes?"

"Now," she told him, breathing in hard, "I have to go to Cochabamba."

"I can't go with you, you know."

"I didn't expect you to."

"I'll help you get to the bus station, if you want me to."

"I can find it."

"Why don't you show me those sentences you wrote in Spanish?"

"You can go now," she said, making him feel like a kid dismissed from class for screwing up. In school it had been his best subject. "I don't need anything from you, Roger."

But he had the time to go with her back to the Empire of the Andes, where Doña Inocencia herself checked Agnes out. The mangled miner was nowhere to be seen; the question of an extra body in Agnes's room for one night did not come up, which saved a little unnecessary embarrassment.

Since he had nothing of his own to carry, he hauled Agnes's neat little backpack for her on the way to the bus station. He could have taken off running. He knew she kept her little cash stash in the bottom of the pack, in a navy-blue canvas wallet with a red-and-yellow stripe. Not real, not realistic. He felt bad enough about the way things were working out between them. He wanted to try to talk her out of going. It would be better for everybody concerned, including the sick old man in the States, for Johnny the Mystical Gringo to stay lost. But the way his sister carried herself down the sloping sidewalks of La Paz was proof enough that anything Roger said would be a waste. Agnes was definitely going to Cochabamba.

"What are you going to do to get yourself out of Bolivia?" she asked him once. Her curiosity sounded honest, and simple.

He reached for a wiseass answer, found it, tossed it away. "Not sure yet," he told her.

"Well, you've been very helpful to me. I wish you all the best, Roger. I'm sure you're going to make it."

At the station—full of traveling trolls with that same fatalistic expression that meant they expected their bus to break down, or slide off the road down a cliff, or their country to be invaded by armed forces with superior firepower—Agnes insisted on negotiating her own ticket. He stood away from her, guarding her pack. The determination on her face when she came back from the window was kind of sexy, if you stood at just the right angle to her and let your mind and your eyes play around a little. But she shook his hand like a high-school principal handing out diplomas.

"I have to wait an hour," she told him, taking the pack. "Listen, Roger," she said, and her clumsiness made him panic. He didn't want the handout he was afraid she was going to offer him; he needed it.

"I've got to get out of here," he told her. "Good luck, Agnes."

She understood him, gave up on her bad idea, which should have been a great idea. He called himself stupid, because he was.

Away from the station, the relief was as good as he expected it to be. Going nowhere, he walked. He thought about going back to El Alto and breaking into Don Eloy's. He would take only as much from the troll lumberman's green metal box as they had taken from him. Then a bus to the border. Except Don Eloy always had a gun around. He thought about hurting himself just bad enough to get into a hospital, where they'd have to call the consulate and then maybe they'd put him on a plane back to Gringolandia. But he didn't have the nerve it took to hurt himself, not even a little. And he realized he could not take the shit they would throw at him in Customs in Miami when he showed up like some international welfare case. He'd say something that would get him into trouble, and his trip home would start off bad. He wasn't superstitious, just realistic enough to know how one wrong thing led to another.

Without thinking about it too much, he was making a circle. The circle brought him back to the bus station, where he spied on Agnes. She was sitting on a hard-backed bench next to a family of trolls for whom she must be the ex-fucking-zotic one. The upright way she read the red leather book in her hands would make people think it was the Bible, though it probably wasn't. Probably it was something like *Basic Phrase Book for Locating Lost Magicians in Third World Dumps*. All the important parts would be underlined so she could go back and review before the test.

He watched her for a long time, until she looked at her watch, closed her book, and tucked it into the front flap of her pack. Then he was there.

"Good luck," he told her. "I hope you find your brother."

"Good-bye, Roger."

"I don't have any money."

"I know that. You told me."

"If you buy me a ticket I'll go with you as far as Cochabamba."

"Why?" she wanted to know.

"The bus is leaving, isn't it?"

"Tell me why you want to go with me."

"There isn't time," he said. "If you want me to go with you, you have to get the ticket now."

From the same pocket into which she had dropped her book she pulled out her bus ticket. Only there were two. She handed him one. He hoisted the pack for her, and they headed for the bus. One thing he liked about Agnes was that she was smart enough not to keep asking him questions he wouldn't answer.

Crossing the Altiplano in a gray bus that had a red racing stripe and a severe case of asthma, there was plenty of time for Roger to explain to Agnes the unusual history of Bolivia, which was related, in a way you wouldn't expect, to the history of the rest of the world. Partly he thought it would help to keep her mind off the trouble her worthless brother was getting into in Cochabamba, and partly he thought he had spent enough time in the country to understand it better than the average gringo ever dreamed. Not as well as Claude, and not with the intelligent words Claude had, but Roger knew some of the things they didn't put in the guidebooks. It was funny how some things you didn't know you knew until you said them.

"It's hostile, isn't it?" she whispered.

The sky was covered with a single gray cloud, thin as tissue and grainy, scalloped in patterns like the backs of seashells. It let in light but hid the sun. It was like driving across the floor of the moon. There was no air on the moon, either. Just flat miles of stone, like the Bolivian high plains, stone stretching to the horizon, which shimmered a little like most places you could never get to. Sometimes they saw a range of the Andes. Sometimes a single snow-capped peak filled up the sky in front of them. They would drive toward it until the road snaked and the mountain disappeared, and all that was left was more flat stone. They passed hills of heaped stones that could have been burial mounds except nobody in the world would have had the energy to haul and stack them that high, not in a million years. And villages made of mud: A handful of square shacks with mud walls, a mud church with a mud spire in a muddy plaza, maybe. The streets, also mud, were full of men in ponchos and kids with ear flaps on wool hats and black pigs and brown dogs. Squatty women scuttled like black crabs. And then llamas, moving like dignified, humpless camels, beasts of unbearable burden. Roger tried to see it with Agnes's eyes; the effort woke him up.

"They're really Mongolians," he told her.

"Who?"

"The trolls. After the dinosaurs died there was an ice age. You read about that in school, didn't you?"

"Keep going."

"Well, at some point during the ice age a bunch of Mongolians tried to get away from all that cold weather in Asia. It took them a couple hundred years, but finally they crossed a land bridge that led them over here to the Andes. The place was deserted at the time, nobody home except the condors. They explored around for a while. That ate up another hundred years or so, I think. But before they could get back to Mongolia there was some kind of earthquake and the land bridge fell into the Pacific Ocean. So they got stuck here. Rotten frigging luck, if you ask me."

"You're amazing."

"They've got this music you hear every once in a while up here. Lots of pipes and drums and wailing. They call it autochthonous. Close your eyes while you're listening to it and you could be in Outer Mongolia. Anyway over the years they stopped being real Mongolians and became Bolivians. There's two separate breeds: Aymaras and Quechuas, and as far as I can tell they don't mix much. You know how you tend to hate the person who's just like you are? Anyway they wound up with all this incredible space up here. It's so big it feels like half the world, doesn't it? But it's the opposite of prime real estate: mountains and no oxygen in the air, and the only thing that will grow is chuños."

"What's a chuño?"

"They're kind of like potatoes, only smaller. When they harvest them they lay them out on the ground until they freeze dry. They last forever that way, but they taste pretty musty. Bite into one in your soup and it's like chomping down on somebody's dirty socks."

She laughed, or came close to it, but he was trying to make a serious point. "You are what you eat, and where you eat it. I mean just think about the kind of attitude toward life you'd have if you spent your entire existence in a place like this eating freeze-dried potatoes that tasted like socks. They're tough people. They lose all the wars they fight, but nobody can really knock them out. The Incas tried. They invaded once but they couldn't drive them out. The Bolivians just hunkered down and chewed on their coca leaves and outlasted them. They'll outlast everybody. But they've got this basically suspicious attitude about foreigners. They assume you're here to invade them, or if you don't want to invade then you want to fuck them over in some way you're trying to hide from them. So they keep quiet and check you out trying to figure out what your master plan is. Everybody's got a master plan."

Roger liked being in the position of knowing more about something than did the person he was talking to. Agnes was the kind of person who respected knowledge, the kind of person who would have read the chapter on Bolivia twice during the plane ride south. While he talked, she shared out cookies from her pack, and the trip, getting out of La Paz, was like minor liberation.

"What do you do?" he asked her, "I mean back home in the States."

"I work in a place called Futures. It's kind of like a halfway house for adults who have been institutionalized, the last step before they can live on their own in the community."

Roger saw her bending down to tuck a row of beaming retarded people into bed at night. For some reason all her patients were bald, and they wore those pajamas with feet in them. He was sure they trusted Agnes with their intimate secrets. He watched her turn out the light, close the door, walk quietly down the hall to the living room, where classical music was playing on the stereo. It made perfect sense, since her brother was a bum: the dark meat and the light of family dynamics. Roger's most brilliant question came without effort, the way good questions should. "What would you have spent the money on if you didn't have to waste it coming down to Bolivia to find your brother?"

She didn't even have to think about it. "There's a place on Martha's Vineyard. I'd go there off season, nobody around. I'd take all the books I haven't been able to read, and in the mornings I'd walk."

There had to be more to it than good books and walking on the beach. She'd be walking with somebody, or wanting to, but Roger knew she would keep that part of her vacation getaway private, and he didn't push. For a while she dozed, and he tried to fantasize sex with her. It should have been easy. She was right next to him, her body bumping into his when the bus swerved. She was wearing her denim skirt and a white blouse, and asleep she was vulnerable in a sexy way, like Sleeping Beauty waiting for the kiss that would put the blood back in her veins. He tried to imagine unbuttoning the white blouse. She was sitting in a chair. On Martha's Vineyard, in a room near the beach with just enough light to let him see her breasts. But it didn't work. The picture fluttered and went out. He was shut down. He had to figure out what it was he needed before he could really want it.

There was a bad moment when they stopped for gas in one of the mud towns along the highway. It was like any of the little nowhere places they had driven through: an uncomfortable camp in a cold place except it had been that way for a million years, since the first load of Mongolians crossed the land bridge looking for a better life that wasn't to be had. Agnes went looking for a bathroom. He warned her whatever she found was going to be below the minimum daily requirement for adults in the way of sanitation. He watched her disappear around the corner of a mud shack then come right back. She was trembling and flushed.

"I told you it was going to be pretty basic."

"It's not that," she shook her head. "It's something else. All of a sudden I'm afraid."

"We'll find your brother," Roger lied. The Mystical Gringo's best trick was his disappearing act. Abracadabra and there was nothing left but his silk handkerchief on the floor.

"This has nothing to do with my brother," Agnes shook her head. "What's bothering me is here." She pointed to the ground. "I feel as though I've stumbled into someplace I wasn't meant be."

"It's not you, Agnes. Nobody should be in Bolivia, at least not up here on the Altiplano. This place isn't fit for human habitation. Look what staying here has done to the trolls."

"I feel as if I'm trespassing."

"That's the way the trolls want you to feel. Fuck 'em. You're here for the right reasons, aren't you?"

The driver honked his horn, and they headed for the bus.

"There's one thing I can't get out of my mind," Agnes told Roger when they were in their seats again and the bus was back out on the highway down the middle of the high plains, the home of permanent stone. She was calmer, as sexy, in a way he couldn't understand, as when she was asleep. "Once we get to Cochabamba, how do we find the Grán Moxo? We don't have any idea how to do that, do we?"

"I'll take care of that part," Roger told her. Finding the house of a major drug dealer couldn't be too hard. "What you ought to be thinking about is what happens after that. Do you plan to knock on his door and tell him to give you your brother back?"

"Yes," she said. That simple.

She made it simple, kept it simple. Maybe that was the secret Roger had never learned for walking straight lines. Cochabamba, when they got there, was a more reasonable city than La Paz. You could actually taste the oxygen in the air, which was warmer than the Altiplano, and there were fruit trees in the streets, and the dogs looked well fed and frisky. They checked into a quiet dump of a hotel not too far from the city center, and Agnes spread her sleeping bag on the floor for him.

"I can't afford to get you your own room," she told him, and he understood that it was a warning. "Wait here."

Too tired to be curious, he lay on the floor on her bag and drifted until she came back with a package.

"You don't have a change of clothes, do you? How long have you been wearing the clothes you have on now?"

That was a personal question. Coming from anyone else it would have ticked him off. Coming from her, he let it go without comment. In the bathroom down the hall he tried on the clothes she had picked out, which fit him: A pair of jeans and a shirt, sneakers and a denim jacket. He looked at himself in the mirror. The glass was wavy, so that his body was all weird angles and unexpected bumps. They were clothes he might have bought for himself, but they made him feel like some kind of impersonator. He was impersonating a reasonable human being. Which was okay as long as he didn't get caught.

She said nothing about the clothes or the way he looked in them, which tact he appreciated. But the trusting way in which she asked him What next? made him uncomfortable, made him restless. He was a guide, and interpreter, and temporary, and he was taking it on faith that she would help him get out of Cochabamba at least.

It was evening. Bats were dive bombing all the plazas in the city, while old people locked up their businesses and headed home and young people cruised the streets looking for excitement or satisfaction, which may have been the same thing. It was like going on a date. Roger left Agnes to order pizza and beer in a little restaurant near the hotel. He was back before the pizza hit the table.

"He lives in a suburb south of the city. We'll have to take a taxi."

"Tonight," she decided.

"All I can do is interpret for you," he told her. She looked at him like she was trying to get to the hidden meaning in what he said, but there was none.

"Tara," she said when the taxi driver dropped them in front of the house of el Grán Moxo.

"What's Tara?"

"The mansion in *Gone With the Wind*. That's what it is, a replica. It's a perfect copy, only bigger, I think. It must be twice the size of Tara."

From the street they stared through the security fence. Floodlights in an enormous yard lit up the face of the building like the Washington Monument or some other public shrine people came in chartered buses to take pictures of. Roger agreed that it was a fairly ridiculous building to come across in a suburb of Cochabamba, Bolivia. Pillars like the ones holding up the front of el Grán Moxo's house belonged in Greece, holding up civilization.

A uniformed troll with a submachine gun stepped out of the guard house at the front gate. Roger wondered what the difference was between a sub-machine gun and a regular one, but he knew, somehow, that this one was a sub. "What do you want?"

"We have to talk to Señor de la Rocha."

"Who?"

"El Grán Moxo."

"He's not here."

"We're looking for the gringo magician. This is his sister. She has to give him an important message." It didn't sound convincing, not even to Roger.

"This is private property. Get lost." The guard gestured with his unslung gun back up the road they had come in on.

"You're going to get yourself in all kinds of trouble," Roger warned him. "If we have to go all the way back into the city and call Señor de la Rocha from there, he's going to ask what the hell you were doing on the gate out here."

"What are you telling him?" Agnes hissed. It was driving her crazy not to understand the Spanish.

Roger thought it wouldn't hurt to let the guard hear some English.

"I'm telling him he's a worthless sack of shit and if he didn't have the goddamn machine gun I'd jump over the fence and show him how a genuine imperialist hardcase kicks third-world ass."

"Good," she said.

"But he's got the machine gun."

"Tell him about my father."

"Do yourself a favor," he told the guard. "Just call up and tell your boss that the sister of the gringo magician is here and needs to talk to him urgently."

The thing was, Roger was never sure when the anger was going to be there, or how it would work. This time it worked the way it was supposed to, and he went with Agnes up the long brick-paved drive to the house with the guard's gun not quite touching his back. Inside, a tall, thin Bolivian with a pocked face, wearing a black silk shirt and white pants, led them into what would have been a library if there were more books. Ugly pictures in gilt frames covered the walls, and a pinball machine with blinking blue lights and a picture of an electric cowgirl riding a UFO stood next to a big rolltop desk.

The man in the black shirt sat at the desk, pointed with a pistol-shaped hand to chairs for Roger and Agnes. "You're not from the DEA, are you." Not a question.

It was a stupid question, meant only to fuck with them a little, but Roger translated, and Agnes shook her head hard enough for both of them. "All we want is to find my brother. His name is Jonathan. He's a magician. We were told in La Paz that he's with Mr. de la Rocha."

"Do you have any idea how often clowns from the DEA show up here? They only come to badger Mr. de la Rocha. They think: He lives in a big house, he drives a Mercedes, he's a Bolivian. Therefore he must be a drug trafficker. That's how their minds work. They don't want to understand that Mr. de la Rocha is from a respectable old family in the Beni, and that he made his money in ranching. Even in Bolivia a person can make a fortune legitimately. In the United States nobody questions that, do they? Who ever cared how the Kennedys made their money, even though they were rum runners?"

"We'd really like to talk to Señor de la Rocha," Roger said. "It will only take a minute."

The Bolivian shook his head. "Unfortunately he's not in Cochabamba at the moment. I'm sorry."

Roger translated.

"Then ask him if he knows my brother."

El Grán Moxo's assistant lifted his hands, turned them palms out in a gesture meant to suggest his helplessness, and the disappointment he felt at not being able to help. "I think you got bad information in La Paz," he told them, looking directly at Agnes. "I work very closely with Señor de la Rocha. If he had a young American friend, a magician or a musician or a bricklayer, whatever, I am absolutely sure I would know about it. And I can tell you with all honesty that I have never heard of this magician your brother."

"Por favor," said Agnes, understanding without the benefit of translation that the door was being shut on them. *"Mi hermano. Necesito mi hermano."*

"It's not a question of wanting to help or not wanting to," the Bolivian said impatiently. He stood up. "For better or for worse, Señor de la Rocha has no North American friends."

Over.

In the street, away from the guard, who scraped his gun hard in Roger's back on the way out to let him know who won that one, Agnes said, "He's lying."

"Maybe. Probably. But all we can do is ask around town for your brother. There are places he would hang out if he was here. I can find those places."

"He's lying," she repeated.

"There's no way we're going to catch a taxi way out here," he told her. He remembered how weak he was, calculated he could walk as far as the hotel in *el centro* if he had to. They walked.

But they were lucky. Before they'd walked a kilometer a taxi happened by and stopped.

"We're going to *el centro*," Roger told him.

The taxi was a little Korean sedan. Folded into the driver's seat the *taxista* looked like he didn't have enough room to turn the wheel. He looked at Roger in the tiny rear-view mirror. "I know where you're going," he said.

"Then take us there."

"Don't tell the woman what I'm going to tell you, not yet."

"What's he telling you?" Agnes insisted.

"He's telling me about his family."

"The magician, is he really her brother?"

"He is."

"Why does she want to find him?"

"Their father is dying."

The driver nodded to himself in the darkness, whistled through his teeth in a way that would have irritated anybody in the world. "He's out of his mind, you know."

"I know."

"His tricks are sick. They're dangerous. That's why the *patrón* likes him. He entertains him. They affect each other. It's as though they are in a contest to see which one is crazier."

"What's he saying, Roger?"

"He's telling me about his youngest daughter. She's crippled. She needs an operation, but he doesn't have the money. He could sell the taxi to pay for the operation, but then the whole family would starve."

It was true for someone, somewhere, probably at that very moment; he knew that much, which justified telling her the story.

"Are they in Cochabamba?"

"They would kill me if they knew I was doing this. Not because it matters, but because that's the way the *patrón* runs his business."

"Then why are you telling me?"

No answer.

"Are they in Cochabamba?"

"Is who in Cochabamba?" Agnes wanted to know. She had a pretty good ear for the language. "His family? Is he asking us for money to pay for the operation?"

"Last week there was a party at Tara Two," the driver told Roger. "Big, with all the people he does business with. The only whiskey they served was Chivas Regal, they had it running in a fountain. And there was cocaine, a lot of it. That's what's different now. That's what makes me think someday it's all going to fall apart. In the old days he said it was white *mierda* manufactured for the nostrils of the gringos, and he wouldn't let anyone working for him use the stuff. Now a lot of them do."

"Does he use it himself?"

"The brother was there. The *patrón* had him do his tricks for the crowd. They ate it up, really. He's pretty good. But he was doing a lot of the drug, and so was the *patrón*. The *patrón* made a toast. He said something about how his five-year goal was to see white shit coming out of the nose of every gringo under the age of twenty-five, and all of a sudden there's the brother with a little pistol in his hand pointing right at the *patrón*'s head. Everybody gets quiet very fast. Bang, the magician says, bang bang. And everybody's looking to see how the *patrón* will take it. You never know ahead of time how he's going to take something like that. This time all he did was take the pistol out of the magician's hand and slap him in the face a couple times. Then he hugged him, and the magician fell on the floor and started crying. People carried him away, and the party kept going. Do you have any idea how much it costs to fill up a fountain with Chivas Regal?"

"They're not in Cochabamba, are they."

"The *patrón* had to go out of town on business. He took the magician with him. Down into the Chapare. He doesn't like to go there much. He's from the Beni originally. That's where he likes to be.

The houses in Cochabamba and Santa Cruz are for the family, mostly. He doesn't like them to have to see the things that happen out in the Beni. And he only goes to the Chapare if things are going wrong. It's a supply problem, is my guess. He makes a commitment to the Colombians and then he has to deliver on time or he's in trouble. Sometimes the paste makers think they're not getting their fair share and they hold back on him, and he has to show up and convince them he's right. He's always right. You know what I think?"

"What do you think?"

"I think pretty soon the *patrón* is going to get mad at the magician. Things are moving in that direction, they have been for a while."

"He's not still talking about his family, is he?" Agnes asked Roger.

"If you're lucky—if the sister is lucky, I mean—the *patrón* will just beat him up a little and dump him off in the Chapare somewhere. If she's not lucky. . . . There's only so many times you can watch the same magic and find it entertaining. Maybe her brother has to learn some new tricks."

They were approaching downtown Cochabamba, which seemed sleepy at night, the kind of place where people wound alarm clocks and put out cats and gossiped into their pillows, where the palm trees were ornamental and the moon radiated the attitude of a trusty caretaker, somebody with good intentions and no criminal record standing the night watch while the city's innocent citizens slept. There was a question to ask. Roger did not want to ask it. The driver slowed, stopped, reached back to swing open Agnes's door.

"Where?" Roger asked him. "Where in the Chapare do you think he took the magician?"

He was standing on the sidewalk. Folk music came at them quietly from an open door. Agnes stood next to him wondering why nobody was asking her for money to pay the driver his fare. The roaring in Roger's head did not quite cover the name of the place in the Chapare the phony taxi driver said before he drove away.

"His daughter doesn't really need an operation, does she?" said Agnes. "It's about my brother."

But she was wrong about that. What it was really about was not being able to get out of the one place you had to get out of. When they walked to the hotel he held her arm to keep himself from falling. Tingo Tingo.

THREE

The road down turned to grease when it rained. The night he spent on the floor of Agnes's room in Cochabamba, Roger had a dream that disturbed him, made him feel scared and amazingly lucky at the same time. If he had been a normal kind of person, the kind of person whose life was like a story that made sense—started somewhere and went somewhere else and was full of good guys and bad guys and bleachers full of roaring fans—he would have interpreted the dream as a response, finally, from God. He would have thought: He heard me after all, back there in el Panóptico when I was talking to him, but he wanted to make sure I was listening before he answered me. Either that or he's running on cosmic time so the difference between when Roger unconsciously started talking to him and when he finally got around to saying something back was, for God, something less than half a heartbeat and shouldn't necessarily be taken as an indication of his lack of interest. Of course Roger was not a normal kind of person. The story of his life was something you would find in a comic book on the bargain rack, one where they didn't pay the writer enough to make him give a shit about the plot so he wrote it one night when he was blitzed on something strong enough to inspire silliness, and none of the important parts were spliced together in a way that made any sense. The upshot was Roger was not sure how he should take the dream.

In it, however, the stone cowboy was sleeping on a pallet on the floor of a cabin. When the woman woke him he remembered having been there before: on the edge of some woods he had been trying to find for a long time. She didn't have to say a word, just stood there in a long white robe, her long hair loose down her back. In the cabin a window was open, in through which wind was blowing. When he stood up he felt the wind on his body, saw it lift the woman's hair, wrinkle her robe a little. He understood that he was supposed to follow her. He did.

Outside in the woods, the wind was stronger. The strange thing was it made no sound in the trees, the tops of which twisted and bent in a way that made him think of children horsing around, pretending they were going to be sick and throw up. Walking behind the woman, who knew where she was going, Roger felt a tremendous anxiety until he realized it wasn't that at all, it was longing, pure and simple. It was just wanting. He was getting close.

They worked their way through a thicket of scrub trees and came out on the shore of an enormous lake. The air was almost cool. The moon shone on the surface of the water, which was roiled by the noiseless wind. For a minute, the longing growing stronger, he looked out over the lake. Then she pointed. When he saw the sailboat, the sail picking up moonlight and throwing it in their direction, relief overwhelmed him until he realized it was not relief but satisfaction. He had reached the place, finally, where he could see, finally, the thing he had been wanting to see. Finally. The satisfaction was strong enough to wake him up.

His neck lay bare on the floor of Agnes's room, which was cool to the touch. He listened to her breathing going in and out. It made a trusting sound, the sound a bird might make in its nest if it thought there was nothing dangerous in the immediate neighborhood. He remembered lying on his cot one night in el Panóptico listening to Claude breathe after the Frenchman's body had taken in a shitload of dope. But that was a different kind of sound; it was more like counting your heartbeats wondering what the magic number was that you could multiply them by to figure out the exact moment you were going to die.

He thought about waking Agnes up to ask her whether she was afraid of anything. He wanted to know what she was dreaming. But if he woke her she would turn the question around on him, ask him whether he was afraid. He wanted to tell her yes but not of what. He let her sleep.

He didn't figure out what it was he was afraid of until the next day, on the bus ride down into the Chapare. His body had always been smarter than his brain.

"You're shaking," Agnes told him. "What's wrong?"

The way she asked the question made him feel like he had made the kind of mistake she herself would never be caught dead making. From all indications she was a normal kind of person, which placed her fairly far away from the stone cowboy.

He gripped the back of the seat in front of him, watched his knuckles turn white. "Checkpoint Carlitos," he told her. "Everybody has to get out and get frisked by the Bolivian storm troopers."

"I don't understand."

Of course not. How could she? The wheels of the shimmying bucket of broken bolts they called *transporte publico* mud-planed, and the bus hunched sideways coming to a skating stop in front of a pole-and-concrete barrier across the road. The trolls were great at following orders. Without even being told to, they filed out and down off the bus into the greasy road, stood there with their I.D. papers in patient brown hands. Rise up, a quiet rabble rouser whispered in

Roger's ear, Rise up and take what's coming to you. Not that he was going to repeat it for their benefit. It was something they had to figure out by themselves.

"You, too," the driver pointed at Roger.

"I'm going," Roger said, but he wasn't. Panic froze up his body. He was embarrassed, then grateful when there was Agnes quoting some of her weird poetry in his face in a distracting voice that was meant to tell him he'd better get moving. Something in the voice. He moved.

It had rained the night before. Ragged flapping strips of fog hid most of what was there to be seen. Which was a greasy one-lane road going too steeply down the side of a mountain with no guardrail. And boulders like petrified dinosaur eggs strewn across the rocky landscape looking like they were waiting for an excuse to work their way loose so they could crunch the nearest bus within terrorizing distance. There were trees with real leaves, and green bushes, and jazzy flowers you never saw in Flint, Michigan. And you could actually feel the air get thicker as you dropped below Cochabamba. There were creeks down which white water ran noisily. There were a few stray llamas, like camels looking for their lost humps, and a donkey with one long-nailed clubfoot dragging its tether. Every once in a while there was a stone shack surrounded by a mud wall, a mud shack surrounded by a stone wall, and trolls in funny hats with sticks in their hands looking out at the world like they were waiting for it to start turning before they made up their minds to do something. Rise up, Roger heard. But behind the fog it was the rock that overwhelmed.

"Tell me what the sign over the driver's seat says," Agnes was saying in her telephone receptionist voice as she helped him get off the bus. *And how may we help you today?* By giving him back his heart. No. Not that, not then or there.

"It says Don't get on my case, only God knows when we'll get there."

"I thought it was something like that."

The bar across the road was attached to the outside wall of a stone guardhouse, inside which shadows moved like men. In front of the guardhouse, Bolivians in uniforms were checking the papers of everybody on the bus.

"UMOPAR," Roger told Agnes. "They're the Bolivian drug cops. The frigging C.I. fucking A. taught them everything they know about shaking down honest, law-abiding citizens."

"Is that necessary, Roger?"

But he saw she meant the shaking, which he had under control, pretty much. A couple of UMOPAR grunts said something to the driver, who stooped to pull open the luggage door on the side of the bus.

"Why are they searching us on the way in, Roger? Don't the drugs go out of the Chapare, not in?"

"Psy ops," he explained.

"What's that?" She took his arm and pulled him into the end of the line of waiting trolls.

"Psychological operations. We learned all about that shit in el Panóptico. There was this bonehead gringo in with us for a couple months. He was in Central America fighting with the Contras. Said he was, anyway, and he was wacko enough to be telling the truth. According to him, psy ops means these goons are trained to hassle people just to remind them who's in charge. The idea is to keep you off balance. They're occupation troops."

"That's ridiculous."

"What do you know about it, Agnes? Where are you from in the States?"

"We're from Greenfield, Massachusetts."

"When was the last time you had a serious occupation force in Greenfield, Massachusetts?"

"Do you have to be so aggressive, Roger? I'm sorry if my sheltered background, if that's what you think it is, disappoints you. I am who I am. I'm here for a reason, and only one reason."

That had to be a lie, but he let it pass. But he couldn't stop ragging; had to be his nerves, which tingled and jingled. Besides, he was right, something that happened seldom enough it was worth making a big deal out of when it did. He didn't tell her it was one more piece of Bolivian folklore he had picked up in prison from Claude, who understood the place better than any three historians of the world put together. To understand Bolivia you had to live it, live in it the way you lived in your skin only closer, tighter, scarier. You had to live it in a place like el Panóptico, where the terror of being totally vulnerable, totally weak, totally a victim, worked its way into your system and made you into a different kind of person.

It's about shape, Claude told him one time. Into Roger's naked ear came sneaking the Frenchman's secret sad wisdom, like that dangerous ant of evil that kids back home always thought would crawl in and down to your brain and make you crazy. If you fell asleep in the grass at the wrong time, and the ant worked its way in through your open ear, it would live out its life cycle tracking around on the gray cottage cheese of your brain, nibbling away at your memories and your judgment—good or bad—and your self-preservation instinct, short-circuiting the electrical system. And then when it died, the ant's little carcass would rot in one of the miniature crevasses inside, one of those almost invisible cracks between your thoughts, and the poison of its decaying body would corrode your cottage cheese and you would do something genuinely insane. Like go to Bolivia. Like paint the word LOVE on the inside of a secret place and then stare at it thinking that would make it happen. Like wait for an answer when you talked to God.

Shape, *hombre*, whispered Claude until he got Roger's attention. They usually talked in Spanish. French was not one of the things Roger had picked up in his travels, and Claude had political reasons for not learning English. He must have given the guard with the key whatever he had to give him—Roger preferred not knowing what that might be, didn't like guessing even though his mind wouldn't let it go—and there was his French friend with his need and his knowing and a fat joint of primo marijuana rolled in pink paper.

For some reason Roger couldn't get up off his pallet on the floor when he became aware that Claude was there in the room with him. The *yanqui* vice-consul had brought him a clean, new striped wool blanket the week before, out of the goodness of his heart was how that expression went, and staying warm in a clean way had improved Roger's quality of life measurably. So staying under the blanket made sense. After a while you could feel a sheet of warmer air around you, and moving your arms or your legs one at a time just a little gave you a pleasant thrill of feeling that was like comfort. Only your body wasn't quite dumb enough to be tricked that easily, it knew better. It knew that what you had was too temporary to count.

"You were born with a shape, Roger," Claude told him. Roger liked the way his name came out with the French accent, softened and more sophisticated than in English. It made him feel like a true world traveler, someone who knew how to sit around at a café in a port city watching sailboats frolic in the harbor and talking with a sexy red-headed spy about the missing microfilm and what was going to happen to both of them if they didn't get it back.

"We're all born with a shape," Claude insisted.

"I don't want to get high, Claude. I can't handle it right now."

"Sure you want to get high. Even if you are not aware of your interest in going up high it is there in your consciousness, at one level or another. The only value of not being high is contrast. It tells you what you're missing, and that's what makes you want to get high once again."

"Maybe, but I don't want to do that number with you."

"What number?"

"That's old-fashioned North American hippy talk. Don't light it, Claude. El Verdugo's been on the warpath. If somebody tells him they smell smoke he'll be here in half a second to knock the shit out of me."

"Fuck el Verdugo. I'm lighting it."

"I can see that."

"Here."

"I don't want it."

"You want it."

That was the thing: He wanted it. So took it. The harsh assault of the smoke on his wet lungs was as sweetly familiar as his own body under his own blanket in his very own isolated cell at the windy top of the semihabitable world.

"You're a sensitive person," Claude informed him.

"I'm not."

"That was your original shape, anyway. Bolivia changes the shape you're born with."

"I don't get it."

"There is nothing to get, Roger. It's what gets you. I mean into you. It goes into, what's the word?, the pores of your skin and into your mouth every time you open it and up your ass every time you open that. Did you know that *bourgeois* is a French word?"

"I'm too wiped out to follow you, Claude."

"No you're not, you're just wanting to resist me even though my logic is irresistible. Bolivia makes a joke of the entire bourgeois world. You can understand that, can't you? I mean all that ridiculosity about working hard and saving money and being monogamous and cultivating the aesthetic virtues and praying to God on Sundays. Tell me what relevance all that has to a place like Bolivia."

Roger could not. The only image that came to him when he thought of the word *bourgeois* was a hamburger, a particular kind of red meat eaten by middle-class people in the developed world. That and the sober expression on their faces while they chomped and swallowed. The nonstop way Claude laughed when Roger told him that made the stone cowboy feel like the smartest man in the history of the universe.

"I'll bet you money," he told Agnes, "that every last grunt in a uniform you see here is an Altiplano Aymara. They send them down here to ride herd on the Quechuas because the one brand doesn't trust the other. You couldn't get valley Quechuas to do what these UMOPAR guys do to the locals."

"Get yourself under control," she told him. "You're still shaking."

"I'm not." He was.

"You'll draw more attention to us the way you are, don't you think?"

"You mean if we stand real still and look sad they'll think we're trolls?"

Too late. One of the shadows inside the guardhouse materialized. He opened the door, stepped out into the fog, and marched in their direction like a Nazi in training. G.I. Joe. He was the actual action hero. Roger recognized right away those baggy camouflage pants with the nifty snap pockets, the green T-shirt, the tattooed lumpy muscles. A big knife in an ugly leather belt. M-16 in a webbed sling across his back. His face was jarhead square, his hair rusty red. Only the eyes looked like the eyes of a real human being. A tawny color was twisted into the outer rim of the green. The eyes kept moving, checking out the surroundings, like a creature way out of its natural element but still too smart to let itself get caught and eaten by whatever dangerous beasts happened to be in the neighborhood it had wandered into.

"Can I see your papers, please?" Roger asked him. He couldn't help it. It would take almost nothing to hate the guy, who was the real reason his body continued to tremble, as though it had known all along that this was what was coming.

"You're reading upside down, pardner," G.I. Joe told him. "You got the whole thing ass backwards. I'm the one that does the asking, and you do the producing."

Roger noticed that there were no markings on his uniform, nothing to identify him. He could club the stone cowboy with his M-16 and no one would ever know enough to come claim the body. Not that anybody would. He tried to picture Danny in Flint getting a telegram, wondered whether he might spend the money to bring his dead friend back to be buried in gringo ground. He realized he had no idea whether Danny would do that for him. His ignorance depressed him, steadied him, reminded him of who he was. He was nobody.

"You're a gringo," he told the soldier. "You've got no right to ask me to show you anything anywhere south of Brownsville, Texas."

"Suit yourself," he shrugged. "I'll ask one of my UMOPAR buddies to do it for me. I thought I was doing you a favor."

He was from some southern state. Roger hated southern accents. They made him think of grits, a food that had gagged him in jail in Georgia. The guy's voice was like honey trickling down a dark tube. In Georgia there had been a trusty with a voice like that, a voice that didn't even pretend to make you believe it when it said Trust me. Roger was pretty sure he was the one who let those twin brothers into his cell to fuck him that one time. He was far enough away, now, from all that noise to draw the right philosophic conclusion from the event, which had to do with balance: There was none, at least none in the world Roger was walking around on. Therefore everything tipped. What other conclusion could you come to if you started thinking how it was that a stone cowboy doing thirty-six hours on a vagrancy charge in a Confederate lockup in some podunk Georgia town would get raped in stereo by ugly, dumb perverted twin brothers whose breath smelled like garlic and grits and their mother's sour milk? Ike and Elvis. He thought he had been able to forget their names. Guess not. Some day he would.

"What do you really want from us?" Agnes asked G.I. Joe.

"Routine check is all. Other than that, just simple curiosity. Who wouldn't wonder what a couple of innocent gringos like y'all are doing on a bus full of Bolivians going down into no-man's-land?"

"Who are you?"

"I'm an adviser. No secrets. We do training."

"Who's we?"

"You know this bus is going to Tingo Tingo, don't you?"

"We know," Agnes said.

"You're not in the coca paste business by any chance, are you?"

"We're not."

"Then what on God's green earth do you want to go to Tingo Tingo for?"

"We're looking for someone," she told him. Roger was proud of her for not saying any more.

G.I. Joe shrugged, pretended not to care. "It's a cesspool is all. Don't say I didn't warn you. If you want, you can wait here with us until a bus comes up heading back to Cochabamba. That's what I'd do if I was you, which thank the good Lord I'm not."

The UMOPAR squad was finished with its psy ops drill. They let the trolls line up and begin boarding the bus again, and a couple of them leaned on the concrete weight that held the barrier down across the road. The pole went up jerking, and Roger and Agnes headed for the back of the line.

"Hey!" G.I. Joe stopped them. He stood in the muddy road looking irritated, scratching the bug bites on his arm with blunt nails. "You ever hear what they say about cocaine? I mean people who really know about it, not the official propaganda types."

Roger didn't know. Neither did Agnes.

"Cocaine is like shit," he told them. His free hand fondled the black handle of the carnivore knife in his black belt. "It's like shit," he repeated. "Whoever sticks their hand in it comes away stinking. Do you believe that?"

"I believe it," Agnes soothed him. She was calm as a coma, and she was a woman who would tell few lies.

"You better believe it," he told her, "because it's true."

⸙

Down. As in low. If you left your brain in neutral, if you forced your eyes to see but not to think, it was like falling down a bottomless well. You went floating down like Alice with a tingling feeling in your arms and legs that meant there was nothing below to break your fall, no end to tumbling, just the slow, sure sense of dropping down. As in lower.

Hours. Slow kilometers. The driver was not driven by the same suicidal impulse that most troll bus drivers suffered from. He went slowly, hugging the mountain side of the road where he could. He made the bus crawl across the washed-out spots where runoff water took mud and stones and litter with it over the cliff, making a treacherous trench in the road, which was miserable to begin with.

The good thing was the air, which got sweeter and more breathable every hour. Roger's window was down. He sucked down the wind that blew in, swallowed it, opened his mouth for more. The lower they dropped the stronger he felt. There were bright birds celebrating something in the trees, and the walls of the canyon were patched with needle-nosed purple flowers that fell like waterfalls.

"This was a good thing to do," Agnes told him once. Mostly she was staying quiet, reading poems in her book with the red leather cover or watching out the window for moral shortcomings on the road ahead. You never knew when something was going to jump out and disappoint you. "I wish it had been something else that brought me to Bolivia. I've been thinking."

"About what?"

"About all this." She waved her hand at the rocks and the jungly green and a tall, skinny waterfall on the far side of the road. The fog had burned off. The sun glazed the water as it came down the mountain. "And about that soldier we met back there. Was he a soldier?"

"He's a genuine G.I. Joe."

"What I was thinking was this: that I could have spent my whole life without meeting a person like him, in a place like this. And I wouldn't have known enough to imagine either one."

"No great loss, as far as I can see."

"That's because you've seen things. The imagination needs nourishment."

He didn't care for the way she said it, but he liked what he thought she was trying to say. She lulled him into making a new mistake.

"I don't understand why you reacted the way you did back there at the checkpoint."

There were two halves to an honest answer. He gave her the half that would get him into trouble. "Insurance."

"Please don't be cryptic. I think it's important for us to try and speak the same language."

Kryptic Krunch—it sounded like breakfast cereal. He hadn't had a bowl of Kryptic Krunch for years. He wondered whether they still made it.

"Before I left el Panóptico, my friend Claude gave me two hits of windowpane acid. It's my insurance. I carry it in case I need it."

Her sense of outrage sat her straight up in her seat. "Do you mean to tell me you're carrying drugs on your person?"

"Two hits of acid. It's nothing. It's on a little piece of paper wrapped up in plastic. There's no problem, Agnes." That was the first time he remembered saying her name. The unfamiliar taste of it on his tongue was sweet. His taste buds tingled. He thought he might get an erection, waited and wanted, but it didn't happen. Shut down.

"I can't believe it." She was shaking her head like someone at a funeral who doesn't want to accept the fact that 'ol Uncle Elmo has finally bought the farm. "I can't believe you would run a risk like that, for no reason."

No reason she could appreciate, anyway, which was the same as no reason at all.

"He wasn't going to find it on me."

"But what if he had? They would have arrested both of us, wouldn't they? They would have sent us both to prison, and I would never have found my brother, and some stranger would have had to call my father and tell him his daughter had been arrested on a drug charge in Bolivia. Is that what you wanted to happen?"

"It didn't happen. I knew it wasn't going to happen."

"Then why did you have the shakes like that?"

That was the harder half of the honest answer. It had to do with a certain way of being vulnerable: on a bus somewhere, anywhere, coasting to a stop at a barrier, cops in uniforms with guns and the power and the desire to hurt you, to look into all the holes your body had to offer, to slap you around because that was how they understood their job and the way people were supposed to be with each other. He'd been shaken down plenty, he'd been violated by bureaucrats with pistols and night sticks and ugly impulses. The only way to avoid getting raped on the road was to keep moving down it. Until you came to the next barrier.

"Malaria," he told Agnes. "I got it in Nicaragua. Sometimes it comes back."

Actually Nicaragua was the only country in Central America he'd skipped, because it was full of communists and communist killers and he didn't want to get in the way of anybody's bullet no matter the politics involved. The psy ops gringo in el Panóptico had come down with malaria there, though, and Roger watched him weather a recurrence once in the prison; the watching was close enough to the real thing to justify, for Roger, what he told Agnes. The guy's name was Herbert, and he claimed he was a genuine internationalist because part of one finger on his left hand had been blown away by a bullet made in Czechoslovakia while he was fighting in the Nicaraguan hills carrying a gun made in the U.S.A. and listening to Radio Venceremos broadcasts out of El Salvador on a Japanese shortwave radio. He'd been saved from dying of the malaria, he said, when one of the Contra *comandantes* showed up with some miraculous pea-green pills he liberated from a Sandinista health post. The *comandante* had a metal plate in his head, from an operation in Miami done by a Republican Cuban surgeon who told him if he stood totally still and there was no metal in the neighborhood he could pick up radio wave signals from outer space, and that the signals he caught would be a message from a highly developed planet in another solar system where they had already solved their communist problem so they were able to get on with the business of space travel and cloning and interstellar sex.

"Throw it away," Agnes told him.

"You can't throw malaria away. It's a permanent thing."

"The LSD."

"I can't. I'm not saying I'm going to use it, but I have to have the insurance. I don't expect you to understand that."

"Please throw it away."

"I can't do it now, not in plain sight of all these trolls."

"Then later. Promise me."

He promised. It was good to have something to hold out on her, something she shouldn't know about. Hanging on to the windowpane made him feel safer with her, too.

Down.

Tingo Tingo turned out to be exactly the kind of miserable hole in the ass end of nowhere he had thought it would be, only more sinister. They had been traveling through coca territory: a million fields, a billion plants, picked leaves drying in long sheets along the roadside.

"I had no idea it was done so openly," Agnes told him.

"Growing coca is legal. They make this tea out of it that's good for altitude sickness. Plus it's sacred. Making cocaine out of it is what's against the law."

"They could float all the ships in the world with the tea they made from this much coca."

"Forget tea. This is all going to be stomped into dope. Someday a bunch of stupid kids in Detroit are going to shove it up their noses and think it's a religious experience straight from the Bolivian jungle."

"What makes you so bitter?"

That was more than he had to put up with, and she knew it. She was quiet for a while, her way of apologizing, and then they were in Tingo Tingo. The driver downshifted, the engine bitched a little, and all the trolls on the bus grabbed their bundles. Out.

The sun had gone down, but there was enough light left in the sky to make out the settlement, which had grown up around a crossroads where two lonesome dirt highways came together in the middle of infinite coca.

"It scares me," Agnes told Roger. They were walking like obvious gringo geeks in a herd of Bolivians carrying bundles. *Pichicata*. It was a bulky, mysterious word.

Tingo Tingo was the troll version of a Wild West town before the sheriff showed up to clean house. What buildings there were were shacky; wood slats, mostly, tied together with what looked like baling wire. No electricity, just kerosene and gas lanterns hung on trees and rafters and resting on tables. People were packing up for the day the things they had come to Tingo Tingo to sell: plastic sheeting and plastic buckets and mountains of toilet paper, chemicals in barrels and buckets and vats. That had to be for the coca maceration pits. The rest was the kind of thing poor people bought when they had a little cash: Japanese radios and sturdy Hercules bicycles, cheap cookware and dishes and sneakers and plastic roses and pictures of puppies with sad eyes. Junk, most of it.

"This is a trading center, that's all," Agnes decided. "It's just people doing business with each other." She was trying to explain it to herself in a way that would take the sting out of being in a place that could spook a reasonable person in thirty seconds.

"What do you figure is in those bundles they're all carrying?" Roger asked her. It felt good to know a little more than she did.

"Bread," she guessed. "Or else the dough to bake their bread. They take it home and bake it at night when they're done working."

They were talking low enough that Roger had a hard time catching what she said, but he could tell that the Bolivians didn't like having foreigners around mumbling in a language that they couldn't understand. He realized he was as uneasy as he had been at Checkpoint Carlitos, except that the threat was different here. It was more spread out in Tingo Tingo, it was hanging in the air, up there with the road dust that the moving bus and a few hundred troll feet had kicked up.

"It's *pichicata*," he told Agnes. "That's what the Bolivians call the coca paste that buys all those nifty radios and shit."

She stopped in the middle of the milling herd, nodded as if that was going to be her second guess, dope after bread dough. Roger stopped next to her, feeling protective and mildly brotherly while a wave of Bolivians broke grudgingly around them. He listened to the unfamiliar sound of Quechua being spoken. The language was nothing like Aymara. What he had learned in prison was about to become totally useless.

"So what do we do now?" she wanted to know.

He could have come back hard at her on that one. It was her brother they were looking for, not his. But her trust, which was like innocence in action, gentled him. A little.

"First we have to find some place to spend the night. We can't do anything until tomorrow morning."

But there was no room at the inn, no inn, and they got the same story Mary and Joseph got under similar circumstances back in the days of miracles and locusts. They went politely from stall to stall, shack to crummy shack, asking with all the respect Roger could muster whether they knew of a person who would rent them a room. Just for the night, for one frigging night.

"The problem is we're tourists," he explained, "and they hate tourists."

"All we really need is a place to lie down."

"They don't want to give it to us. We're either tourists or else we're spies. They probably think we're working for the DEA and we want to steal the fucking *pichicata* out from under their sweaty armpits."

"Keep trying, please. But if no one will rent us a room, we'll find a clean place on the ground and sleep there. On a piece of wood. I'm sure we can find a clean piece of wood. With all these people around there won't be any snakes."

Snakes . . .

People had begun to light their lanterns. By blind instinct Roger moved toward a table on which a dozen portable cassette players were stacked in an attractive pyramid, a neat little monument to troll consumerism, below a lantern hung in the crook of a tree branch. There was enough light to see the kid with green feet grab one of the cassette players from the pyramid and run.

And get caught. The stall belonged to two women who looked like sisters. They had the same long wild black hair, the same wide waddling bodies, the same bare brown feet with the toes turning up. They screamed Thief! together in high-fidelity stereo.

The kid was stupid, or maybe he just panicked. Or maybe his brain had rotted out from too many *pitillos*, so there wasn't enough left inside to do any serious thinking. He held the cassette player over his head and ran toward the intersection, right where the crowd was thickest. Somebody stiff-armed him in the chest, somebody else tripped him. He dropped the cassette player, which brought out a stereo wail from the sisters chasing him, and fell like a humbled sinner at the feet of the crowd.

If Agnes wanted food for her imagination, there was plenty in what happened then. The trolls made a tight circle around the kid on the ground in the middle of the road, and the two sisters ran up, stepped through the bars of their neighbors' bodies to inflict revenge, judge and jury in a hurry. They kicked the kid hard with their hard bare feet. They spat on him, they cursed him out in Quechua and Spanish, they bent over and slapped him in the face he couldn't hide with the flat of their horny hands. One of them drove her heel into the small of his back, and the sound that came out of the kid's mouth was the sound a deer would make when it knew the hunter had it in his sights, if deer had just a little more vocal range.

Roger went up close enough to see the blood coming out of the boy's mouth stain the packed earth of the road.

When it was over, the kid lay unconscious and the crowd moved away. The door of the cassette player had come open when it hit the ground, and the sisters were arguing about whether the hinge was broken or just a little loose. The kid bled quietly.

"Why are his legs and feet green like that?" Agnes wanted to know.

He was pretty sure she was close to heaving. He took her arm and led her back toward the stalls, all of which were closed up for the night by then. Behind wood slats, quietly hissing lanterns cast a mellow light that reminded him that they had no place to lie down, and not much prospect of finding one.

"I have to sit for a minute," Agnes said.

Roger found two empty apple crates, temporarily unclaimed, and dragged them off the road onto a patch of stiff, dusty grass. People were disappearing fast. Hard to know where, except for the few who had a shack. Roger thought maybe they went into the woods to hang upside down like bats. That would solve the scientific mystery about where trolls came from, anyway. Their ancestors were bats that had mated with the Mongolians after they got trapped when the land bridge back to Asia fell into the ocean. He had another of those funny visions that were the product of thinking too much and about the wrong things: He saw the last Mongolian horseman on the western shore of the continent. The sun was going down making it hard to see, but his eyes were blurred anyway with bitter tears. Behind him on his big black horse, hugging him because she was afraid, a bat-woman whispered *Too late*, in a low, sexy voice. They were on a high cliff with a long view, and the horse stomped its hooves in fear when it felt the tremor in the ground as the land bridge crashed into the water. There was no boat in the world strong enough to take them all the way back to Mongolia. The bat woman, ancestor of the trolls, was right. It was too late.

"It's awful," Agnes said, and for a minute he thought she was seeing the same vision.

To get away from the vision he forced himself to think of something practical and close at hand. He could knock the crates apart and lay out the wood for her to lie down on.

"The kid's been out stomping coca in the maceration pits," he explained as he thought about logistics. "If they don't wear boots the chemicals and the leaves and all the rest of the shit turns their legs green, eventually. You okay?"

"I'm okay. I guess I'm seeing more than I ever expected to see. Maybe that's what makes people . . ."

"Turn out like me? We can sleep right here," he told her. "No snakes, no trolls. It's safe." Maybe it really was.

He was worn out, as though he had been running all day instead of just sitting on a bus. Agnes was tougher, in a way, but she was in a kind of shock from seeing the boy with green feet get the living shit beat out of him. Maybe you couldn't say you had really lived until you saw blood come out from an unconscious person's mouth like that onto the dark dirt, like the guy's best-kept secret spilling out of his body while he lay there surrounded by neighbors who walked away.

Agnes fell asleep sitting up, so Roger did guard duty. For a while the combination of quietness and darkness made him edgy. He was a person, he assumed, who needed just the opposite: noise and light and something weird going on to keep from getting unnecessarily agitated. That was why it was good to keep moving, bad to sit in jail anytime, anywhere. In el Panóptico he noticed that being stuck and still caused his mind to play tricks on him, remembering things with a piercing, painful clarity that might or might not have happened to him. The farther back in his life he remembered the sharper the picture and the more doubtful the memory. Now, in the dark middle of the Chapare, which was the same as nowhere only more humid, after a time the edginess went away and he remembered a place.

It was a porch, must have been in Flint, and April from the feel of the sun, not that any crumb-snatching rug runt would be thinking about the month. The boards of the porch were warped and needed paint. Somebody like Roger was sitting off to one side of that porch, which was the halfway zone between the house and the street. He watched an angry man haul suitcases and grocery bags full of all kinds of personal household stuff out of the house, across the porch, down to the street to a car with big fins. Every trip the man made the screen door slammed—a flat, wooden sound—and a woman inside screamed something that was a cross between a threat and a victim's lament. Despite his anger the man whistled. There were tattoos on his biceps, wiggling women with oversized purple nipples and fleshy hips that moved with his muscles. Once, he stopped, stared at the kid on the side of the porch, said something cheerful and stupid and beside the point like Tough times in the big city, sport, but she'll get over it.

Maybe it happened, maybe it didn't. Maybe to him, or to someone like him. He stared into a dark place on the road hoping to catch himself talking to God. It wasn't something you consciously tried to do; your deep-down better half was in charge of all that. But instead it was an angel that appeared in the road.

"Buy from me," the angel told him in Spanish. She was a miniature. Everything about her was small, and fine, and gave him the impression of being breakable. Her wings, he assumed, had already snapped off in some sort of flying accident. She came closer, and there was just enough light from somewhere or other that he could see her face. Her black eyes had the blank, bright gravity that adults usually mistook for kids' wisdom, but Roger knew better. What lit the angel's eyes was only terror, kept under control by her instinct to hide the important things. Her black long hair was combed and tied into a tail, and the dress she wore was shiny from being washed on the rocks too many times, and her miniature brown feet were bare in the road dust. "It's what you want," she told him. "It will make you feel good."

"What are you selling, little angel?"

But she couldn't believe that he wouldn't know, thought he was being mean, or just cheap. She shook her head impatiently. If he tried to just a little, he could make her angry. He didn't try. "Tell me how old you are, first."

She was eleven. "All the others will cheat you if you buy from them," she warned him. "They will laugh at you and talk about you in Quechua, and then they will cheat you."

"So teach me some Quechua so I can defend myself."

One miniature foot stamped in the road. What she wanted was a sale, not small talk with an ugly, fairly hairy gringo. "I'm not lying, you know," she told him. "You think I'm lying to you, don't you?"

"You haven't told me what you're selling."

Agnes was awake. "What an extraordinarily beautiful child! She looks like a china doll. What does she want?"

"She wants to sell us some dope. You want any?"

"Don't be cruel, Roger."

"I'm serious. That's what's in that bag she's carrying. *Pitillos*. Here we are in the Chapare on the cutting frigging edge of the international capitalist economy. Supply and demand. Gringos up north demand to get high, and trolls down south supply what they need to get there. It's a clean deal, if you think about it."

"Ask her who her people are."

He asked.

"They need the money," she told him. "My father is angry."

"Why is he angry?"

She shrugged her angel-wing shoulders. If Roger had had a little money he might have bought a *pitillo* from her, out of charity. But he was living on charity himself, in a way, though he was working hard enough for the little he was getting. He had an idea. "Does your family have a house?"

"It's a house."

"Take us there."

"Why?" Her Spanish was good: clear and not hesitant. Besides being an angel she was smart.

"I'll give your father some money and maybe he won't be angry any more, if he lets us sleep at your house. We need a place to sleep."

It must have seemed like a reasonable deal. Without waiting to see whether they would follow, she took off down the dark road away from the settlement.

"I'm exhausted," Agnes told him as they went after her. "I can't absorb any more tonight. Do you understand that, Roger?"

He understood it well enough. His first months in Bolivia had been like that for him, more than one person could swallow in a single sitting, but there was more to take in at the house of the little angel, which was maybe a kilometer away from the Tingo Tingo crossroads, down a dirt path that sliced a big field of coca, over which fireflies were gathered in a shifting, shimmering cloud. A house it wasn't, but the shack the girl led them to looked pretty good, looked almost inviting, compared to the apple crates Roger had figured he would knock apart for Agnes to sleep on.

He let the girl go inside and explain the deal in Quechua, waited in the patch of dirt that served for a yard while her angry father stormed a little. Roger caught *hijo de puta* and a few other expressions in Spanish, but listening to the rest depressed him. The idea of a world full of languages you couldn't hope to understand if you spent your whole life learning seemed like calculated cruelty, some cosmic king's idea of a bad practical joke.

"They won't let us stay," Agnes predicted, but after the angel had talked and listened for a while the whole family came out to look at the homeless gringos. The father was a small, defensive-looking man in old pants and a long-sleeved white shirt with no buttons. The mother could have been the sister of the sisters in the road who had kicked the boy unconscious. There were half a dozen sisters and brothers, older and younger than the angel, an average troll family into which it seemed impossible that an actual angel could be born. In the orange light of their one kerosene lantern they looked like the victims of some kind of disaster, survivors milling around hoping their world would get put back together before they died.

"You're not from the DEA, are you?" the mother asked them.

It was the question she had to ask. She knew better. It looked like the father didn't speak Spanish. The angel stood apart from the others, proud to be the one to bring home the daily bacon. Her name, Roger picked up, was Esencia. He could think of no prettier name in any language.

"I hate the DEA," Roger reassured the mother. "Back at home, in the United States of North America, they killed my brother."

The mother translated for the father, who sucked in his chest in what might have been a gesture of sympathy. Roger wondered whether he should tell them that it was true that gringo astronauts had made it to the moon, and when they got there all they found out was that it was made of green cheese. People should know that; it wasn't fair for the North Americans to keep all the good stuff to themselves just because they were more technologically advanced. That far at least Roger could go toward sympathy with Bolivia and all the places like it Danny couldn't imagine no matter how free alcohol and video products made his imagination.

"Why did the DEA kill your brother?" the woman wanted to know. "Was he a drug dealer?"

Roger shook his head. "They killed him because they're the ones that have the guns, that's all." It was among the truest things he had ever said. He hoped Agnes would believe him, was glad she had as little Spanish as she did. "Will you let us stay the night? We can pay a little. Not a lot, a little."

"How much?"

"Do you have room?"

What they had was one hammock, big enough for both of them. Roger decided to worry about the arrangement later. He accepted what he knew was a reasonable price, and the woman, whose hostility was just the mask she wore—he knew that, but he didn't like thinking about that, didn't like imagining he might like a troll—led them into the shack, where the furniture was made of apple crates. There were pallets with blankets spread across the dirt floor, and everything the family owned, which wasn't much, was hung on nails pounded into the walls in no conceivable pattern. Against the back stood what looked like a dresser, with claw feet and drawer pulls with tattered braid tassels and a cracked mirror. From the top of the dresser the woman took a fire-blackened pot, served them plates full of what had to be mush.

"What is it?" Agnes wanted to know before sticking the broken fork they gave her into it.

"It's mush," he told her. "It's the Bolivian national dish. If you don't scarf it down you'll hurt their feelings and they'll have to kill us to save their pride." He had no idea whether what was on the plate he was holding was animal, vegetable, or mineral, but it tasted pretty good to him. He scarfed.

Watching them eat, Esencia's father said something in Quechua, which the mother translated. "He says in the morning you'll have to leave. He says if you stay the DEA and the UMOPAR will show up looking for you, and even though we have nothing to hide from them they'll tear the place apart looking for *la pichicata*."

"We'll go," Roger told her. It wasn't going to be like getting thrown out of Paradise or the Ritz Hotel, even though the mush was tolerable. "My sister is tired," he explained. "Can we go to sleep?"

"Your sister?"

The hammock they were renting was out back, tied to a couple of banana trees. Esencia's father was rattling on in Quechua, the kids listening like they were afraid not to. So it was only the angel herself who followed them out and watched.

"I'm sorry," Roger told Agnes. "This is the way it has to be. It's not like there's all kinds of options out here. I won't touch you."

"How can we lie in the same hammock without your touching me?"

"I mean I won't bother you."

"I wasn't going to say anything," she said.

She climbed in first; he went after her, uncomfortable to be forced so close.

"Do you want to smoke a *pitillo*?" Esencia asked him. "If you want it, I'll give you one. For free."

"Don't you know what happens when you smoke those things?"

"They make people crazy, and then they get real sick. The youngest son of the family down the road smoked too many and died."

"Then why do you want me to smoke one?"

"The other gringo liked it."

"What other gringo?"

But she changed her mind, shrugged her wings.

"What does she want?"

"She's wondering if you want to smoke a *pitillo*," he told her. He didn't like the way she was always hovering over him; he was an on-demand translation machine. "She'll give you one for free, she says. I guess the deal down here is a free smoke with every hammock you rent."

"I have to sleep now."

"Are you unhappy?" he asked her, even though he knew she wasn't. When she hesitated he knew it was because she was looking for the precise word she needed. She was good at that kind of thing. She found it. "What I am," she told him, "is porous."

Maybe that was why he felt himself beginning to disintegrate lying next to her in the hammock. He told Esencia they didn't want any *pitillos*, and she went away without giving away anything: no surprise, disappointment, satisfaction. Staring at the black space she left empty, he wished he had something good to give her: a doll with a Bolivian face, or a kid's book in Spanish that had pictures in bright colors that would show the girl something that wasn't the Chapare and a world filled with *la coca*. Then he noticed that he was beginning to come apart. He was seeping, cell by cell, into Agnes's porous, warm body, on which the sweet smell of her sweat was better than anybody's phony perfume. Whatever it was that was happening left him feeling peaceful, and he had a two-second vision of spending the next five years or so tracking the Mystical Gringo around the world's weird spots in the company of his porous sister Agnes.

Loud ragging in Quechua woke him, brought him back to his sense of separate self.

"What is it?"

When they came out he hadn't noticed the little room back behind the cleared patch of earth on which Esencia's family lived. Now there was a light like a flashlight that showed the outline of the room in a thicket of banana trees. In front of the room Esencia's father stood ragging. There wasn't enough Spanish thrown in for Roger to pick up what he might be talking about.

"I don't like that man," Agnes whispered to him. "It seems impossible that anything as beautiful as the little girl could come out of him."

They listened until he wore himself out, turned around and went back to his shack. When he was gone, the sound of a woman's sobbing came out of the little room in the banana patch. She made a low sound that made his flesh creep, repeating herself in an unconscious pattern that made Roger think of old-fashioned women in black dresses at a wake he had never been to in his life. Maybe he was remembering a movie. She went on for a long time.

Overhead, the sky was as clear as it had ever been, a blue so deep you couldn't tell it from black unless you let your eyes go out of focus for a while. And the stars. He had forgotten about stars. A doper into cosmic fantasy and fiction had told him once that they were messages, and the real reason for human sadness was because no one remembered how to read them; the knowledge died in you when you were born, and all you could remember was that you had lost something valuable. Bullshit. *Caca de vaca*. But in their indifference they were beyond beautiful.

"Roger," said Agnes.

"Did you notice all that stuff hanging on nails in the shack?" he deflected her.

"It's because they don't have money for anything else."

"Did you notice the black hat?"

"I wanted to ask them what they were doing with a top hat in the middle of the jungle, but I didn't want to embarrass them."

"That's your brother's hat. I saw him use it in his act, the one time I watched him in La Paz."

"It doesn't mean anything," she told him. "All it means is he has been here."

He wanted to shift his body a little, put an arm around her. But he was not the kind of person who comforted. None given, less taken; a fair trade. He did the best he could do, which was to rock the hammock a little. They rocked on their backs in the blue-black dark listening to the woman in the little room sob. At the peak of the hammock's arc, the stars shifted their course, and under the banana trees Roger felt the world turn quietly upside down.

§

It was a lucky thing, after all, that Agnes didn't speak enough Spanish to get herself in any serious trouble. In the morning Esencia's family woke up friendly. The mother, Doña Blanca, gave them breakfast for nothing, and Agnes wanted to pay her back with honesty.

"Just tell them who we're looking for," she insisted. "We have nothing to hide."

Roger could tell from her voice that she thought he was trying hard to be contrary, that he lied because he liked to, that she was putting some distance between them after their cozy night side by side in the swinging hammock. It occurred to him that maybe his body had given off some of the same mysterious heat hers had, had leaked onto her skin where she couldn't help touching him. The possibility, faint as it was, encouraged him, set him apart from himself for as long as he considered it. The idea of being someone other than who he was was like a physical craving. You could want it, he discovered, the way you wanted sleep, or drugs, or food and drink.

It wasn't much of a breakfast, but he had eaten plenty worse: bananas and oranges, and a cold, pasty glop that might at one time have been beans. The coffee was a real treat: super sweet and hot, a whole potful to share. But on balance the meal wasn't worth giving away the little they had.

"It's not lying," he told Agnes. "It's being careful. It's no good if you don't hold something back." If she was smart she would take the warning for what it was worth.

"I'm telling her," he told Doña Blanca, "that you are the friendliest people I ever met in my life."

Drinking his coffee standing up, her husband, Don Serapio, snorted once. With his free hand he grabbed his machete and hacked away at a bush. There were kids in the trees, in the dirt of the patio playing games that were nothing like Monopoly, in the house making sounds that made Roger think of intelligent birds.

"Please ask them if they know what's happened to my brother." Agnes lifted her arms in frustration, as though she wanted to pantomime the truth but couldn't come up with the first telling gesture.

Chopping, Don Serapio said something out of the side of his mouth to Blanca, who translated. "He says you have to go, but he wants to tell you something before you do. He'll talk. He wants me to put it into Spanish for you. He says he can't say it right in Spanish."

Which meant that what he said probably wasn't exactly what Roger wound up translating into English for Agnes, but the general idea came through. It was another story, Roger understood, of small potatoes.

Don Serapio couldn't sit still and talk. To get his story out he had to keep moving, fidgeting around the yard hacking at innocent bushes, drinking coffee and spitting it back out in a thin brown stream. He came from one of the high valleys above Cochabamba, a place called Condorito made famous in the big revolution of 1952. One of the important battles took place in Condorito on the *latifundia* of a landowner who also owned tin mines around the country. The place in the country was his hobby. Serapio was a kid during the revolution, but he remembered seeing the body of the landowner carried out on the carved mahogany door people had ripped from its hinges at his big house. They made a giant bonfire, propped the million-dollar door above the flames until it caught fire, and watched the corpse of injustice go up in smoke.

Except that what took the place of the bad old ways was less than perfect justice. Serapio's father was given a chunk of land high in the valley, and that was better than working as a serf for the landowner. But the remote property he wound up with was small and rocky, and the life the land produced for the family was in most respects hard to tell from the life they had suffered before. They had chuños, a few animals, a stone hut, and a stone fence, not much more. Nevertheless,

Serapio's father died believing that he was a free man of property and things could hardly get better.

Things could get worse, though, and they did. When he died, the father's land was divided in half. Serapio's older brother Filomeno got the better half because he was older and tougher and whispered something corrosive into their father's ear before the man bought it. Serapio took what he got, which was the short end of the family stick, and practiced resignation (that was the Bolivian national sport, Roger added for Agnes's benefit when he got to that part of the translation). Blanca came from a family who had no more land than the husband she married, so she expected little more than the little she got.

But if bad people could make a hard situation worse—this was Blanca's own addition to the story being told, Roger was pretty sure—they would. They did. What had been barely enough land to support the father's family turned out to be less than enough to provide the minimum for the two growing families of his sons. Both Filomeno and Serapio were blessed with lots of kids, and every year it became more difficult to fill up all the mouths under their roofs with freeze-dried potatoes and quinoa and the other low-grade delicacies highland trolls made out on.

In his own telling of the story, Serapio coped by eating less, working more, gearing down. From his father he had inherited a certain independence, the ability to be happy, more or less, in the high hills, even though when he thought about his father's satisfaction with the way the revolution had turned out a lump of sadness formed inside his body, pressed in on his vulnerable lungs so he had a hard time drawing air down into them. His brother Filomeno, meantime, just got hungrier, which made him meaner.

As often as he could get away from his own place, Filomeno visited Serapio to argue what was obvious: that both brothers and their families were going to get poorer with the passing of every year. Filomeno's solution to the problem of small potatoes was for Serapio to sell him his half of their father's land and leave to try and make a life somewhere else.

"But Serapio told him he had as much right to stay as his big brother did," Doña Blanca told Roger.

The kids had heard the story before. To them it was the history of the world. They ignored the flow of adult words in three languages, except for Esencia, who sat rigid by the coffeepot on the open fire wearing an expression that made Roger think of an angel overhearing ugly things she had a hard time picturing. Agnes was caught up in the story, wouldn't wait for a break so Roger could translate. She kept pushing him to tell what he was hearing.

Which had enough sadness in it for several families. Filomeno did what rotten brothers usually do. He pulled a fast one, made a deal with a local magic man, who messed around with his llama shit and coca leaves and whatever else the local hustlers used to beef up their act. Then the magician had a vision, or maybe it was a dream. In the dream-vision a terrible bird of prey came circling the sky above the valley of Condorito, and everywhere the shadow of its wings touched the earth the crops shriveled up, the animals died, the ground dried up hard as a kiln-fired plate. People came out of their houses to watch the bird destroy with its shadow everything they had, which wasn't much. When it reached the end of the valley it made a slow turn and came back for another pass, taking out another swath of life and livelihood, and another, until eventually there was nothing left of Condorito worth staying around for. On the last pass the terrible bird made, it flew low enough that people could see plainly that it had a human head, and on the head was the face of somebody they all knew: Serapio the unlucky.

"You can guess what happens after this," Roger told Agnes, who had a sick look on her face that meant she was feeling sympathetic; she could guess.

Because the drought in the valley had gone on for a number of years, people in Condorito were desperate to blame it on someone, and Serapio was handy, and helpless, and meek. The Earth Mother and the sidekick gods who worked for her weren't cruel enough to make all of Condorito suffer for no good reason. Someone had ticked her off in a big way. It was obvious: To get back on her good side they had to offer up a sacrifice.

At that point, when people were working themselves up to do something nasty and terminal to Serapio and maybe his family too, Filomeno showed up with a deal and an idea. The deal was he would take his brother's land off his hands for a promise and enough cold cash to get drunk on. Then Serapio was supposed to head for the Chapare while he could still get away from his pissed off neighbors. There was money to be made in the Chapare growing coca and stomping it into paste.

"So is there?" Roger asked Doña Blanca.

"Is there what?"

"Is there money to be made in coca?"

She looked at her husband, who shrugged his shoulders and walked away in the direction of the Tingo Tingo crossroads. Roger saw the man's frustration in the way he swung a green stick at the weeds in his path, and he felt sorry for him. His story was over. All the rest was his wife Blanca's contribution.

"We were doing pretty well," she said carefully.

"But something happened," he helped her out. They were the kind of bad-luck people that something was always going to happen to. It was as predictable as the afternoon shower in the rainy season, and it made Roger think for a moment about fairness, which in Bolivia anyway was as scarce as oxygen on the Altiplano. People needed to breathe a little of both to survive.

"We don't want to do this forever," Blanca told him. "Grow coca, I mean. We know what they use it for."

"It's your sacred leaf, right?"

She shook her head. "It's not sacred after they mix it with chemicals and make it into a drug. There's nothing good about drugs."

"Then how come you grow the leaves if you know they're only going to make it into drugs? You hate the gringos? You want all their kids to die?"

This time when her head shook slowly he saw the pride there, disguised as defense, and he regretted ragging on her.

"You keep forgetting to translate," Agnes reminded him.

"This is just time out," he told her, "a word from our sponsors."

"What would you do," Blanca asked Roger, "if your neighbors were going to burn you out and maybe kill you and you had no money at all but you had this many children," she waved to the trees in her yard, "and you heard of one way—just one way—to make a little money, and you could get to the place where it was to be made, and it didn't require a lot from you except the work of planting and tending and harvesting, and when you lay down in your bed at night and listened to your children breathing all the noise you heard was their hunger? What would you do?"

Roger translated. Better that than answer the question. He knew Agnes would have something to say, and she did. "Tell Doña Blanca I would do the same thing she has been doing, and I wouldn't think too much about what happened to the leaves I sold."

"Does this mean," Roger wanted to know, "that you're changing your mind about drugs? Traveling broadens your horizons, right? You're going to go home and write a letter to the editor saying legalize the shit . . ."

"Just tell her."

He told.

"When you go back home to North America," Blanca said, "you tell the people you know there that we don't hate them. We're sorry that their children are addicted to cocaine. But it's not our fault. You tell them all we're doing is trying to survive, because we don't have factories to work in like they have, we don't have anything that they have."

What they had, he didn't tell her, was small potatoes, freeze dried and tasting like old mold. "What went wrong for you, Doña Blanca?"

She stood up from the stump on which she had been resting, paced the way her husband had paced, shaded her eyes with a cupped hand, and looked in the direction of the shack behind their shack.

"This is the part he didn't want me to tell you," she said. "That's why he went away."

"He went away," Roger corrected her, "so he wouldn't have to hear you tell us, that's all." He knew he was right, and so did she.

"There was a gringo."

"The one who left the hat that's inside your house."

"He showed up with the buyer we were working with. He's a buyer for the big one."

"El Grán Moxo?" That was a mistake. Agnes's ear was good enough to catch that one, and she wound herself up tighter still. "Cool your jets," he warned her. "If you want her to keep talking you have to stay mellow."

"Why won't you translate?"

"I will," he promised. In the case of Agnes, he had learned, it was good to make a promise you knew you weren't going to keep.

"Our plan was to put together enough cash to get ourselves to La Paz. If you're smart and you work hard you can make money in La Paz. You can go into business, but you have to have enough money to get by on until your business starts feeding you. That's been our idea from the beginning. I wouldn't go back to Condorito anymore even if Filomeno died yesterday and left all the land to us. If your neighbors hate you it changes you. Their ugliness wants to make you ugly, doesn't it? "

She was having a hard time staying on the subject of the Mystical Gringo, but Roger knew if he was patient she would get to the place he wanted her to go.

"What was this gringo's name?" he asked her.

She shrugged. If he had a name it meant nothing to her. "We're not like the rest of them, you know."

"The rest of who?"

"These people, the ones who grow coca and make the paste. All they want is enough money to buy something that makes them feel good."

"That's bad?"

"It's bad if you want something better like we do. We worked real hard. The kids, too. Esencia works the way an adult works."

"Who is the person in that little room back there, Doña Blanca?"

No dice, not yet. She wanted to tell her story her way. "We've been saving it all. Serapio said if we tightened our belts now we could sell all the paste at once when the price was good. Then we were going to go La Paz on that money."

"What did the gringo do to you? Did he steal your paste?"

"He might as well have. Esencia has an older sister. Her sister's name is Paloma."

"That's who is in the room."

"The gringo who showed up with el Grán Moxo's buyer is a magician."

It was time to take a chance. "I know," he told her. "I know who he is."

"There was a problem. The Moxo himself was here for a while. He scared people. While the Moxo was working things out the magician was at loose ends, so he did all kinds of tricks for people. He was the free entertainment they brought along, and at first people really liked him. The things he did were amazing, they were real magic. That's what people here thought, anyhow. He could make a white dove appear in that hat, and make coins appear in children's ears, and tricks with cards, all kinds of them."

"Paloma liked his magic . . . "

"She liked him. That was the reason he was able to put a spell on her."

"What kind of spell?"

"The night after the buyer made his deal he gave people a party. It was supposed to be just for the people who were selling their *pichicata* to him, but everybody in Tingo Tingo wound up there. There weren't three sober people in the settlement. The magician was there. He was taking some kind of drug."

"Was he smoking *pitillos*?" If Flame the Mystical Gringo had gone that far, they would be better off not finding him.

"I don't know what drug it was, but he was drinking, too. Someone gave him *chicha*."

"That's Bolivian moonshine," Roger told Agnes. "They spit in it to make it ferment. If the Bolivians had a space program they'd use *chicha* for their rocket fuel. It's too strong for regular human consumption."

"The gringo played that game with the pistol where you put it to your head and pull the trigger and if you're lucky you get one of the empty chambers. For money. People are mean, aren't they? I watched poor people, people who have nothing, hand over their money to him just for the chance of seeing him blow his own brains across Tingo Tingo. For a while I felt sorry for him because what was happening to him made me think about what happened to us in Condorito. It's the same idea, right? People want to bring you down. But he was lucky, and after a while he got tired of the game. He did some more magic, and then he disappeared. We didn't notice when he left, it wasn't any of our business, we thought, but it was."

"Because Paloma went with him."

"He put the spell on her so he could get our coca paste."

"He stole it from you?"

But she shook her head. "How come you're so interested in what I'm telling you?"

"Go ahead and tell her he's my brother," Agnes was urging him.

Roger thought maybe if he ever got out of Bolivia he would go to the United Nations and offer to be their official translator. The effort of doing justice to what everybody said was wearing, but he had to keep his brain thinking in a straight line. He knew what he was doing, thought so anyway.

"The magician took something from us, too," he explained to Doña Blanca. "That's why we came down to the Chapare. We have to find him and get it back."

"What he did when he put the spell on Paloma was get her to show him where all our paste was. Then the two of them must have moved it somewhere. Anyway, it's gone."

"What makes you think he didn't take it with him when he went?"

"Too much to haul. Besides, afterward we saw him take off in el Grán Moxo's airplane from the *pista clandestina*, and he didn't have it. Paloma was gone for two days. When she came back she was crazy."

"And she won't tell you where they hid your *pichicata*."

"She won't talk at all. That's the spell. He did it to her on purpose like that."

"So you locked her up in that little room out back?"

He had offended her. Give him a long enough conversation and he could offend the pope, or a saint, or anybody else whose business it was not to let the world's unending shit get them down.

"You think we'd lock up our own daughter?" Doña Blanca wanted him to say. "She went in there herself and won't come out, except maybe after everybody's asleep I think she comes out and wanders around, at least when there's moon enough to see by."

"What was Serapio telling her last night when he went out there?"

"The same thing he always tells her. That it's not her fault the gringo magician put a spell on her, and it would be good if she all of a sudden remembered where they hid our coca paste because her sisters and brothers need the things we can buy with the money we get from selling it to el Grán Moxo and maybe we can even get our whole family out of this hell hole to La Paz and start to live a human life, but it's not her fault. Didn't you hear the sadness in his voice? You don't have to understand Quechua to hear the sadness."

"What I heard was Don Serapio sounding mad."

"That was just his frustration. Wouldn't you be frustrated?"

"Let us stay with you for a while."

"Why should we let you stay?"

"Because I can take the spell off Paloma."

"What are you doing, Roger?" Agnes said. "The girl is obviously emotionally disturbed. Why don't you just tell her mother the truth about us and my brother Jonathan. All you're going to do is dig a hole we can't climb out of."

But he would not take away the small smile of satisfaction from Doña Blanca's work-worn face. Esencia, sensing something important might be happening, came and stood gravely in her mother's shadow. "He was right," said Doña Blanca.

"Who was right?"

"My husband. The last thing he said before he went to Tingo Tingo was maybe you knew how to take the spell off Paloma, and if you did I should make sure you stayed. Esencia?"

"Sí, Mamá."

"Walk down to the crossroads and see who will give us a little more coffee on credit."

"We'll stay," Roger told Blanca in Spanish and Agnes in English. "It will take some time, but I know how to take the spell off Paloma." He told each woman what she needed to hear: Blanca, that after the spell was gone Paloma would tell them where their stockpile of paste was hidden. And Agnes, that when Paloma came back to sanity she would be able to tell them where her brother had gone, and maybe how to get there. He earned, he figured, the second pot of coffee they were going to make him.

"You're thinking about your father," he told her, even though he knew she was going to say she wasn't. He had spent enough nights next to her in the troll family hammock to understand Agnes's body language. When she thought about her father back in Gringolandia her body stopped being porous. All the holes in her skin silted over with something hard that kept everything out, including the stone cowboy.

"It isn't going to work, Roger. Whatever happened between my brother and Paloma left her a disturbed woman."

Roger realized he had begun to hate her brother. "Give me a little more time," he told Agnes.

Since he had made his promise to break the spell Flame put on Paloma, Don Serapio, who believed Roger really could, had quit going out to his daughter's room at night. The silence there was creepy; it was the sound of a crazy woman holding her breath so she could hear all the noise that wasn't there. Worse tonight because the sky had clouded over and dense gray fog dropped down on the Chapare. His skin felt clammy. After the Altiplano it was like being at the wet, dark bottom of the world, where sluglike creatures crawled across your naked body leaving a trail of slime, and thinking about the way God might look, if he had a face, only brought up pictures of the devil.

He wanted to be helpful to Agnes. "If you want to write a letter to your father maybe we can find somebody going out to Cochabamba that'll mail it for you."

She shook her head. "There's nothing to say. Not until I find my brother."

"Your father is the kind of guy that doesn't like to be disappointed, isn't he."

"Before my mother died, every year the four of us used to rent a cabin in the woods in a state park in New Hampshire that my father liked. His father had taken him there when he was a boy. One year, I don't remember how old I was, I met a boy. He was a musician, he played the cello, and he knew all the constellations in the sky, and he told amazing long complicated jokes. My father liked him; he let the boy take me out alone. That was a first."

"He wouldn't let me take you out, would he?"

"One night we went out to look at the stars and we both got kind of carried away. One minute we were looking at Ursa Minor and the next minute I was lying on my back on the forest floor and the boy was taking off my bra."

"Felt pretty good, right?" Roger felt a slow glow of sex spread in his body. It was like sparklers going off under his skin. He had forgotten not the feeling but the reality of it, the actual sense in the skin.

"It was a wonderful way to begin," Agnes admitted. "But after a few minutes I had a horrible feeling that something was wrong. Not between me and Jeremiah, that was his name. It didn't have anything to do with us or what we were doing. I just knew that something bad was going on. So I got up and left Jeremiah sitting there thinking he had offended me and I ran back through the woods to our cabin. There was a police car parked in front."

"Your brother screwed something up."

"He had made friends with a local tough guy, the son of a very strict Methodist minister. They stole a car, took it for a joy ride, and crashed it. It was like stabbing our father with a knife, Roger. He thought he must have been doing something wrong. He had two teenagers: One of them was stealing cars and the other one was out in the woods being groped at by a cellist with the gift of gab and his eyes on the stars in heaven."

"I know what happened next. You dumped Jeremiah because you felt guilty, and then you had to feel guilty enough for two since your worthless bum of a brother didn't feel anything at all except sorry he got caught."

"Jeremiah wrote me for a year. He sent poems he had written and books he thought I would like. And a star chart. And at Christmas he sent a pair of expensive lapis lazuli earrings. They were beautiful, the most beautiful earrings I ever saw."

"And you stiffed the poor guy to keep your old man happy. And you stopped letting nice boys play with your underwear." He didn't mean for it to come out sounding the way it did, but it did. He recognized the place he'd gone; it was called too far.

"There's something mean and ugly in you, Roger. I believe you get pleasure from hurting people. My brother is like that. I appreciate what you are doing for me. Don't make the mistake of thinking I don't understand what it means. But after we find Jonathan it will be time for us to say good-bye, because I don't want to be around someone who takes pleasure from hurting."

She rolled her schoolmarmish body, which was stiff with anger and rejection, out of the hammock, then disappeared in the clammy fog toward the shack. He didn't worry about her. They would make space for her on a family pallet. What ticked him was what she took for granted, that he was the same kind of planet scum her miserable brother obviously was.

He couldn't sleep, which turned out to be a break because, rocking alone in the damp, dark night, he had his inspiration. He knew what he needed to do to break the spell on Paloma. It was easy: All he had to go was go where she was. The hard part was figuring out where that was, and then how to get there.

Seeing her the first time had been a shock: It was like looking at an older version of Esencia, but an Esencia who had been through the Bolivian mill. She was twenty, maybe twenty two, and she was still pretty, but her small-potatoes life up in the high valley, where the visionary bird of destruction wore her father's face, and down low in the Chapare, where nothing meant anything except coca, had blunted her, worn her down and a little wild. He knew he had to be patient and he was. Every day he went back to her mini-shack and talked. Not with her, because that took two and she didn't want to be one half of anything he had to offer. And not really at her, either, because he could see that was what everybody else was doing: Her mother and father and every once in a while one of the brothers or sisters went back under the banana trees and talked at her the way people talked at cats, without expecting much in the way of a response. So he just talked alongside of her. Sometimes he borrowed Agnes's red leather book of poems and read a few of them to her. He didn't worry about the meaning of the words; what he wanted to get at was their rhythm, and he found that much, thought maybe she heard it too.

But no response. She sat in the threshold of her little cell and watched the trees around her wilt in the heat. Or she swept the dirt floor, or combed her hair looking at the wall as though there was a magic mirror on it instead of just a knothole with the knot knocked out. There was something pathetic in the way Paloma dressed: in jeans with a phony gringo trademark meant to make you think of high style but that only suggested the cheap imitation it was. Even in the heat she wore her white blouse buttoned to the throat, and the lace on the sleeves was ridiculous. He watched her carefully paint her toenails fire-engine red, working away as though she was sure nobody in the world could see her doing something private. Her parents didn't have enough cash to eat on, and their daughter, under a strange gringo-induced spell, sat in the shack painting her nails in the privacy of her own universe.

Once, after he had read a long, rhythmic poem by Tennyson that bored him, she stood up from her pallet on the floor, looked right through him, and said something in Quechua that might have been Tennyson, or Che Guevara, or a knock-knock joke, or the weather report for the Eastern Chapare. Or else it was a question, because she was irritated waiting for an answer he would have given a lot to be able to make. "Dove," was all he was able to come up with, her name in English because that was better than nothing. She turned away, grabbed her broom, and swept a skin of dust across the dirt of her floor.

But he kept trying. Doña Blanca and Agnes were the skeptics. Neither one thought he was going to be able to get through to Paloma, but Don Serapio, maybe because he was desperate, seemed to think it was only a matter of time. Which it was.

Without Agnes in it, the hammock was a less than middling bed.

Roger rolled out of it, walked a few steps in the fog, which was getting thicker, toward the family shack. But he turned around, felt his way back to where Paloma was sleeping. He knocked on her door.

No answer. He pushed on the door. It swung inward, and he walked in singing. "I've Been Working on the Railroad." He wanted to let her know he was coming but not to think he was one more stranger come out to rag her into surrendering her secret. If she had one.

"Dove," he said after the second verse. Too dark to see, but he thought she might be sitting upright on her pallet. He wondered whether she was dressed, tried to imagine the expression that might be on her face. "I was dreaming," he told her. Agnes wouldn't be able to see the difference, probably, but it was not a lie in the usual sense of the word. Even before he started he realized it was truer than most things he saw with his eyes closed.

"In my dream I'm a bird, and I'm unhappy. I'm sitting on the branch of a tree in a place that's a lot like the Chapare. I'm afraid, because someone's firing a gun and I figure it has to be at me. So I fly. Straight up. High. Higher than I ever flew or thought to fly. I fly up so high the whole *maldito* Chapare shrinks down to almost nothing." He almost lost it, couldn't remember the word in Spanish for shrink until it was out of his mouth. *Achicar*. It was a useful word. It kept him going.

"I keep going until the Chapare is shrunk down to the size of one little leaf. It's a coca leaf. I hang in the air for a while, looking down at that coca leaf. Then I hear a voice talking to me, and something tells me it's the voice of the bird god."

"Pacuri," Paloma said. That had to be what the Quechuas called their bird god. Roger felt a huge satisfaction. He had made a connection they thought he couldn't make. She was talking back. One word, anyway, which was one word more than anybody else was getting. Satisfaction clarified his vision, kept it growing when it could have fallen apart.

" 'Burn it,' the bird god is saying into my ear, and I know he means the Chapare, the leaf I'm looking at. But I don't know how. It doesn't make any difference, because while I'm looking at the leaf it burns up anyway. Smoke comes spiraling up in my direction and I breathe it in. It makes me strong. I can feel it in my wings. Now I know I'm strong enough to make it over the mountains, all the way to the Altiplano. The high plains. So I go. I fly up higher, over the mountains, and I don't come down until I see this gigantic eucalyptus tree on the edge of a big lake. I land in the tree and look out over the lake, and I have this great feeling of being in a place where nobody can get at me. None of them. Nobody. You know what I mean?"

She stood up from her pallet, walked toward him in the doubled dark of the cell, traced the outline of his face with her hands the way a blind person might: his ears, his hair, his cheeks and chin, his lips. The moment had come, he figured, not to ask any questions. "I'm going back to sleep now," he told her.

Satisfaction rocked him in his hammock like an easygoing baby. All he needed was a little more time.

In the morning, if the real dove was meant to be a message, Roger believed it had to be for him. Esencia was first up and the one to find it: pure white except for a black medal on its chest. It was sitting on Doña Blanca's favorite stump, and it wasn't going anywhere. Somebody had clipped its wings.

The dove made Serapio nervous. Ever since his face had turned up on the bird of destruction in a visionary dream in Condorito, he had no use for birds of any kind, Blanca explained.

"It means you're going to have to leave," Serapio worried. "People at the crossroads are talking about you. They think you're a spy for *la DEA*."

The DEA. In the Chapare it had quit being a string of gringo initials, become something else: a hammer, or a club, something hard and powerful that could hit you over the head and wreck your plans for the future. Without the DEA, according to the leaf farmers and paste stompers of Tingo Tingo, the UMOPAR were nothing. The traffickers would buy them off, or scare them off, find ten different ways to run them off, and in a week and a half the Chapare would go back to being what it ought to be: a genuine free-trade zone.

"I already told you about me and the DEA," Roger reminded him. "They murdered my brother Robert. Poor little Roberto. The bastards put a gun to his head on a dark street in Detroit and pulled the trigger, and I guarantee you they never lost any sleep over it." It would have been nice, actually, to have a brother named Robert, in Detroit or any other major American city.

But what Serapio said worried Roger. Most days he got restless hanging around the family shack watching the coca farmer and his wife worry. He walked into the crossroads, watched people buy and sell and bullshit each other, thought about Agnes, killed time. He thought people's hostility was just the normal troll suspicion of anything or anybody that looked different from what they were used to. But maybe it was more than that. In a certain kind of mood he would have appreciated the idea of being considered a DEA spy, but he wasn't in that mood. He took Agnes for a walk into Tingo Tingo to see whether Serapio was right or just a pessimist, converted by hard luck out of his natural hopeful way of looking at the world.

"I'm sorry I was upset with you last night," Agnes told him as they walked.

It was a better day than they were in a position to enjoy. The fog and the clouds had burned off, taking the humidity with them. The morning sky was the shade of blue that made you think of vacation, of being in a place good enough that there was no reason to want to be anywhere else. Ahead of them on the shady side of the road a lone monkey pointed its hairy finger at them and laughed, and birds that looked like wild parakeets fell like pastel confetti from the top of the canopy to a midair point they all agreed on, rose again, and disappeared into the thick, green-black woods.

"I'm not asking for anything from you, Agnes." He wanted to say something simple about the way it felt to lie in the hammock with her, about the good thing that being next to her was slowly doing for him, but he had made that kind of mistake before.

"Well, I'm sorry anyway."

"She talked to me. Last night, after you left."

"What did she say?"

"She said she'd tell me what we need to know."

"Does she know where my brother is? Did she say that?"

He couldn't bear to disappoint her. He nodded, felt like a hero. Everybody deserved that feeling once in a while. What he really wanted was to be sure she came back to sleep in the hammock.

"Part of it is I'm not used to telling people important things," she told him.

"You don't have friends?"

"I have friends, but when you live alone you get wrapped up listening to yourself, telling yourself the same things over and over. You start hearing your own echoes. So it becomes difficult to be accurate about the things that matter. You're always qualifying everything, and editing it, pushing it around and around. The only way I've found to get rid of my thoughts that really works is to write them down."

Which meant, he supposed, that telling him was not like telling a real person. To her he was the gringo equivalent of a troll, or else a notebook with legs, anyway something that didn't count the way people ought to count. The idea angered him, not a good thing, because it took him off his guard so that he didn't realize the guy unloading cases of soda pop and beer in front of Tingo Tingo's one and only restaurant was a gringo until the guy said *spies*.

"Fuck you," Roger told him. It felt great to say it in English to somebody who understood exactly what he meant.

"Peace, *hermano*," the guy told him. He took off his blue-striped cotton work gloves, held up his fingers in a V. "You got a guilty conscience or what?"

He was red: his face swollen and sweating red in the heat, his scraggly beard red at the edges, his red hair in a ponytail that hung down his back like a Davy Crockett coonskin cap. To keep the sweat out of his eyes he wore a blue bandana around his head. He looked more like a pirate than somebody you'd find in the Chapare driving a delivery truck that said Bebidas Samapa—Samapa Kola, Cerveza Samapa, Agua Mineral Samapa.

"Carl Kelleher's the name," he told Agnes, looking past Roger. "Purveying healthy beverages to thirsty Bolivians is the game."

He dropped the peace sign, stretched his hand to shake hers. Roger knew the look that was on her face: It was the one that meant she was feeling grateful for seeing something else she would never see back home. Chalk up one more for Flame, the Mystical Gringo, a.k.a. Jonathan the deadbeat brother.

A Bolivian midget came out of the restaurant and took the hand truck from Kelleher. "This is the Nugget," the American introduced him. "He's my partner. Even if you speak Spanish you can't talk to him, though. He's deaf and dumb. We get along real easy."

The Nugget squinted in the sunlight at Agnes, then at Roger. He wasn't interested. He wheeled away half a dozen cases of Samapa Beer into the two-room shack somebody had converted into the settlement's greasy spoon. He looked like a cross between Speedy Gonzalez and the mayor of Munchkinland, only with drooping jowls.

"All I'm trying to do is give you a heads-up," Kelleher said. "They think the DEA sent you here to check out who's moving what. They think you're drug spies. It's very sexy, if you think about it. If you survive, you can sell the movie rights to Hollywood. That kind of thing is very big, from what I hear."

"We're not spies," Roger told him.

"I didn't say I believed them, I'm just passing on a hot tip because we're *compatriotas*. Right now the entire Chapare is running with rumors about the next big bust the Yankees are putting together with the UMOPAR. The local yokels think you two have some kind of fancy radio transmitter hidden somewhere, and every night you're passing dope intelligence back to the base camp so they know who to hit when they come through."

"Bullshit."

"Don't shoot the messenger. I'm trying to do you a favor."

"Will you give us a ride out of here?" Roger asked before he knew what his question was going to be.

"We're not leaving," Agnes corrected him. "Not right now."

"I'd like to help you out," Kelleher told them, "but it's an insurance thing. I got this great deal from Lloyd's of London—no deductible, payable in pesos—but they say I can't take any suspicious riders. I'm really sorry."

"Do you know an American, a magician, down here in the Chapare?" If asking was a mistake, it was Agnes's to make.

"What do you want to know about him?" Kelleher said. He pulled bottles of Samapa Kola from a case, opened them, and passed them around like a host who remembered just a little too late what his duty was. The sweet, hot liquid tasted terrible. Roger drained his bottle in a hurry.

"He's my brother."

"Then you don't want to know what I heard."

"Tell me, please."

Kelleher shrugged, gestured to the Nugget, who was settling up with the owner of the restaurant. He moved them to the shady side of the truck. "Your brother's name is Flame, right?"

"His name is Jonathan."

"I only met him one time when we were doing a delivery in one of the settlements over east. When I saw the guy he was extremely high. He told me this long, far-fetched story about how he's on a holy quest for genuine magic, that you can still find it in places like Bolivia, if you know how to look, places that aren't part of the Industrial Revolution and the ecological assassination of the planet. He was getting close to what he came for, but he'd been close before and didn't quite make it. When I talked to him he was worried. Somebody was after him. He didn't really care if they caught up to him and killed him; it was going to happen sooner or later because the magic was a major threat to the first-world power structure, but he wanted to find the magic and touch it once before they got him and put him out of his misery. When I said what power structure is that? he looked at me like I was the *loco*, not him. I heard he travels with el Grán Moxo and his buyers; he's their dancing bear. Anyway it pains me greatly to tell you your brother is totally crazy. One of my customers at the other end of the valley told me one time the magician wanted some *pitillos*, but he didn't have any cash on him so he wrote the guy out an IOU in his own blood."

"Do you know where he might be now?"

"Sorry. My advice is quit looking for him, 'cause if and when you find him he's only going to break your heart."

"Maybe you're the spy," Roger decided. "Otherwise there'd be no reason to spend your time in a place like this."

"Bolivian Buddha say, Create no unnecessary grief for innocent suffering brothers and you won't get dumped on by the gods of retribution when they come through the green valley looking for victims. You weren't there, were you? I don't even have to ask; I can see it in your eyes you weren't."

"Weren't where?"

"In the exploding rice paddies."

But the Nugget was done collecting cash. He hauled the hand truck up onto the back of their Mercedes diesel, strapped it down, and he and Kelleher climbed into the cab. Partners. From behind the wheel Kelleher rolled down his window, looked down at Roger and Agnes in the road. "You'd be better off looking for your magician brother someplace else," he told them. Roger watched his wheels. They were rolling wings. Gone.

Roger had a car once, back when Danny got him a job on the line in Flint that lasted for ten and a half months before he called the foreman a fuckface and did something ingenious but ugly and permanently damaging to the guy's lunch bucket. It was a used Camaro, black with a silver stripe running all the way around the body, and Danny helped him put in lifters. It was the lifters, and the memory of the pirate-skull shifter Danny talked him into buying, that started him laughing until Agnes thought something was seriously wrong and he had to tell her nothing hurt, which was the simplest lie he could come up with.

So he knew it wasn't just his normal paranoia when he saw the threatening scowl on the face of the troll who sold them a music box with a plastic ballerina that danced across a tiny mirror floor when you wound it up. The music box was a bribe for Paloma, an expense and a tactic Roger didn't particularly like sinking to, but even if the people of Tingo Tingo were afraid to hassle them because they thought *la DEA* was protecting them, if there was going to be some kind of operation he wanted to be out of Tingo Tingo before it happened.

Back at Don Serapio's everybody had gone off to work a new coca field they were starting because they didn't know what else to do. Roger made Agnes wait in the shack, where she read her Tennyson's Greatest Hits, while he took the music box out to Paloma.

Paloma was working on her nails, filing and painting and studying them. He wound the music box, put it in her hand. Arms over her head, hands clasped, the ballerina in a blue tutu danced jerkily across the little mirror, spinning in time, more or less, with the music, which was, according to Agnes, a Strauss waltz. You couldn't prove that by Roger, and he didn't know the Spanish word for waltz, but the whole idea was what it might do for Paloma.

"They all think that the gringo magician put a spell on you," he told her.

No response, none was expected.

"It's not a spell, though, is it, what he did?"

She pointed one red-nailed finger at the reflection in the mirror of the jerky ballerina.

"Do you believe in the magic that the magician is looking for, Paloma?"

She shook her head.

"But you love him just the same."

The movement of her head might have been a nod, the motion equivalent of a whisper. The stone cowboy, Roger told himself, was not quite as dumb as he looked.

"He needs the money," she explained. Her voice startled, not just because it was the first time he had heard it but because it was deep, a rich-sounding voice like maple syrup and coffee stirred together in the bottom of a deep cup. Jonathan was a genuine bastard, had to be, for hustling and then dumping her. That was one important difference between Roger and the magician: Roger had only messed up his own life.

"The Moxo treats him like a slave," she told Roger. "He won't give him any money. He makes him beg for everything he needs. He doesn't even have enough money to get out of Bolivia. That's wrong. It's terribly wrong."

"That's why you told him you'll share your family's *pichicata* with him."

The music stopped, the ballerina quit dancing, and Paloma looked fiercely at Roger. He wound the box again.

"They can make more. They've got the time. They'll never go to La Paz. That's just my mother's daydream. If she didn't go on thinking that they're going to get out of here and have their little business in La Paz she'd go crazy."

"Will you tell me when he's coming back, Paloma? We don't give a damn about the *pasta de coca*. That's between you and him. I'll tell you a secret: Agnes, the woman with me, is his sister. She came all the way from North America to see him."

"He's taking me with him back to North America."

Lying, son-of-a-slug bastard. It seemed impossible that anything as decent as Agnes could be related to anything as low and crawling as the Mystical Gringo.

"Dove," said Paloma quietly, her eyes on the ballerina. "He taught me how to say my name in English. That's why I knew what you said when you called me by my name the other night. We're going to sell the *pichicata* to get the money for airplane tickets."

"When is he coming back to pick up you and the coca paste?"

She stared at him, not trusting, and he understood that the reason she was going along with the idea that Flame had put her in a spell was the guilt she felt for robbing her family, which made it impossible for her to be around them.

"I'm asking," Roger told her, "because we have to see him. That's all we want to do is see him and talk to him. Their father is sick. He should know about that before the two of you get back there."

"I'll tell him."

"Everybody in the settlement thinks the DEA and the UMOPAR are planning a big raid. They think they're coming here. If they do, they might find your stash, and if the magician is around they'll pick him up and take him away because everybody knows he hangs out with el Grán Moxo. So the DEA will think he's a drug trafficker, and they'll lock him up in jail in New York City."

He stopped, breathed three times deeply, told her what had become true by repetition. "The DEA killed my brother in the United States. They put a gun to the side of his head and pulled the trigger. Bam, just like this. It was all a mistake. My brother was no drug trafficker, and they apologized afterward, but saying you're sorry doesn't bring him back, does it?"

Paloma wouldn't look at him. She picked up the ballerina from the music box, ran a curious finger across the base of the magnet that attached her to the mirror, closed the top of the box. Strauss stopped waltzing, and she tucked the ballerina into the pocket of her lacy blouse. She was speaking a different sort of language, which Roger considered himself lucky for understanding.

"Dove," he said softly, pronouncing it with a blurring Spanish accent the way Paloma herself did. There was something disturbing about her bright red nails when her fingers curled around her broom. She moved away, swept up a private little storm, and Roger wondered whether the monkey laughing outside in the banana trees was the same one that had pointed its finger at him and Agnes on the road to Tingo Tingo. Dove.

By the time they noticed that Esencia was trailing along behind them it was too late to send her home. The way she hung back in the tree-choked darkness of the path bothered Roger. It was like being followed by your guardian angel just closely enough that you couldn't even think about committing the sins you'd like to commit.

Everybody in Tingo Tingo knew how to get to the secret landing strip in the jungle that the Moxo's men had built. You couldn't move major quantities of paste on the roads out of the Chapare. Bad as they were, the UMOPAR sometimes stumbled across the *pichicata* hidden in truckloads of merchandise or the bundles of bus passengers. Some stuff moved by boat, but the important shipments went out by air. It was faster and safer.

Paloma had to be taking the longest way around to the *pista clandestina* that she could find. They went quietly, no flashlights, the sweat drying cool on their skin as soon as it leaked out. There was enough of a moon to make out shapes and distances, and Paloma knew the trails around Tingo Tingo as well as she knew the high valley territory back in Condorito.

Not that you could have gotten a word out of Agnes anyway. She didn't approve of the version of events that it had been necessary to come up with to put Don Serapio and Doña Blanca at ease. Agnes wanted everybody to win, or else be guaranteed an individual happy ending: herself to find her wacked-out brother, then convince him to go back home and make peace with their sick old man. That was primary, of course. But at the same time she wanted Doña Blanca's family to get their stash back and sell it now, while the price was fairly high, and escape into legitimate business in La Paz. She thought if they got Paloma out of the Chapare and into a healthier environment the girl would forget her diseased fantasy about traveling with the Mystical Gringo up to the land of electric can openers and blue-light specials. A mean part inside Roger had felt pretty good about laying out the case for Agnes: it's either you find your brother or they get their dope back, but not both.

She had cried when he did that, but she quit trying to make everybody happy. She quit talking. And now she moved lightly through the Chapare woods. From a certain point of view she was the ideal companion to go on an adventure in Bolivia with.

"We'll get your *pichicata* for you," Roger had told Serapio, who believed him. "But let us go alone. If half of Tingo Tingo shows up they'll panic and take off and nobody will get anything they want."

He would live with the guilt he felt about that one. He could tolerate it, as long as Agnes got to see her brother. The bad part was Esencia tagging along behind them, worse than a conscience, really, because prettier, more fragile, more valuable. In another world she would be dancing across her own mirrored floor in a blue tutu, her hands arched over her pretty head gracefully, gracefully, while a real band played Strauss, or the Bolivian equivalent, just for her.

Flame's plan had been to have Paloma hide her family's stash close enough to the *pista* that they wouldn't lose any time loading it onto the plane. One of the trafficker's pilots, according to Paloma, liked the magician. He was a real friend. Enough of a friend, anyway, to fly one of the trafficker's planes to the hidden strip, land it long enough for Flame and Paloma to throw their bags of paste on, and take off again. The pilot would help them sell the paste to some Colombians he knew, and then, according to Paloma, they were going to fly to Miami and live on the beach for six months eating shrimp and lobster and

Alaskan crab. She wondered what all those sea creatures tasted like; she wasn't sure she was going to like them even though Flame had told her she would love the taste, that she had to at least try the stuff if she was going to go with him.

"They'll only stay on the ground five minutes," Paloma had told Roger. "After that the pilot will get nervous. So we have to be completely ready."

Which was a royal pain. Paloma had spent the two days she was gone from the settlement digging holes, burying the paste, covering the filled-in holes with branches and leaves and enough general jungle shit that nobody was going to find her hiding place. And nobody did, but digging up the dope and hauling it to the edge of the dirt *pista* without making any noise was hard work, harder than working on the line in Flint knowing you weren't even going to get minimum wage after they took taxes and your life out of you. It made Roger think about working at Don Eloy's lumberyard, and the money the troll lumberman had stolen from him. He could have been back in Michigan learning Japanese, putting money down on a black Camaro, training his personal robot in the privacy of his own home, making unstopping love to a yellow-haired gringo woman who would be impressed by the sweet Spanish nothings he whispered into her willing ear. Instead, this . . .

They finished hauling and stacking the bags of dope early enough that they had to wait, and they had to wait long enough that everybody started thinking What if he doesn't show up? The little dirt landing strip had been built in the middle of a played-out coca field, on one edge of which a ravine fell down into the dark woods, which was where Paloma had buried the *pichicata*. The less-than-half a moon was going down fast over the ravine, but it still gave enough light to make out the packed dirt runway, weeds poking up high the length of it, and a single buckle-branched tree far enough to the side it hadn't been worth anybody's trouble to fell it. The ravine was a black gash. The cooling air was peaceful, making a temporary comfort you had to be sitting still to appreciate. They sat.

Roger worried that Paloma might have gotten her knots wrong. Because there was no calendar, before he left Tingo Tingo Flame had tied loose knots in a length of waxed twine. I'll be back the night of the day you untie the last knot, he told her when he gave her the twine, but she could have been confused, forgotten a day or untied two the same day. Or else, more likely, Flame had no intention of coming back, and he had only given her the knotted twine and made her go through the labor of hiding the stash out of sheer perverse evil and so she would fuck him. Or the pilot would chicken out, or el Grán Moxo would figure out what was going on, or the Mystical Gringo would get so wasted smoking chemically enhanced coca paste cigarettes that he would forget which planet he was on, not to mention the fact that a woman named Dove was waiting for him at a *pista clandestina* with a load of negotiable dope.

Roger had no idea how much the stack of black plastic bags stuffed with paste would be worth to a Colombian trafficker who would refine the shit into cocaine. Paloma probably didn't know either. It had to be worth a bunch of money, and for a few moments he fantasized what it would be like to have that cash himself, and what unlikely things would have to happen for him to get it. Fantasy always stoned Roger, put him into a coma of slow thought that lifted him out of the boring space his body generally inhabited. Agnes was sitting on the ground with her legs crossed, hands folded in her lap, her back against the stack of *pichicata* bags. She was rehearsing the things she was going to say to her worthless brother if he showed up, wondering whether he would be temporarily sane, working herself up to defend her sensitive self against his full-bore hostility. Paloma was too nervous to sit. She was cooing quietly to Esencia, running her fingers through the little girl's long hair, saying good-bye through her to everybody else in the family she was about to rob and abandon.

Roger was the last one to hear the sound of the airplane engine.

Agnes jumped up, Paloma began pacing, and they watched the small plane come in low and fast without running lights. It hit the far end of the dirt *pista* and shuddered a little, the engine whining loud enough to wake the Bolivian dead, and rolled bouncing toward them across the rough ground. It was a time when everybody in the Chapare knew enough to stay away from the strip unless they had business there, so it was kind of surprising to hear a human stir from across the field when the engine died, the door swung open, and the propellers wound themselves down to idle.

Flame was smaller than Roger had imagined him to be. He climbed down from the plane with a showman's flourish: It was the first half of a really convincing disappearing act, and he wanted to make sure everybody in the neighborhood realized how lucky they all were to witness him. Paloma ran toward him, the pilot jumped down, and Agnes moved in behind Paloma. Roger hung back. He didn't like even the idea of a family reunion.

"Jonathan," said Agnes. It was a sound that hurt, and the Mystical Gringo froze before Paloma got to him.

"Agnes?"

"It's me."

"I don't fucking believe it. I do not fucking believe it. Do you have any idea where you are here? Do you have any fucking idea?" Only a brother like him could get ticked off like that when he learned his one and only sister had tracked him down through the Bolivian jungle.

"Everything's broken," she said to him. Not what Roger expected, but it made a sense to him that he would have to stop and analyze later. Nestling into the magician like a homing pigeon, Paloma was whimpering, and Agnes was moving in close enough to touch her brother to prove he was real, and then they were all the object and intention of an UMOPAR raid.

"¡Alto!," somebody yelled in Spanish, but instead of stopping to get arrested, the pilot, a chunky man with a hard belly and a monster-

sized mustache, pulled out a pistol and blasted at the shadows, which were filling up with antidrug police.

"Shit," said Flame.

"Don't go," Agnes begged him. "Please. We can fix it, Jonathan."

"You're out of your tree, Saint Agnes."

"No te vayas," Paloma was crying, but she was more accustomed to significant disappointment in her life's principal desires than Agnes was, probably, and the hopelessness in her voice was clear.

"Out of here," said the magician. No trick. He was gone. The pilot was already back inside the plane revving the engine.

"Jonathan!" Agnes called again, but he must have thought she was only part of his bad dream.

Afterward Roger blamed the pilot. If the guy hadn't started blasting away like a trigger-happy cowboy from his window, the UMOPAR might not have shot back. Which meant one of them might not have fired low enough the way he did to hit little Esencia, who fell silently. Her sister screamed, ran over to the place she had fallen and covered her with her own body. The plane was already taxiing; it was amazing how little time and runway they needed to get the thing up. Not so amazing if you remembered how much money traffickers like the Amazing Big Moxo had to put into operating expenses.

There was shooting going on from both sides. Roger heard bullets thunking into the *pichicata*, a satisfying sound that made Roger wish you could kill cocaine, destroy every last stash in the world.

Agnes was paralyzed. You wouldn't expect anything else. It was not the kind of situation a woman like her should let herself get into. The moon had sunk below the rim of the blackened woods, and the darkness made everything that was happening seem not quite real. It was like being on the edge of the place where a movie was being made and getting caught up in the fake excitement. He heard bad Spanish being barked. *La DEA*. He remembered the brother he never had being assassinated by a rampaging agent in Detroit. He slapped Agnes in the face, dragged her by one stiff hand off the field, down into the ravine, up the other side, and into the woods.

He waited without looking for the plane to lift off. Without lights maybe it would be a harder target to hit. For a long time, weak legs pumping, he could hear Paloma wailing. He tried to listen for a quieter crying, which would mean Esencia was still alive, just hurt, and maybe it was there, but in the confusion of sounds and the fear he couldn't hear it. Agnes was in better shape than he was. She had no trouble keeping up with him.

If you ran far enough without taking a bullet in the back, eventually you would have to come to a place where the woods ended, and there was no coca, no dope, nothing lethal. There was such a thing as a safe place. They ran. There had to be that kind of a place. Running.

FOUR

Chop-ita chop-ita: It was the sound of alien metal invading your private dreams, cold steel blades that wanted to slice your hot heart and no place to escape. When Placido Macdougal's giant pet pig bolted and ran off into the jungle, it proved something to Roger and also taught him something he did not want to learn. Bobby Burns was swallowed by the dark Chapare in one fatty mouthful, which proved that bad luck was not a random thing, like lightning. It hit certain people over and over again, and Roger was one of them. But he resisted what it taught him: Bad luck was what he had in common with the trolls. In el Panóptico one of the other prisoners, an angry egghead political type who spent his free time reading hard books and raving about all the injustice there was in the world, had taught him just enough history for Roger to accept the fact that Bolivia had had more bad luck than any three countries of equal size put together. The thing was, he did not want to have anything in common with any Bolivian.

It was an optical delusion: You ran like a nonstop maniac trying to get close to the thing you wanted, or needed—in this particular case it was Flame the Mystical Gringo—until somebody switched the binoculars around on you and instead of gaining on your goal all of a sudden you realized it was still a million miles away and tiny, too small and too far away to get your hands on.

Running away from the *pista clandestina* Roger had been sure he could get back to the path down which Paloma had led them, on the far side of the ravine. But the ravine was like Smoky the Bear's nightmare. The moon down, it was totally dark, and the pathless growth they waded through was so thick and ungiving that the only way through was to throw themselves at it and crash. Once Roger stumbled and fell, but the bushery was so dense it held him up so all he did was cut his face on an unfriendly branch with spines. He held Agnes's hand but that was only to be sure they didn't get separated.

Coming up on the far edge of the ravine they stopped to breathe. They weren't that far away from the landing strip in the coca field, but the thicket they had just come through was as good as a wall, on the far side of which they could still hear Paloma wailing, though what reached them was faint and sounded slightly unreal. There were a few shots going off, but the plane was in the air by then, and there was no reason for the drug cops to think two suspicious gringos had escaped to the far side of the ravine. Unless they had those high-tech eyes, night-vision goggles that would make Roger and Agnes appear like guilty blurs of moving red light. Was that how the things worked? Plus it was probably standard DEA operating procedure to send out patrols to sweep the area after a raid, street cleaners mopping up the neighborhood after the action was over.

Agnes was not the kind of person who cried much, but she was crying now. He guessed it was not so much because she had come within spitting distance of her brother, had actually touched and talked to the bum and been hassled by him, but because of what happened to Esencia. The sound she made was mechanical, two big sucking breaths in, one out; two in, one out.

"Bastards," Roger said, but that didn't help at all. "She'll probably be okay, Agnes. Paloma is freaked is all." His own voice sounded strange. It was wavery and thin, somebody else's voice, somebody with the courage of a crippled rabbit being tracked by a starving wolf with a better-than-average sense of smell. "We better keep moving is all."

He could tell Agnes was going to start an argument with him. But before she had time to gear up, he pulled her hard by one arm, which went limp, and they moved through waist-high grass toward the path that would, with luck, take them back to a recognizable road. The only luck Roger had, however, was troll luck, which guaranteed he was going to miss the path. The one they took seemed right, felt right for the longest time, until it forked in the woods where there should have been no fork. He played his flashlight up and down both paths; the canopy overhead blocked out whatever starlight or left-over moonlight there might be. He guessed the brush and bushes were dense enough to hide their little light from anybody coming behind them.

"This isn't the right way," Agnes told him. "There was no fork the way we came in, was there? I don't remember this way, Roger." Her voice went notching up the panic ladder.

Roger stopped himself from saying what came to his tongue, which was Fork off, baby, it's your asshole brother's fault, not mine. Behind them he thought he heard, distantly, the pursuing noise heavily armed antidrug police with night-vision goggles would make tromping through the jungle after fleeing suspects, second-class global citizens on the run. Maybe not. Anyway, they couldn't stand there. The same sick fear that had undone him at Checkpoint Carlitos weakened him, wobbled him. It was worse this time because there was no doubt they would nail him if they tagged him. The fear, he understood, had to do with el Panóptico and all the places like it that he had seen and imagined and worried about being stuck inside for the length of his traveling career, which was his life.

"Pick a path," he said, and they moved off more slowly down the one she chose.

He was coated with sweat, and his skin had swelled up all over his body. Snapping sticks went off like guns when they stepped, and birds that had their own version of night-vision goggles hooted and screamed at them, eager to give them away if they could, if anybody was there to pay attention to them. He supposed there were monkeys, too, because monkeys made the same kind of racket, or did they sleep at night? He realized he knew nothing about anything in the world around him, the world that surrounded him, and even in the middle of his fear it burned like new knowledge. His bottomless ignorance shamed him.

Until they came to the next fork—could have been a kilometer, or a half kilometer; Roger had no skill in estimating distances, and the darkness stretched everything out in a weird way, so that it was like trying to trot hamstrung through the scenery of your own bad dream—he maintained the hope that they were going to intersect with the right path, and the God who never talked back would somehow give him the grace to be able to distinguish it. But at the second fork the only thing he could think to do was to ask Agnes to pick her choose again. So she understood that they were totally screwed up and picked the path that looked a little wider, but that was only more of the same optical delusion.

This one led to a stomping pit. They could tell they were approaching one by the stench of chemicals leaching out into the innocent air. When the trolls finished stomping their leaves into mash they let the chemicals leak out of the pits into the woods, which smelled bitter, caustic, the Bolivian version of bad factory air. At the site they stopped long enough to look for drinking water, but all they found was a heap of plastic jugs, and some trash half buried in a hole in the ground, and then the pit itself, lined with plastic sheeting but empty and already filling up with fallen leaves.

"I don't think they're chasing us anymore," Agnes decided. "I mean if they were." Her voice was hoarse, sweet, vulnerable. He shone his flash in her face. It was filthy, streaked with dirt and tears and pain. The light made her squint, and Roger wondered how a person could survive in the jungle wearing contact lenses.

He felt bad, because hitting her with the light was as brutal as kicking her. Fork you, Agnes, he didn't say. He turned off the flash, and she lost what she had to lose, bent over and heaved into the empty coca-stomping pit. The wet, raspy sound she made throwing up, crying at the same time, was worse than fingernails scraped on a blackboard. For a moment he had to fight the impulse to turn and run, to leave her where she was and run back to Flint, Michigan. She would find her way out eventually and be better off alone than with him. But he was selfish. He stayed, left the flash off so that she could heave in privacy, more or less. He closed his eyes, became aware that his arms, his legs, his hands were trembling. It was, he thought, the world's strangest wake, and they were never even going to know for sure whether Esencia had died.

"She is the most beautiful child I ever saw," Agnes told him when she was through.

That she was. An actual angel, with little nubs on her back that showed you where the wings had been. The unusual thing happening to Roger was crying. "We can't go back to Tingo Tingo anyway," he said.

"We have to. I have to know about Esencia, Roger. Even before . . . "

"Even before what?"

"He's crazy now, isn't he? It's gone way past his fantasy adventure of looking for magic in South America. It wasn't like seeing Jonathan, my brother. It was more like seeing . . ."

"Like seeing what?"

She was breathing almost normally, but there was still a rasp when she exhaled, something that wanted to come up and out that maybe wasn't words, it was the thick, dark stuff words were made of. "It was like . . . like seeing the magician. It's as though he has quit being his father's son and Agnes's brother, and he has let himself become a character, a joker: the gringo magician in Bolivia."

"What did you expect if you saw him in the middle of an UMOPAR raid? Nobody can be at his best when he's being shot at and his sister just popped up in the middle of the Chapare like some kind of cosmic bill collector. Give it up, Agnes. Give him up."

Though he couldn't see her in the black he was sure she shook her head. Stubborn. What had to be a monkey with insomnia laughed at him, and Roger decided he hated the animal kingdom. When it came down to it, animals were no better than people, no more charitable or tolerant or helpful.

"Those guys didn't just happen by that landing strip, Agnes. They knew something was going down. And they had to know it was coming out of Tingo Tingo. If we go back, the real spies will let the UMOPAR know we're there, and then it's all over. And even if that didn't happen the trolls would lynch us. No one is ever going to believe anything bad about you, but there's such a thing as guilt by association, right?"

"Meaning?"

"Meaning it will take them about three and a half seconds to decide I'm some kind of small-time trafficker down from Gringolandia to make a killing in coke. And you're with me, aren't you? As far as they're concerned we probably think we're the new Bonnie and Clyde, out to make a name for ourselves in cocaine."

"My pack," she said.

It took a minute for him to catch it. Her pack was the place she kept the things they needed. Like cash, and the passports, and Tennyson's Greatest Hits.

"Fuck me," he said, regretted it immediately.

"I had it at the landing strip."

Roger tried to think whether at any time in his down-tending life he had been harder up than they had just become: chased by drug police of two different nationalities in the middle of the night through hostile jungle territory they didn't know, broke and passportless and no prospects for getting out, let alone saving the day by finding Flame and converting him into a human being. The answer was no.

What awed him was Agnes's strength of purpose, which gave her peace of a kind he recognized but never lived in himself.

"If you don't think they're coming after us," she told him, "the first thing to do is find a place to sleep."

Snakes, he thought but didn't say. They didn't like the ground around the coca stomping pit. The fouled air was nasty, and the whole place seemed like the abandoned scene of somebody's terrible secret sin. If there were monkeys in the trees overhead they would have the devil's face, or the face of an UMOPAR grunt, or Don Eloy, or el Verdugo from prison. They moved slowly down the path through the woods, putting a little more distance between themselves and the troops that might or might not be on their trail.

Which ended unexpectedly on a lip of higher ground overlooking a quiet creek. The water sound was soothing, reassuring, and the lip was covered with low grass that had no spikes. Agnes had a plastic poncho she was wearing in a Girl Scout-type holster strapped to her webbed belt. They stretched it out on the high flat ground but couldn't decide whether it was better to lie on the poncho or cover themselves with it. Agnes thought it would be better under them, but Roger wanted the shelter of something over him, and he was right. They lay on the grass, heads toward the water, wrapped arms around each other without deciding to, shut out the Chapare with a piece of blue plastic that made Roger think of the troll families he had seen living that way in El Alto above La Paz. But the trolls up there on the high plains had a few things, at least: water buckets and cooking pots and maybe a knife, a little money in a pocket one or two days a week. And some kind of hope that the tin-mining business would pick up again and they could go back to work, or imperialist prospectors would find gold in the Bolivian hills or oil in the salt flats or something else valuable enough to change their weather. That was how you could define low: when you were living under a single sheet of plastic with less to get you by than an out-of-work Bolivian tin miner had.

"It can't get worse," Agnes decided.

"That doesn't mean it has to get better."

"We're not going to die here, if that's what you mean."

"Do you believe in God?" he asked her. The question made him anxious. He had not planned to ask it.

Even a few days ago her answer would have ticked him off, but he was beginning to understand her better. She was a person whose thoughts made her careful, slower than most because so much was going on inside and she didn't want to make a mistake, say something that was not one hundred percent the thing she wanted to say. "It's not the kind of question I know how to ask myself any more, Roger."

The way they were lying wrapped, if he moved his hands just a little he could have brushed her breasts with his palms. He wanted to do that. He imagined what they looked like under her shirt—the pale brown color of her nipples, the little mysterious pleasure-producing bumps around their edges, the white resisting give as his hands moved against them—and the feeling that seeped through him mingled sex and respect in a way that was unfamiliar to him. He owed something to Cherokee, the fortune teller gringa in La Paz, but he was not sure what. He wondered whether Agnes was a virgin. He had assumed the only virgins left in North America were the daughters of Bible beaters in the deep South, and then only because they were afraid of being caught committing acts of illegal pleasure by their righteous fathers. He wanted to ask her but could not. His palms itched, ached, wanted, but he did not move his hands.

"Just before they let me out of jail in La Paz," he told her, "I heard myself talking to God."

Saying it embarrassed him, but when she did not react he went on. "Maybe not all of me, just a part. And not with words."

He needed a way to explain it. "It's like," he decided, "there's layers inside a person, lots of them. And all the layers are connected to something, to you, the real you, which is like an invisible cord, even though most of the time you think one of the layers is all there is. You go along like that. That's how you live your life because that's what it takes to survive. But every once in a while something will happen that makes you notice there's a person in there listening to all the noise you're making. That's the one that was doing the talking. Not that I got any answers. I didn't really expect any. You don't get answers the way people do in movies, do you?"

For some reason that question was enough to make her kiss him, or at least come grazing close with her virginlike lips. He tried to remember the last time he had felt this kind of hard wanting for a woman. Before he quit, there had been a girl in high school. She was one of the reasons he wound up leaving, because both her parents worked and she had a car, so they started skipping classes. They went to her house. In the attic was a space fixed up as a guest room nobody ever used, a lumpy queen-size bed and the air full of dust motes that made the light coming in through the little window above their heads thick as bright jelly, and it quivered. They made all kinds of love, all the time, until he figured out that she didn't really like him. He was a dildo with a body attached, a bunch of moving parts some of which made her feel pretty good when she closed her eyes and fantasized. One time he got her to admit she was pretending that he was John Lennon. The worst part of that was he always hated the Beatles. They were millionaire phonies wrapped up in their own anxieties making music to get richer and feel better. It was therapy with a back beat. So he quit going with her to the attic, but by then he was so far behind in school it wasn't worth going back, and he didn't.

"Sorry," she said. It sounded like she was apologizing to herself, not him, so he didn't tell her it was okay.

He listened to the night racket of birds and bugs and animals with see-in-the-dark eyes. It rose and fell, rose and fell. If you left a tape recorder running you could make the soundtrack to a Tarzan movie. He could tell by the way she held herself, tensed, that Agnes was thinking about Esencia again. But behind them through the hostile unknown woods came no DEA agents, no UMOPAR trolls. There was nobody, for the moment, close enough to hurt them.

"It's safe to sleep," Roger told Agnes. "We better, anyway. Are you scared?"

"He didn't even look like my brother."

"What do you mean?"

"It was Jonathan, I'm not saying that. But he scared me. I used to get angry with him, but he never scared me before."

"Even if you get to talk to him in a reasonable place, in a reasonable way, he's not going to go back with you to see your father. No matter what you decide to do next, you'll be better off if you assume that's the way it's going to turn out."

"You're right," she decided, and for a moment he was pleased to think he had convinced her of something important, but the satisfaction passed when he realized she meant he was right, they should go to sleep.

There were no snakes, no trolls, no UMOPAR agents or low-watt foremen in Roger's dreams, which moved like a river carrying colorful garbage, dropping trash in the dangerous eddies where it bent. The fish that fed in those eddies had teeth, and when they opened their mouths to grin there was blood on their teeth. Coasting on the surface of the water in a flat-bottomed boat with low sides, he watched the blood leak out in murky, shaky lines, dissolve and disappear in the invisible undercurrent. But the damn fish kept grinning. Wanting his vulnerable human ass made them happy, kept them happy. It had something to do with the survival of the fittest, with feasting on the fattest, with the hunter's instinct and the runner's instinct and another strong, appealing instinct to close your eyes and forget you had a body and a brain that lived inside it. He forgot.

They woke early. They were stiff, sore, ugly. Their hair was wild, their bodies dirty, their clothes a mess. He was used to thinking of himself as ugly; it wasn't a condition you were born with, like an extra toe, but a way of being that you acquired if you weren't careful in the right way. That was one of the hazards of being a rolling stone cowboy; you couldn't always get your hands on the basic things you needed to stay civilized, like clean underwear and a hairbrush. One way or another, one place or another, there was always sand in your shoes, wax in your ears, snot crusted in your nose, sleep grunging your eyelids. But he felt bad for Agnes, and something close to halfway responsible, because up until then she had been able to maintain something, a connection with her past that would lead, eventually, back to her future and that made the crumminess of the present tolerable. He assumed she was still wearing her contact lenses.

"What is it?" she asked him, understanding the appraising way he was looking at her. "I look terrible, don't I?"

They crawled down the bank to the stream, washed their bodies in the cool water, and that helped a little. Roger watched the water soak into her shirt, which clung to her skin showing the outline of the body beneath. It was a fairly interesting body, a fairly pure vision.

"Too much," he told her.

"Too much what?"

"Your brother did too much dope. It makes the pieces of your self get loose inside you. In his case the pieces have been floating around loose so long they won't go back into place. They're stuck in a screwed-up order, and now he doesn't even remember it can be any other way. He thinks bad is normal."

It had to be the outline of her private body against her wet shirt that kept him at it, twisting his finger in the hole of her hurt. He knew all about his shortcomings, but being cruel for its own sake was not among them, not usually.

Still in the water, Agnes was whining now. But at least it wasn't about her brother. "She died, didn't she, Roger."

He shrugged, turned away, and climbed up the bank so he didn't have to see her in that condition. He was remembering the way Esencia had appeared in front of him on the road in Tingo Tingo that first night offering to sell him *pitillos* she knew were poison, and her perfect innocence, which was the same thing as beauty, if you thought about it. Better not to think about it.

Behind him, Agnes was making up a story to make herself feel better, although she should have known it only worked if you actually believed the story you invented, and she didn't believe hers. "I'm almost sure I heard her crying when we were running away. It was hard to hear because Paloma's voice was so much louder, but I also heard Esencia. She was hurt, and I'm sorry she was because it was our fault, but now I remember distinctly hearing her voice."

If Esencia's getting shot was their fault, in Roger's opinion it was only because of the generally defective way the universe was glued together, or wasn't. Not because of anything specific you could go back to and undo in your mind and feel sorry for. Should he have stopped and tied her to a tree trunk before they got to the landing strip? He didn't even have any rope.

When they were cleaner they left the stomping pit, retraced the trail back to a fork and moved in a direction that felt right. On top of being ugly they were hungry, and their dirty clothes chafed their skin. Roger felt a lump of soreness forming inside his throat. It was like being on the road during a stretch of bad luck, except there was no road. It got hot early, but the white sunlight that worked its way down through the canopy to the bushery and the grown-over trail they were following was important, something they needed in the absence of food and a clear destination. Sweat crept on his body, and his ears hummed.

The only thing to do was get to a road that would lead them back to the road out of the Chapare. They could hitch a ride to Cochabamba. Without telling Agnes, Roger would steal them some food, hustle what they needed, just enough to survive without getting lightheaded. In Cochabamba he would force her to make a distress call to the American Embassy in La Paz. The consul would be willing to help out a person like Agnes, and Roger could tag along back to the city of his imprisonment. Back to square one. The way up was the way down, which so far showed no indication of being the way out.

The only problem was finding the road. The jungle was full of trails and half paths, slightly worn tracks that led from one place to the next in a way that lulled you into thinking there was an overall design, and if only they had thought to bring a Chapare road map. But neither Roger nor Agnes had any sense of direction. They moved on instinct. At a fork, or a turning, usually one path looked a little wider, a little more traveled, than the other, and usually they chose that way. With some frequency they passed abandoned coca-stomping pits, and every once in a while a shack disintegrating while the jungle grew back up around and inside and over it. But no people, no trolls, nobody they could ask directions from, let alone help.

Once they found some trees with ripe grapefruit, and the sun-warmed fruit tasted good enough that for a while things didn't seem as bad as they actually were. When Agnes said her head hurt Roger realized his did, too. But the grapefruit staved off the hunger, blunted the ache in his temples, made him think about paradise as a place a person might be able to walk to, a place on some luckier body's map.

He assumed the reason Agnes was able to keep her spirits up the way she did was because she couldn't really imagine anything but a happy ending: getting out of Cocalandia and back to the Bolivian equivalent of civilization. Her little adventure was getting longer and more complicated, it was more of a hassle than she had thought it would be, but adventures ended; they had to. You closed the cover on the storybook and did something else, like baking cookies or going to the movies or throwing stones at ducks in the lake at your favorite park while little kids in short pants let their balloons go up into the air and pretended it was only an accident.

But still she amazed him. She sang songs. He remembered some of them, and they reminded him of being rocked on a lap, wrapped in female, comfort-inducing arms, even though he personally did not remember ever being rocked by anybody in his life. It was more the idea of rocking, the possibility, inside which there was something sexual. And she recited poems, by heart. Some of them were long. Amazingly long. Roger had assumed people quit memorizing poems after television was invented, when their memories started to corrode, and probably that was ninety percent true. But there must be exceptions, and Agnes was one of them. Before she began a new one she would tell him the name of the guy who wrote it and something about his life. That was how he learned that Thomas Hardy was a miserable individual even after he had money in the bank and a statue of himself put up inside Buckingham Palace. And Keats did drugs with Shelley, which probably made the poems sound better than they actually were when they got together in the English woods and blew a few Jamaican numbers. Wordsworth had a sexual thing for trees and flowers, it sounded like. And William Blake honestly believed in the possibility of a natural high. Roger liked the Blake poems best, even though he had no idea what they meant, if they meant anything. He thought he might sit down and try to write a poem himself someday, except he would not want his poem to rhyme the way Mother Goose did, which Agnes told him was acceptable. Rhythm yes, but no rhymes.

It was the rhythm in her songs and her poems that kept them moving, actually, both of them. Roger didn't want to mention it to her, but he was pretty sure it was aerodynamically possible for them to keep walking around in the Chapare until they fell over exhausted from hunger and flesh-eating insects nested in their eyes, after which a herd of wandering trolls would stumble over their bones and make up a folk tale about them. It wasn't even necessary to go in a circle. Following the trails, which all looked more or less alike, they could move in long loops and zigzags or strange, off-kilter triangles or rhombuses. Where did that word come from? He must have been in school the day they taught that one. The girl who fantasized him as John Lennon was out with the flu, or the potato famine, or syphilis, or else she was home fucking some local up-and-coming rock star in that attic room on the same lumpy bed on which Roger had lost his virginal belief in romantic love, so Roger got the benefit of a new and unusual word.

They would never get anywhere. Anytime they came to a place where it was possible to go in more than one direction Agnes stopped, expected him to know which way was better. But he had no idea, no sense of one place over another, and he forced her to make the decisions. She thought it was part of his plan, which irked him a little. He did not want to be responsible, any more than he was responsible for Esencia's getting shot.

It was somewhere in the middle of the afternoon when they came through an unending forest of squatty banana trees out onto a little road. They stuffed themselves with bananas and finished off the grapefruits they had been carrying while they stared at the tire tracks in the fine, sandy dirt of the road. Fruit salad, kind of, nothing like the fruit cocktail in a can that Danny was probably sitting down having in Flint with his wife and their brood of greedy crumb snatchers. Roger was dizzy. He closed his eyes and saw one blood-red cherry fall from the can onto a heap of soft, innocent chunks of pears and peaches in Danny's plastic bowl. Who said visions had to mean something besides the pictures they were?

"They go that way," she pointed.

"So which way is out?" he asked her, "the way they went or the way they came?"

Roger wondered whether a person could die from eating only fruit salad, the way they said you could die in the Arctic Circle if you only ate rabbit meat because it had no fat, which may have been the reason God invented blubber. A balanced arctic diet. It was one more question Roger would want to ask him if he ever started answering. Without talking it over, he led Agnes in the direction he thought the tracks took. Forward. And she followed. The way things were glued, which was not real well, whatever happened was going to be his fault.

Before the sun went down they limped into Pes Volado, Placido

Macdougal's settlement, no home away from anybody's home. They were the walking wounded. The tracks belonged to Macdougal's snazzy Toyota 4-Runner, bright blue with a red band around the body. That seemed unfair. If Macdougal was getting rich selling coca paste to Colombian traffickers, who made their money by selling the finished coke to gringos, the least he could do was buy an American car. The circle didn't quite close, in Roger's opinion, but he had no mind for economics.

Pes Volado wasn't even a settlement, really, just a few huts thrown up more or less in the same neighborhood, which was close to a noisy creek the stompers drew their water from. Placido Macdougal didn't believe in spoiling his workers with all the conveniences of an isolated Altiplano mountain village. The place was a shit hole of human trash in the middle of weedy nowhere. Not even a banana tree. Macdougal trucked in everything they ate, and the little else they needed, in his 4-Runner—it was a company store on chrome wheels—along with the chemicals and supplies they needed to take the sacred weed and stomp it into unsacred drug paste.

When Roger and Agnes arrived, Macdougal was ragging. From what Roger could pick out from the red-faced man's rave, which was a river of words in Spanish and boss-man Quechua, a bunch of the workers he had hired to make paste had gotten tired of the living conditions in Pes Volado and split, leaving an unstomped mountain of coca leaves. Having frequently been shat upon by Neanderthal foremen who thought of him as expendable scum, Roger understood what was happening. It didn't matter that the ones who stayed behind to work weren't the ones who needed to hear the sermon; they were there, they were scum, they had nothing better to do with their free time. They hung their heads and listened. They were like Don Serapio, Quechua Indians from the high valleys around Cochabamba who had come down into this green hell to put a few pesos together because there hadn't been any action in their hometown in the mountains since the Incas invaded. They were small-potatoes people, to a man. Roger tried not to feel any amount of sympathy for them, but that was hard because he had sat where they were sitting, in a manner of speaking.

Macdougal's rave also had something to do with a pig.

"*¡Jesús y Maria!*" he said when he noticed Roger and Agnes, and the Quechua stompers stared open faced at them, unable to hide their curiosity. The name of God's only son and his son's mother came out of Macdougal's round red mouth sounding like a dirty joke.

"We're lost," Roger explained to him, "and we're hungry. We have to get out of the Chapare. We just learned my wife here is pregnant, and she's starting to feel sick. She needs to get to a doctor." He liked that; even saying it sent sexy little pleasure points like needles running through him. It was comforting to realize that Agnes had no idea what he was telling them about her. "Look sick if you can," he told her in English. "Don't smile and look friendly like that."

But Macdougal shook his head, frowned like a man in a hurry. How could you be in a hurry in the middle of the Chapare? He was obviously uncomfortable, not built to last in the tropics. Sweat slicked the surface of his fatty body, made his clothes hang, his skin shine. His blue eyes shone in a face that resembled a dried-out ham hock, and the humidity frizzed his blondish hair. The hair was the color of a dog Roger pretended to remember having once. In his memory the dog had been run over by a car.

"Did either of you ever take care of a pig before?" Macdougal wanted to know. Roger thought it was some kind of joke he was not supposed to understand. He didn't.

"Please," he whined—he hated whining, but in certain Bolivian circumstances it worked, got you what you wanted—"we've been walking all day and we haven't had anything to eat or drink." He was gearing up to finish the story of how he and his pregnant wife happened to be innocently in the Chapare when certain shady characters with bad intentions took advantage of them, robbed them of every last cent they had, but Macdougal waved a fat hand at him to shut him up. He didn't care.

"I know who you are," he said. "You're *la borra*."

Roger didn't know the word; his face showed it.

"Picture the United States of North America as a giant vat of wine," Macdougal told him, eager to teach. "The best wine money can buy in the world today. You follow me?"

The stompers looked relieved, and Roger understood that, too. That was why they used to like having him around in Don Eloy's lumberyard up in El Alto. When the dumb gringo was there he collected all the shit that usually flew in their direction. He told Macdougal he followed him.

"*La borra* is what you find at the bottom of the vat."

"He says we're the dregs of American society," Roger translated for Agnes once he figured out what the word meant. If he had been in a slightly better position he would have been mad at the guy. Not for himself but for Agnes, who had forgotten more quality poetry than a guy like Macdougal could even imagine was to be found on the planet.

"Tell him we'll pay him to take us to Cochabamba. We'll give him whatever he asks."

Roger liked that. It showed she was learning things, such as when to invent; he had taught her something worth knowing. But Macdougal didn't want to hear about Cochabamba. He told the stompers to get lost, which they were happy enough to do, and Agnes and Roger to follow him. They went down a path back into the woods—even going that far back into the jungle, which was already going black while the western sky glowed religious red, made Roger sick with apprehension—to a fenced clearing where Bobby Burns was resting after a heavy meal.

It was the biggest pig Roger had ever seen, not that he bothered to keep track of things like that. It had to weigh four hundred pounds. Its hide was bristly black, the kind of handsome black horses could be. It raised its snout in their direction, squinted its suspicious piggy eyes at them like they owed it another free meal. From the beginning Roger hated the animal. Bacon, he thought. Placido Macdougal's prize pig deserved to be so many pounds of cholesterol-laden bacon wrapped in plastic in some Bolivian butcher's freezer.

"Did you ever see anything so beautiful in your life?"

He made Roger translate the question for Agnes, who shook her head.

"It's a pig," Roger said. "It's a big pig."

"You see a pig," Macdougal corrected him, "but I see what's really there: proof positive that breeding counts. This animal is the brilliant outcome of intelligent experimentation, of scientific planning. This pig justifies the distinctions about people everyone is too timid to make these days."

So Roger knew the guy was a racist. He was willing to hear him out, but not for nothing. They stood admiring the pig just long enough to humor the breeder, then worked the conversation around pretty directly to food, and Macdougal fed them. While his hired coca stompers sat together in quiet little groups in front of their shacks, eating troll food and sharing bottles of beer in the peaceful darkness, beneath the glow of a kerosene lantern Roger and Agnes ate molded meat from a tin that tasted like dogfood only better, and salty soda crackers, and dill pickles, and canned peaches. The price was listening to Macdougal while he sat on his own heavy duty camp stool drinking Johnnie Walker Black Label straight up, jungle temperature. He was the kind of person who got drunk very slowly; he had to work for his buzz.

He was hiding the pig in the Chapare, it turned out, until it got as big as it was going to get. Then he was going to haul it back to Cochabamba and win a thousand dollar bet with his rich neighbor, a soft-headed liberal who believed in the moral regeneration of Bolivian society.

"What Ortíz doesn't want to admit," Macdougal told Roger, whose translation was half assed because he was tired, "is that genes matter. There's such a thing as quality stock, right?"

Roger nodded. He was used to picking paths; this time he took the one of least resistance.

"Well? If you concede the existence of the superior, then you're tacitly acknowledging the inferior. Am I right? Of course I'm right. The Europeans that colonized North America knew that. That's why they massacred every last Indian they came across. Strong drives out weak, and that's good. It's very good. That's how the Almighty designed the world to work, for reasons of His own that it isn't for me to question. They made one big mistake up north, though, when they brought those slaves over from Africa. The blacks are why the U.S. has the problems it has today. But at least the Europeans still run the place, even if they pretend otherwise."

He winked like a lecher at Agnes, but his dirty secret had nothing to do with sex. "Is it true they give all the blacks a day off from work on the birthday of Martin Luther King? That's smart, see? That's very intelligent. Give a little, get a lot back. That's what keeps the wheels of industry turning. Wave that African flag once a year and you'll keep them contented and dull down in the factories. We should be so smart on this side of the equator."

"But you're Bolivian, aren't you?" Agnes made Roger ask him. He drained the syrup from a can of peaches, felt temporarily strong. When Macdougal offered him a hit of his Johnnie Walker he took it. It was a taste Danny in Flint would never experience: expensive Scotch whiskey chasing peach juice in the Bolivian Chapare, served by a ranting racist.

"An accident of history," Macdougal told him; Roger could tell it was a sore point with the man. "My grandfather came over from Glasgow to work in the mines. He was a highly qualified engineer. But he wasn't careful enough, and he married a local. The blue eyes and the blond hair won't last another generation, though. It's a fluke they came out on me. That's why I won't have children. Strong only drives out weak if there's enough of it. If there's not, the strong drowns in the sea of mediocrity, which is the biggest body of water there is in this godforsaken country."

Since Roger didn't, Macdougal laughed at his own joke.

"You were lucky up north, even though people like you will never understand it." He wagged his finger in Roger's face. "You were colonized by the Anglo Saxons, by and large. They killed all the Indians and built the strongest nation in the history of the planet. Never mind that there's dregs, there's dregs in every vat. Georgia, I read, was settled by convicts; that doesn't make any difference. But poor unlucky South America got colonized by the Spanish. The goddamn *conquistadores* got down from their boats, looked around, and saw the possibility of a soft life with household help and fruit falling from the trees, so they decided not to kill off their Indians. Instead they turned them into gardeners, and maids, and butlers, and shoeshine boys, and they built one of the most worthless semicivilizations in history."

Macdougal's historical vision, and the Johnnie Walker Black, and the dark Chapare night, made the man sad. Roger wanted to maneuver him away from the subject of breeding and toward his immediate travel plans, but Macdougal was working himself up for a long, moody rave. From the cabin of his 4-Runner he pulled his grandfather's bagpipes and began to play soulfully to the stars. Roger had never heard bagpipes played before, so he had no idea whether Macdougal was doing it well or terribly, but the windy complaining sound they made filled up the Chapare and shut up the stompers, who seemed to want to cover their ears, something they couldn't do, given their master-slave relationship to the sour Scotsman. The music drowned out all the normal night sounds, which couldn't compete. Once, during a pause, Roger heard Bobby Burns snorting sounds that had to be some kind of pig-beat accompaniment.

When Macdougal ran out of air he stopped, put the instrument carefully away in his truck, and went back to drinking. For a long time after it was over, the music seemed to fill all the available space in the air, so there was no room for crickets or monkeys or owls or any of the other creatures that were supposed to be up and working at that hour. Macdougal looked like he might cry.

"They won't honor a contract," he complained.

"Who won't honor a contract?"

"The Bolivians. I've got mountains of leaves to stomp. I have a buyer I can count on, and a reasonable price for my *pasta*, and a production schedule to meet, but the filthy bastards I hire to do the labor keep running out on me. It's the same problem every time. I can tell you. You're North Americans, at least, and that's worth something: It's the same goddamn dregs problem. I'm surrounded by human dregs."

He leaned on his camp stool confidentially close to Roger's face. Roger breathed in the whiskey fumes, experienced a small rush, tried to keep his mind on Macdougal's nonstop rag. "If any of these human wrecks had half a brain in his body he'd grow his own leaves and make it into paste and then sell it. You can make fairly decent money doing that, you know, and it doesn't require a whole lot of muscle power between the ears. Everybody does it. The ones who don't are the lowest of the low, they're the bottom rung on the evolutionary ladder, but they're the only ones I can get to stay out here and work for me. They never last. They think they'll make it. They think they'll put together a little money and move on to something better, but they don't have the discipline. They disappear into the Chapare like . . . like blind monkeys. So here I come out to check on things and half my people are gone and my pig is seriously neglected—I think he's lost weight—and there's all this unworked coca. I can't meet my production schedule."

"Tell him he's a drug trafficker," Agnes said.

"No way."

"Tell him."

"What's she saying?"

"She says to tell you you're a drug trafficker."

He shook his head. He wasn't offended, but he did want to clarify for her. "I'm a businessman. Supply and demand. Anyway, it's the Colombians who actually make the drug. And all the serious profit, for that matter."

"Ask him if he feels guilty," Agnes prodded him.

But Macdougal felt no guilt. "The ones who ought to feel guilty are the ones who let the greatest nation on the face of the earth run down to the point that anybody with five dollars in his pocket all of a sudden wants to spend it on drugs."

"Are you going back to Cochabamba in the morning?"

He shook his head. "I can drive in the dark. That's what the whiskey's for. You won't catch me spending a night in the Chapare."

"Then take us with you. We'll pay you. We'll pay you whatever you want if you take us with you."

"Something tells me you couldn't buy a bus ticket from here to the next tree. Anyway, I don't need your money. I'm making a comfortable income catering to the degenerated youth of the northern empire."

"But you'll take us out with you."

"I'll tell you what I'll do," Macdougal said. He put a fat hand on Roger's knee and squeezed. Roger counted to ten slowly in Aymara, then in Spanish, so that he wouldn't react. He was, for the moment, the most mature individual in the Southern Hemisphere, dictators and priests not excluded.

"You stay out here for a week and stomp," was Macdougal's deal, "and take care of my pig, and keep this human trash in line, and when I come back I'll not only take you back with me to Cochabamba, I'll give you enough cold cash to get you back to La Paz. From there you're only a stone's throw from Disneyland."

"Tell him we're sorry," Agnes said when she heard the offer, "but we have something we have to do, so what we really need is a ride out now."

Roger translated, but he knew already what it was taking Agnes a little longer to figure out. Besides being a racist and a lousy bagpiper, Placido Macdougal was mean and calculating. He knew they had no options. He knew he had them in a spot tight enough he could get what he wanted, which was his leaves stomped, his pig petted, his theory about social dregs confirmed. He wanted to take out on them his anger at his grandfather for having stayed in Bolivia and married a troll. Roger tried, and he let Agnes keep trying, but he knew it was no good. By the time Macdougal finished his bottle of Johnnie Walker and handed out survival supplies to the Bolivian stompers, who had the patience of stones, they were saying one week. No more than one week. Not that saying it was going to do them any good. If Macdougal didn't show up for a month they were stuck in the place they were stuck.

"Trato hecho," said Macdougal from behind the steering wheel of his 4-Runner when he was ready to take off. "It's a deal." He stuck his hand out the window for both Roger and Agnes to shake. They shook. They could forgive each other later for that. They watched him open another bottle of scotch and cradle it between his legs.

"Any of these bastards gets out of line while I'm gone," he told them, "and you have my permission to shoot them. Set a good example. Listen, I appreciate your willingness to help me get past this temporary labor shortage. The drug addicts of North America will be in your debt."

Gone. In the dark they couldn't see his dust. They went to look for an uninhabited shack.

⸙

So there really was a place called hell. And it was as low down as they said it was, and just about as hot, at least in the daytime. They had left out of the Bible some of the details, like the sweat that never quit running on you, and the anxious way you felt being surrounded by people who would just as soon see you dead as look at you. That anxiety took its toll on your mind and your body, which sometimes you wanted to lay down to dead rest but never could, quite, because you could never let your guard completely down. The stompers of Pes Volado were close-mouthed men who seemed always on the verge of violence, tinder smoldering in the tropical heat. If you thought about it, it was harder to blame them for being perpetually ticked off about the miserable way their life was working out. For sure, anyway, they resented the fact that Macdougal had left rubber boots for Roger and Agnes to wear while they stomped; even the dregs of gringo society got a better deal than they did. It had to make you see the world with a certain amount of bitterness to watch your feet and calves turning slowly green while you kicked around all day in a bath of poisonous chemical shit trying to make enough money to quit kicking but you knew—in that quiet blind place into which your lies couldn't penetrate—that it wasn't going to happen, not in this lifetime, not in this particular place.

At least Roger had Agnes. And she had him, for what he was worth. Actually it was worth a lot to have somebody to talk to; talking could keep you sane if you got past babbling. Plus Agnes had the kind of developed brain he himself might have had, if things had gone a little differently for him. She helped him understand the nature of hell. To the extent he understood it, her theory went like this: Everything in the outside, physical world was the picture of something in the inside world people had quit believing in.

"Everything?"

"Everything."

"Including the Chapare?"

That made her think for a minute, but she nodded. Yes, the hell on the outside was connected to a hell within. So, the way Roger saw it, there had to be two of everything: every jungly bird sound, every smell of green rot and wet growth, every banana frond and army ant and coca plant in the world had its magic twin in a secret, undiscoverable place you were always trying to get to whether you knew it or not. The idea of that much life doubled and doubling made Roger wobble. Break time. He stepped out of the pit, sat on the mashed-down grass with his back against a tree. Agnes was tougher, stronger. She kept stomping, because she thought they had to have a certain amount done by the time Macdougal came back or else he would refuse a second time to take them out. Roger was too tired to try to convince her that wasn't how it worked.

It was like working in a factory, in a way. It smelled almost as bad, and the work itself was the same brain-numbing monotonous movement Roger remembered from the line in Flint, back before the world as it really was began. One of the stompers, less hostile than his *compañeros* in crime, had helped them dig a pit in the ground. Then Gregorio, who had the irritating habit of whistling when he stomped, when he worked, when he did anything, showed them how to line their pit with plastic sheeting. How to mash up the leaves in the pit, add water and some potassium carbonate, throw in some kerosene, then stomp to get the juices going. Agnes understood what was happening. Alkalines precipitate alkaloids, she told him, which only meant to Roger that some hotshot business kid in Chicago or Dallas or some other big city full of high-rise buildings was eventually going to get a big-time buzz when he shoved their end product up his deal-sniffing nose. Roger must have skipped chemistry class the day they talked about alkalines precipitating alkaloids.

All that work drained the drug juice from the leaves, which became useless, though it occurred to Roger he might be able to give Bobby Burns a world-class stomach ache if he fed the selfish animal enough of them. Then they had to drain off the good juice—*agua rica*, the trolls called it—and add some sulfuric acid to it, which according to Agnes pulled the alkaloids out of the kerosene, which they saved to reuse. Then they added lime. (Every time they dumped lime from a sack into the pit, Roger wound up inhaling the cloud of lime dust that rose around him. He assumed it was taking some days or months off his life, but that couldn't be helped.) Their shit was starting to become cocaine, in a way. All they had to do was filter out the paste, which was as gray as your brain, and lumpy moist, and bag it. Coca paste. And paste was what it was all about in the Chapare. It was what brought the traffickers' planes down on hidden airstrips and DEA agents down on Bolivia from the streets of Newark.

"Stop, please," Roger asked Agnes. Against the tree his back ached. Inside the knee-high rubber boots his feet, his legs itched like fire. It was not his imagination, the way Agnes thought it was. The skin on his feet and his calves was creased, chafed red, rubbed raw. He had seen an ugly sore develop on Gregorio's ankle where juice from the mash he was stomping had soaked into a cut the size of a thumbnail. Every time he stepped into the pit he was pretty sure his boots were going to leak, his sensitive skin get infected, his legs turn as green as Gregorio's. The troll didn't seem to mind as much as Roger knew he would mind if it happened to him, but Bolivians, he had learned by observation, were expert hiders, so maybe Gregorio was only going crazy quietly. Hell was the place where your legs turned green. When he thought about Macdougal he envied him, hated him, fantasized killing him. If it wasn't for his pig and his big investment, the racist Scot-Bolivian who didn't have word one of the English language would never come back to a place like Pes Volado.

Agnes stopped stomping, straightened up, her hands on her hips. They had talked Macdougal out of a few necessary items from his company store. They had a hairbrush, and one toothbrush between them, so they were staying halfway civilized. But there were no extra clothes, and washing what they had in the chemical-fouled creek never quite got all the dirt out. At rest she was beautiful. "I'm a drug trafficker," she told Roger. She started stomping again, but more slowly now. Something was going away. She was wearing down.

He had to distract her so she would rest. He knew he would never convince her, but the amount of paste they produced would make absolutely no difference to Macdougal, who took too much pleasure in leaving them stranded in his settlement to change the arrangement. It had something to do with revenge, even though he was wreaking it on the wrong victims. "This thing about there being two of everything," he said.

"Something like that."

"I was thinking about it. If you're right—and I'm not saying you're not—then the things you don't see kind of make the things you do seem second rate. You know what I mean?"

She looked at him with real curiosity, as though he had said something worth saying. For a change. She stepped out of the pit, wet chemical juice dripping from her brown boots, and sat in front of him on the stiff grass. Behind them in the jungle the creek water ran quietly, and a million birds twittered, and on the far side of the settlement one of the stompers barked once. It was supposed to be a laugh. The sun was going down as slowly as it ever went, which was not very, leaving light that looked electric seeping into the sky like water into a broad, flat pool. A frog threw a stone. The stone sank.

"I threw away your LSD," she told him.

He expected to be angry with her; she expected it, too. When he was angry, the things that came out of his mouth could be fairly interesting. But the only thing he thought to say was, "I want to go home."

It was not something he would have expected to say. It was only a feeling created by the loss of his insurance from Claude, which when it happened turned out to be not much worse than the loss of any of the other things he had misplaced in his travels, which was just about everything. Home. Saying the word made no particular sense since there was no such place he could get to, but it was still true, and Agnes hung her head because she knew it was a confession the equal of her own.

She tried to distract him. "What you see in the world isn't second rate, Roger. That's the mistake people always make. You're thinking too literally."

What was that supposed to mean? For a moment Roger resented his ignorance, which he had worked so hard to cultivate over the years.

"What I'm talking about has to do with where perception begins. The world wouldn't exist if we weren't here to imagine it, that's all. And the way that works is the feeling that we've seen a place like this before, and it was good, and wouldn't it be wonderful to get back there again?"

Because he had nothing worth adding to the conversation, Roger decided it was time for the surprise.

"Soap!" she said, and he felt responsible for the pleasure in her voice. "Where did you get it?"

"From Gregorio," he told her. Actually he had lifted it from the shack of one of the other stompers when everybody was out at the maceration pits, but he did not want to dilute her enjoyment of the soap by making her think she was cleaning her body with stolen goods. They left their leaf mash to ferment, or whatever it was supposed to do, and went toward the spring they had discovered in the woods above the settlement. A small creek had its start there, feeding into the larger creek that was the reason Pes Volado had been settled where it was. None of the Bolivian stompers ever seemed to go there. Roger and Agnes had gotten into the habit of spending evenings at the creek because it made her nervous to be around the trolls when they started drinking. The fierceness that they talked when they were drunk was nothing like Beethoven, or Tennyson, or any of the noises he knew from experience that Agnes could appreciate, or tolerate.

She was either ignoring or not noticing the fact that some of them also smoked *pitillos* when they stomped in their pits. Up in the tin mines in the Andes, Bolivian miners had been chewing coca leaves for hundreds of years, mixing them in their mouth with a foul-tasting black resin that activated the drug. It was the troll equivalent of a coffee break, not much more. Roger had tried it a few times, felt a low-grade lift wrap his tongue in sleep, felt at the same time maybe a little bit less terrible than he would have otherwise felt. But the *pitillos* were something else. They could keep a person going when he had to work, but the odds were he would keep on going into wacko land and not come back. It was funny, or maybe just a question of luck. He had seen people smoke them and survive, seen others inhale one and disintegrate. If Agnes was right, then all the shit you saw around you in the world—the shit you stuffed up your nose, or inhaled in a joint, or shot into your veins—was only the visible half of the shit inside you. The possibility that she might be right sobered him. Not that he needed sobering.

It had been hot all day, clammy-skin hot, the kind of humid heat that made it hard to breathe, there was so much moisture in the air you took in. But when the sun went down it sucked with it the worst of the heat, and just a little breeze began blowing, cooling and drying their skin. At the pond, something was different that had nothing to do with the soap, or not much. The place, or everything in it, was breathing. The spring was in a low, scooped-out hole, so you had to climb down through the brush to get to the edge, which was mucky. Roger had liberated a plank from the settlement, laid it across the water so they had something to stand on to wash from. Around the circular spring, stumpy palms grew at strange, bent angles, their trunks roped with waxy green vines that wanted to choke to death everything in their long, twisty reach. The breeze was making everything tremble. It was as though everything there was waking up at once and watching. Roger felt spied on. It was a pleasurable sensation.

Different, too, for both of them to sit at the same time on the same plank, letting their legs dangle in the cool, sticky water. Usually with Agnes you talked things through. She was that way. She wanted to understand what was happening before it happened, and to have the right words for it, so that she understood her feelings. But this time, the Chapare breathing around them and watching, there was no discussion of what was important. Which was Roger unbuttoning her shirt buttons one at a time, pulling her arms out of the sleeves, laying the shirt on a branch God had conveniently caused to grow there for a hook. He leaned low, cupped water and dribbled it on her back, a handful at a time until her back was wet enough to lather. He lathered. The lemon smell in the soap drugged him.

Agnes's eyes were closed, which he appreciated because he had what had to be the biggest erection in the history of the world and he wasn't sure how that would affect her. He lathered. If they had given him the choice, he would have said okay, I'll spend the rest of my life here soaping this woman's white and tender back. He looked with his fingers, learned the bumps, the contoured small of her back, the long arch, the tiny raised spot on her shoulder blade that might be a mole. But there was nobody with cosmic power there to offer him any choices at all, and after a long while of slow and perfect lathering her back he moved his hands around and found her breasts, which he also soaped. He moved slowly enough that he could tell that it was okay with her for him to keep soaping.

When he was done he rinsed her breasts, traced with his fingertips their outline, rested the palms of his hands on her nipples, which were standing up in a gratifying way that must have had something to do with him, or at least with who he was at that particular moment. A bird whistled. Roger heard five different notes come out of its mouth and wondered whether that was normal. The brush and the palms were still trembling.

They slid off the plank and into the spring, which was shoulder high and startlingly cool.

"Do you want to open your eyes?" he asked her. There was just enough light to see shapes.

She opened them. They were standing face to face, their feet up to their ankles in the comfortable muck of the spring bottom. She pulled him to her and they wrapped their arms around each other's back. Her eyes were closed again. He had taken off his own shirt also, so he felt the pointed pressure of her breasts against his chest; the skin-to-skin touch came close to undoing him. She had to be feeling his erection, which was aimed approximately at her navel the way they were standing, but it didn't seem to bother her, which mildly amazed him.

"Roger?"

"What?"

Knowing Agnes, she was going to force them to talk over the idea of sex, or love, or whatever it was that was happening between the two of them. If he had to, he could talk about it with her, but his tongue was lead.

"This is pretty good, isn't it?"

He nodded.

"I want to tell you something."

He waited.

"Ever since we left Cochabamba, ever since La Paz, really, I haven't stopped feeling afraid. The fear is down inside me, down deep. It's there when I lie down at night and it's there when I wake up. I can feel it there like some kind of terrible Bolivian wild animal just behind my shoulder ready to jump at me if I relax for a second. Have you ever felt anything like that?"

No comment.

"It has to do with all the things that are going on, not just this." This, he understood, was the Chapare, her bad-seed brother, Macdougal's maniac bagpipe serenade, the infected cut on Gregorio's green legs. And the worst of much bad: Esencia the angel shot in a drug raid. "It's as though I have been waiting for years for something to happen that was big enough to contain all my fears, and now here it is, in Bolivia. I remember lying in bed at home, a lot of times, not being able to sleep because the fear was there—it was nearby—and wanting, in a way, to let it inside, to let it get at me, but I couldn't do that because I was too afraid of the fear. Am I making any sense? Am I being logical?"

Roger wondered what logic had to do with anything.

"Agnes . . ."

She put fingers on his lips to shush him. He shushed.

"What I mean to tell you with this round-the-fence explanation of my own personal history of fear is that just now, for the first time, I stopped being afraid. You did that, Roger. Do you understand what you did?"

He had nothing to say because nothing to think. He put his head down, kissed her neck and then slowly down to her breasts. He found one pebble-like nipple with his tongue, sucked for a long time with his eyes closed.

Then when he moved his mouth she said quietly, "Let's go back to the settlement," and he knew that for the moment, something good was over.

In Pes Volado the troll stompers were restless. One of them had a guitar and another one some kind of drum, and they had come together in front of one of the shacks, built up an unnecessary bonfire, and were singing what sounded to Roger like Quechua protest songs. When they noticed their gringo neighbors were back in town they started hooting like outraged wolves, and there was no reason in the world not to feel the kind of fear that Agnes was talking about at the spring. Roger opened some cans and they had a boring supper, sitting side by side in the threshold of their own shack listening to the Bolivians wind up and party down.

After a while Gregorio came by to tell them not to worry. "They always get this way when they're left out here too long," he told them.

Roger was sorry he had nothing to offer the man, who took a chance by being decent with them. Roger appreciated Gregorio's ability to stand up to peer pressure, which was pretty much the same thing as mob rule.

"Ask Gregorio what it is they want," Agnes told him.

But the question took Gregorio by surprise; it was a hit over the head with a blunt instrument. That was the thing about cross-cultural communications, Roger had learned, you never knew when what you said was going to offend somebody, and once you did, you were never sure why, or what the consequence was going to be. All you knew was you blew it.

Gregorio offered Roger a drink from his bottle of cane whiskey. It burned, felt good in a medicinal way going down his gullet as if it was burning away a lot of greasy shit clogging his system. He realized he had not been drunk or high, really, since meeting Agnes. The wine at El Monticulo with Cherokee the fortuneteller didn't count, since all he got out of it was warmth and temporary comfort, and there hadn't been enough of Macdougal's Johnnie Walker to take him anywhere but sideways.

"What do they want?" Gregorio said, as though he had to make sure he got the question right.

In the dim orange glow of their kerosene lantern Roger watched the man who was almost their friend blink, his cheeks puff out, the cords in his neck tighten.

"I'm sorry," Roger told him. *"Lo siento, amigo."* But it was too late.

"They want a life, that's all. They want to get the hell out of this devil-ridden place and back to some other place with people who talk, and normal food, and women who care, and real work. Is that wrong? You think they should want to stay here forever and die in this hole making money for Macdougal?"

It worried Roger to see Gregorio wind up like that. It showed him how thin the line was keeping him on their side, more or less. He wished he had something to give the man, who had been generous. But he had nothing, and he felt helpless to stave off anything ugly that came their way. It had been a week, and no Macdougal. Roger was not surprised, but he had to live through Agnes's disillusionment, and that cost him.

Agnes was smarter than Roger. She went in the shack, came back out with their last can of peaches, which the three of them shared slowly. Gregorio was pacified, as much by the gesture as by the sweet fruit itself. He went quietly back to his rowdy *compañeros*, and Roger felt more relief than he was entitled to.

What happened in the middle of the night with Agnes was not something that could be explained. Not to him, and probably not to her. It didn't quite cut it to say he was sleepwalking, because he wasn't walking. It didn't have a word, but it was blind and full of need.

From the beginning they had been sleeping fairly close together on the lone pallet whoever had abandoned the shack left behind when he went. Closeness was comfort, for both of them. That was okay. But then how explain waking up on top of Agnes with his hands twisted inside her clothes and the zipper on her jeans down? When he woke up—if he had really been asleep, and he had to have been asleep because it couldn't have happened any other way, but how could a sleeping man do something so deliberate?—she was making little squirming noises that meant irritation more than fear.

"No," she was saying.

As soon as he understood what he was doing he stopped. He took his hands out of her clothes, let her zip her own zipper. They sat up like wrestlers on the mat. The palms of his hands burned, ached, gave him away to himself.

"I'm sorry, Agnes." He wanted to tell her he had been asleep but was afraid she would think he was lying, which would make things at least twice as bad as they already were. So he said nothing.

"It's okay, Roger."

"No it's not."

"I mean it. What happened at the spring was real, and it was good."

He wanted to say So then what? He didn't.

"But there is something in me that is stopping me from going any farther, Roger. It has nothing to do with you. It's in me. Do you believe that?"

Didn't make any difference whether he did. He didn't want to think about it any more, at least not until he understood how it happened. She wanted to hug him to show him he was forgiven, but he wasn't going for that. No consolation prizes. There was noise outside. He went outside to follow it.

"Roger," she said distinctly, with that particular Agnes-like determination to make herself understood, but he was gone. Had to be.

It was a radio broadcast. La Voz del Chapare. The Voice of the Chapare. He had heard it a couple times while they were back in Tingo Tingo but paid no attention. The guy had a great voice. His Spanish was rich and easy to understand, molasses on melting ice. But Roger hated politics on principle, because he hated the difference between what people said and what actually happened, so he had tuned out the Voz del Chapare announcer the way he used to tune out Ronald Raygun and other professional liars like him back in Gringolandia.

The trolls had calmed down, drunk themselves into passivity, which was exactly the position, according to Don Eloy at the lumberyard, where the imperialists of the world wanted them to be. They were lying on the ground in front of Gregorio's hut listening to the broadcast, which for some reason was harder to ignore than it usually was. Uninvited, Roger sat on the edge of the little crowd and listened. Without turning around he knew Agnes was there behind him. He surprised himself, found nothing serious to hold against her. His fingers, on their own, remembered unzipping her jeans.

> . . . *Objetos* . . . that's what they would like to turn you into. Both sides: the traffickers and their buyers, on the one hand, and on the other hand the government and the gringos. You're not people for them, you're not individual bodies with souls inside lighting up your personhood like miracle candles. Not by a long shot. For the traffickers, who are you? You're the wheels driving their money machine. Round and round. And they'll pay you for your trouble all right, they'll pay you just enough to keep the wheels turning. Round and round. But lift up your heads, lift up your voices just once to let them know you're not happy

(how could you be happy doing what you're doing?), and watch and see what they'll do. There's a problem with the wheels on our money machine, they'll tell each other, and they'll send somebody down to fix it.

I'm not telling you anything you don't know, am I? Of course I'm not. You knew all this before you packed up your things and left your valleys to grow coca here. All I'm doing is giving you a platform, and I wouldn't be doing it *clandestinamente* if my message didn't scare them. Both sides. Because what we're saying—what you all are saying through me—scares the government and the gringos as much as it does the traffickers. You're still not people, are you? You're a problem. You're dots on a strategy map in some cabinet minister's office in La Paz. You're little bright dots on some Pentagon planner's computer screen. If they started thinking of you as people they couldn't do their jobs, which is to solve problems such as these: For the government, how do we convince the gringos we're serious about stopping cocaine so they don't cut off their financial aid, especially if we're not really serious? And for the gringos themselves, how do we keep this deadly white powder out of our country, since so many of our sons and daughters can't seem to resist it? How do we obliterate all those troublesome dots from the screens of our computers?

Close your eyes for a moment, and see what's there to see: This could go on forever. There is no indication that the children of the industrialized North will ever tire of consuming drugs. Why? Some will tell you it's a symptom of the decadence of capitalistic culture, that consuming something that might kill you is the ultimate sick expression of a sick consumer society. But let's not be too quick to take comfort from that story, which sounds far too full of self-righteous rhetoric to be true. Haven't we all seen ten-year-olds on the streets of Cochabamba wretched in their absolute addiction to *pitillos*? Haven't you yourself been tempted to smoke one to help you get through that last rugged hour in the maceration pit? And if you said yes and smoked and survived, it certainly was not because you were a capitalistic consumer. Hardly.

More likely we are all of us a little weaker, a little more frail than we would like to admit. Likely there will be a certain number of people in any society who just can't turn down temptation. Maybe that person is your sister, or your father, or your nephew, and they don't know it but they have something in common with the kid in New York City who can't say no to the temptation powder, either. Maybe it's a mistake to see this phenomenon of cocaine as North against South. Maybe the enemy isn't who you thought it was.

I like to ask questions and let you come up with your own answers.

I like to reach a point where people stop spouting the easy rhetoric and start thinking on their own.

I like to believe people are not stupid.

If the government and the gringos stopped thinking you were stupid maybe they would come up with a better solution to their problem.

As long as there is this much money in growing coca leaves and stomping them into paste, I don't care how hard they try to convince you to grow pineapples or macadamia nuts or asparagus, you're not going to do it, are you? You're too intelligent to become their experiment. They call it alternative development, but what's that? That's their rhetorical way of saying they are desperate and can't figure out what they should really do. They are grasping at straws.

Maybe you should think it through for a while and then tell them what they should do.

Here's one more thing to think about, now that you've engaged your mind: The UMOPAR are an occupation force in the Chapare. Don't blame the bullet-headed soldier in his cheap shiny uniform who prods you with his rifle barrel when they make you get down off the bus to check your luggage. It's not his fault. He's an Aymara, for one thing, and you're a Quechua, and don't think that's any sort of accident. He's a victim the same way you're a victim, which is to say only as long as you let yourselves be victims instead of victors.

And the DEA? Let's talk about *la DEA*. The history of this particular place on the planet is a long, sad story of occupations, and here we are in the late afternoon of the twentieth century and it's still going on. Why? Maybe because you let it go on. Because when you try to get yourselves organized you allow yourselves to be bought out by trafficker money. Which of you who are listening now doesn't know that the unions are just one more way that the buyers make sure their wheels keep spinning? . . .

La Voz del Chapare went on for a few minutes before the signal faded, the mellow, entrancing voice disappearing down a hole of silence.

"That means they had to shut down," Gregorio said. "They have to keep moving. If they don't, somebody will track their frequency."

To Roger, the silence that followed was like the tranquil quiet that came after church, or should come after church if church was what it was supposed to be, which it wasn't.

"He's right," one of the stompers said, but nobody was in the mood to talk, and Roger and Agnes went back to their shack.

"Agnes," he told her, whispering for some reason that made no sense unless it was not to give himself away even to her.

"Lie next to me," she told him, and he heard in her voice the unphony acceptance he needed to do that. They lay like spoons, their bodies curving on the crummy pallet, and Roger thought about ugly things—the prison food in La Paz, Don Eloy's monster-mouth garlicky breath in the morning at the lumberyard, the feeling of being glazed in factory crud he used to have after eight hours on the line in Flint—hoping the erection went away.

"Agnes?"

"Is this going to be a hard question, Roger? I don't know whether I can give you an acceptable answer to a hard question. Not right now. Do you understand that?"

"What did you mean when you told your brother that everything was broken?"

"Simple truth."

She didn't ordinarily play games like that, which meant his question was, in fact, one of the hard ones. But he didn't want to let go of whatever it was he had hold of.

"What's broken?"

"One time while Jonathan and I were still in high school a policeman brought him home. This was six or seven months after our mother died, and we were all going through the kind of pain you can't tell from shock. The policeman was a great admirer of my father. They had gone through school together, and he respected the fact that my father wrote articles that were published in journals and newspapers and sometimes people quoted him in their own articles."

"What did he write about?"

"About the impossibility of knowing God, and the impossibility of stopping trying to know God, and the division that creates in the psyche or the soul."

For the first time the guy seemed a little interesting to Roger, although he didn't trust his choice of words. "So what did your brother get picked up for, shoplifting?"

"They found him in a city park wandering around a patch of woods with a flashlight in his mouth. That was the reason they saw him in the first place, the light from the flash."

"He was blitzed."

"They found enough marijuana on him to put him in jail. Anybody else they probably would have. But Jonathan was lucky. This same policeman recognized him as our father's son and brought him home with a stern, old-fashioned lecture and a warning to Father to straighten him out because if there was a next time they would be obliged to arrest him. I remember he asked Father a question about existentialism, and Father sputtered out something indignant about superficial twentieth-century pseudophilosophies that didn't deserve the name, they were only twaddle. But that was just an act, it was the price he paid to keep Jonathan out of jail, and he and the policeman both knew it. It was their ritual, and they both loved it and hated it at the same time."

"So then you had your heart-to-heart family huddle. At the kitchen table."

"In the living room, with the lights out so that no one had to look at anyone else's face. All the predictable clichés were repeated, by all of us. We played our parts perfectly."

"What was your part?"

"The part of the good daughter, the necessary counterpoint to the troublesome son. The only thing different was the extra pain of our mother's loss, which was so fresh I almost fainted. I couldn't take it."

"But?"

"As we sat there in the dark talking and listening and hurting and being confused I started to feel something terrible, something I didn't want to be feeling. At first I thought it was just resentment of Jonathan because he had done his usual sterling job of ruining things, and if it weren't for him things would have been fine, we could have spent our time getting past the grief of losing Mother. But maybe because I couldn't see anything, I could only hear, after a while I realized that what I was feeling was envy. In a way, I mean. Maybe that's not the right word."

"You mean you wished you were the one the cops brought home with dope in your pockets?"

"No. I mean I wished that I was the one who had been able to do that to our father."

"Do what?"

"Pound him and have it hurt. Make him falter a little, and doubt."

"So, how come you didn't?"

"I didn't know how."

Not trusting the memories of his own prelife, which was full of shadows that had unusual shapes, big heads with large mouths that made sounds he couldn't interpret, Roger didn't know what to tell her. It was possible that other people's pasts were just as doubtful and therefore just as open to reinvention as his.

"What's broken," she finally said, "is the way we're supposed to feel about each other. Think of a flower."

He was thinking.

"It has a stem, straight, and then petals at the top. When the stem snaps, the petals drop off."

"Agnes?"

"What."

"I'm sorry I had my hands in your pants."

"It's okay."

"Felt real good."

"What?"

He let her get away with that. Maybe there really was a roaring in her ears that made it hard to hear, and Roger admitted his voice was low as a criminal's. She lay facing him on her side on the pallet. He put one hand on her hip. She let it stay there. If it had been somebody else's hand he would have said it was where it belonged.

In the morning, the *chop-ita chop-ita* noise while the sun was still coming up drew him awake into a state of receptivity he would have enjoyed if he hadn't been sure that Pes Volado was under attack. In fact it was. Terrified, he thought about Agnes's theory of doubles. The *chop-ita chop-ita* of the Vietnam-surplus helos in the blue Bolivian sky was an echo of something just as ominous inside his soul. For lack of a better word. There was no Agnes.

He rolled off the pallet, pulled on his jeans and sandals. Absurd to be meditating philosophy in the middle of an attack by death-dealing drug helicopters, or were they drug-dealing death helicopters? But it had rained a little while they slept, and the poorly thatched roof leaked. Going for the door he slipped in a mud slick, stumbled, and a yellow dog with chewed-up, pointy ears, which he had never seen before, dove at him, nipped him in the leg with diseased teeth. He cursed it in Aymara, and it went out the door before him with a put-upon expression on its long, miserable face.

"The pig!" In front of their shack, fetching as the woman with electric hair on the clam shell on the postcard from Italy he had seen one time, Agnes had figured it out, but it was too late.

There were two of them. Like dragonflies looking for a target, the helicopters hovered, spitting their ugly metal sound. Then they made pass after pass over the defenseless little semisettlement. They were looking for maceration pits, a reason to swoop down like storm troopers and kick Bolivian butt. The troll stompers huddled in the doorways of their huts, more afraid, and with more reason, than Roger himself. Shading his hand, Roger saw the black barrel of a long gun—it must have been a machine gun, the complete one, though who could tell when it was pointing at you—aimed out the open door of a helo when it came to temporary rest above him. Behind the gun, motionless, a black helmet with goggle eyes shaped like black bulbs, and a cable running out of the helmet back up to the roof of the aircraft that meant the gunner was talking on the radio to the pilot. *Move off to the left just a curly cunt hair, will you, Slim, and I'll blast that worthless frigging shack clear into another time zone.* Something like that anyway. Roger knew the mentality: how it worked, what gave it job satisfaction, moral satisfaction, all kinds of satisfaction in all kinds of circumstances when they were the ones with the guns. He knew the guy with his hand on the trigger was feeling virtuous, and slightly sad, and that the next time around he was going to vote Republican.

"The pig, for God's sake," Agnes said again, and it snapped Roger out of the trance he had fallen into, which was like waiting to be martyred. The helo with the bug-eyed gunner angled off, and he ran with Agnes under the covering trees to the shelter where Bobby Burns passed his pampered days.

Used to pass. Because there was no pig, none. In its panic over the foreign noise of the drug helicopters, the animal had kicked or shouldered a hole in the wall of the pen, which had not been built to house crazed beasts.

"It's over," Roger told Agnes.

"It's not," she contradicted him. But that was just her personal necessary reflex, the kick a frog's leg made after the animal was gigged.

"If Macdougal comes back and the pig isn't here he'll shoot us. I'm not exaggerating, Agnes. He's going to shoot us."

It sounded like the helicopters were moving away. Either they hadn't been able to see the settlement's maceration pits from the air, or they were just fucking with the humble population of Pes Volado because it gave them pleasure to do that, or the gringo government had called off the drug war and everybody was going home to get high together. But it didn't matter. Bobby Burns was now an ex-resident of the settlement, and Placido Macdougal was going to shoot the gringo *borra* when he came back.

"The pig will come back when it gets hungry," Agnes decided. "It's not used to living on its own, and it's lazy. It will come back."

But Roger couldn't handle her optimism, or the electric radiance of her hair, or the memory his hands had of being inside her pants, or the thought of being shot by Macdougal. He left her standing looking at the hole in the pen. She was the kind of person who would wait all day to prove she was right, the pig was coming back.

Bobby Burns the prize pig didn't come back to Pes Volado, but neither did Placido Macdougal. Roger wanted to quit stomping. What was the use in producing a million pounds of grade-A *pasta* if they couldn't produce the necessary pig? Macdougal had already proven he cared more about his pet than about the human beings who were making his sticky money for him and getting green legs in the process. But Agnes would not stop working.

"What are you going to do all day?" she wanted to know. "Lie around on the pallet and fret?"

Roger couldn't remember anybody ever using the word *fret* in any actual sentence in his presence. She continued to surprise him, and the surprise, he noticed, was always doubling his desire. It was because she was someone, she was something, that he was not. He wanted her—no sense pretending any different to protect his feelings; his feelings were going to be stepped on, stomped on like so much coca paste in a hidden pit. His self-defense antenna picked up danger when it was inevitable—he wanted her more than he wanted an uninterrupted flow of oxygen to his brain.

"I'm going out to look for the pig," he told her. "You keep stomping if you want to. But it's not going to do us any good with Macdougal."

He went, but even the idea of beating the jungle for an AWOL animal with a tiny mind of its own was ridiculous, and after an hour or so of wasted wandering along the trails through the woods that surrounded Pes Volado he wound up back at the pit. He needed not her company but her presence.

"Don't stomp unless you want to," she told him, which missed the point.

Wanting to had nothing at all to do with why he climbed into the pit and tromped cramped miles in a rank stew of precious leaves and industrial-strength chemicals. He stomped because he stomped, and now only because he felt guilty sitting comfortable watching her work. She wiped sweat from her forehead, blinked when it burned her eyes. The look on her face meant she had just remembered what she was always forgetting, that he was another species, something more closely related to bugs with hard shells and eight legs than to her. He stomped. She stomped. We stomped he she they. Stomp.

For three days no Macdougal, no pig, and not much left in the way of food. Gregorio, as decent a troll as Roger had ever met—and being decent in indecent circumstances such as you found in the Chapare was an amazing accomplishment, if you thought about it, the kind of thing that should win you a Nobel Peace Prize but never would—brought them a little troll food to supplement what Macdougal had left. And they found plenty of oranges and grapefruits and some bananas. Basically it was boring food, but Roger was used to long stretches of eating boring food, and Agnes was the kind of person—he hadn't met many but knew they lived in the world somewhere—who didn't concentrate much on what she ate, or care.

Then, on the morning of the fourth day after the helicopters buzzed Pes Volado, Bobby Burns came back. The sound of piggish snuffing and rooting outside the shack woke Roger, and he ran out without his pants to make sure it was the right animal.

It was. It wasn't. It was. Pigs also, to judge by appearances, had souls. Because whatever happened to Bobby Burns during his three-day ordeal in the wilderness of the Chapare had been enough to try the animal's soul, which couldn't be tried if it didn't exist in the first place, right? The proof was visible, undeniable: Its hide, which had been the sleekest glossy black, had turned completely white. Spotless.

"I can't hate it anymore," Agnes told him. She handed him his pants, and behind the movement Roger saw the ghost of intimate wifery appear, disappear. Invisible wings flapped. Not even the ghost, really, just an illusion. Never in a million years. Not in the Chapare, not anywhere. Passion was weakening his ability to think clearly, which hadn't been, in recent years, his main outstanding personal quality. "This pig has suffered, Roger."

He zipped up his jeans. It was true. The blanched white bristles made the dumb look of wonder on Bobby Burns's squint-eyed face all the more pathetic. Roger hadn't known that she also hated the animal. It was one of maybe two things they had in common.

The troll stompers came by to be amazed. They were subdued in the presence of a natural miracle; almost all their muttering came out in Quechua. Roger worried that the noise would spook the pig again, so he carefully coaxed a rope around its neck to lead it back to its pen, the walls of which he worked carefully to repair and reinforce. In a place like Pes Volado it was impossible to guarantee anything, but he was pretty sure Bobby Burns wasn't going to smash his way out a second time in any kind of helicopter-induced panic.

The Bolivians took the miraculous instant bleaching of the pig as a sign, but they couldn't agree on what the omen was intended to tell them. Some of them said it predicted the ultimate financial ruin of Placido Macdougal. Eventually, one way or another, the pseudo-Scotsman they hated was going to go broke, which would make the whole settlement happy, especially if it meant losing their jobs. Others saw the blasted pig as proof that the Earth Mother, la Pachamama, was offended by the presence of foreign forces buzzing like metal gnats over her territory. The warning was meant for the gringos, not that anybody believed they would heed it. Gregorio, more thoughtful than his neighbors, thought the whiteness of the pig was mysteriously connected to the white powder that their gray paste was eventually going to become. That was a sign if you wanted a sign, he told Roger, but the trouble with signs was people always wanted to invent a single, simple meaning for them. What the temporary population of Pes Volado ought to do was meditate on what the transfiguration of Bobby Burns might mean to each and every man among them.

Roger liked Gregorio's interpretation the best, but it turned out there was no time to meditate on much of anything, because next morning the helicopters came buzzing back. Three of them this time. It was the combination of frustration and anger churning up in him—it left in his throat an acid taste, a copper taste, a taste of here-we-fucking-go-again—that led Roger to make his big mistake. Not that he needed excuses for screwing things up. It happened naturally.

There was one gun in Pes Volado, an old lever-action Winchester with a pitted barrel, a cowboy rifle that had belonged to Butch Cassidy or the Sundance Kid before they kicked their bucket in Bolivia. It hung on pegs in the shack of one of the stompers. While the Bolivians huddled again in their doorways waiting for the plague to pass, Agnes ran off in the direction of Bobby Burns's pen in the wood. And Roger stepped into the empty shack and lifted the Winchester.

He had watched the stompers play around with the rifle—load and unload it, shoot a few rounds at bad-luck birds they almost never dropped—so he knew what to do. He wasn't thinking, didn't want to think. What he wanted was for the sky above his particular location in the Chapare to be helicopter free.

Every last troll in the settlement watching, Roger aimed at the nearest helo and fired. More recoil than he expected; a little pain spasm traveled through his shoulder. There might have been a *ping*, masked by the overpowering engine whine of the aircraft. He fired again. *Ping.*

He watched a bulb-eyed gunner grab the handle of his own meaner, more serious weapon. The barrel of the machine gun swung (did it gattle? what did that mean?), fixed on Roger. Rooted to the sandy dirt floor of Pes Volado, the Chapare, Bolivia, South America, Roger the stone cowboy wished, during one flash of brilliant clairvoyance, for death. The solution that was salvation. The moment passed, and he ran, throwing the gun down.

The helicopter gun, he was pretty sure, did not follow him. Your back would have to know. Instead, the aircraft angled off to join its brothers in formation, and they all disappeared into the eastern sky, which glowed milky white while it absorbed them.

They didn't give Roger time to feel delivered. Before the noise had completely faded on the placid air the stompers were moving toward him in one congealing pissed-off group. Having been cornered in his career a handful of times, Roger knew enough to pick up the gun he had thrown down at the scene of the crime.

They were all shouting at him at once, even Gregorio, whose pleasant face had gone purple, the color of outrage. From what Roger could pick out of their noise it seemed that they were convinced that his useless, wimpy attack on the helicopter was going to bring down on their hatless heads the combined wrath of *la DEA* and UMOPAR. Why the pack of them took off when they did without torching the settlement when they were already in the neighborhood was a mystery but irrelevant. They would be back. They would strafe the air, they would land, they would shit green soldiers who would roll out and burn the place to the ground. Fast. Fact. Completely.

He was aware of Agnes coming up behind him to tell him about the pig. Roger had quit caring about Bobby Burns. If he could draw it into his sights, he would shoot the animal, convert it to Bolivian bacon.

"What's wrong, Roger? What did you do?"

She was assuming, of course, that he was the one at fault, that he had done something stupid. He was, he had. Convicted.

"We're leaving, Agnes." He had to shout to be heard over the angry roar. They had stopped in a clump to rag at him, waving their arms and pointing loaded fingers in his direction, flapping their angry lips. It held that way for a few minutes. Then, when the clump started moving again toward him, Roger's arms decided for him. On their own volition they cocked the Winchester, raised and aimed it at the heart of a shifty stomper he had never liked. The clump of trolls stopped moving like magic. But the gun, it was obvious, was making them seriously angry. By the itch in the soles of his feet Roger knew he had stepped over a line.

"¡Te vamos a matar, gringuito!" somebody yelled.

Killing him was a possibility.

"We're leaving," he told them. His voice cracked like a teenager's. "I'm taking the gun. Now listen to me."

They listened. It was the closest thing to a speech he had made in his life. Maybe that was because the way things stood between them and the trolls was so clear, you couldn't help understanding it. "If any of you come after us I'm going to have to shoot you. Do I want to shoot you? Of course I don't. I don't even want to think about it. If it was up to me I would just as soon give you back the gun and watch you shoot Macdougal. But if I don't mean what I say, then any of you who want to kill me will just go ahead and do it because there's nothing to stop you. I have to mean it when I tell you I'll kill you. So I do. Do you see that? Do you understand my situation?"

The question, for some reason, quieted them. But their unvented anger was more combustible inside them. He saw that with a level of calm he had never expected to feel in his life. After having wished, a little, for his own death, he felt capable of pulling the trigger. If that was only an illusion it was the one he required.

"Hijo de puta," someone called him. Son of a whore. He had been called a million times worse than that in a bunch of languages. He didn't care. What he cared about was what he had, which was temporary control. Agnes staying behind him just the way she should, without being told, Roger backed his way slowly out of Pes Volado. The stompers believed him, which made Roger respect and fear something hard and unpredictable inside himself. *When it all came down to dust he would kill them if he must.* Maybe.

But at a certain point—a quarter mile away from the entrance to the settlement, back down the road that Macdougal had left on, the same road they came in on—he realized he could stop wondering what he would do when push finally came to shove. The stompers of Pes Volado were letting them go. Good riddance to gringo rubbish.

"Where are we going?" Agnes asked him. Her voice was velvet cool.

But the question bugged him. Everybody always wanted to know where he was going. That was what the Swedish mercy nurse in el Panóptico had asked him, too. What's your plan, Roger? Gotta have a plan. People seemed to get pleasure out of crowding him, pushing him, leaning on him, making him do what he was not inclined to do.

He was the kind of loser, they figured, who had to be reminded to put one foot in front of the other down a certain clearly laid-out path; otherwise he would fall off the track into the swamps. No matter where you went there were always swamps. And he was that kind of person.

"Going," he told Agnes. After his speech to the stompers, his voice came out in a cross-grained whisper.

Left foot right. In the swamps, dangerous animals made frightening noises and licked their leathery lips. Not that he was going to fall in. They moved slowly but steadily in no direction whatsoever.

FIVE

Somewhere along the line—probably in an exploding rice paddy, or else in those first maximum-stress minutes when he was yanked from his mother's womb—Carl Kelleher got bent. As in out of shape. That was the obvious reason he was spending his life hauling beer and soft drinks from Cochabamba to the Chapare and other hindparts of Bolivia, which was the hindquarters of Latin America if you could visualize the continent as a body. Permanently bent out of shape, he no longer fit in the United States of North America. If he ever had. Roger could not see the guy, say, selling tires at Goodyear: standing around the coffee machine talking about that sudden-death overtime play and the scarcity of pussy with a herd of local nerds who never thought about anything that didn't happen on the triangle drive from home to work to the handyman's store that ran glossy ads in the Sunday paper pushing Black and Decker drills and resin-treated two-by-fours.

Takes one to know one, he heard himself comment to nobody in particular who might be listening, because no one was.

Kelleher was one outstanding example to prove Roger's point, which was that some basic balance was seriously out of whack: People were always trying to get out of the place they were born and into some place they fit better. Up north, Mexicans and Salvadorans and Nicas were risking the nothing they had crossing a dangerous desert to get to the border of Gringolandia, where they might or might not make it safely across into the land of plenty of plenty. In Central America one time Roger heard a story about a Salvadoran carpenter who let a grungeball Mexican coyote fuck his seventeen-year-old beauty queen daughter as part of the price for shepherding the family across no-man's-land into Texas. Once he had the family across the line, the coyote turned them all over to a Border Patrol agent as part of some kind of deal to keep himself out of prison. More than once Roger had wondered what went through the carpenter's mind the instant he figured out he had been double-fucked.

While meantime restless, bent-out-of-shape gringos like Carl Kelleher who couldn't find a slot to slide into in the U.S. left a life and luck the Salvadoran carpenter would have killed to own. Walking away from convenience stores and flavored-coffee boutiques with topless waitresses and cable television installed in their bedroom ceiling and robots programmed to satisfy the strangest sexual desires, they came out to camp for good on the minimal edge in places like the Bolivian Chapare, where survival was success and anything more than that probably meant your sins were not misdemeanors.

This was philosophy, for Roger. Not what Agnes would consider philosophy, although maybe by now she had traveled enough, broadened her horizons enough, that she could get into a real give-and-take discussion of the subject with him. Some other time. Thinking philosophic thoughts was only possible because he no longer thought they were going to die unmourned from overexposure in infinite fields of coca. He was letting down.

"Don't have any extra hammocks," Kelleher told them, "but you can nap in the cab if you want to."

They watched the Nugget string two hammocks between trees on the edge of the clearing where Kelleher had parked his big Mercedes delivery truck.

"Spies," was what Kelleher called them again when he drove up behind them on the road Roger and Agnes had finally found that led somewhere. The word and the ugly accusation behind it were starting to get on Roger's nerves, since he knew himself to be the kind of person who was spied upon, for inscrutable reasons having to do with his lowdown position in life, not the one to do any spying. As the Bolivians said, anybody with two fingers' worth of forehead would know that. Kelleher, however, thought he was being funny. "You're the DEA snitches from Tingo Tingo, right?"

Without being asked to, the midget jumped down from the cab, climbed onto the back of the truck with the cases of rattling bottles, and Roger and Agnes were delivered. It felt like being delivered, anyway. Sitting in the cab as Kelleher drove slowly uphill in the general direction of Cochabamba, Roger felt a powerful lassitude drag him down. All the weight in his body sank downward, to his butt, his feet, leaving him light-headed, too exhausted to be tired. Next to him, Agnes had to be feeling the same sensation of drain. Neither one of them had the head to talk to Kelleher, who chattered like a talk show host having problems warming up his guests.

"If I were you I'd stay away from Tingo Tingo," he told them. "I hate to be the one to break this to you, but if there's a vote, you two probably won't win most likely to succeed in the Chapare. They think you tipped off the DEA and the UMOPAR to hit the landing strip that night when the little girl got shot."

"What happened to the girl?" Agnes sat up.

"So you *were* there . . ."

"What happened to her?"

"What do you think happened to her?" Downshifting on a grade, he flipped his ponytail upward once in a girlish gesture that irked Roger.

"She's dead, isn't she," said Agnes. Her voice was flat, too low for Kelleher to hear over the sound of the diesel engine.

"One more victim of the drug wars that won't make the *Times* obituaries." Kelleher shrugged. "Hey look, there goes a jaguar." He pointed with a red finger into the woods, but there was nothing to see. Agnes was degenerating. Nothing Roger had or could do would give comfort.

"It's our fault," he heard her tell herself.

"No it's not," he corrected her, but the lethal look she gave him stopped him from going any farther. The pressure in his head was fierce, causing his thoughts to slur. It was the only way he knew, at the moment, to interpret the loss to the world, and him in it, of Esencia, unwinged angel. It occurred to him that maybe she had been a messenger from the God who wasn't answering Roger's calls. But if that was true, how come she hadn't passed on any messages, and what did it mean that she was gone?

"I apologize," Kelleher told Agnes when he finally noticed, but the fact that he meant it didn't mean much. "Listen," he said, trying to divert her, "you got to keep your eyes open for jaguars. Jaguar spotting is a basic part of this whole business. It's something me and the Nugget take very seriously, and if you're going to ride in our truck you have to, too."

Roger didn't think there were any jaguars left in the Chapare, if there ever had been. But the territory they climbed through was designed for wild creatures: lush, spiky, sweaty, full of slit valleys, the world's hidden sex furred with slender trees. Dry, the road was covered in a fine, thick cap of red dust that hung in the air behind them forever when the truck stirred it. The stompers they passed carrying family-size loads of *pichicata* looked fatalistic when they stood aside. They never got quite far enough off the road to stay clean, and the dust coated them like fine flour. They took it the way they took rain.

"Where you from?" Kelleher asked Roger, who was too slow to answer. To say Flint would have been the same as lying; the city and everything that went on there was another existence that happened to somebody else. The stone cowboy, who was still Roger in some fundamental way, had no permanent address and never had. What he had was lacerations, a.k.a. memories that might or might not be trustworthy guides to get at who he was, which was the fault of who he had been, which may or may not have been his fault to begin with. He must have committed, back before his memory kicked in, a not very original sin.

"Me, I'm from Tibet," the drink distributor told him. He was trying to be friendly. "It's a good place to raise a family, and I wish I was there right now. I mean you didn't lock your front door when you left the house because there was nothing inside to steal, so people were honest. I was happy there. It was a satisfying non-consumer-oriented lifestyle, if you catch my drift. All that stuff you used to read in books about the spiritual power of the East is for real, by the way. Some people are good at sports. The Tibetans are good at spirituality. They're world class. But I had to get out. When the Red Chinese heard my first cousin was the Dolly Llama they were all over me. Listen, I know what it means to be persecuted."

Agnes looked at him, blinked, looked away. She was hearing the blur of bullshit, but she was thinking about Esencia. Something punched Roger in the stomach from the inside out, and he flinched.

Kelleher was happy to have the company. He went on, sure that his riders were as interested as he was in what happened to him in Tibet. "The two of us went to grade school together; we shared a pencil case. Anyway, when the Chinese Communists heard I was a closet capitalist they came after me with their long knives. Remember what Jimmy Carter said when he clubbed that attack rabbit way back when, that time it went after him in the boat? Life isn't fair, he told the American voting public, and for once by Jesus the man was right. I mean I'm not really a capitalist, or if I am it's only because of the indoctrination they gave us back in the fifties. But I could have adapted to the regime, I'm flexible. I would have gladly traded any principles I had for a couple acres of land with a view of the Himalayas. No dice, though. The Communists didn't deal that way. They were hard-liners. The upshot of all that was when the time came to leave Tibet, I asked myself why not Bolivia? Why not the Chapare? Give me one good reason why I should have gone somewhere else."

When Roger didn't answer, Kelleher began crooning softly, "In the magic mountains of Tibet, when the yaks begin to quack, my love comes to me on a cloud. My Buddha baby, Buddha baby boo . . . Hey, I'll teach you the lyrics if you want to learn it. It's kind of a drinking song the Dolly Llama and I used to sing, but I can't remember all the verses."

Roger didn't want to learn the words to Kelleher's Buddhist drinking song, but he could put up with anything just by thinking about getting out of the Chapare. The roads in Cocalandia were supposed to be impassable at night, but Kelleher was going to push on through to the city. In some ways it was safer at night, he told them. That is, if you were careful. Most of the crazy truckers and resentful bus drivers pulled off to sleep after the sun went down, and the jaguars came out to play on the highway, such as it was.

Just before dark Kelleher downshifted into first, maneuvered the Mercedes onto a half-moon shape of open ground on the mountainside of the road, turned off the engine with a flourish supposed to mean something.

"Forty winks," he told them, "for safety's sake, then we'll eat something. Then, my fellow Americans, we're out of this vale of fears. We'll make Cochabamba before the sun comes up. The little woman will be waiting for us with a hot pot of java. The kids will come running out to tell us they missed us, and the dog will frisk around the yard, and the neighbors will look out their windows and envy us our domestic contentment. Sounds great, does it not?"

It did. The Nugget hung their hammocks, and Roger and Agnes took the cab, but Kelleher didn't get his full forty winks. After about twenty or so, a bus plowing by in the thick, stringy twilight blew its horn, and the former classmate of the Dolly Llama tumbled out of his hammock ready to fight.

"Who the fuck are you?" he asked Roger, pounding on the door of the truck cab. He didn't seem to be faking it. Roger was pretty sure he could not remember them. He had brought Agnes stone cowboy luck, which was a lot like Bolivian luck: The only one around to pick them up on the highway and drive them out of the Chapare was an irritable psychotic who thought oppressed Tibetans had a lock on spiritual progress in the twentieth century. Roger thought he remembered seeing a picture of the Dalai Lama in the newspaper once, back in the U.S. If he was right the guy wore round glasses and a saffron robe and his shoulders were rounded, and the look of aggressive benevolence in his eyes was the same look you saw in the eyes of Hari Krishna beggars in airports. Love me and my brown-rice boogy, or else go to Krishna hell. Fuck that noise.

"I'm from Tibet," Roger told Kelleher. It was not his first experience with a psychotic, or with someone who wanted to hurt him, or bully him, or otherwise do damage to him. "I was persecuted by the Communists, so I had to get out. Why not Bolivia? I asked myself. Why not the Chapare?"

Kelleher looked at him and nodded, accepting the justice of Roger's argument. He blinked several times, wavered a little on his feet. Then he took a tin basin and a bucket of water from the truck, washed his face and hands daintily. Afterward he offered the basin full of clean water to Agnes, who had stepped quietly out of the cab.

"Get out of my truck. How come you didn't go to Vietnam?" he asked Roger.

"Nobody asked me."

But Kelleher didn't like that answer, which was the simple truth. He walked around to the back of the truck, hauled down a case of Cerveza Samapeña and opened bottles of warm beer for everybody. It was a party. Roger hadn't been to a party in a long time.

Kelleher sat on the lip of the beer case and pointed his bottle first at Agnes; Roger was an afterthought. "The first thing you got to realize is I voluntarily gave up my deferment to go to Vietnam. That puts me in a distinct minority, if I'm not mistaken, doesn't it?"

Agnes told him it did. Good for Agnes. The only thing Roger could hold against her was blaming him, or both of them, for the death of Esencia. The real reason Esencia was shot had to do with space limitations. There was no room on the planet for angels.

"When I went for the physical," Kelleher was going on, "they classified me 4-X. I didn't know it at the time but there were only a handful of guys in the whole country who got the 4-X."

"What's 4-X?" It was Roger's turn to lead him along the way he wanted to be led. It was going to be a long trip to Cochabamba, but they would get there. Patience, the kind stones had. If stones had faces the eyes would be closed, even in sunlight, and the expressions on the faces would be serene and smooth; nothing could get at them, get to them, get them. If stones had faces, which they probably did.

"4-X?" Kelleher asked him. He was ticked off again. He made it sound as if Roger had been the one to invent the classification and now he was denying responsibility. "During the Vietnam draft, 4-X meant you were a saint. You didn't know that? Where were you, man? I mean where did you stand on the primary political issue of the Coca Cola generation?" He shook his head, disgusted with Roger's indifference, which was the source of his integrity, if he had any.

Nothing was going to stop Kelleher from saying what he had to say. Roger understood how good it could be, for a long-time expat, to run across somebody you could talk to in your own language. In Spanish at least fifty percent of anything worth saying got lost in the translation.

"To get a 4-X," Kelleher remembered, "you had to have the blessing of the Catholic Church, plus on top of that you had to demonstrate your holiness quotient. The pope was in on it from the beginning;

don't let them tell you he wasn't. Those John Birchers were right, by the way, even if the secular humanist liberals don't want to face the facts. The year John Kennedy was elected president he had this secret cable installed that ran from the White House under the Atlantic Ocean directly into the pope's bedroom at the Vatican. People who knew about it called it the Aquinas Connection. The two of them talked every day until Kennedy bought it in Texas. Then when the spooks popped Kennedy and Johnson took over, he said, What the hell, it worked for that oversexed son of an Irish bootlegger, it'll work for me. He was wrong, as it turned out. Some day historians will put these pieces together: The day the pope decided to withdraw Vatican support from him is the same day LBJ lost any chance he had of reelection, and the son of a bitch knew it. That's why he announced he wasn't running."

"I've heard of the Aquinas Connection," Agnes offered. "I read about it in an underground magazine years ago. But the story I read had it wrong, I think."

"Of course they had it wrong. All anybody knew back then was rumors. The truth was too hot to handle." The gratitude with which Kelleher smiled on Agnes ignited a slow burn in Roger, who smoldered. "Anyway the trick on the 4-X deferment was you couldn't actually go out and try to demonstrate how holy you were. Lots of guys tried that and it backfired on them. They wound up in the exploding paddies just like everybody else. But the government had all these undercover agents at the time—some of them went over to work in DEA after the war, I heard a couple years ago and it wouldn't surprise me—and it was the job of these agents to check out who the actual saints were. I assume one of them followed me around for a while because I got the 4-X when I didn't even know it existed. It was supposedly a classified classification, very hush hush, but word usually gets out on that kind of thing, and there were draft counselors who knew about it that were always trying to coach people on how to get it. Never worked, that I knew of."

"But you gave yours up?" Agnes asked him. Roger heard two clots thickening her voice: Esencia the innocent was dead, and Jonathan her brother had become, from what she saw of him at the landing strip, a resident alien in the maximum wacked-out beyond.

"Not for your standard patriotic reasons. I want the record to be clear and straightforward on that. Who are you, by the way?"

"I'm the woman looking for her brother the magician."

"That's right. I remember you now. How come you're traveling with a guy like him?" He pointed at Roger.

"Why did you give up your 4-X classification?" Agnes was learning. Keep him on his fixation and off of Roger.

"How come the bear went over the mountain?"

"To see what he could see."

"Exactly. Only I went over the ocean and landed in an exploding rice paddy. And there wasn't a damn thing to see worth the seeing. All that stuff you hear about men secretly loving war is bullshit. It's phony folklore instigated by the ruling class to keep the sons of the lower orders signing up to defend the national interest. They think they're getting themselves into this exclusive men's club of some kind. Members only, but you have to kill a gook to get your lifetime membership card.

"Never mind about that, though. When I got back to the States, I remember visiting this friend of mine who stayed behind and went to graduate school. He was living in a miserable little apartment in New Haven full of mounds of dried-out dog shit because no one would take the trouble to walk the goddamn Russian wolfhound when it had to crap. So you had to kind of map your way around inside, if you wanted to keep your shoes clean. I had this thing about clean shoes. It's a genetic defect. I tried to get the residents to open a window to clear out the air, but they were totally paranoid. They thought the neighbors would smell their dope, which by the way really did rob them of their ambition. Chalk up one more for the Birchers. Anyway, while I was there we smoked some hash, and when my friend passes me the pipe, without thinking too deep he says something like, 'Well when you get down to it, Vietnam is really just a metaphor, isn't it, for the sickness of the Western soul.' I can't remember the exact words but that was the general drift."

"And that made you angry." Agnes was good and getting better at pulling him along. She could see he had to speak his piece before they could get back on the road.

"A metaphor? A goddamn metaphor? I spent eighteen months of my half-life in an unjustifiable war in a for-shit Asian country doing outrageous, insane things twelve or fifteen or eighteen hours a day, and my former best friend Waldo the flatulent philosopher calls it a metaphor?"

"If it wasn't a metaphor, Carl, what was it?"

He didn't hesitate. You could tell he had thought it through. "Vietnam was the great purge. And I'm not talking about any kind of metaphorical enema. What I'm talking about is totally physical. You opened your mouth and swallowed it and one of two things happened. One was it killed you. Two was you were purged."

"Purged of what?"

Kelleher liked the way Agnes was able to follow him. Roger felt unnecessary; he was. He worked not to hate the soft drink distributor. Too many long miles still.

"Purged," said Kelleher, "of all the rhetoric, all the illusions, all the backed-up shit in your system that was keeping you from seeing how things really worked."

"How did they work?"

"You mean how do they work. Nothing's changed. The world is at war, that's all I'm saying. And the war moves. It's a moveable frigging feast. It was in Vietnam for a while. Then it moved to Central America and Afghanistan. Now it's here."

"But you served your time," she egged him on. "You're a veteran. You don't have to follow the war, not unless you want to."

"Who wants to?"

"Then go home. Where are you from in the States?"

"You weren't there," he shook his head. "You're an intelligent woman. I can tell that about you already. But you weren't there, so you can't understand it."

"Explain it to me anyway."

He tried. "As long as the war goes on, and it's going to go on forever, no matter where it's happening at any given moment, it ruins the peace. I mean we could be in Nebraska right now, couldn't we?"

"That's where you grew up, isn't it?"

"We could be standing on the edge of a ten-mile cornfield, flat as the day is long, and the sun is warm on our backs, and there's half a dozen red-winged blackbirds riding the telephone wire, and the shadows of clouds come rolling over the corn like pirate ships, and we can smell the corn growing and the clean dirt and something tasty inside your picnic basket."

"But?"

"But then we remember the war is going on, and our own little idea of Nebraska goes up in smoke. It's ruined for good. This isn't something I'm making up, it's a proven fact. So what happens then? You come back out to watch the war, wherever it happens to be happening at the moment. It's seductive, I admit that, and even though you hate it you get seduced because you remember how it felt the first time, that clean and empty feeling you had inside after your first big purge. What I'm talking about has nothing to do with loving it, loving the war I mean. No one loves it."

"It doesn't have to be that way, Carl."

Agnes, from the sound of it, had decided to run Kelleher through her quickie therapy course: how to put the eternal war behind you, in ten do-it-yourself easy installments. Roger didn't like the attention she was so quick to pay him. Kelleher didn't deserve it, when all he was doing was licking self-inflicted wounds. "From here," he asked Kelleher, "how many hours' drive is it to Cochabamba?"

In retrospect, it was a question he would have passed on. No way he could have known, though, that it was going to be the thing that made the guy snap.

"Who," the big reddish guy was suddenly asking him, up off the beer case jabbing at Roger's chest with his finger, then shoving him with the flat of his hand hard enough to knock him over into the dirt, "who the fuck do you think you are to be asking me that question?"

Alone, Roger would have walked the rest of the way out of the Chapare rather than answer the question. But he wouldn't do that to Agnes. Or was it that he couldn't help imagining her riding away in the Mercedes with Kelleher leaving him in the hanging dust? He picked himself up, rubbed his chest where Kelleher had hit him, told him to fuck off in Aymara.

"What's all that noise about?"

"Nothing. It's not about anything at all. Let's go, that's all I want to do is get the hell out of here."

"You got to be someplace by a certain time?"

"Please," said Agnes, but Kelleher ignored her. He was in Roger's face again, saying something about swearing him to secrecy.

"Do you swear?"

Roger swore. Agnes swore.

"If you ever say a word about this I'll hunt you down and cut out your tongue. That's not a metaphor, either. I mean it. I'll cut it out and stuff it down your throat and you'll never betray another human being in your life."

Roger wasn't sure what it was he was going to have the power to betray until Kelleher lifted up the hood of the truck. He watched him disconnect the battery terminals and unscrew the cover. It was a big, heavy-duty battery, the kind of extra insurance you would want to have if you were traveling through one of the world's wild places, the kind of places that didn't have corners to have gas stations on. "I'll cut your tongue out," Kelleher repeated. He lifted the cover off.

The Nugget, who had fallen out of his own hammock when Kelleher did, stood respectfully next to him.

"War," Kelleher told the midget out of the side of his mouth in Spanish. "They have to see what they're wrapped up in as war. No metaphors, just fact."

The Nugget gave no indication of anything, none to give.

The top and all four sides of the battery cover were hinged. Kelleher was unlocking panels on the inside walls of the cover, unhooking and unhinging the walls, turning them inside out and then reconnecting them. "If they keep thinking about coca as some kind of quick-fix economic solution to their problems they'll never get out of it. It's war in the Chapare, Pepita, and they have to understand the morality of war, which is nothing at all like the morality of peace. If they don't, they'll stay victimized victims until the sun burns out and it's the end of the world and they're standing around waiting for Jesus to come scoop them up and take them to some happier planet."

The Nugget held the transmitter while Kelleher closed the hood, and Roger and Agnes followed the two of them into the woods. There was no path except for the temporary hole Kelleher's big body made crashing through. He was babbling to the Nugget, practically frothing at the mouth, and Roger understood that it was like scriptwriting. Kelleher was thinking through, aloud, the general shape of the message he wanted to convey, laying down the line against which he could improvise, the way jazz musicians did.

Roger was not really surprised when they started broadcasting that the Nugget was not a deaf mute, that the man had, in fact, the richest voice in Bolivia. It was a voice made for radio, a voice that crawled into a person's ear, infiltrated the brain, echoed off the walls and circuits inside and made him shiver. It was the Voice of the Chapare.

This is la Voz del Chapare broadcasting from the heart of the region where ninety percent of the leaves that go into making Bolivian cocaine are grown. Those of you who have been listening to us for a while—our regular audience, the people we would like to be our friends if only we could go public—know that we're never sure when we go on the air just how long we can broadcast. So we'll talk for a few minutes, but if we fade out you'll know it's for safety's sake. What we wanted to talk to you about tonight has to do with war, the war you're fighting right now, the war they are obliging you to fight. . . .

The voice alone was enough to hook Agnes, although her Spanish was coming along, and Roger had the sense she was following a fair amount of what the Nugget said. Roger himself felt like a witness, a pretty good feeling actually: in the middle of the cooling Chapare woods listening to a deaf mute midget send his sweet, hypnotic sound out on the airwaves of the blackish night, knowing that both the traffickers and the government would love to get their hands on him and Kelleher and their nifty, high-tech, disguisable transmitter and shut down the Voice of the Chapare for good. Agnes took his hand while they listened, and goosebumps ran down Roger's forearms.

The broadcast seemed to drain the poison from Kelleher's valves. Sitting on a stump, he listened like a baby to what his friend was telling the coca farmers, which was Kelleher's own message: his passion, his obsession, his vision of the history of war in the world. It couldn't have lasted ten minutes. When it was over they humped it back to the truck, turned the transmitter back into a battery cover, and headed uphill again for Cochabamba. The Nugget, likewise mellowed out by what he had accomplished, which was a highly creative performance and required great concentration, rode in the back with the bottles.

"You're involved now, both of you," Kelleher warned Agnes and Roger. "I mean you always were, even before you came to Bolivia, because that's the way the thing was designed by the powerbrokers, but now your involvement is clearer in your own minds, isn't it? You have this great sharp image to take home with you. Never mind, what I told you before still holds. I'll cut out your tongue if you ever tell what you know. Not even in your memoirs. Not even in your dreams; somebody might be listening, and they might be a spy for the other side. What you just saw has to die with you."

Roger was thinking the guy was out of his mind, but Agnes asked him why.

"Why? Because the war is eternal. It's going to go on long past the day we're all dead, all four of us."

"Who is the Nugget? I mean who is he for real?"

It turned out he had been a miner in Potosí, a mining city on the cold, bare top of the world. He was born in the little settlement of houses carved like caves into the mountain across from the big hill out of which the Spanish had sucked enough silver to keep their rotten empire running for a couple hundred years. His father, small but not a midget, was killed when a mine shaft collapsed, and his mother wore mourning black for the rest of her life. Which may have been one reason why people in the settlement thought she was part witch. The other reason was she had been seen on more than one occasion flying through the night air over the *cerro*, her long blowing hair glowing a strange, fiery blue, her skin phosphorescent, her obvious destination destruction.

The Nugget was his parents' only child. From the time he was twelve he had been in great demand in the mines because of his pint size. He could crawl down doubtful passages nobody else could squeeze into. The miners also thought it was useful to have him along with them underground because, his mother's son, he was at least one quarter diabolical himself. The devil who lived in the bowels of the mountain considered him a kind of distant cousin and, by extension, looked more charitably on the men he happened to be working with.

The way the Nugget explained his story to Kelleher, it was that same devil who was the cause of his leaving the mines and practically getting himself thrown out of Potosí. He was working with a group of men trying to open a branch off the main shaft in a played-out section of a mine called La Democracia. They dug their way to a ledge in the rock, at the back of which was a hole perfect for someone as compact as the Nugget, who went in because that was his job. He crawled for quite a ways until he came to what looked like a scooped out hollow in the rock, and there sat the devil of the mountain himself, hands folded on his belly and a sour look on his face that didn't change when he laughed. The devil was a small individual, smaller than the Nugget. He didn't speak either Aymara or Quechua, let alone any Spanish, but somehow he let the Nugget know that there was going to be an accident the following day. Don't tell anyone else, the devil cautioned him, and something forbidding in the way he commanded him to keep his mouth shut held the Nugget to the promise he hadn't quite made.

The Nugget played sick the next day, and at first everyone in the settlement considered his being saved when everyone else in his crew was swallowed by the mountain as simple luck. But by the second day after the accident it occurred to some of them that the family relationship between the devil and the Nugget, however distant, might have meant what in fact it did mean, which was that the midget got a heads up that he didn't pass on to his *compañeros*, who consequently died. His mother had passed away by that point, which robbed the Nugget of his basic protection; they were reluctant to hassle the son of a witch only as long as she was alive to defend him. The anger in town built up to the point that the Nugget sneaked out of Potosí in the middle of the night in the back of a delivery truck whose driver didn't know he had a small diabolical creature stowed away with his canned goods and cooking oil and wool ponchos. The Nugget wrapped himself in a poncho and tried not to think about his mother, or the smug look he had seen on the devil's face, or the ease with which people were willing to believe the worst about someone.

"Does he believe he actually saw the devil inside the mine?" Agnes asked Kelleher.

"He does," Kelleher told her, "because he did. I never went down in the mine myself so I can't prove there's no devil, which as far as I'm concerned proves there is one. Follow?"

To Roger, the second half of the Nugget's story was even sadder. He washed up in a small town in Chuquisaca, in a pleasant valley south of Sucre, and fell in love with a plain-faced woman with three fingers on her left hand who worked for the owner of the local grocery and hardware store. The surprising thing was she loved him back. Roger was disturbed for a minute, and mildly thrilled, by a vision of the Nugget nestled snug in the lap of this woman, who apparently had light-brown hair and squinted continuously. She had been sweeping the walk in front of the store. When she saw the Nugget come down the street she leaned her broom against the side of the building, led him around back to her room. It was twilight. There were bats. The bats swooped gracefully, catching mosquitoes in their front teeth. She sat on her narrow bed and pulled him onto her lap, closed her squinty eyes while he undid the black metal buttons of her yellow dress one by one. He felt her breasts with his tiny hands, closed his eyes, and sucked gently on the erect pink-brown nipples until the mild, enveloping Chuquisaca sky went completely dark. . . .

It was a Bolivian love story, or maybe that was the way love stories everywhere had to be, but the end was bitter, and things went bad. The Nugget didn't know it, of course—why should she have told him? The closest of lovers had to keep back a few important secrets from each other. It was unlikely that the Nugget told her his mother was a witch—but the woman who loved and sheltered him was married to a man in Oruro who had beaten her hard enough to drive her into hiding. One way or another—Kelleher didn't have this part of the story completely clear—the husband showed up wanting his legally sanctioned woman back. There was an ugly showdown, which the

Nugget lost, and he had to hit the road again, in the process becoming deaf and dumb as a kind of self-defense mechanism and to avoid complicated personal entanglements. By the time Kelleher bumped into him in Cochabamba he had developed a view of human relationships that was on the skeptical side, but he was still a romantic, and the Voice of the Chapare gave him an outlet for his choked-off passion and his hope for a better Bolivian future that kept him, at least, from contemplating suicide.

Back on the road, Kelleher drove slowly, the rage temporarily burned out of him. He sang his Tibetan love songs in a remember-all-that-great-stuff way that made you think he really had been there, really shared a dorm room with the Dolly Llama, really been driven unwillingly from the country he loved by Chinese Communists who were threatened by a mysterious spiritual power they didn't understand. Stranger things happened all the time.

Such as what happened next, which was, from a philosophical point of view, yin and yang in action. It was as clear to Roger as a towerful of clanging bells. Hanging around with Agnes had made him smarter, quicker, more capable of on-the-spot analysis. (The opposite was also likely true, that prolonged contact with the stone cowboy had probably done no good at all for Agnes's mental powers. She must have lost a few million brain cells since that first day when she showed him her brother's picture in the Plaza San Francisco in La Paz. He felt sorry for her but not sorry enough to walk out of her life for her own good.)

One reason it was easy to see the yin and the yang in what happened was the fact that Kelleher and G.I. Joe had a lot in common, which made their differences stand out. They were both fairly reddish individuals. They both had big Northern Hemisphere bodies that sweated a lot in the south, in exotic places where the sun was cruel and injustice rode on the back of a small brown donkey lashing the beast's haunches with a stinging quirt. G.I. Joe was a square individual and Kelleher was round, which also helped bring the difference into focus.

What happened was a roadblock. One minute the yaks were quacking in Tibet and the next, Bolivians in antidrug uniforms were shining flashlights in their faces telling them to get down from the cab with their hands in the air. "I'll cut out your tongue," Kelleher told Roger.

They got down. Their hands were in the air. They followed orders as well as the most completely oppressed Bolivian peasant in the history of the republic.

Quake. That was the word for the motion Roger's body was making. He stood next to Agnes, who had to be thinking that finding her brother couldn't possibly be worth the grief she was getting trying to reach him; either that or she was thinking she needed a better guide, one who knew how to keep her out of unnecessary trouble.

Kelleher made it worse than it probably had to be, or else his going crazy was supposed to keep the troll storm troopers from thinking about looking for a radio transmitter cunningly disguised as a heavy-duty battery cover. They punched his button, and he wound up on the Geneva Convention, which apparently had a clause, or an article, or a whole chapter, in plain black and white protecting Tibetan tradesmen from search-and-seizure operations conducted after the sun went down. The UMOPAR squad leader—maybe he was a sergeant; Roger had never bothered to learn how to tell military ranks from the gaudy gizmos on their uniforms—ignored Kelleher, smoked a cigarette peacefully while he supervised the shakedown. He sent his men up the sides of the truck, where they lifted and shifted random cases of Cerveza Samapeña and Samapa Kola to see whether Kelleher was hauling *pichicata* along with his innocent drinks. Buzzing, Kelleher was a nonmalignant gnat, or less, to the sergeant.

Without waiting for an order, one of the UMOPAR grunts lifted the hood of Kelleher's Mercedes, aimed his flash and peered in. For one long, weak moment Roger saw his future relived in El Panóptico, sentenced to death in life for inciting the natives to riot, or whatever the authorities in a position to fuck them over felt like calling the Voice of the Chapare.

The battery cover was too obvious. The grunt looked right past it, at it, around it, then slammed the hood down disappointed. But even before he knew they weren't going to find the transmitter, Roger experienced a fairly Buddha-like sensation of not caring. Agnes next to him, he stood off to the side of the narrow road, at least two automatic rifles pointed more or less at his unprotected heart, such as it was. In the black Chapare woods frogs twanged rubber bands, bugs ground their millions of little teeth, and the night birds talked to each other in phony falsetto voices that rose and fell like gusts of wind. The woods seemed much bigger than the road. The Chapare was a throat, the devil's throat maybe. If you waited long enough it would swallow anything, everything on the puny, temporary road. Roger's back tingled; there, behind him, was the real vulnerability. But he felt, for a moment, serene and untouchable. It was a feeling worthy of the Dalai Lama.

And it was an illusion. Because out of the shadows on the far side of the road stepped yang. In action. There was something in Kelleher's nonstop Spanish rag that G.I. Joe couldn't take, rules of engagement be damned.

"Shut the fuck up," he told Kelleher in English, the universal language of diplomacy and command. The UMOPAR commander looked relieved.

"Who are you?" Kelleher wanted to know, as if he didn't.

"I'm your friend. You don't know it yet, but I am."

"Bullshit. This is Bolivian soil we're standing on, pal, and I'm a Tibetan national with permanent resident status. You're obviously a Gringo Ranger. You've got absolutely no jurisdiction here. Those are the facts, and they're incontrovertible."

"I don't care what kind of car you think you're driving, let me see your passport."

"Fuck off. I know you. I've seen you around. There's a million of you. You think you can rule the world because you've got superior firepower and an organizational flow chart and you know how to talk in secret codes. But you're wrong. You're absolutely frigging wrong. One of these days all the people you've been stomping on with your steel-toed boots are going to start stomping back, and they've got long memories, let me warn you, they've got memories that go back to the first day somebody like you shit on somebody like them and got away with it."

G.I. Joe came back at him with something about soft underbellies and misplaced intentions. Yin and yang. Ponytail and brush cut, round and square. For a long time they went back and forth, and it was clear to Roger that they were two halves of the same strange character who didn't fit in the U.S. of North America anymore so they had to come out here to the Bolivian jungle to play out the weird family drama they couldn't act out at home.

It was also pretty evident that G.I. Joe and his UMOPAR henchmen didn't really expect to find any coca paste on the truck, and that they had no idea they had unintentionally stopped the one and only clandestine philosophical liberation portable radio station in the Chapare. The idea was to hassle Kelleher because that's what the guys with the guns did. When G.I. Joe got tired of going back and forth with the transplanted Tibetan he told him to move on. "But your two gringo riders stay with us."

A small noise came up out of Agnes's throat, died before it reached her lips.

"Bastard," Roger said silently.

"They're my guests," Kelleher tried. Had to give him credit for trying real hard. He spent fifteen minutes of his own time lobbying G.I. Joe to let Agnes and Roger go on to Cochabamba with him and the Nugget, but all of them knew he was only doing it because it was the right thing to do. Roger stopped hating him.

"When I get back to Cochabamba," Kelleher threatened G.I. Joe, "I'm going to call the American Embassy and tell them this American Nazi in a suspicious uniform with no identifying emblems is holding two innocent American citizens hostage at gunpoint down here. They'll send down a congressman in a helicopter, and your law-and-order ass is weed. You're compost."

"I'm not holding anybody anywhere," G.I. Joe corrected him. "This is a Bolivian operation. I'm here with the blessing of the Bolivian government. I'm an adviser."

"We heard that one before."

In the exploding rice paddies, Roger completed the sentence for him. But it was no good. G.I. Joe thought he was being a decent human being by booting out the UMOPAR grunts from his jeep, driving it himself with Agnes and Roger bouncing in the backseats like suspects in a squad car. Roger had made similar trips before.

Down. Again.

"Where are you taking us?" Agnes asked G.I. Joe, who thought he was being even more decent blowing his cigarette smoke out the window and not into the backseat to choke them.

"I'm not taking you anywhere. My Bolivian comrade-in-arms, Major Fretes, is taking you back to the base camp to answer a few questions, that's all. What I'm doing you is a favor."

"What favor?"

"Trust me: You're a whole lot happier driving along with me for company than you'd be with my UMOPAR *compañeros*. They're a group of basically resentful individuals. You'll see what I'm talking about at the camp. The U.S. government and the Bolivian government want them to spend their productive lives chasing bad guys through the jungle, which is okay, it's a living, right? Except they don't pay them shit, and the bigshots are always worrying that my buddies down here are going to turn the next blind corner and get corrupted by the bad guys. Which is a definite possibility. I mean, wouldn't you like to make ten thousand bucks just for not showing up on a certain stretch of a certain road on a certain night? Of course you would. It's a quality-of-life issue. But what you get instead is people driving nifty government vehicles on per diem coming down for a day to tell you you're saving Bolivian democracy and North American youth from eternal damnation from the white poison."

"I don't care where we are," Roger tried. "We're Americans and we have rights."

G.I. Joe looked at him in the rearview mirror and nodded enthusiastically. "No argument from me. Even in the godawful Chapare people have their Adnarim Rights."

"What's that?"

"It's Miranda, backwards," Agnes told him quietly.

"Complete-amente correcto," said G.I. Joe. "You've observed the toilet bowl phenomenon, I assume? You notice in the Southern Hemisphere that toilets flush backward? It has something to do with the pull of the moon, I think. Well, backward is the way everything works down here. Your Adnarim Rights guarantee that people will presume you're guilty of the worst crime they can imagine for you, and that you will get no slack from anybody that could cut you any, and that your court-appointed lawyer will be on the take from the other side. I'm sorry to be the one to break all this to you, but better it comes from a fellow American than from a Bolivian that's got no reason to care."

"Please," Agnes said. It was as close as Roger had heard her come to pleading, but it did not detract a thing from her. "You can't really believe that we're drug dealers. We don't even use drugs, let alone sell them. We're here looking for my brother."

"There's such a thing as guilt by association, is there not? Your brother is on the UMOPAR's top ten wanted list. He may not know it yet, but he's a major hit. He's the missing link to all kinds of major connections back at home."

Down. Again. Disaster. In the low, dark place where dead dreams stacked up, the bird that had carried Roger out of the Chapare to the high plains stirred in its sleep, shifted, went back to a sleep so deep it had to be hibernation, had to be the bird's response to danger. Roger didn't blame it, even though he felt abandoned. G.I. Joe drove them down.

Hard to keep track of the time it took them to reach the base camp. Anyway, who cared how far it was from the roadblock back down to bad luck? They did not pass Go. Eventually G.I. Joe got tired of hassling Roger. He drove as though he'd forgotten he was hauling prisoners of war in his backseat, he was on his way to the corner store to pick up a six pack before the game started on TV. Next to Roger Agnes sat rigid, too outraged to speak, too intense to relax, too full, still, of Esencia dead and her brother to unbutton.

This kind of free-form, falling-from-the-sky abuse didn't usually happen to people like Agnes. People like her lived behind a wall, and on the wall were flowers. The way they were protected without trying or knowing was unfair, from a cosmic point of view, but Roger had no desire to see Agnes go through grief just so there was a fairer distribution of good and bad, of roses and shit, of rewards and punishment on the planet. Besides, he had a certain advantage. He had been in custody before, plenty of times. He knew you got used to whatever shitty situation was there to get used to. In some ways the idea of what was going to happen to you was the worst part, though not the only bad part. He was flexible, so flexible he was limp. He slept.

Even in the dark Roger knew that the Chapare base camp was going to be like prison. Through the gate onto the compound what he saw was eyes. Bare flat chests, and kick-ass black boots, and green fatigues, and commie-killer knives. But mostly eyes, hard eyes, eyes that were calculating, measuring, looking for the stone cowboy's weak points, the point of easiest entry. It was like getting raped in their minds, by their meat-eating eyes, Bolivian and gringo both. Kelleher was right, in his twisted, peace-loving way. It was war, and the bad guys had captured his flag. Roger was in the Cocalandia equivalent of jail, which was greener than el Panóptico but not much better in any other important regard.

What hurt most was being pulled away from Agnes. She went without a word, and her toughness, which was serene, made him want to fall at her feet and kiss them. Even if it was only because she thought she was still behind the flowered wall. But his helplessness burned, shamed him. He hoped they would let her get some sleep, at least, while they grilled him.

It was just like any other place where people were held against their will, except no hot white lights. Roger was a cheese sandwich, he was grilled. The interrogation shack they led him into looked like the portable campaign headquarters in the rolling drug war. Maps with color-coded pins in strategic places were hung all over the rough board walls. On the one steel desk, a messy heap of file folders—maybe they had a file on him; if they did he would like to know what was in it, and who invented it—and an upscale black radio with blinking lights and buttons. Every few seconds it made an electric fart noise, clearing something from its system. In one corner, a Bolivian grunt with the face of an Aymara highlander slept in an olive green canvas chair with his rifle across his knees. No one woke him.

Major Fretes was a classic. Roger understood him right away, because he had been dumped on and dicked with by the man's brothers-in-arms up and down the continent over a period of years. The main thing, for Major Fretes, was not to let Roger know what he already knew: that this whole show was a gringo operation, even though his job description said he was in charge of everything that went on in the camp, and even though G.I. Joe took one of the slat-backed wooden chairs pretending to be just the audience. It was a question of national pride, and vanity, and whose balls were swollen up the biggest. In Major Fretes's hidden heart he wanted to kill G.I. Joe, the gringo empire's hard-ass messenger of conquest and superiority. But he couldn't, couldn't even kill a stone cowboy of no account, so he did the next best thing, which was to work out his frustrations on Roger, making it look like a legitimate interrogation.

Fretes had been in the Chapare a while. His fifty-year-old body showed the traces of the exertion it went through getting used to jungle life after fat city in the capital. And there was still some fat on him. Thin sheets of it hung on his gut, in his jowls, even in his biceps. But most of the congealed grease had been scoured off his body by his tour of duty in Cocalandia chasing traffickers and living a genuine soldier's life in the base camp. His bright black eyes were set close together. They tended to focus inward, toward the middle of his nose, which made it look like he wasn't paying attention to what anyone said, he was listening to something more interesting that people around him couldn't hear. He had let a little military-regulation mustache grow out; it was completely silver, a hairy minnow. And he had a bad habit of stopping talking midsentence to stretch, or scratch different parts of his body, or pick at his teeth with his long brown fingers.

Roger and Agnes were there, it turned out, because UMOPAR had reason to believe.

". . . that you came to Bolivia to set up a major deal with el Grán Moxo. We have an intelligence report that says he is getting greedy. He wants to cut out the Colombian middlemen and deliver his product directly to a network in the U.S. There's more money to be made in HCL than in the paste, a lot more." Fretes stopped, blinked, scratched his crotch absently. The grunt in the canvas camp chair mumbled something in his sleep. Outside, the normal night noises of the Chapare sounded like filler, something added at the last minute.

"Who is this *chico* who claims to be a magician?" Fretes wanted to know.

Name, rank, and serial number, thought Roger. One out of three. He remembered a nifty curse in Aymara, rolled it out on his tongue, and then didn't say it. He could have gotten away with it. Fretes was the kind of guy who wouldn't admit he knew Aymara even if it was the language he sucked in with his mother's sweet milk. He was a modern man, a mid-career professional with an ambitious boss to worry about, and a wife who spent more money than he made every month, and children who were embarrassed to admit to their friends that their father was a cop, and a mistress who understood his individual needs and just how he had been getting shafted by everybody else in the world. Aymara was for the Indians. And they said the gringos were racist . . .

"We have reason to believe," Fretes repeated, "that you and the woman—what's her name? Agnes—were notified by the magician that el Grán Moxo is ready to try his experiment of cutting out the Colombians. He dreams of controlling the entire operation from the leaves to the paste to the base to the final package of HCL. You are here to help him make the connection with distributors in the North."

"Bullshit," Roger told him. *"Caca de vaca."*

"Do you deny that Agnes is the magician's sister?"

"That doesn't have a damn thing to do with anything."

"So you're suggesting that this woman came all the way to Bolivia to see the sights, and you are her tour guide."

G.I. Joe slumped in his chair, tilted his head back against the wall, pretended to sleep. He was a bad actor.

"She came to Bolivia," Roger told Fretes, "to find her brother. She has to tell him that their father had some kind of major heart attack or something. The guy is in very bad shape. So she wants her brother to go home and see him. She thinks that will cheer him up, and maybe that will do his condition some good. I came down with her because I spent some time in Central America, so I had the Spanish. I hate the Sandinistas, by the way. They stole the revolution. I sent in my absentee vote last time, and I voted for the Republican. Agnes is a friend, that's all, and when a friend needs help you help them." It was a risk worth taking; he doubted they would know he was actually a graduate of el Panóptico.

The radio crackled and farted, and the Bolivian grunt woke up, his wide black eyes round and blinking. He ran his hands up and down the stock of his rifle, came to attention when he saw Major Fretes there. The base camp commander told him to make himself scarce. He went out the door looking guilty, and Fretes went back to work. G.I. Joe's imitation snore was a joke.

Roger was a piece of dirt; dirt was what you stepped on. Fretes went up one side of him and down the other talking all kinds of garbage he couldn't really believe, except that Roger had a sick intuition that he did, or he might, or he could make himself believe it if he tried. The UMOPAR major repeated himself a lot, but that was part of the standard investigation technique, which had to do with wearing a person out, boring into him enough times that even if he had no contradictions being tired would lead him to invent a few. G.I. Joe, coca-control adviser to the national antidrug effort, continued to play dumb. He got up out of his chair and poured a drink of water for himself, settled right back down to pretend not to listen. His big boots stood out in front of him like warships on the board floor. Even distracted by the hazing he was getting from Fretes, Roger could see just how much it cost the American to stay out of it.

After a while Roger realized he was exhausted. Fretes's questions were coming at him like soft-point bullets shot from a great distance, traveling across a long wavy space to ping him in the head, the neck, the shoulders, the gut. As often as he could bring himself to say it, Roger repeated that he was not a drug trafficker. What he didn't tell him was that he was a stone cowboy. That was something Fretes wouldn't be able to understand even if he strung it out in one-syllable words for him.

It was getting light. Outside the interrogation shack soldiers were making getting-up noises. There were chickens in the base camp, future soup for the troops. Their alarm clock calls were homey sounding, creatures of comfort, and Roger wondered whether he was ever going to be allowed to sleep. Fretes didn't seem to be tired at all, but maybe he had slept before they showed up at the camp. His brain in first gear, grinding down, Roger told himself he would last what had to be lasted. Then the door opened.

Martin was a civilian, and a gringo, and from the beginning something set him apart from the aggressive ignorance that seemed to move and motivate everybody else in the base camp. He had to be about forty, but it was a young forty, the kind of forty that assumed the better, the more interesting and rewarding and satisfyingly mysterious half of his life was going to be the second half. He was wearing clean khakis, a white cotton shirt that had been ironed, tan sneakers with unmuddy laces. His face reminded Roger of the face of a shrink, or the way he imagined a shrink ought to look: craggy, and deep enough to cause shadows when the light was bad. It was the face of someone who had been watching the world's uglinesses for a while but was still holding back any final judgment. His black hair was a little long, which also marked him out in the herd of bullet-headed cops and *militares* who peopled the camp. Roger hadn't smoked for a while, but he felt the old nicotine craving tingle in his mouth, down his throat, watching Martin drag on a brown-paper cigarette, exhale slowly, smile at the whole room in a convincing way that could have meant every separate thing everybody present wanted it to mean.

Fretes nodded once in his direction, then ignored the new guy, of course, but his indifference was as bogus as the Bolivian government's anticoca rhetoric. The interrogation of the stone cowboy went on for a few more minutes, for form's sake and not to wound more Bolivian pride, but basically round one ended when Martin came through the door.

On the way to jail Roger looked around for Agnes, but it was part of the UMOPAR's psy-ops plan to keep the two of them apart and wondering about each other. They probably thought they were depriving them of sex and love as well. In the sleepy blur in which he stumbled across the camp he saw soldiers moving in ragged lines, a kitchen with smoke and steam rising at the same slow rate, a line of temporary shower rigs, a motor pool full of two-door Toyota Landcruisers, what looked like a boot camp obstacle course, rows of temporary tents set up on permanent wood platforms.

The Chapare base camp, Roger eventually understood, was built on the illusion that the place was a short-term necessity. As soon as they won the drug war, the gringos were going to shake hands with their Bolivian *compañeros*, strike their tents, and haul out all that valuable equipment to the next battle site. Even thinking locally, it wouldn't have been smart to make the camp look like a long-term arrangement, a done deal. The buyers and the agitators working with the coca-growers league and anybody else who didn't want the gringos in their Chapare could point to permanent-looking structures and say See? We told you they're an occupation force and they're here to stay; the time has come to rise up and throw them out. So the little room they locked Roger into wasn't exactly the kind of cell you found in a genuine jail, just a separate space with walls and the same grim feeling that you couldn't go anywhere until the guys with guns said you were free to leave. There was an army-green camp cot, more bed, and better, than he had had for a while.

He had never noticed before that you could sweat while you dreamed. No windows in his cell, nowhere for the stale air to go. In his dream also he was sweating in a closed-in space he could not get out of. It was like relief when Martin came quietly through the door and woke him. Roger disliked not knowing which part of the day it was. He could have slept half an hour, or six or seven. His body couldn't tell him what it didn't know. It was on strike anyway for all the abuse it was taking in the Chapare, which was, in its own way, as inhospitable as the Altiplano.

"I wouldn't mind one of those smokes," he told Martin, who lit one of his thin, unfiltered cigarettes for him.

"They're Bulgarian," Martin said. "I did a tour there a few years ago and got hooked on them. It's a pretty foul tobacco, actually, but hey, it's what you get used to, isn't it? They're not easy to get, but I have a friend who sends me a few packs every now and then. Did you ever get to Bulgaria?"

Dragging slowly on the smoke, Roger knew he had made a mistake. He had been away from cigarettes for long enough that he could survive without smoking. But the impulse to do something stupid and destructive was strong in him, as strong, some times, as the impulse to survive.

"Where's Agnes?"

"Agnes is okay. One strange thing about a macho society is they're a little intimidated by women, really, so they build castles for them. She's got her own private suite. Her room has a window, and somebody brought her a fan, too. She's a tough woman, isn't she? I mean calm. Very calm. She's the kind of person who can take whatever they throw at her."

"Why don't they let her go? They can hang on to me until they get tired of fucking me over, but not even those UMOPAR sludge brains are stupid enough to believe she's involved in anything ugly."

"Your timing is bad."

The tobacco rush was sweet, intense, brief. Then it was just a smoke. "What do you mean my timing?"

"The Bolivians are sensitive right now."

"Sensitive about what?"

"It's a sovereignty question. They're asking themselves who's really running this operation. It's their country, even though we forget that in the course of a workday. And it's their drug trade and their antidrug trade. The gringos, in case you haven't noticed, have an obnoxious tendency to come into a place like gangbusters. My way or the wrong way, you know what I mean? You've seen it. They're hyperorganized, and they have all the latest sexy equipment—they've got their own brand of gadget macho—and they think they can do everything that has to get done better than the locals can do it."

"So the natives get restless."

"Do you blame them?"

Only for being trolls, Roger didn't tell him. "Who are you?" he asked him.

"I told you, my name is Martin."

"Who do you work for?"

"Do you want a smartass answer or an evasive one? My guess is you've already figured out that I'm on your side in this."

"Then get us out of here."

"Normally I could, and I would. But Major Fretes is asserting his authority, has been for the past couple weeks. He's calculating that we won't care enough about the two of you to make a stink."

"He's right, isn't he?"

Martin shrugged sympathetically, offered him a second cigarette. Roger took it. He knew all about slippery slopes. He had slid down a few just for the buzz you got when you let go.

"Writing my congressman isn't going to do me much good, is it?" he said.

"The mail's been pretty slow lately."

"So what does Fretes want to do to us?"

Martin's theory confirmed Roger's. "It makes him feel good to have a couple of *yanqui* citizens under his thumb, however temporarily. He needs somebody to get back at. I wouldn't worry too much, Roger. Odds are he's not going to hurt you. There's almost always a bunch of gringos around the camp. But he's probably going to ride your ass for a while. You can pretty much count on that. He's got all the moral support he needs to do that."

"How long is a while?"

"If I knew I'd tell you."

"What about getting him to let Agnes go back to Cochabamba?"

"You ever hear of a phenomenon called national pride?"

"What about it?"

"It's been wounded. That makes the situation unpredictable. I could tell you that time heals all wounds, but I won't, because I'm not sure the empirical evidence bears that out."

"What about G.I. Joe?"

"Who?"

"The red-haired commando."

"Albert is a true believer, Roger. He stands for the restoration of the monarchy and the primacy of the Orthodox Church. Anything less than that, for him, is godless communism in one form or another. Don't let him know that you know it, but he reads Dostoevski in his bunk at night."

This wasn't too much, though it could have been. Roger had a small idea of what Martin was getting at, which was basically that Agnes and the stone cowboy could expect no support, sympathy or interest from G.I. Joe, who thought fighting drug traffickers was the work of the Lord and would get him into Heaven.

"So now that I've figured out you're on our side," Roger guessed, "you want me to tell you everything I know about Agnes's deadbeat brother."

"It wouldn't hurt. It might help."

"He's a loser. He's the kind of guy you run into on a bus somewhere in Arizona, and he drives you crazy for the next two hundred miles telling you about how his life is going to work out much better now that he's getting his shit together."

"That's all?"

"He's also a decent magician. I saw him perform once. He has whatever it takes to make you quit looking for the trick. After you watch for a while you relax and start enjoying the magic."

"Keep going."

"The unusual thing about him is that he really believes there's some kind of special magic in Bolivia."

"What about you, Roger? Do you believe there's magic in Bolivia?"

There was. If you woke up in the middle of the night and there was nothing in your ears you could hear la Pachamama breathing in and out, slow slow. But that was a private question, not something you asked a person face to face even if you had him in your custody. "How come you care so much about the guy?" he asked Martin. "He's a zero."

"Are you in the right frame of mind to take some advice, Roger?"

"What advice?"

"Put some effort into convincing your friend Agnes to give up her quest to find her brother."

"She won't. She's stubborn."

"And you're loyal . . ."

"Fuck you, Martin."

"You can't offend me, Roger. They pay me not to get offended. So don't waste your breath. Want to hear a story?"

Roger was willing to hear a story. He had the idea that the more he listened to Martin, the likelier he was to get out of the Chapare.

"The Grán Moxo has a ranch in the Beni, right? Paititi. It's popular history, the stuff of legends. He's more popular than the president right now. Why do you suppose that is? Some day they'll make a movie about de la Rocha. They'll make him out to be some kind of Robin Hood. He's got houses all over the place, but Paititi is his real home, and the Beni is where he does his real business."

"El Dorado."

"What's that?"

"The City of Gold. That's what Paititi is supposed to be."

"Something like that. De la Rocha's grandfather was a rubber merchant. Fairly big-time but not one of the real barons. The Moxo himself grew up on a cattle ranch in the Beni. He loves the place. And he's been careful to make sure nothing even remotely resembling cocaine or lab supplies or chemicals comes near Paititi, which apparently is a real palace of pleasure but hard to get to. There's a road, but any time it rains the road floods, and it rains a lot. The labs where he makes his drugs are scattered across the Beni on no-man's-land."

"I can't figure out what this story is about, Martin."

"He's hauled in by river everything a genuine drug magnate needs: thoroughbred ponies, a video arcade, a satellite dish to pick up the Brazilian porno flicks. Anyway, the other day we got a report from one of our snitches."

"What?"

"What do you mean, what?"

"What'd your snitch tell you?"

"That the Big Moxo is into magic in a big way these days. He's been converted by Agnes's brother. The eternal Flame, the Mystical Gringo, is giving him lessons. From what we hear it's becoming a regular obsession. The two of them go at it every day for hours. They started out with card tricks and simple stuff like that, but it's gone way beyond that. Don't ask me how, but your friend Flame has convinced de la Rocha that he was missing out on all the magic that's available in Bolivia, right in his own backyard, so to speak. All these years he's been wasting his time making a billion dollars selling cocaine when he could have had the magic for nothing. If he had the right attitude. Now he's got the attitude."

"If you know where the ranch is, how come you and G.I. Joe and the Bolivians don't jump in your helicopters and go get de la Rocha?"

"What are the Bolis going to charge him with, breeding ponies without a license? I told you the guy is careful. Anyway the Beni is wild. It's wilder than the Chapare. The minute the worker bees at the labs hear the helos coming they melt into the forest like sylvan legends. This is a supremely frustrating way to make a living, Roger, if anybody ever crawls up your back and asks you. You want another smoke?"

Roger took another cigarette, let Martin light it for him even though he knew he was only being nice to him because he thought it might get him something.

"I have friends with mutual fund portfolios and time-share condos in places with beaches. And what do I have? Perpetual challenge. The bad guys are better armed, and they have more high-tech gear than the USG, and they're operating on their own turf, and they have enough money to corrupt a saint, let alone the Bolivian legal system. So what do you do? You can't blame a solid citizen like Major Fretes for being a little short tempered every once in a while."

Roger could. He did. "What about kidnapping? Tell the Bolivians they can charge de la Rocha with kidnapping a gringo."

"Patience, Roger."

"Martin?"

"What?"

"Tell Fretes we don't know anything. Come on. You know we don't know shit. We're nothing in this. We don't even know what's going on."

But if Martin could have said something to Fretes, it was almost for sure that he didn't. So Roger hunkered down into his survival mode, which meant going minimal. Fretes, it was obvious, didn't like people like Roger, didn't like Roger himself, the particular example at hand of whatever kind of person he was supposed to be. The man rode him pretty hard. Three or four or even five times a day he had Roger marched under armed escort across the grounds of the camp to the interrogation room to answer the same repetitive rosary of questions he asked the first time, the answers to which never satisfied him. The major wanted to wear him down. The interrogations lasted a long time, long enough, it always seemed, for butterflies to mate and fly and die and their bodies to decompose on the jungle floor. Sometimes G.I. Joe or Martin or both were there, sometimes stiff-faced UMOPAR officers who never contributed a word to the conversation. Sometimes Fretes worked on the stone cowboy alone. The only thing that didn't change was Fretes's antagonism, which reminded Roger of his days in Don Eloy's lumberyard, where he was held up as Exhibit A of gringo decadence on display to the Bolivian jury. Guilty. He was experiencing negative imperialism.

Not that it was more than Roger could handle. Since stepping outside el Panóptico a freer man he had acquired three things he had lost a long time ago, if he ever had them: some patience, some strength, and the ability to visualize a life, some kind of life, after the crisis of the moment had passed. He knew he had to answer Fretes's stupid question the seventeenth time it was asked with the same level of unriled cool he did the first time. After a while it turned into a contest, or a game: seeing how long he could hold out without snapping, how long the major would hold on before giving up on him as a hopeless, brain-dead gringo druggie who knew nothing the UMOPAR wanted to know about the movement of cocaine across their violated national territory.

They thought they would make it harder on him with the P.T., but that was only more psy ops from the military mindset. It smelled to Roger like a G.I. Joe contribution to the breaking of the stone cowboy, although Martin wouldn't admit that when Roger asked him. Roger knew how it worked anyway: After a hard day hammering at their prisoner with the same boring, unimaginative questions, the two military hardheads, brothers in antidrug arms, stopped by the local commissary for a cold brew and some shop talk. (Did the base camp have a commissary? Roger hadn't seen anything that looked like one, but the point was the same no matter where they did their drinking.) Tossing back his half-cold Paceña beer, G.I. Joe confidentially tells Fretes Back in 'Nam (or Laos, or Nicaragua, or undercover on the streets of downtown Beirut, it didn't matter where) we got good results by stressing out their bodies at the same time we were messing with their minds. And there it is, a little unwrapped present for Major Fretes, who accepts it with an ugly smile of gratitude on his face.

If for no other reason than to maintain his self-respect, Fretes had to come up with his own particular variation on the physical hassle theme. What he did was simple: he forced Roger to do high-intensity workouts with a herd of sullen UMOPAR grunts who'd rather be kicking back and cool up on the Altiplano. Push-ups, jumping jacks, running in place, running through a phony maze of bald truck tires, climbing fake walls and jungle-vine ladders that led nowhere. *Uno dos tres* let's do it again you worthless sacks of llama shit. Etc. He was in Bolivian boot camp. At any moment he could expect to be awakened, pushed outside by Bolivian soldiers making bark-like military noises in his face, worse than garlic breath, and drilled. He drilled. They drilled. He drilled again. He was a sack of llama shit, worthless but burnable for ceremonial purposes.

But their plan backfired on them. It was hard work, and for the first few days Roger was so beat he wasn't even coherent during the interrogations. If his thoughts were like letters of the alphabet he couldn't get past A all the way to B because there were too many strange and unknown letters between them that he couldn't quite make out. He put the little mental focus he had into the effort not to contradict himself, not to strike out at Fretes with a punky answer that would have the effect of keeping them longer in camp custody than whatever minimum sentence the Bolivian goddess of vengeance had decided on. But after those first few miserable days his body responded. Not strong but stronger was what it got. His head was not clear but a little clearer. There was virtue in stones.

The only thing that threatened to twist him back out of shape was the separation from Agnes, the most effective part of Fretes's master plan. He didn't want the two suspects to get together and synchronize their alibis, or whatever it was hardened criminals did when they had a few free moments together. He didn't want them to build up any hope by making some love and remembering they were human beings. Every time Roger was marched out for P.T. or to be interrogated he kept his eyes open, and every once in a while he saw her: sitting in the shade under guard, standing with her arms hanging limp at her sides, at a table in the mess hall eating slowly. Most of those times she seemed not to notice him, or else, more likely, she was a mirage, and if they had let him go toward her she would have disappeared the way palm trees did in a desert.

They never let him get close enough to talk to her, so the one time they were left alone for a little while he assumed that also was a conscious decision by Fretes. Maybe the idea was for Roger to see how it was with her and worry enough to break down and spill the secrets he didn't know. Or something.

It was like walking up to the edge of a cliff, looking down and seeing deep below you the only green valley you ever wanted to pitch your tent in. And then not being allowed to go camp there. They left them with a single grunt guard who scarcely spoke Spanish sitting at the same wood plank table outside the mess, after everyone else had eaten and left. The grunt's nickname was Halcón Negro. Black Hawk. He was a squatty, powerful Aymara from Patacamaya, a marshy flatlands place on the Altiplano with little single-lane dikes along which the campesinos' cattle and llamas migrated to graze. Halcón Negro was famous for sniffing out maceration pits; it was a gift of the Pachamama, who favored him. The UMOPAR never went on a helicopter raid without him. In camp, though, out of action, he was bored. Ten degrees cooler and he would have been restless. As it was he ignored Roger and Agnes completely. He leaned his rifle against the table, practiced twitching his face into weird, exaggerated expressions: intense, brief imitations of fear and anger and pride and joy that didn't go below the skin but were still impressive.

Roger had lost track of the days, but he had the feeling it might be Sunday. The Chapare weather felt like Sunday, at least. It had rained the night before, clearing the humidity from the air. The sky had that painful blue color that made you think about Easter eggs hidden in tall, soft grass somewhere and your first girl friend sleeping half naked on a blanket in the woods while you sat next to her looking head on at a red deer that had showed up to stare at you through the spring leaves. Not that anything like that had ever happened to Roger, but it could have, might have. Should have. His memory was not to be trusted. Sitting next to Agnes on the bench accounted for half the depression he felt. The other half he wasn't sure about. Behind them, behind the camp, the Chapare woods were loud with bugs and birds.

"They can't keep us much longer," he was telling her. "It's a game."

She was calm, the way Martin had said she was, and she was strong. But being a prisoner had done something to Agnes. Some necessary valuable fluid was gradually leaking out of her, a little more every day of their confinement, leaving her dull and indifferent.

"Agnes?"

She looked at him from farther away than he could stand. "What is it, Roger?"

"One of the Americans is okay. The quiet one, Martin. He's not a military hardhead. He explained it all to me."

He waited for her to ask him to explain it to her, but she seemed more interested in Halcón Negro's facial contortions than in listening to him.

"They're just jerking us around because we're here and we can't fight back. But they'll get tired of that and let us go. They have to. When they do, we'll go back to looking for your brother. For Jonathan. Okay?"

"Okay," she said quietly, but she was only putting him off.

"Are they hurting you, Agnes? Are they doing anything bad to you?"

She shook her head.

"Then what is it? What's going on?"

Halcón Negro had begun to make little musical noises to go with the facial expressions. He was a one-man band: percussion and slinky strings and something back deep in his throat that was like a French horn. (Roger wasn't really sure what a French horn sounded like, but he had an idea, and he liked the name because it made him think of French kissing, something the girl who pretended he was John Lennon used to be very big on.) Under different circumstances Black Hawk would have been worth watching.

"It's like," Agnes began dreamily, and Roger wondered whether they had given her some kind of drug to sedate her. Not likely. It was only from being cooped up, which was hard on a high-strung person like her who had no major sins or crimes to make up for, so what they were doing to her was a waste of punishment, and it had the effect of spacing her out. "It's like . . . like I've been cut off."

"Cut off from what?"

"From everything I knew."

"Well, you are."

She shook her head impatiently. He wasn't getting it. That bothered him, but he told himself it was only because he was out of practice. All he needed was to be around her again, and he would begin to understand her language.

"Not everything I knew, everything I am. Or that I was. I keep thinking about what Kelleher told us."

"Kelleher's a lunatic. He's been on the road too long. He doesn't have a thing worth saying to a person like you, Agnes."

"Remember Nebraska?"

He didn't remember Nebraska, didn't want to.

"He said after Vietnam he couldn't stand in a cornfield in Nebraska anymore. Something like that, anyway. And now I understand what he meant."

"You're letting all the shit get to you, Agnes. You're giving in to it.

Come on, please, don't." It was the first time he remembered begging anyone for anything.

"I sit on my bunk in that awful little room when it's dark, and it's as though. . . . I don't know. It's as though the world has stopped moving. And I play this little game that every time I breathe out, another piece of myself is exhaled and lost. So if they leave me long enough inside that room there won't be anything left to breathe."

"You're not the kind of person to let yourself go downhill like that, Agnes."

"I'm not?"

He told her she was not. Something in his voice must have alarmed Halcón Negro, who froze his face in a gesture of disgust, looked over at them suspiciously.

"I'm losing my discipline, Roger. That's something I never thought would happen, not to me."

"It's only because you don't have anybody to talk to."

"So your character is a function of your circumstances?"

"I don't follow you."

"I mean you can be a sterling, upright individual as long as you have an unthreatened middle-class existence. You wouldn't think of lying, and when the cashier gives you too much change you'll walk back inside the supermarket to return it to her even if you're in a hurry and it's only seven cents, and you don't eat or drink too much, and you're kind and generous to people, especially people who have less than you do. And when you go to bed at night you pull the covers up over your head and the feeling of being safe is real."

A different person would have been trembling. What Agnes did with her stress was turn it back in on herself, and the force of that made her body rigid. Roger felt helpless. He was.

"It'll only be a few more days," he lied. "Martin told me they're getting tired of us."

"Martin isn't here," she told him, which was probably true. He hadn't come by Roger's cell for a couple days. "If he was here he'd be talking to us."

The thought that the only sane and unmilitary man in the base camp had left, the only man who might stand up to Fretes if the Bolivian decided to get tougher on them, was not something Roger wanted to think about.

"You know what I can't tolerate, Roger?"

"What?"

It had to do with him. It didn't.

"I can't tolerate the possibility that the person I was—that plucky little woman with a rewarding career and a lifelong commitment to social service work, the woman who listened to Mozart every night before she went to sleep and never forgot to floss her teeth—that she was a fiction. She was an invention, and she only made sense in Greenfield, Massachusetts."

"For Crisssake, Agnes," he told her, "don't make what's happening to us into some kind of do-or-die adventure. You're taking yourself too goddamn serious. That's the only reason you think you might crack up."

He had gotten out of the habit of being mean on purpose to her. It felt good to bring a little ugliness back into their relationship; it felt clean, but it also scared him. She looked at him as if she couldn't believe he was capable of saying what he had just said to her. Her mouth was open, and he wished his tongue was inside it, exploring. She started laughing. Halcón Negro had given up practicing his nervous habits; he was watching them the way Bolivians watched a soccer game, all wrapped up in the action to see who was going to get the next goal. Then Agnes was through laughing because she was crying. Sobbing, really. It was the first time in his life Roger had needed that word, but it was the only word to describe the wet, rhythmic sound she was making.

"All I want," she told him, "all I want, Roger, is to find my brother. I've come this far, I've done this much, I have to find him. My father . . ."

"Would never forgive you . . ."

That made her angry, which he supposed was healthy, just then. "What do you know about my father? You couldn't even begin to imagine what my father is like. He's so far away from the life you live he wouldn't even recognize it. My father lives on a different planet, Roger, from the one you're on."

"All I'm saying is you're only doing this because of your father. I didn't say that made it bad, or you shouldn't do it, Agnes. Jesus, cut me some slack."

"Go away," she hissed at him. "Now, please. I don't want to see you right now." Her mouth was clamped closed; the words came out like thin little snakes of sound and bit him. The erection he was getting made no sense, but there it was, long and long lasting.

He would have obliged her anyway, gone away to his cell to meditate on how easy it was, really, for a person like him to fuck things up, but Black Hawk would have shot him in the back. He did as much as he could to help her out. He moved to another table and sat there listening to her sobbing and the noisy woods and the distant, cadenced shouts of a unit doing P.T. on the obstacle course until an UMOPAR escort came to march him away.

One thing about prison—about being locked up by people who had it in for you—was it made you seriously paranoid. In el Panóptico, the first few times Claude had come close trying to talk to him, when Roger was still new, and raw, and scared, he thought that the French doper was pumping him for some kind of information that he could sell to the troll guards. In exchange for what didn't make any difference. Maybe Claude's idea was to barter his way out before serving his full sentence, or maybe he just wanted free cigarettes. In Roger's paranoid state of mind the motive didn't make any difference; what mattered was not giving anything away. It turned out that Claude was the closest thing he had to a genuine friend all the time he was in jail in La Paz, and that proved the point he was making to himself: paranoia struck deep. Into his heart, or what was left of it, it did creep.

Otherwise how explain the fact that G.I. Joe showed up the same afternoon of the morning they let him get close to Agnes out at the mess hall? He was inviting Roger to a poker game. They were still trying, from the looks of things, to break him: in half, preferably, so that his secrets bled out into their tin cup. If he had any, he thought they must be red.

"I don't play poker," Roger told him. "I don't play cards, period."

"You can learn. It's not like you've got so many social engagements you can't work us into your social butterfly whirl. Besides, this is strictly a friendly game, gringos only."

"Fretes won't let me."

"Major Fretes gives his official UMOPAR antidrug fighting force blessing to this particular poker game. It's in the Bolivian national interest. It's been approved in advance by Underwriters Laboratories and the South American SPCA. You can trust me."

G.I. Joe was standing in Roger's doorway. The sun was at an angle low enough to catch his chunky silhouette, outlining his shape on the late afternoon air, which had an odd greenish cast to it. The light was thick and moldy, as though you would have to punch your way through the air to get anywhere. What he saw caused a reflex wish in Roger not to be there: in the base camp jail, in the Chapare, in Bolivia, in trouble that never went away, just got more complicated. For a minute he let himself wish he was three years old, sitting in some soft protector's lap. The protector would be a woman, and she would smell like lilacs and soap, and the only words she would whisper in his ear would be murmurs like shallow water running through innocent woods. No such. She wasn't there. He wasn't, either.

"I don't have any money," Roger said. It embarrassed him to admit that to a guy like G.I. Joe. It was another new way to go naked in public while people laughed into their hands making fun.

"You don't need to worry about any cash up front," the soldier told him, shaking his square red head slowly back and forth. "In this poker game you can get all the credit you need and then some."

"Not interested," Roger told him.

G.I. Joe went away, but Roger knew he had no choice.

Slopes were slippery. No such thing as Velcro strong enough to hold you fast to the safe side when your body and your brain wanted to go down. That was the original purpose of guardian angels, apparently, but Roger's angel had walked off the job years ago. He remembered hearing the crinkly noise its wings made going away mad. Bourbon was the problem.

He had never been much of a boozer. In the bad old days on the line in Flint, he and Danny sometimes got drunk together at the end of the shift, but that was only bad factory habits, and mostly beer. For Roger the main value of alcohol had been the texture it could give to a drug buzz. He liked variety, and the right amount of the right substances, mixed at the right time, sometimes produced peace, and wisdom. Temporarily, oh so, but better than the usual nothing.

"You ever hear of truth or dare?" G.I. Joe asked him.

A couple of Americans in sterile fatigues came to get him after the sun went down. He walked behind them like a tame dog on a leash. The way they swaggered in front of him gave Roger the impression that they were new in town. They had to strut whatever invisible stuff they thought they had, to keep off the Bolivian swamp monsters. They led him to the row of tents where the gringos slept.

In the light of a Coleman lantern, he saw in front of the longest tent a bunch of folding canvas chairs arranged around a low, collapsible table on which there was a deck of cards, a bottle of Wild Turkey, and one glass. How many times could the same person be executed?

"What we're playing tonight is like truth or dare, only it's different. It's called truth or bourbon. Neat, huh? You want me to explain the rules?"

"No."

The soldier shrugged. "You ever hear of something called enlightened self-interest? You'll probably make out better if you know the rules."

Troll-less. That was the strange sensation Roger was brushing up against. There wasn't a Bolivian within spitting distance. He was surrounded by Yankee patriots. It was like crossing another border into a country you remembered having escaped from way back when, and your relief at getting free.

Truth or bourbon turned out to be a game for two players only. One of them had to be a raving military fanatic. The other one had to be a stone cowboy with limited options. Straight five-card draw poker, nothing wild. Bets and raises were done with matchsticks. If Roger won the hand, they gave him a double shot of Wild Turkey, straight up and jungle temp. If G.I. Joe won the hand, Roger had to answer his question with truth, which they were thinking was secret, and valuable, and what they wanted to know. So much for military intelligence.

Roger won the first hand with the pair of jacks he was dealt. He thought about tossing one of them so he would lose, but a competitive instinct he was unfamiliar with made him hang on to the pair hoping for a third jack from the draw, which he didn't need against G.I. Joe's king-high nothing. One of the drug soldiers watching poured at least a double slug of the Wild Turkey, brought the glass up to Roger's lips in a hurry with the flourish of an executioner who liked his work.

"Easy, Marlon," G.I. Joe told him, "give the guy a chance to catch his breath. He'll drink what he won when he's good and ready. This is a friendly game, remember?"

He was right. Roger drank. It burned going down the way a person's first ever drink of whiskey burned, scalding his throat and making his gorge rise and causing his body to understand its own mortality in an intimate and totally convincing way. But by the time it trickled down into his stomach the vapors were making him feel good. It was like being rubbed in a sensitive place by somebody with just the right seductive touch.

"He's a natural-born juicer," somebody said, and everybody laughed in the dirty, guilty way jocks in locker rooms laughed. At least nobody had a towel to snap at his butt.

It was pathetic if they thought their plan was going to trick him into cooperating. Maybe they didn't, but they acted as if they believed he was blindly on his way to some kind of major truth binge with their bourbon taking the place of sodium pentathol or lysergic-whatever-the-d-was-acid that the master spies used to make their victims confess their classified info. So it was something else that made Roger react the way he did. He was tired of being patient, of playing the idiotic back-and-forth game he was playing every day with Major Fretes. One part at least of his interior watching self realized that he might spend the rest of the drug war as a prisoner in the Chapare, and that might be a hundred years, time he didn't want to give away to anybody. All the bourbon did was lubricate the slide, which he took because it made him feel good to take it and because Agnes's anger from the afternoon was curdling something sweet he had needed. He could not handle being abandoned.

He won the second hand with even less, a pair of fours that beat G.I. Joe's second round of nothing. "Fuck you," he told the soldier who passed him the second glassful of Wild Turkey. He was smiling when he said it; he felt the stiffness in his face.

"Careful, vermin breath," the guy came back at him, "you ain't in any position to get lippy with us."

Hard to see his face in the shadowed dark, but Roger heard the ignorant aggression illuminate his voice, which sounded like Jersey City on its day off. The bourbon released him, and when he finally lost the third hand—G.I. Joe made a big, noisy deal out of three queens, two of which he picked up in the draw—Roger was ready to talk.

"What do you know about el Grán Moxo?" G.I. Joe asked him, shuffling the cards over and over again like the hustler in a fancy vest in a Western. Somebody brought out round blue cardboard cans of pretzels and French onion dip in tins, which seemed as out of place in the

Chapare as the drug agents themselves, and Roger ate a small handful of undipped pretzels before he opened his mouth to answer. The taste brought back memories of junk food, and money in his pockets to buy it. Danny, he was sure, would not be able to picture much of this, although maybe Roger wasn't giving his friend enough credit.

"The Grán Moxo is the biggest trafficker in cocaine paste in Bolivia. His operation is as big as some of the major Peruvian operations. He's an albino, and he hates gringos."

"Tell us something we don't already know. Who sent the magician down here to Bolilandia? What's the name of his contact back home?"

You dove for the feeling of impact, because shock was a good thing in itself, better than sleep and most other common forms of satisfaction.

"Pure luck," he told them. His reluctance was an act, one of his better ones. Too dangerous to play himself, that naked nothing.

"What do you mean luck?"

He shrugged. "The magician was working at a restaurant in Miami. He's pretty good. Good enough to make a living at it. One night he was performing for this big noisy table full of rich greasy creeps from south of the border. They were trying to prove something, drinking champagne out of the women's shoes and burning twenty-dollar bills to light their Cuban cigars and bossing their waiter around. The waiter was this rabbity gay guy from Cleveland with AIDS. At the time, nobody except the magician knew he had it. Anyway the guy had something more important on his mind than taking a load of shit from a bunch of macho Latino businessmen with hairy chests and gold watches. Once they saw he was gay they rode his ass real hard."

"Where the fuck you going with this particular song and dance, pardner?" G.I. Joe wanted to know. The troops were grumbling; Roger wasn't sure what it was that was bothering them.

"Nowhere," he told him, glad to take a break.

So they played another hand, which Roger won too easily. G.I. Joe was a lousy poker player. He discarded decent hands thinking he was going to draw into something better but almost never did. More bourbon, more pretzels, more shuffled hands, more locker room muttering from the rest of G.I. Joe's unit, who were bored because all they got to do was watch. More truth, the kind of truth you had to make up for it to be real but once you did you saw that it was something that should have happened all along, had been happening in a place you didn't recognize.

"El Moxo Grande was at the table," Roger told them after he lost another hand.

"Don't bullshit us," somebody warned him.

"He was traveling on a Chilean passport. Undercover, isn't that what you guys call it when you do that?"

"Drink." More bourbon, more truth.

"I told you. The tableful of businessmen el Moxo was with were getting down on their gay waiter pretty bad. The manager of the restaurant saw what was going on, but he didn't want to piss off his customers and he didn't like the waiter anyway so he let him eat their macho shit all night. The guy couldn't walk away from the job because he didn't think he was going to get another one, not once the AIDS started showing on him, I mean, his hair falling out and all that. He needed to keep his health insurance. The magician felt sorry for him, I think is what happened. He did his best tricks trying to distract the fuckers. Like I say, he's pretty good. Which for some reason got el Moxo Grande interested in him. Next thing you know there's the three of them up on the roof of the restaurant looking out at the Miami night life and the palm trees and smoking joints and talking about magic. The gay waiter said he only believed in black magic: True love turns you into a disease. De la Rocha said Watch us! Down in Bolivia we've got the most powerful white magic in the history of the human race. Give us a few more years. We're going to sprinkle white powder all over North America and make the whole goddamn empire disappear. Poof, just like that." Roger snapped his fingers. The bourbon in him sloshed and settled. No more patience.

They were ticked, which must have been what Roger had been wanting, been working for.

"You know something?" G.I. Joe told him. He was on his feet, hands planted on the table, his face up against Roger's face, his breath smelling like onion dip and pretzels and something more insidious not worth naming. "You're so full of shit there's not enough room inside to stuff any more fecal waste. You're the kind of individual that's dragging our society down into the gutter."

"He's a frigging animal, he's a freak. We ought to put him in a cage for the show," someone behind him said.

Roger was drunk but not drunk enough to ask them What show? He listened, his head wobbling on his neck, and figured out that somebody called the Administrator of the Drug Enforcement Administration was coming in on a helicopter with the American ambassador and a bunch of bigshots from Washington and some Bolivian cabinet ministers. They were going to inspect the base camp, give a pep talk to the troops, then burn a big load of paste the UMOPAR had seized the week before.

"It's what they call a photo opportunity," G.I. Joe explained. He had been drinking some of his own truth serum, and his tongue was looser than it usually was. "It's a kick. They bring in reporters and photographers on their own special helo, and then two days later you see a picture on the front page of your hometown newspaper with the DEA Administrator burning drugs in Bolivia and there's a headline that says something like TROOPS BUST COKE TRAFFICKERS IN THE CHAPARE—DRUG WAR FINAL OFFENSIVE LAUNCHED, DEA CHIEF SAYS."

Listening as the poker game fell apart and everybody started mixing bourbon and beer and talking cheap and greasy, Roger got the impression that the presence of gringo prisoners while the Washington bigshots were touring the camp was going to be a problem.

"Put him in a fucking cage," the guy who'd had the original idea was insisting. Roger couldn't see his face in the darkness, didn't want to. The voice was enough. The face it was coming out of had to be even uglier. "Let those fucking firemen from Washington see the ass end of the cocaine feeding chain."

"They won't even know they're around, if we keep them inside," somebody else told him.

But the problem with that, evidently, was the possibility that the Administrator would decide to make a sudden snap inspection.

"He's been known to do it," G.I. Joe agreed, "and he's got the right. Picture this: The head of the DEA opens a door with one of those made-for-TV smiles on his face, cameras rolling right behind him, and he trips over a gringo scumbag that's laying chained to the wall with UMOPAR whip marks on his back."

"The cage."

"Fuck you, you ignorant bastard," Roger said suddenly into the darkness. This time no smile, no stiff face. Amazing that you could be this calm when you were that drunk. Amazing that you could give away, just like that, all the patience you'd worked to acquire and all the good your patience gave you. Amazing that you could get this angry at the bad guys, after all these years of being manhandled by them, as though you were seeing them in action for the first time and couldn't quite believe how bad they really were.

"What'd you say, pal?"

"I said fuck you and your dog-faced, cock-sucking, dick-loving mother the whore, you ignorant bastard." That was maybe the one good thing that had come out of working on the line in Flint. Some of that stuff could be useful, if you really needed to get in trouble, which apparently he did.

This also was a place he had been to a few times before, back at home, traveling around, around: undefended in the center of a circle of muscle-bound goons who thought they were the good guys, thought the good guys owned the right to violence, thought they could fix or save the world if they smacked the bad guys hard enough, often enough, and they had an arrest warrant. Didn't make any difference that they had the whole thing back-aswards.

He didn't know whether the guy who hit him first was the one he had called an ignorant bastard but he hoped, for some reason, that it was he. Before he absolutely had to he hit the ground, rolled himself into a ball that exposed as few of the tender places as possible. Which meant his backbone was vulnerable and got the shit kicked out of it by U.S.-manufactured drug police boots. The fear made the actual pain worse than it had to be, but the pain on its own was considerable.

I lost, Roger admitted to himself. He was being kicked. Fretes had outlasted him. Not that it was a fair contest, since Fretes had everything and everybody on his side, even Agnes, in a way. He was not as drunk as he would have expected to be, drinking that much Wild Turkey. It was only truth or bourbon, only a game. They should have given him some points for creativity.

Roger gave G.I. Joe the credit he deserved for stopping the stomp as fast as he did, before any major damage was done to the stone cowboy. That was all he bothered to remember about the rest of the night, except being dragged back to his cell and somebody, maybe two of them, giving him another ration of shit before they walked away satisfied with the feeling that they had done the morally correct thing in police-brutalizing and abusing him.

In his cell there was somebody talking. Turned out it was Roger himself. Not talking, exactly. More like mumbling: semi-words, half-thoughts, little dripping clots of feeling aimed unconsciously at the empty space God inhabited. Out there, the wild black yonder. Off we go. God, to judge from the way it all got swallowed, was like a kind of suction pump. Sucked everything you had out of you and wanted more, wanted what you didn't have to give. And even then you didn't know whether you were going to get an answer. Probably not. Not. A more disciplined person would have been able to stay awake to see. Not Roger. He felt his mind collapse. His body had already collapsed. Some other time. He slept with the sensation of being watched over, but only in his dream did he realize that the one watching him was la Pachamama, and that she really cared about him. As an actual individual, somebody with a face.

The morning was torture. Nobody brought him anything to eat or drink. He could feel the whiskey floating like pond scum on the surface of his bloodstream, and the small of his back was badly bruised where somebody's boot had nailed him hard. The sweat on his skin, on all of it, was like the sweat that used to leak out when he got sick in el Panóptico. He kept expecting Fretes himself to show up, for some reason, maybe to haul him back to prison in La Paz for failing to show the proper respect for all those uniformed citizens of the Yankee empire who were cooperating with the troll forces deployed to win the drug war. What he didn't expect was Martin.

"You're an idiot," Martin told Roger, but he already knew that.

"It happened."

"Because you made it happen. Because you wanted it to happen. Because you decided you didn't want to ride it out a little longer. Now they're ticked off in a personal way at you, Roger. Before last night, you had some kind of sympathy factor working in your favor. They didn't particularly like you, because they don't appreciate your style, but you're an American, and we're all in this place together, and that bought you some safety even if you didn't know it. Now they hate you, which I assume is what you wanted all along."

"So you decided to come by and bang on my head a little more. When did you get back? Where did you go? Can you get me an aspirin and a glass of water? Who are you, Martin?"

"I came by to tell you to keep quiet and cooperate when I show up this afternoon. No questions, no noise, nothing. You follow me? You have to be inert, completely inert."

"What's that mean?"

"Don't take any of this as a joke. Just spend the rest of the morning imagining what it would be like to be a duffel bag. Work at it. Can you do that?"

"I can do it."

No use pushing him for more than he was willing to say.

So Roger spent the rest of the morning and the early hours of the afternoon pretending to be a duffel bag, which was not as hard as a person might think it was going to be. Eventually a UMOPAR grunt showed up with some stale rolls, hard on the outside and chalky, crumbly on the inside, a mugful of coffee, and a banana with only one bad spot, which made the world seem like a habitable place again. God would not speak to duffel bags. They let Roger outside to wash his face in a bucket of clean water, and he shaved, something he had only done once every couple weeks for as long as he had been in Bolivia. He didn't want a beard, really, but shaving required looking in a mirror, which had consistently been a negative experience for as far back as he could remember.

What Martin came back to play was a kind of a shell game: hide Agnes and Roger under baskets and keep moving the baskets until people got so confused they would quit looking if they ever started. He marched them to an undecorated office Roger hadn't been inside before, then pointed the way out a back door toward a tent with the flap door snapped open. Where they stayed, imitating male and female duffel bags, until a Bolivian in an unusual uniform stepped inside, put his finger to his lips, then led them out along the perimeter of the camp behind the mess hall. Around to the motor pool, where a jeep was parked with the motor running, rear door swung open. Roger and Agnes climbed into the back, lay like accomplished duffel bags, let the Bolivian and a driver pile real duffel bags and boxes of supplies and a muddy spare tire on the tarp with which the pile of gear and gringos was covered.

Hard to calculate how long they lay there sweating under the tarp. It felt like hours, but maybe it was only half an hour. The angle at which Roger was wedged caused one hand to come in contact with Agnes's waist. The touch was what kept him alive. He got hard, and his eyes teared slowly, and his tongue got dry, and the tarp held in all the sick sweat that came out on his body. But he was able to move his hand around just enough to get past her shirt, get his hand on the skin itself, and the touch anchored him inside a darkness that would otherwise have been intolerable. Then the jeep started moving.

Out the front gate. Roger had to guess the actual moment when the ass end of the vehicle was past the gate, out of the camp, but he knew. That little, that much, he knew. How could you not know?

The jeep had no suspension to speak of. Riding stretched out in it the way they were was almost like being dragged down the road. He was happy to be dragged. It hurt, it lulled, it dulled him. He waited for Agnes to say something to him—it was safe, had to be—but she said nothing. She allowed his hand to stay clamped close to her waist, which was better than conversation.

He heard the helicopter before the jeep came to a stop. Heard the preoccupied, businesslike sound of men shouting in Spanish all the important technical things they needed to say to get the machine off the ground. Felt the spare tire and the other camouflaging gear being lifted off them. They came out from under the sweaty tarp like sin giving itself up to final goodness.

Martin was waving them toward the helicopter. They hunched instinctively away from the engine noise, the whooshing wind of the rotors, crawled through the door and let men in black, bug-shaped helmets strap them into canvas seats. Up. Away. Martin, sitting across from both of them, smiled tranquilly. Not his first time in a helicopter. He was the kind of guy who always got away.

Roger knew they were not flying to Cochabamba because they didn't climb. The helicopter flew straight and level across long green miles of Chapare coca, Chapare wild woods. Past thatch-roofed shacks in the raggedy yards of which troll planters lifted their heads and prayed it wasn't a raid, and if it was a raid that the UMOPAR troops and *la DEA* wouldn't think their little patch of plenty was worth the trouble of dropping down to destroy. Every once in a while they passed over a maceration pit, a briefly visible blur below them, just ugly gashes in the ground. From one of them, Roger noticed, the runoff of chemicals had burned a brown stream in the earth down to a small creek, a stain that was like evidence, for some reason, the proof of something for which he had no adequate words.

They landed at the military airport in Santa Cruz. Martin handed two fifty-dollar bills to Agnes. "This is all I've got on me at the moment," he told her.

Surrounded by busy soldiers on the tarmac, which steamed in the late afternoon heat as though it would bubble and melt, Agnes was falling apart. As the rotors wound slowly down she told Martin thank you, wiped her face the way a little girl would when she forgot her handkerchief. Martin took her arm, walked them both off the airfield, through the ground floor of the control tower, out to the edge of civilian territory. The great thing was nobody caring enough about them to watch, or even to notice. It was like liberation itself, the actual event you thought you were only going to live in a dream.

Martin kissed Agnes's cheek, shook Roger's hand. Roger could not remember the last time he had seriously shaken hands with anyone. Doing it now embarrassed him. Even though he had come out of the Chapare in a helicopter, Martin looked clean, cool, competent. If anybody owned him you couldn't tell by looking at the man. Dark sunglasses kept his eyes private. Out of his chino pockets had come a hundred American dollars, a miracle as startling and necessary, just then, as Jesus' loaves and fishes. Roger, by contrast, was a duffel bag that sweated. He had come out from under a tarp the way slugs came out from under rocks.

"If you could say one thing to your brother Jonathan," Martin asked Agnes, "what would it be?"

She looked at him, waiting for the punch line. Roger wished she would quit crying. "Where is my brother, Martin?"

He looked at her for a long time. Martin was the kind of guy you could never force to say a word he didn't want to say. In Vietnam with bamboo shoots shoved up his butt he'd still look at you with the same expression of calm control, and he wouldn't open his mouth.

A taxi heading for the city came by, slowed hoping for a fare, gave up and drove off honking angrily, disappointed. He asked her again what she would tell the magician if she had the chance.

"I'd tell him," Agnes finally decided, "to make his peace."

"Hey," Martin said, making more noise than had to be made. But he was being phony for a good reason. "Enjoy Santa Cruz. It's the town that cocaine built. My advice is you should go to Los Tajibos and rest up. It's the best hotel in town. I recommend it to all my friends."

Then he was gone, and Agnes herself flagged down the taxi that took them into Santa Cruz. No more Chapare. Being out of it, for Roger, was like being alive again. No more. All he needed now, he told himself, was a way to Flint. Just that. Simple. In the backseat of the taxi he made sure his leg touched Agnes's leg all the way into the city.

SIX

The first day in Los Tajibos Hotel in Santa Cruz Agnes called their room a way station, which meant she knew it wasn't going to last. As way stations went, though, this one was highly tolerable. The luxury of the place was like downing too many cheeseburgers too fast after a month of roots and berries in the woods. They had one of those brown mini-refrigerators in their room, and inside the refrigerator there were soft drinks and gaseous water and little bottles of brand-name booze and packages of peanuts and candy bars. Every morning an invisible Bolivian maid came in and changed their sheets while they ate a tropical breakfast outside under awnings that protected them from the morning sun, which was friendlier than it had been in the Chapare. Roger couldn't get enough of the sliced pineapple, and the mangos, and the sectioned grapefruits, and the butter that slid through his unaccustomed system, and the coffee that didn't stop coming until you wanted it to stop.

They wound up in Los Tajibos because Martin had said the name, and when they got off the helicopter they were too dazed to think two connectable thoughts on their own. In the lobby no one looked twice at Agnes, who looked like the normal kind of person you would find in a place like Los Tajibos even though she and her clothes were both worn out. She had learned some things in the Chapare, one of which was not to give herself away. The clerk at the desk, who spoke pretty good English, signed them both into the hotel under her name.

"How will you be paying for that?" the clerk asked Roger. "Cash, credit card, or traveler's checks?"

"Cash," Agnes answered for him, and Roger wondered what cash.

Inside the room, Agnes slept the way Roger remembered sleeping his second night in el Panóptico, when he realized he was as close to home as he was going to get for the foreseeable future. He sat in a chair in a corner of the room and watched her diaphragm go up and down, trying to make the pace of his own breathing match hers. Outside, over the air conditioned hum he heard the party sounds of Brazilian tourists frolicking in the gigantic swimming pool.

Roger had seen people like them before, though not up close. They were beasts not of burden but of pleasure. They would be drinking piss-colored Scotch, the ice melting fast in the heat, and wishing, behind all that neighborly noise they were making in each other's slap-happy faces, that they could fuck each other's wives just once. Or maybe twice. Twice, or else two different women one time each, and then they could go back to the rest of their lives content and willing to work like blind, deaf, and dumb dogs of industry to make the big money they all needed to afford these high-cholesterol vacations.

Being in that cocoon of a room—buffed white walls and a tame picture of a parrot with a hooked orange beak, and air that licked your skin cool while the unprotected world out there was still murderously hot, full of bugs that bit, and snakes that spit poison into your bloodstream if you didn't watch where you put your foot down in the uncuttable weeds, and resentful trolls who thought all gringos were decadent capitalists and so any amount of shit you dumped on them was holy revenge and more than justified, it was settling a historical score—was as good as Quaaludes after all the time they were stuck in the Chapare. What cash? he wondered. Not that he cared, not all that much. They could slide out of Los Tajibos anytime they had to. They could do a disappearing act as good as anything Flame the magician had in his bag of evil tricks.

He must have slept, because there she was, sitting up on the bed, her legs crossed, the muscles (or ligaments or rubber bands or whatever they were) of her throat stretched tight as she cocked her head to one side, looking out the window. The late afternoon sun coming back at her lit her up, showed the exhaustion, like beauty on a rack. The fabric of her white blouse was worn thin after their time in the Chapare. It took Roger a few minutes to realize that what was keeping him in his chair in the corner of the room was an erection the size of Mt. Illimani.

"Why don't you call room service?" she asked him.

What cash? He hesitated.

"Tell them we want yogurt, and peaches, and buttered toast with marmalade—strawberry marmalade—and hot tea with lemon and sugar, and two bars of chocolate. Large."

"They're not going to have peaches here, not fresh ones."

But Los Tajibos also had fresh peaches. They were almost as big as grapefruits, and the waiter who brought them everything Agnes asked for on a pewter tray was courteous, and not curious or offensive, and his black Bolivian eyes were as gentle and penetrating as Esencia's, who was still dead. Roger signed the bill he handed him, added ten percent because that was what you did in a place like this. Maybe ten percent wasn't enough, but it didn't matter because they had no money anyway, so the tip he scribbled on the bill was one of those thoughts that counted.

It was like a dream, except in dreams there was always something with horns and a snout lurking offstage that threatened to pull you out of the pleasure you were experiencing, the satisfaction you were sucking down in your private action-packed adventure. But on the big bed under the startled eye of the unrealistic parrot there was nothing, just then, to get in the way of the food—luxury itself—and letting their exhaustion out without a leash, and feeling with their tired eyes the unfiltered sunlight raining at a slant through the single window, and soft inoffensive music on the radio, and the certainty that nobody like Major Fretes was going to come barreling through the door to haul them back into custody, and the pleasant little miracle of their bodies next to each other. Not touching, but close enough that the heat radiating from Agnes's met and mingled in midair with the heat from Roger's before either had a chance to cool.

Afterward, enough energy to lift the tray from the bed, lay it on the floor. Just that much and no more. They slept again, beyond hard, beyond deep, down past the colorful middle levels where dreams hatched and you could still be surprised and terrified, down to the black floor. Except that it wasn't a floor, it was a bottom in which you stayed suspended and free, untouched and untouching, healing if that was what you required.

Love happened, finally, because neither of them was responsible. If there was a first move that needed making, impossible to know who made it. This was pure romance but temporarily acceptable to the stone cowboy, who had the rough equivalent of an open mind after so much traveling and was willing to believe that pretty much anything could happen, to pretty much anybody. Better to think that their sleep cycles coincided, so that they pushed off, lifted up from the black bottom of sleep at the same time, woke together and moved toward each other in the Santa Cruz night at exactly the same instant, as if . . . But there was no as if, because this was the real and only thing.

They were unbuttoning each other's shirts, pulling arms out of sleeves. She kissed him so hard he thought his lips were going to bruise, and he was kissing her back just as hard. Her tongue in his mouth was pointed, sharp, just like Agnes herself asking probing questions he couldn't possibly have an answer to. His own tongue, he thought, must feel flat and thick to her. It was the tongue of a person who lacked all kinds of words. Her spit leaked into his mouth; the foreign salt-water taste stimulated his own saliva to run. After a while she began rocking, her mouth still inside his, her body leaned hard up against his, her hand brushing the little bit of hair on his chest.

One of the things he had forgotten in the past several hundred years of unrewarded solitude was how a woman's breasts could swell up when she made love. Agnes would not stop rocking. It was something in her whole body, and whatever was there comforted and excited him at the same time. He put the palms of his hands on her nipples, brushed them until both nipples were standing up, then took them between his thumb and a finger and rolled the hard flesh he felt. This had something to do with him, had to have. Amazing.

Neither of them was saying anything, which was all right with Roger. He thought of the loud and desperate sounds he sometimes woke to in el Panóptico when lovers of all descriptions let what they were feeling come out through their mouths. This was different, and it was better. It was his, private as a person's most demanding need.

Eventually they helped each other slide out of their jeans, then their Chapare-rotted underwear, which they tossed onto the floor. Then their hands started slowly asking each other questions. Roger's questions were simple ones that mostly had to do with remembering. He thought maybe Agnes's did, too, though he didn't know about that part of her life, didn't need to know or want to. What his hands remembered was feeling. Amazing that you could forget; that your hands, which had their own memory, under the skin, could also forget. Not what this was like; your mind was always remembering, always reinventing what it felt like. What they remembered, though, was not what it was like; it was the feeling itself. Touching, his hands moving slowly around the inside of her thighs remembered, reminded the rest of him that this was why you had hands, and thighs, and spit in your mouth, and a cord running up into your brain: to feel, this.

"Agnes," he said once. She must have understood it wasn't any kind of question, anything that needed response.

When their hands had answered all the questions for their curious pleasure, she rolled him gently, nurselike, onto his back, climbed onto him. He wished, for an instant, that he could see her: the way her breasts looked, the angle at which she held her head, whether her eyes were open or closed, her tongue inside her mouth or out. But the fact was he didn't need that sort of seeing. What he needed was what he had. For the longest time, long enough that you couldn't notch it on any stick, they rocked together in the air-conditioned dark.

She made noises when she was coming, human noises that were kind of like barking but made more sense. Otherwise he might not have been able to open his own mouth and say whatever it was he said, which was probably just his own equivalent of the barking so she took it for what it was worth, which was, at the moment, enough.

He didn't remember falling asleep again afterward. They had to, though; he understood that much psychology. Nothing to say and too much to contemplate.

In the morning water dribbling on his penis woke him.

"Clean," she said. With the wet end of a towel she was slowly swabbing down his chest, his belly, his penis, which was mountain size again and unfamiliarly sore. She was naked, and all her many guards were down, and the sleep she was coming out of was still around her head like a halo protecting her from thinking any dangerous thoughts like, The man in my bed is a stone cowboy and a loser. He's a convicted liar and a troll hater, not the kind of man I should be sleeping with.

He took her breasts in his hands, looked at her lips to see whether they were bruised. His own, he felt with his tongue, were puffy.

"Clean," he told her.

Los Tajibos also had a shower with plenty of hot water, and pressure in the pipes driving it down in a needle spray that massaged your back, and a tub long enough to lay your body down into, and soap that smelled like civilization and actually lathered, and colorful little tubes of shampoo with the hotel name printed on them. They made themselves clean before they made love again.

It was different, being able to see. Sometimes their eyes locked onto each other and he recognized that she was a stranger, and that he was a stranger to her, and the shock of seeing that was almost enough but not quite for them to look away. Sometimes her eyes squinched closed, and he took it as a compliment that she felt free enough to concentrate on what she was feeling to ignore him. When her eyes closed he watched her face, watched a line of sweat appear on her forehead at the hairline, beads of concentration, watched the cords in her neck go taut and slack again as she moved her head in one direction or another. He thought he could see faint pink marks on her breasts, fine lines of passion, where his hands had touched them the night before. Maybe. He wondered if she hurt, and what that particular kind of hurt would feel like. She was a stranger, and she was inviting him in. Amazing.

He thought his luck was changing. Once when Agnes was out by herself taking a walk through the city, Roger sat at the side of the swimming pool disguised as a normal vacationing-type human being, a gringo with good credit and time to get sunburned, and thought about luck. Not just his own but luck in general, anybody's luck, the luck of the draw. If anything was possible, then at one time or another probably everything that could happen was going to happen to somebody. Which meant, when it came to luck, that there were all kinds: people who were born lucky and died that way, peacefully in their sleep after receiving the Nobel Prize for inventing a cure for cockroaches. But there also had to be people who never got a single break, never got what Roger was getting, which was a breather in a sheltered, peaceful place in the tropics with a woman who had enough imagination to love him. Temporarily, anyway; with her body and—this was the mysterious and hard-to-explain part—with her mind.

Poolside with his shirt off to catch the available rays, he watched three thin, sexy women in bikinis wag their beautiful asses in the pool, their arms out flat like unfeathered wings resting on the sides of the pool. They were all tanned the same way, and their sun-buttered butts were identical, and the tinkly Spanish sounds coming out of their mouths were so alike you couldn't tell them apart, not sound not sense. On the edge of the pool in front of them were three identical glasses of something expensive and fruity with colored straws and ice and those ridiculous paper umbrellas jabbed into hunks of lime.

Roger watched the women for a long time. He recognized the men coming to claim them before they were out the door. Gold and muscle, dark sunglasses and careful mustaches, money and sweet, sweet aftershave. They walked over to the women, who tinkled their expensive noises up at them out of lips that pouted and made fun of them at the same time.

A waiter in a white jacket shucked his way over to take the men's drink orders. In the heat the poor sucker must be sweating up a storm, but part of the training for waiters in a place like Los Tajibos was how not to sweat in a visible manner that might offend the guests. With a little practice, they got to the point that no telltale water marks stained their uniforms, which relieved everybody concerned including the waiters themselves, who thought something was wrong with their bodies, the way they leaked. Behind the people at the pool, a bunch of trolls in uniforms like Harold Handyman outfits brushed the grass, killed unacceptable weeds, watered banks of flowers that cost more than the Bolivian minimum wage for a month.

That was the way the luck was distributed at that particular time in the history of Bolivia, which had more in common with the history of the rest of the planet than Roger liked to recognize. What got to him, watching the women's buttery rich asses and the men's cocky cool, was the way they totally tuned out everybody around them. They had their own planet, and no room for ugly people on it. Actually it wasn't a bad place to visit if you had plenty of money and could appreciate what it did to the women: the way they talked, the way they dressed, the confident way they came at the men. But next to them, behind them, under them, all those waiters and workers, people with tools and brooms and hoses in their hands: invisible, as in ghosts. They had their own planet, too, but it wasn't a place tourists were dying to get to. What you needed to do if you were going to be a rich person in a place like Bolivia was learn how not to see certain things. You fixed your eyes on the easy pretty, the pretty easy.

Roger had been out of el Panóptico long enough to admit that the prison did him some good. Not that he would go near the place again, if he had any choice, but it had turned out to be a highly educational experience. It had to do with what you couldn't help seeing.

The Bolivians don't really want democracy, Claude told him once. He was arguing with the resident political nerd, who got drunk on his pallet the day he found out he had the clap. He drank a bottle of Singani by himself, then took out after all the foreigners in earshot, lecturing them on how come they were never going to understand Bolivia; you had to be one to see one.

According to Claude, the trolls on top of the big mountain had no reason to want democracy, which meant they'd have to wash their own dishes, shine their own boots, water their own imported grass. And the ones below them in the heap, which was everybody else, their brains were stuffed so full of superstition, so weak from malnutrition, that they thought up was down, hell was heaven, black was white. Democracy, Claude told Roger after the nerd had run out of gas and gone to puke in private, was for democrats.

Roger didn't particularly care what happened to Bolivia, at least not once the country uncurled its claws and let him go. When he was president of the USA he was going to send down a specially trained CIA hit squad to rescue a few people: Gregorio, and all of Esencia's family including her father Don Serapio, and Doña Inocencia, and Eloy the lumberman's wife. He would put them all on pensions but make them do some kind of work for the money they drew. They'd be happier working anyway. Serapio could work in the garden at the White House, which would be a good deal for the American taxpayer since the hard-luck Bolivian leaf grower could knock down all the grass in the yard with his machete, no need to spend money on gas for a lawn mower.

Meanwhile Roger's varsity scientists would be working on an ecological bomb big enough to wipe out everybody with a Bolivian passport but leave the mountains standing, the fish smiling in the rivers, the trees healthy in the woods. Still, free now and reasonably alert, he couldn't help seeing what was there in front of his eyes: rich Bolivians blind and pampered next to poor Bolivians locked into some kind of permanent daze, too beat from too much work to put two and two together and come up with revolution.

With an effort he looked away from the row of bikini'd butts. There was another woman coming down the covered corridor between the reception desk and the pool area. Something light and sexy in her legs. She wasn't bouncing, exactly, but the adult equivalent was there. Her light white sundress hung on her hips. She was smiling in his direction. At him, actually. It was Agnes.

"Do you like it?" she wanted to know, meaning the dress. "I bought something for you, too." She handed over a package tied with twine.

Swimming trunks, blue with a red racing stripe like Macdougal's Toyota 4-Runner. And sandals, and a T-shirt with a macaw on the pocket and SANTA CRUZ DE LA SIERRA below the bird in tropical letters.

"If you're going to live a life of leisure you have to look the part, Roger."

The hundred bucks from Martin wasn't going to last forever. He appreciated the gesture (or was she embarrassed to sit down in a place like this one with a stone cowboy?), but it would have been smarter to invest the money in token payments that would stretch out their stay at the hotel.

"Agnes."

"You don't like them. Is it the color? Are they too jazzy?"

"I like them."

"Then what?"

"The money," he explained. Amazing. There they were in palm tree paradise, the sun was shining, and they were on the ugly edge of an argument over money. Like, say, Danny and his wife Rhonda on a Friday night after payday when Danny came rolling in plastered because he drank up money that was supposed to do other things: buy food, and shoes for the crumb snatchers, and an oil change for the car, which was overdue and when it threw a rod it was going to be Danny's fault. Amazing.

But a slow smile was spreading across Agnes's face as she understood something Roger did not. She sat down, called a waiter over. "Tell him we want papaya juice," she ordered Roger.

"They don't have papaya juice."

"Tell him. With lots of ice, and some strawberries on a plate."

The waiter wrote down papaya juice with lots of ice and some strawberries. On a plate.

"You're worrying about that money Martin gave us, aren't you?"

He was.

"It's gone."

He had guessed that much.

"I called a friend of mine at home," she told him, "the other day while you were taking a nap. I didn't tell you. Actually she's kind of a cousin. She told me they fired me at work. Not maliciously or anything, but they had to have somebody there, and they never heard a word from me. I don't hold it against them. In their position I would have done the same thing."

"And that's what's making you happy?"

"What's making me happy is the fact that my cousin had my bank wire me some money. All the way to Bolivia, to Los Tajibos Hotel."

Money in the bank. He recognized the failing for what it was, but there was no getting past it: Here he was: sunk low in a fancy lounge chair, poolside at a dream hotel, in the company of a woman in a white sundress who had money in the bank and enough independent judgment to overlook his shortcomings. It was the situation, and thinking about all that, that gave him the hard-on. They went back to their room and made love that was painful, the satisfaction was so big and round and hard to get out. And Roger shaved.

He had been shaving a lot lately, almost every day. This time, standing shirtless in his new swimming trunks in front of the mirror in the white-walled bathroom, razor in hand, he panicked. The person in the mirror was nobody he recognized; he had no right at all to be inhabiting Roger's body, which no longer felt like his own.

For a long time, the shaving cream drying out on his unfamiliar face, Agnes in her underwear on the bed reading poetry out loud (she had found a paperback with what she claimed she needed, which was somebody named Auden), he stood there trying to face down the man in the mirror, who resembled a stone cowboy in no observable way whatsoever.

It wasn't like he had anything against the new way he looked, except for the shaving cuts, and that was mainly because the chlorine in the pool left every last nick ragged and tender. It was the difference itself, which he felt in his skin. Set him down in El Alto next door to Don Eloy's antiimperialist lumberyard and the trolls who worked for him might not even recognize him. . . .

Yes, they would, and they would laugh like Andean hyenas at the stone cowboy's attempt to impersonate a regular human being, any old gringo you'd pass in the street and envy for the money in his pockets, the ability he had to jump on airplanes and escape to places where life was less hard to live.

"What is it?" Agnes wanted to know. In the doorway she stood holding her new book of poetry up to her chest. The thin and delicate white straps of the new bra she had bought in Santa Cruz cut her shoulders neatly, beautifully in half. The shoulders were pink from the sun. Looking with hungry eyes, he realized it was the intimacy as much as the sex that went along with it that was making things blur.

"Something is wrong," she decided.

He told her nothing was wrong.

That night in bed he figured out a way, trial and error but mostly error, to tell her something she might want to know. "When I was a kid in Flint."

It was a salsa band that woke them up. The P.A. system burped a few times, and then here came loud salsa that had nothing at all to do with Bolivia. In a landlocked country salsa sounded saxa-phony.

"When you were a kid," Agnes reminded him, "in Flint."

"My father was a traveling salesman." The important part of that was true: Traveling salesmen traveled. The rest—the image of a tattooed man carrying boxes of junk across a wide porch, smoking and joking while a woman inside the house cried and a kid watched him work—the rest wasn't something you would talk about because maybe it wasn't even true, and even if it was, maybe it happened to somebody else, and Roger had only picked up the memory of it because it was out there floating loose in the atmosphere at brain level. More than likely the person it happened to was dreaming one time, and the dream equivalent of upchucking happened to him, and the memory shot out of his brain like some kind of weightless, invisible vomit and hung there until Roger—more bad luck—happened by and inhaled it without realizing what he was doing. Stranger things happened all the time.

"What did he sell?"

"Who?"

"Your father, Roger."

Careful. "He sold tools."

"Tools?"

"You know. Hammers and saws and socket sets. Wholesale, to hardware stores. He used to have this silver tieclip with a little chainsaw on it. The saw came off the clip, and when he was in a good mood he used it to cut my meat up at the dinner table. Not that he was in a good mood all that often."

He couldn't tell if she thought he was lying, or if it mattered. Lying wasn't an accurate word for this kind of truth.

"So what about your father?"

"One time he was in an accident. Down near Detroit on the interstate. A tractor trailer mashed up his Buick. He didn't die, but my mother had to go down to Detroit and stay with him for a long time in the hospital while he recuperated."

Saying it brought back another image, fuzzy as the first and therefore just as unreliable. This one also had a porch in it. It was a farm. The long, even-rowed fields around the house, which was white with green shutters that needed a coat of paint, were full of corn and sugarbeets. There were cows, too, a little herd of those black and white ones with the German name he couldn't remember. They were stupid animals, lifting up their moony faces to stare at the car coming down the driveway; a person could run up and whisper *Hamburger!* in their ears and they still wouldn't catch on.

On the porch was a swing. When the wind blew, the swing rocked a little making a pleasant sound of complaint. In the doorway, a woman stood smoking a cigarette. She had a face like the face of the tattooed man, who was not there. A joker's face, smart and with a tall opinion of the person it belonged to, the kind of face that would be looking down at you whenever you decided to look up at it. The woman's arms were folded across her chest, which was covered by a checked apron. There was kitchen dirt on the apron, and a long smear of flour. She watched the dust the car raised down the long drive. When it stopped, she threw down her cigarette, ground the butt with the heel of her shoe.

Out of the car came another woman. Her voice gave this one away; it sounded exactly like the voice of the woman who was crying in the other house while the tattooed man carted his stuff away, if that woman had decided to talk instead of cry. She stood with her bony hands clamped down hard on the shoulders of a kid on the porch step. I've got things to do, she was telling the woman with the apron. Yeah, I know, and places to go. Can I ask you a question at least? Shoot. When he was a kid did he used to clean up the messes he made? Bet not. Well, here's another one.

The band switched out of salsa into one of the standard Bolivian folk hits, El Condor Pasa, and Shits as it Goes Over the Mountain. Roger closed his eyes in the dark and imagined the same crew of rich Bolivians he had seen at the pool that afternoon. In the loud, glittery bar they were dressed up like dolls, drinking scotch and dancing whatever was in style, shaking those buttery butts, and spending enough money to feel like they were still on top of the world even in the Santa Cruz lowlands, which they also owned.

"What are you thinking about, Roger?"

"About luck."

"What about it?"

There were times when Agnes was still a fairly dense person.

Luck. It was where they were. In a temperate place. They ate the things that pleased them—fresh fruits and salads with interesting crunchy things in them and sweets that went down smooth with coffee—and they swam slow, out-of-sync laps in the pool. After laps they lay in the sun and ordered two of every fruit juice the hotel had. Papaya was good, pineapple better, orange cut with carrot the best. When it occurred to either of them they went back to their room, showered even when they weren't sweaty or dirty. They made love that was sometimes slow, sometimes faster and blind, sometimes free fall and scary. It was the closest Roger had come, since the age of dinosaurs, to being in a place with both feet on the ground at the same time. Luck. There was plenty of it around.

Then one night he woke when his sleeping body rolled over expecting to bump into hers and didn't. Some kind of alarm was set off in his brain. He sat up startled. And there in the chair in the corner, Agnes crying. He listened. It was not the kind of crying you interrupted. It was a sound like the sound the darkest river in the world made coming out of the deepest cave, the one you never managed to locate but you knew was there, somewhere, the one that could suck you down.

That was what made Roger start thinking, in a serious way, about the magic, which was not the same thing as luck. The magic happened on a separate plane. How else could Agnes know what she didn't know yet, unless it came in the form of a flash from the Pachamama? It was the kind of flash that woke you up and made you cry deep. And he was right about what la Pachamama whispered to Agnes while she slept. Because in the evening of the next day, the sinking sun softening the city into a tolerable blur of long-armed trees and dusty streets and low adobe buildings, Flame showed up at Los Tajibos.

The unexpected part, for Roger, was how good the magician looked. He was skinny in his black T-shirt decorated with a silver moon and a ring of stars looping like flowers. His hair was the same shade of yellowy brown as Agnes's. The long shape of his bones was like hers, too. On the back of his left hand a small green snake was tattooed. Its tongue was a red knife. The plain silver hoop earring was a necessary decoration. His small feet wriggled in sandals the way a kid's feet would. But he was strong and healthy, pumped up in a way that didn't necessarily have to do with cocaine. It had to be the magic. It was. It filled him up, and he filled up the room.

"Jesus, Agnes. I never thought I'd say this, but I'm saying it: It's good to see you. My little sis. Even in Bolivia. I mean especially in Bolivia. You look different, though. You look kind of sexy. I like your South American look."

"I have to tell you something, Jon." She was working not to cry. The Pachamama's heads-up must have helped. She was doing pretty well.

But Flame held up a hand. "Me first, little sister. We don't have a lot of time." He was a movable sort of person. He switched from Agnes to Roger in a way that didn't tune either of them out. "Hey, you were in La Paz. You had a transcendental experience up there in the magic mountains. I remember. I saw the afterflash in the sky."

"Jon." Agnes wanted to insist. She wanted to get the bad news over with. She had been the kind of girl who ate her vegetables before thinking about dessert.

"There's no good way to tell you this," he said, "but you have to know it. Our father's dead."

She slumped in a way that made Roger want to catch her. It was hard to make out her words. She was talking head down, hands on her face. "You called home. Did you talk to him before he went, Jon?"

The magician shook his head. "Not before, afterward."

"What do you mean?"

"Now I get it. He was sick, wasn't he? That's why you're in Bolivia. You wanted me to know. Hey, I appreciate that. Jesus, I really appreciate it."

"What do you mean afterward, Jon?"

"The question is: Have you been in Bolivia long enough to take me seriously?"

"Say what you mean, please."

Roger heard the echoes of old-time sisterly brotherly bickering. He was glad he was an only child, if that's what he was.

"I have this acquaintance. He's kind of famous."

"El Grán Moxo."

"Try to keep an open mind about this."

"He's a drug trafficker."

Flame shook his head enthusiastically. "That's the one. But he's also a magician. Sort of, I mean. I mean he really wants to be a serious man of magic, and I'm doing the best I can to help him achieve his career goal. We've had our ups and downs. He can be hard on a person. He likes to let you know who runs his show. But all that's behind us now. We're into the magic together. The man has learned, finally, to respect me. We're making serious progress."

"Keep going."

"Well, this is Bolivia, isn't it? What you have to realize is how powerful the magic is in a place like this. I mean it's industrial strength. I've seen things here. . . ." He trailed off into remembering to the point that Roger envied him, a little.

"What about our father, Jon?"

"Last week de la Rocha and I were working on this transubstantiation thing. It's very complicated, very intense. We didn't make it all the way, but all of a sudden I find myself in this very strange space. Right away I realize it's kind of like a cosmic waiting room. It's the place between life and death that some people get stuck in."

"You went to purgatory?"

"Come on, Agnes, I'm being straight with you. For once. What I wanted to tell you is I saw Dad there. That's how come I knew he was gone."

"That's ridiculous."

"Lots of true things are ridiculous. Are you going to hear me out?"

She heard him out. Roger, whose open mind was susceptible to being opened farther, was also happy to hear him out.

"The first thing he does when he recognizes me is he launches into this classic paternal rap about the molecular structure of blueberries and how he never found anything he liked in his whole life the way he used to like the blueberries he picked from his secret patch in the New Hampshire hills. I knew things had definitely changed, though, when I said Enough, and he shut up. He never shut up when he was alive. I said, Let's not waste this opportunity, Dad. We both know this is it, don't we? I knew I was only passing through, and I had no idea what was going to happen next. I could feel de la Rocha behind me waiting for me to haul him in, which I couldn't do. You'll see after you meet him, he's not the most patient guy in the world. Anyway, the old man started talking to me, and I started listening."

"What did he say?" Roger asked. He wanted to be helpful.

"All kinds of stuff. I can't remember it all. He said he was wrong, for example. That's something I never heard him say when he was alive. I mean about things not having souls. He said everything has a soul, even fenceposts. Once upon a time they had the soul of a tree, and when they rot they'll have the soul of dirt. He said the distinction between animate and inanimate is noxious and wrong-headed, and that was where he started going wrong when he was alive. All the dogs that ever lived have souls, he told me, even the dogs in India. Even carp. Did I ever stop and think about what the soul of a carp might look like?"

"What else did he say, Jon?" Agnes asked him, but it was clear she didn't have the kind of open mind required to learn from her brother's experience. Roger felt a little disappointment on her behalf, because she wasn't going to feel it herself.

"He said there's a hundred dollar bill in an envelope taped to the back of that picture his grandmother painted of the Holstein cows, and you and I should split the hundred. He said he was sorry his philosophy got in the way of enjoying sex more, because Mother enjoyed the hell out of it, no questions asked. He said he should have started wearing bifocals at an earlier age, and that music is actually and literally divine. And that in his most important dream he was lying in bed with Emily Dickinson during the day time. It was fall, and the air outside was nippy, and every time Miss Emily opened her mouth the words came out in colors and evaporated into clouds on the ceiling, and she told him that she had no major regrets. Christ, he told me all kinds of stuff I wished I'd heard when he was alive. If I sat still long enough I'd remember it all, and I'd tell you, Agnes. Believe me, I'd tell you. But there isn't time now."

"Why isn't there time?"

"Because we have to go kill a drug trafficker."

He explained that it wasn't that he wanted to kill anybody, or even to see anybody killed. But it was going to happen no matter what Flame said or thought or did about it, so he saw no harm in taking advantage of the man's death to send a message to their father up in the waiting room.

"What message?" Roger asked him when Agnes wouldn't.

"That it's okay."

"What's okay?"

"His kids forgive him all the bullshit he put them through when he was alive. If he doesn't get the message, he's going to be stuck in the goddamn waiting room forever, and I wouldn't wish that on my worst enemy even if he was my father, which he's not. Not really. You know how he frets things, Agnes."

In Roger's opinion there was nothing in any of that to cause Agnes to break down and cry the way she had cried the night before. If you accepted the basic idea, and there was no reason not to accept it, then it made sense to use the dead trafficker to send a fairly important message to her father. What Roger didn't like was the thought of getting closer than he had to get to any troll traffickers, dead or alive.

"Who is it that the Grán Moxo is going to kill?" he asked the magician.

"A competitor, some stupid zero. That's *cero* in Spanish, in case you were wondering, and it still adds up to nothing. He's just some guy that didn't respect the rules of the game. He cut a deal with a major buyer in the Chapare for some paste that was promised to de la Rocha."

"Business."

"It left the Moxo short on this commitment he had with some Colombians."

"So he's going to waste the guy."

Flame lifted his palms in a gesture that Roger guessed was supposed to mean that the drug trafficker's murder was inevitable. It was on the day's schedule of had-to-happen events, and anybody with half a brain knew enough to be reverent in the presence of death, and the message to their father following the trafficker up into death was the kind of miracle a person could understand the use of.

They both spent time working on Agnes convincing her she had to go with them. Flame believed that the message wouldn't get through unless she was there when it got sent, since it was basically a family thing they were dealing with. He was no good at all with his sister; too many fights in the background over who got the bigger bowl of ice cream. She forgot about their father, and the Grán Moxo, and focused on all the things she remembered she didn't like about her brother, now that he was there to irritate her.

Roger was better, because he'd been working at it, but in the end he didn't wind up convincing her, either. She went along with them because she went into a slide that was part daze, part maximum withdrawal. For the first time since she came up to him on the street in La Paz with a picture of her lost brother, it looked like she was giving up.

Roger was disappointed in the car that Flame had come to pick them up in. It was an old Citroën, black and boxy, and the driver behind the wheel was just a driver, the kind of faceless guy in brown pants and crummy shoes that drove the rich women around town in La Paz so they didn't have to worry about the traffic, and they could keep their minds on the things they were going to buy when they went to meet their lovers in Buenos Aires.

"This magic thing," he said to the magician, who sat in front next to the driver like a chaperone for Roger's and Agnes's first date. Roger wondered whether he knew the stone cowboy had been making some amazing love with his sister, and if he did, whether he would care.

"What about it?"

"Who owns it? I mean who does it belong to?" What he really wanted to ask about was la Pachamama, and what her relationship might be to the God who never answered, but Roger didn't have the words in the order they needed to come out to be able to ask the question.

"Doesn't belong to anybody. It's just there. In certain places, that is. Bolivia is one of them. And if you're lucky, and you work at it, you can get at it. That's what this gig is about."

There was nothing left of the evening. The city they drove through was gearing up for night. Salsa music and sambas and high-plains pipe music floated on the air in individual layers that didn't slosh around and mix. Waiters in white shirts and black pants fussed with the tables at the open-air restaurants while the carcasses of many chickens turned on power-driven spits, and women in rooms you couldn't see poured perfume down the front of their sexy dresses, and the tigers in the Santa Cruz zoo paced their cages, and poor people down from the Altiplano looked around to see whether what was going on at sea level was any better than the nothing they had left behind them in the Andes.

Roger would have been happy for the ride to go on. He liked the feel of waiting for something important to happen even though he had no particular wish to watch anybody die, either, even a Bolivian cocaine dealer. It was that sense of anticipation that made the things around them—the things he saw and the things he didn't see—mean something more than they usually meant. But the driver was already turning the ugly black car into a cul-de-sac that Roger knew had to belong to de la Rocha, and it did, and a metal gate on a motor was slowly opening, and then they were inside one more of the Grán Moxo's houses, which was big and splashy in the wrong way.

De la Rocha's Santa Cruz semimansion reminded Roger of the big expensive house-barns he had seen outside Miami one time hitching through on his way to a lower-rent district to meet a woman who wasn't there when he got there. There was only one floor, but it covered an acre or so of ground. There was central air conditioning, and quiet ceiling fans swished the cool air around. There was a game room with video games, and a TV room plugged into a satellite, and a bar with a pool table big enough to hold the eight-ball world series on it, and an indoor swimming pool with an artificial waterfall with real imported rocks, and a knotty pine sauna.

"About time," de la Rocha said to Flame, but his attention was on the entertainment. He didn't seem to notice Agnes and Roger, which Roger interpreted to mean that Flame had told them they were coming, and he had agreed.

Pedro Lopez and the Cholos Vagabundos were sorry they ever took the job playing for Ivo de la Rocha. It had sounded like a deal, but whatever they were getting paid wasn't going to be enough. Roger figured it out right away: The Moxo's idea was to keep the musicians bopping until they dropped, which was going to happen sooner rather than later from the looks of the band. It had been going on for a long time.

Their leader, Pedro, playing a hairy-backed *charango* and doing a decent job on vocals despite the fact that his voice was getting seriously hoarse, had a desperate, faraway look in his black eyes. His *compañeros* were worse off than Pedro. They held onto their instruments—a *quena*, a bunch of pipes, a guitar, and a flat, one-note drum of some kind—as though that was the only thing keeping them propped up and awake. All they wanted out of life was to stop playing.

The song ended, the musicians lay their instruments down on the floor, de la Rocha snarled, and a herd of his hired goons made similar sounds of sympathetic evil.

"Again," said the drug trafficker. "We want to hear it again."

Pedro did his best. His band was wobbling, and he was willing to beg for mercy. But desperation led him to make a mistake. He shook his head no in a way that you could mistake for being stubborn. It was the same expression the Bolivian Indians put on when they saw the Incas climbing up the Andes after them. De la Rocha knew that expression. He shot the musician's *charango* with his pistol. The goons clapped, because that was what goons did.

"Play," said the drug trafficker.

"It's broken, Don Ivo," whined Pedro. "It won't play any more."

"Play the damn song, I told you."

The musician nodded, and the song started out again for maybe the ninety-seventh time since he made the mistake of taking the job. Not that he could get much music out of a *charango* with the back shot out, but the rest of the band filled in the hole he couldn't help leaving.

De la Rocha didn't look like a *loco*. Unless you paid attention. Then you could see he was wacked out in a quiet, intense way. Part of what disturbed about the guy was the lack of color, of course. Except for being an albino he would have been a decent-looking individual. He was built like a boxer in one of the lighter-weight classes, the kind that didn't get overly musclebound. He was in his early forties but he looked tough, tough enough anyway to keep Pedro Lopez and the Cholos Vagabundos playing the same dozen Bolivian folklore songs for the rest of their lives, unless or until he got tired of hearing their music. But the chalky white skin, the pink-rimmed eyes, the stiff-bristled hair that was neither white nor yellow gave Roger the creeps. Not that he was prejudiced against albinos, but the lack of color in the man somehow made him more sinister than the average drug trafficker.

"You ready?" the Moxo said to Flame.

"We're ready."

"Keep them playing until I get back," he ordered one of his goons, a guy with a thin-ribbed chest who wore his Seattle Supersonics cap backward and looked like the kind of person who would shoot the Cholos Vagabundos in the back if he thought they were trying to escape before the concert was over.

"If they're not playing. . . ." De la Rocha didn't finish his sentence. That was something tough guys liked to do, Roger had noticed.

They went in two cars. Roger and Agnes had to ride in the Citroën again, which disappointed the stone cowboy again. In the front seat rode a goon wearing a Chicago Bulls cap. The driver of the Citroën followed a long blue Mercedes with de la Rocha and Flame and another goon, whose hat said Phoenix Suns. They went back across the city, where the people they passed seemed to know something was going to happen, although how could they? They really couldn't. It was just the same feeling of excitement in Roger that made him see something unusual, a way of waiting, in the caution with which a waiter set a salt shaker down on a long wooden table in a barbecue restaurant, the way a woman sweeping lifted her eyes from the sidewalk and watched the dangerous cars go by.

More than being stuck in the junior varsity car, what bothered Roger was not hearing the conversation going on between Flame and the Moxo. They were moving toward a critical moment. Flame would be explaining things to the drug trafficker that Roger wanted to know about. It was probably the kind of conversation in which you could ask that question about la Pachamama and who she was related to, and how. As it was, he had to be content to watch things happen from off to one side. He wondered what you were supposed to feel about one drug trafficker bumping off another one.

Apparently the paste competitor who'd left de la Rocha short with the Colombians had no idea that he had made himself a serious enemy. Business is business, he would have said to himself when he cut his own deal, but sometimes it was something else. It was clear to anyone watching that his guard was down. His nickname, Roger learned from the goon, was el Pajero—the Jackoff—after the deluxe Japanese four-wheel vehicle he drove. Probably the Japanese drones who worked in the part of the factory where they invented names for their cars didn't have much of an understanding of South American slang. You wouldn't expect them to.

They found el Pajero coming out of his own driveway, behind the wheel of his own car. Next to him in the front side was a girl of maybe eight with long hair in braids and bright ribbons.

"Jesús y Maria," he probably said to himself when he figured out who was in the car that pulled up behind him while he was still in reverse.

Roger watched him kiss his daughter for a long time before he sent her back inside the house to tell her mother Papá couldn't take her over to her friend's house to play. Something had come up.

El Pajero was a realist. He didn't fight getting into the blue Mercedes, much, although there was something pathetic in the way his shoulders fell down when he listened to the Moxo rag on him. The Citroën followed the Mercedes again, out of the city this time, to one of those nowhere natural places the world was full of: It was a wide open space of scrabbly field surrounded by palmettos with skinny arms, poor excuses for trees, in Roger's opinion. Frogs and crickets were making their normal noise, which in different circumstances could be a pleasant sound. Part of an orangish moon made the high grass look more interesting than it looked in the daytime. A horse moved away from the noise they made arriving and went on grazing in the clumped shadow of some palmettos. It was not the kind of place where innocent bystanders hung out.

In a way it was hard to pay attention the way a person ought to pay attention to somebody who knew he was going to die in a couple of minutes, because of what was going on with Flame and the Moxo. While Agnes and Roger and the goons and even el Pajero watched as if they didn't have anything else they'd rather be doing just then, the magician rummaged in the rucksack in which he hauled around his magic paraphernalia. At the same time he was lecturing the trafficker; teaching him, really, but the Grán Moxo had a hard time taking orders from anyone, even though he recognized that the American knew a lot more about the subject than he did.

The magician pulled up the grass by the roots in a space in the middle of the field and built a fire. Whatever he put into it made the flames and then the smoke turn colors you didn't see in a normal fire. Ordinarily Roger would have said that was nothing but showmanship, but he was working to keep his mind as open as it needed to be.

"See that, Agnes?" Flame said to his sister. "That's the difference between here and up there. Up there when you make a fire it's to cook hot dogs and those gooey things the Girl Scouts eat on their campouts."

"S'mores," said Agnes. She couldn't help it; if you knew the right answer, you wanted to be the first one to give it to the teacher.

"Far as I'm concerned s'mores is less. Down here you get colors, and you get magic. It's the real thing."

"You could stop this, if you wanted to," she accused him. She was talking in her schoolmarm voice, and Roger didn't like it any more than Flame did. It was the kind of voice that tried to convince you that the things of the world were supposed to work a certain way, and the fact that if you opened your eyes and looked around and saw that they didn't made no difference in what the voice wanted you to accept. Because he was a backwards-working sort of person Roger felt suddenly sexy toward her. He would have liked to take her away to a part of the field where nothing ugly was happening and make love with her.

Flame shook his head, wouldn't buy what Agnes wanted to sell him. He couldn't help looking at el Pajero, who had to be wondering what a bonfire in a vacant field had to do with wiping him out. Maybe he thought they were going to barbecue his body and serve it to the Colombians.

When he was ready to operate, Flame made it clear that nobody else except de la Rocha was supposed to get near the fire until he was ready. Then he called Agnes, who went because the daze had made her passive. El Pajero had to be pushed a little by the goons, but he went, because he was still a realist. Nobody begrudged him the tears dripping out of him or the noises he couldn't help making, which were also like drips. They were drips of sound, and they were a drug trafficker's equivalent of prayers.

It went fast, which Roger supposed was better, more humane. Flame placed Agnes's hand on el Pajero's forehead, then pulled her back while the Moxo himself shot the man through the head.

"It worked," Flame told them before the body hit the ground, fast dead. "It fucking worked!"

He fell down into the grass near the fire, and de la Rocha sat more or less humbly beside him, and the moment that he'd been working to create happened the way it had to happen. To the extent that Roger understood the process, Flame had enough control of the Bolivian magic to send his message of forgiveness to his father in the waiting room between life and death. The message went up with el Pajero, who had no choice except to carry it when he went.

"I saw it," de la Rocha told him.

Flame's success made him feel generous. "Of course you saw it, Ivo. Didn't I tell you that you were going to see it?"

But it turned out that de la Rocha hadn't seen the whole thing: just the flash when the life went out of the man he shot—nobody else saw it, but nobody else had worked on the magic, so how could they expect to see it?—and then something that might have been a transfer of power. There was more, though, and the vision of freeing his father to finally die, and even seeing it happen, seeing him go up liberated and happy to his final resting place, filled up the magician with a satisfaction it would have been better to hide, taking into account the effect it had on the Moxo.

The goons were busy hauling away the dead body to a swamp they knew about that would absorb the evidence. Agnes was busy falling apart. An adventure through the Chapare was one thing. Watching a murder was another thing, not one she could chalk up to experience and write about in her memoirs. Roger wasn't busy at all, so he saw plainly the resentment in de la Rocha that Flame was too buzzed-up to notice, let alone appreciate.

"You're good," el Moxo said to him quietly. Roger didn't like the way the orange moon made his eyes look in the scraggly wildness they were standing around in.

"I'm good," Flame agreed.

"You're getting better."

"I'm getting better. You are, too, Ivo. A month ago you couldn't even have imagined this whole thing, let alone see what you saw. Patience, *papito*. You'll get there."

"I want to get there now."

"What can I tell you, Ivo? It comes when it comes. If I could give it to you, I would."

"You can help me get it."

Apparently de la Rocha had talked over his idea with Flame before. They both knew what they were talking about, so Roger had a hard time following the conversation. His only advantage was in knowing it was not a good idea to get into the Grán Moxo's airplane with him and fly back up to the mountains to find the Andean magic man he knew about. Flame, unfortunately, thought it was a great idea. He had heard about the guy in La Paz. He lived on one of the mountains outside of Oruro. Even the name sounded wrong to Roger. But among people who knew about Bolivian magic, the guy from outside of Oruro was famous.

"I just killed a man," Agnes told Roger in the Citroën on the way to the Santa Cruz airport. "I committed murder. There's blood on my hands, Roger."

"For Chrissake, Agnes, you didn't commit any murder. Come on. You saw somebody else kill a guy. There's a difference." He wondered why it felt so good to be mean to her again.

At the airport, which was closed for the night unless you were a drug trafficker and had your own plane parked there waiting like an old-fashioned mobster's getaway car except with wings, Roger thought about slipping off into permanent fade, vaporizing himself into a place they couldn't see him, couldn't get at him anymore. He was tired of being gotten at. But everybody there seemed to think that he was part of the party. On top of that, the goons standing around the Moxo's airplane all had Uzis or whatever they called those snub-nosed guns on camouflage slings; the way they held them couldn't help making a person imagine the guns as some kind of metal penis, a permanent cold hard-on.

But the main reason he didn't disappear was that he wanted to see. He admitted it. Sticking by Agnes out of loyalty a little longer was the smaller part of it. What he wanted to see was what the magic man in the mountains could do. Roger had figured out Flame's master plan: They were going up into the Andes to summon la Pachamama. He was, however, the last to climb into the airplane.

The pilot was the same one who had flown into the Chapare the night Esencia got shot, which made him guilty in a bystander way at least. Roger remembered him as a shadow with a belly and a mustache, but he was apparently the best small-plane pilot in Bolivia, from what Flame said. He had to be. He knew enough, anyway, to avoid hanging the airplane on a peak in the dark on the way to Oruro.

Sitting side by side like army buddies who'd seen combat together, Flame and de la Rocha did a couple of lines of cocaine on the way up. They took turns holding a penlight over a round makeup mirror so that their noses could get at the wiggly line of white dust. They were talking about magic. Most of it was technical stuff, way beyond Roger. But his instincts, for what they were worth, told him that they were not talking bullshit. Apparently Flame had been trying to get at this particular magic man since he came to Bolivia, and all the time de la Rocha knew who he was and how to get there. Roger listened with a certain amount of respect, waiting for a space to open inside which he could ask the questions he wanted to ask. The space didn't open, but maybe that was the coke happening between them.

As drugs went, Roger had never like cocaine much. He had tried it a few times to be sociable and because he had an open mind, but he preferred substances that helped him get out of himself, which in his experience was a fairly boring place to spend much time. He liked to travel. From what he had been able to observe, the main thing cocaine did was swell up the person inside his own body and make it rave and rattle around in its cage until the high went low, after which the person was worse off than when he started. Fuck that white noise, he said quietly to himself.

His body was starting to wear out on him when the plane touched down at a private strip near a mine in Oruro, and his brain was several steps behind his body. The feeling of being back there—back in the Bolivian mountains as though he'd never left, never escaped Trollandia at all, and never would—almost undid him. He had lost any sense of time going anywhere except around. The Bolivian sun, never friendly although sometimes indifferent depending on where it caught you, was coming up over the Altiplano and the ridged Andes with the kind of glow that made the flat things of the world look promising. Roger knew better. He knew, for example, that it was a mistake to be where he was, and that he wanted to make that particular mistake. He knew he would make it again if he was given the chance, so what was the good of knowing?

Apart from the airplanes and the talented pilots that flew them, one of the other advantages of being a drug trafficker was having cars waiting to pick you up wherever you landed. It was not, however, a trip that required any goons. Pumped up in the same intense, out-tuning way that Flame was, Ivo de la Rocha left his hired hands behind at the strip. They didn't mind that, Roger could see. They would kick back without the boss around, look for a little trouble to cause so they could pass their free time entertained. Having seen a lot of it, Roger understood the goon mentality the same way he understood the military mind. In some ways there wasn't that much difference.

Flame next to him in the front seat, the Grán Moxo drove his own Land Rover across the high plains outside of Oruro up onto a mountain. He followed a one-lane track that needed a guard rail but didn't have one. The road was dirt, with short and then longer stretches of gravel that washed out and down the cliff in a dirty dribble that Roger, in the back seat with Agnes, had no inclination to follow down. Looking out the window at the fall below made him dizzy.

"I've been waiting for this, for something like this that I think had to be this, for a long time, Ivo," Flame said. He was a Bolivian Buddha, a cat's smile on his healthy-looking face, and the idea was for everyone to feel good about his confession.

"You're good," Ivo admitted to him, "and you're getting better."

By cocking his head at a certain angle, Roger could see the man's eyes in the rearview mirror.

"This is a mistake," he admitted to Agnes in English.

"I killed a man," she insisted. "Maybe I didn't pull the trigger, but I'm responsible just the same. So are you. So is my brother."

It wasn't worth pointing out the mistake in her train of thought a second time. What could she have done, thrown herself in front of the bullet that brought down el Pajero? Besides, Roger was having a hard time breathing again. He had forgotten, because he wanted to forget, how hard it was to breathe in the Andes, up on the high plains. Spanish invaders, someone in el Panóptico had told him, stole all the oxygen hundreds of years ago. They put it in bottles and loaded the bottles on ships and took it all back to Spain where they sold it at a tremendous profit. If you looked at things from a Bolivian perspective you could see where their paranoia came from. Roger understood a few things like that. He wondered if the knowing was worth the price he had paid to find them out.

The sun was almost straight up by the time they got to the place where they wanted, most of them and mostly, to be. But it was doing nothing to warm the air, which was like winter on a postcard. They went through something that would have been a village if there'd been any people there: round shacks of stone with roofs made of something you would have called thatch if you found it at sea level. But there was no one there, not even an animal. Desolate; that was the word. Desolation was the kind of thing that happened frequently in Bolivia, which was not really meant for human habitation.

After the empty village, the road degenerated into something less than a track. It climbed again until they came out onto a flat plain. They must have been at sixteen thousand, maybe seventeen thousand feet. You could gauge the altitude by how scarce the air was. The plain, which seemed to Roger to wobble, in a geographic sort of way, was beautiful if your taste ran to bare and simple things. Roger realized that his taste had changed; lately it ran to bare and simple things. He had not thought about Danny in Flint for a long time; even the name of his friend hurt, because of the distance, which was not a thing you could count in miles.

The plain covered a mile or so across a landscape of bright ice and old snow, then ran up against a shelf of rock that looked like shale except the color varied more. It went from smoky gray to steel and then almost black, and from a distance the patterns confused your eye into following them. On the side of the rock was a stone shack with a chimney from which smoke rose and evaporated quickly; no air to hold it. The gray of the smoke was a different color from any of the grays in the rock.

When de la Rocha killed the engine of the Land Rover, Flame leaned forward in his seat a little and closed his eyes. "I can't believe it," he said. First in Spanish, then in English, then in Spanish again.

"You stay here," de la Rocha told them. He left them behind, walked across the ice-crusted ground to the little house.

"Does he speak Aymara?" Roger asked Flame.

"Shut the fuck up, will you?" Flame said. "We're at the fucking door. Don't distract me with chatter. Not now."

After all the travel she'd done, the word *fuck* still had the capacity to wound Agnes. Roger felt it poke at her in the side, and she moaned a little in discomfort. Don't spoil this, he wanted to say. He didn't say it.

As it happened, the Moxo had picked up enough Aymara at some point in his career to carry on a reasonable conversation. Because he knew how hard that was, Roger appreciated the accomplishment. The magic man at the end of the road to whom the Moxo spoke his Aymara was like a human raisin. Dry and brown and small: too much time under the sun, which at that altitude was always closer than it should be. His face was dried into a permanent pucker, and the black eyes were little raisinettes. It was the eyes, when the Moxo finally gestured for them to get out of the car, that spooked Roger the most. They weren't the eyes of an animal; the intelligence of animals was a different thing. But they were not like human eyes, either. They were black lasers, and they sliced.

Flame approached the man with what Roger thought was a ridiculous amount of reverence, but this was what the Mystical Gringo had come to Bolivia to find: the genuine man who had the genuine magic, the real thing, the kind of magic that had been lost in Gringolandia ever since the invention of the cotton gin. It made some sense: that you would find it here, at the end of the road that went pretty much straight up to the top of the world. What you lacked in air you made up for with atmosphere.

It was a quietly pleasant thing to understand some of the Aymara going back and forth between the magic man and the Moxo. Roger had assumed that his abused mind was leaking so badly that none of what he'd learned would stay inside. But it was there, although knowing what they were talking about helped a lot. Some of it was in Spanish, which made it clear to Roger that the Moxo was presenting Flame to the raisin man as a Yankee magician, a professional like the Bolivian himself, not a huckster. No one would expect a gringo to have the same level of skill or access that a Bolivian like the raisin man had, but anybody who understood a little how it worked would also understand that the magic would also be there up north, inside the empire. Listening, Roger imagined it hanging in pockets, in invisible clouds that a lucky person might stumble into even in a place like, say, Flint, Michigan.

Agnes was freezing. Along with the stress, it made her teeth chatter, and mottled spots of blue came out on her skin. They hadn't brought winter clothes. She couldn't follow anything at all of the conversation, and eventually she went back to the car. She sat in the backseat hugging herself, which made Roger want to hug her also, but not enough to miss what was going on with the magicians.

The raisin man asked de la Rocha what his own interest in the magic was. The Moxo, when he gave his answer, seemed temporarily human, not the kind of man who would take another man away from his hair-ribboned daughter and shoot him in an empty field just because he made a business mistake, which was after all only a mistake in judgment. The magic, for the Moxo, had something to do with religion, although it was not like religion in the normal sense of going into a church and crossing yourself three times with holy water. It had to do, as far as Roger understood, which was possibly not that far, with what you saw, and what the seeing made you feel, and what you did with the feeling.

Flame knew enough not to rush anything. Why would he want to? If this was the place you'd been pushing to get to forever, why would you want to hurry it when you finally got there? It was evident that he was impatient not having a clue about the Aymara, but even that must have seemed, to him, like crossing over a bridge he had to cross.

After a while they ate. Roger, wanting to feel loyal but not quite succeeding, carried a tin plate of chuños and plain boiled quinoa to Agnes in the Land Rover. He would have called it food for animals, if he himself hadn't been caught up in the place and the sense of magic, which was really a sense of thinking that anything might happen. Inside the car she was still blue, but she refused to turn on the engine and heat up the inside.

"I want to go home, Roger."

"This is home," he told her. It was a true statement, at the moment, but he knew he did not have the skill to make her understand the truth of it. She looked at him with the same expression she had put on her face when he told her about the two hits of acid when they were going down into the Chapare.

"My father is dead, or he might be, and my brother is insane. They fired me from my job, and I'm sitting inside a frozen car in the middle of nowhere in Bolivia."

Exactly, he wanted to say, but he knew she wouldn't see it. He urged her to eat the quinoa and the chuños. He went back to the magician's shack.

Flame's idea had been to summon the Pachamama. However, with the assistance of the Moxo, the magic raisin man was generous enough to make him see, in the course of a long conversation in Aymara and Spanish that lost Roger around every second turn, that his wanting was wrong. You didn't summon her up just for the pure enjoyment of seeing, just to brag about being a witness. In any case she was there all the time, so how could you summon her? That didn't make any sense, not logical or magical.

Understanding how stupid he had been, Flame went into a dangerous slide of his own. He knew the superior magic man was right, and for a few minutes he faced down the fact that maybe he had come this close, all this way, carrying a mistake that would prevent him from getting what he needed to get. But the raisin man—el Moxo called him Don Eulalio—was old enough to have outgrown the temptation to fuck around with a person just for the sake of fucking around. Talking on and on in a flat voice that soothed all of them, he made Flame see that what he needed to do was figure out what it was he really wanted. Roger got lost again trying to understand, but the Moxo's Aymara wasn't good enough for that, either, and it came out in translation: *el objeto legitimo de tu deseo,* the legitimate object of your desire. Flame was grateful; Don Eulalio had just saved his life. His eyes teared, and Roger watched the Moxo's face to see how all of it was hitting him. But Bolivians had the ability to turn their faces into stones when they wanted to, and that's what the Moxo's was now.

Something, however, was happening to Roger. He assumed it was the company he was keeping. That, maybe, and also the tea that Don Eulalio had brewed up for them. Roger called it clarifying tea, because that was what it did to you when you drank it. He was beginning to see certain things, in a way that he hadn't known a person could see. He became aware of it when he noticed one very small red ant crossing the floor of Don Eulalio's shack. Roger saw the individual working legs going like a machine, the small, domed back, and maybe—he was not sure, and he didn't want to fake himself out—the expression of concentration on the red ant's tiny face. Everything was standing out in a way that made him weak and happy at the same time. It had to be Don Eulalio, who was helping them all along.

Not until sometime in the middle of the afternoon did Flame figure out the *objeto legitimo* of his desire. "I'm tired of being a person," he said quietly in English. Not to Roger, but not to himself, either. Surprisingly, the foreign sound didn't bother Don Eulalio at all, which made Roger admire him even more. In addition to being a major magic man, he was an individual with an open mind.

It was Roger who translated for Flame, who seemed temporarily to have lost his Spanish. No one took the stone cowboy's intervention in the wrong way, which caused a gush of gratitude to well in him that embarrassed him, for himself. He concentrated on his translating.

"He wants to be a bird. He knows that much. But he doesn't know what kind of bird. He knows that it would be a big mistake just to say that he wants to be a bird, without being specific. You can't come this far and not know what kind of bird you want to be."

Don Eulalio nodded peacefully, and the Moxo hung his head. Agnes came quietly into the hut to get warm., but she didn't try to ruin what was going on. She sat to one side on the floor and held her knees in her hands. Don Eulalio got up and gave her a mugful of clarifying tea and a handful of something else they had all been eating. They were something like nuts, brown and furry on the outside and with a slightly bitter taste when you bit into them, but Roger wasn't sure they were nuts. He called them the magic berries because the name seemed to fit, although he wasn't a hundred percent sure they were berries, either.

"He says," Roger translated, "that he thinks he has done as much as he needs to do, by getting to the point that he understands what he wants to be. Knowing it the way he knows it makes him feel confident."

"Confident about what?" the Moxo said, but it wasn't an interruption. He was chewing on a magic berry, and the taste made his lips twist into an expression that looked like sarcasm but probably wasn't meant to be.

"Confident that he can ask la Pachamama for help," Roger explained, because he was pretty certain he understood. Flame, at any rate, didn't contradict him. The gringo magician was too wrapped up in listening to himself to contradict anybody.

"Now," said Roger. "Not before. He knows there is a huge difference between being a condor and a crow, for example. Or between an eagle and a dove. Making a mistake about the kind of bird you needed to be would be fatal. It has to do with who you are as a person, which is the hard necessary part of the process you have to go through to get to where you can ask for help."

All of that made sense to everyone, at that point, except Agnes, who didn't care any more. No, that wasn't being fair to her. Roger admitted that she was numbed past feeling, due to circumstances beyond her control. There was no point judging her.

When Don Eulalio stood up, finally, they all stood up and followed him outside to a big flat rock shaped like a giant ashtray that was still in the sun, although the day wasn't going to last much longer. When the sun went behind a mountain in the Andes it was all over.

But the raisin man was in nobody's hurry. He made a fire as though there were all the time in the world left, because there was. He let Flame hold the ratty gunnysack out of which he drew the magic things he added to the fire according to a recipe nobody else in the world would ever know enough to be able to imitate and follow. It was clear that the honor of helping was about as much satisfaction as the gringo magician could bear. The excess streamed out of him and raised the temperature of the air around him a degree you could measure if you wanted to. Roger didn't want to. It was just as clear to him that the Grán Moxo felt left out and resentful, and for the first time he showed it.

When the fire was right, Don Eulalio sat next to it and started chanting. It was the sweetest music Roger had ever heard, ten times better than all the phony pipe music they played to the tourists in La Paz. It got down inside him and irritated him awake. It was being awake in that particular way that gave him the eyes to see what happened.

Flame seemed to have an idea of what he was supposed to do. He waited the way a man about to be married who knew he was making the right choice would wait, with a combination of patience and expectation that a person would want to stretch out for as long as he could make it last. Every other minute he closed his eyes, and when he did Roger envied him the condition of innocence into which he had climbed. When the signal came—it had something to do with the announcing way the chant went down in Don Eulalio's voice—he went to the fire and held his hands over the flames. The two men were communicating in a code of some kind that the rest of them could see but not catch. Roger wondered whether Agnes was finally going to understand that her brother had something real, something that went way past the street magic he had started out with years ago at home.

The Bolivian magic man said something that didn't sound like Aymara or Spanish or any other human language. Maybe it was bird talk. Whatever it was, Flame understood it, and he raised his arms to the sky, which by then had fallen down close enough, almost, to touch. He opened his mouth, and the same sound that the Bolivian magic man made came out of it. Not quite as good, but not bad.

It had to be the company that was giving Roger the ability to see what he was seeing. He knew better than to assume it was something he had earned on his own. But it was there, and it didn't matter where it came from. When the Moxo stood up on the other side of the fire and drew out a pistol Roger saw it perfectly. Short as the distance was, he saw the silver-gray bullet go across over the fire. He saw the scar the bullet left on the thin air, a diamond scratching glass. He saw the bullet go into Flame's body, and the bird that was in the gringo magician fly out and up, straight up, fast.

At first he thought what he saw in the sky was another bird, like the bird he had dreamed about in the Chapare, a rescuing bird. For a moment the screaming of Agnes distracted him. But he kept watching, and he saw that what he thought had been a bird was really the Pachamama, her great gentle arm and shoulder bending down from somewhere else, scooping up the small bird that had been inside Flame, taking it with her.

Roger understood that this was his chance, the one he was going to get. He took it. At what he knew was still the right moment he did what Flame had done with el Pajero. He used him to send a message. He sent it to the place into which the Pachamama was quickly disappearing. Not that you could call it a place, really, but that didn't matter. It was a message with a request. He thought the same way Flame had been thinking, that he had finally gone far enough to ask for help. With the unusual clear vision that the company he kept had given him, he watched his message go up like a stone, thrown. He watched her catch it and knew it would be delivered. Funny how it all fit into one sentence.

Don Eulalio had retreated into the kind of blind isolation that Bolivians on the high plains were used to putting up with. There wasn't room for anybody else where he was going. Ivo de la Rocha, who must be realizing that he was a better drug trafficker than he was a magician, was looking at the body of Flame, which had fallen away from the fire when de la Rocha shot him. Agnes was wrapped up in herself, learning, Roger figured, how to live broken. It was going to take her a while. Before it all went away, Roger himself, still the stone cowboy in a manner of speaking, repeated the message he had sent up with the Pachamama. Not because he doubted it would get where it was going, but for the easy pleasure of the words themselves: Give me back my heart, he heard. He was tired. He looked around for a place to sit down.

HARTFORD PUBLIC LIBRARY
500 MAIN STREE
HARTFORD, CT 06103
HPL

Date Due

OCT 02 1997	
FEB 20 1998	
MAR 20 1998	